### Praise for *The Goblin Emperor* by Katherine Addison

"Addison patiently and tellingly paints in the backdrop mingling steampunk elements and low-key magic with imperial intricacies. There are powerful character studies and a plot full of small but deadly traps among which the sweet-natured, perplexed Maia must navigate. The result is a spellbinding and genuinely affecting drama. Unreservedly recommended."

—*Kirkus Reviews* (starred review)

"This is a beautifully told story, and has cost me much-needed sleep these past few nights. (And I'm not just saying that because, as we all know, goblins are awesome!) *The Goblin Emperor* made me remember why I fell in love with the fantasy genre."

—JIM C. HINES,
bestselling author of *Goblin Quest*

"A luminously realized steampunk fantasy unlike anything you've ever read."

—ELIZABETH BEAR,
author of the Eternal Sky trilogy

# BY KATHERINE ADDISON

*The Goblin Emperor*

# THE
# GOBLIN
# EMPEROR

**KATHERINE ADDISON**

A TOM DOHERTY ASSOCIATES BOOK • NEW YORK

This is a work of fiction. All of the characters, organizations, and events portrayed in this novel are either products of the author's imagination or are used fictitiously.

THE GOBLIN EMPEROR

Copyright © 2014 by Katherine Addison

All rights reserved.

A Tor Book
Published by Tom Doherty Associates, LLC
175 Fifth Avenue
New York, NY 10010

www.tor-forge.com

Tor® is a registered trademark of Tom Doherty Associates, LLC.

ISBN 978-0-7653-6568-2

Tor books may be purchased for educational, business, or promotional use. For information on bulk purchases, please contact the Macmillan Corporate and Premium Sales Department at 1-800-221-7945, extension 5442, or write to specialmarkets@macmillan.com.

First Edition: April 2014
First Mass Market Edition: March 2015

Printed in the United States of America

0   9   8   7

*For my parents,*
*Katherine on one side,*
*Addison on the other*

# CONTENTS

PART FOUR
WINTERNIGHT

PART FIVE
EDREHASIVAR THE BRIDGE-BUILDER

—∞∞∞—

# PART ONE

# The Crash of the
# Wisdom of Choharo

# 1

## News Comes to Edonomee

Maia woke with his cousin's cold fingers digging into his shoulder.

"Cousin? What . . ." He sat up, rubbing at his eyes with one hand. "What time is it?"

"Get up!" Setheris snarled. "Hurry!"

Obediently, Maia crawled out of bed, clumsy and sleep-sodden. "What's toward? Is there a fire?"

"Get thy clothes on." Setheris shoved yesterday's clothes at him. Maia dropped them, fumbling with the strings of his nightshirt, and Setheris hissed with exasperation as he bent to pick them up. "A messenger from the court. *That's* what's toward."

"A message from my father?"

"Is't not what I said? Merciful goddesses, boy, canst do *nothing* for thyself? Here!" He jerked the nightshirt off, caring neither for the knotted strings nor for Maia's ears, and shoved his clothes at him again. Maia struggled into drawers, trousers, shirt, and jacket, aware that they were wrinkled and sweat-stained, but unwilling to try Setheris's ill temper by saying so. Setheris watched grimly by the single candle's light, his ears flat against his head. Maia could not find his stockings, nor would Setheris give him time to search. "Come along!" he said as soon as Maia had his jacket fastened, and Maia followed him barefoot out of the room, noticing in the stronger light that while Setheris was still properly and fully attired, his face was flushed. So he had not been wakened from sleep by the emperor's messenger, but only because he had not yet been to bed. Maia hoped uneasily that Setheris had not drunk enough metheglin to mar the glossy perfection of his formal court manners.

Maia ran his hands through his hair, fingers catching on knots in his heavy curls. It would not be the first time one of his father's messengers had witnessed him as unkempt as a half-witted ragpicker's child, but that did not help with the miserable midnight imaginings: *So, tell us, how looked our son?* He reminded himself it was unlikely his father ever asked after him in the first place and tried to keep his chin and ears up as he followed Setheris into the lodge's small and shabby receiving room.

The messenger was maybe a year or so older than Maia himself, but elegant even in his road-stained leathers. He was clearly full-blooded elvish, as Maia was not; his hair was milkweed-pale, and his eyes the color of rain. He looked from Setheris to Maia and said, "Are you the Archduke Maia Drazhar, only child of Varenechibel the Fourth and Chenelo Drazharan?"

"Yes," Maia said, bewildered.

And then bewilderment compounded bewilderment, as the messenger deliberately and with perfect dignity prostrated himself on the threadbare rug. "Your Imperial Serenity," he said.

"Oh, get up, man, and stop babbling!" Setheris said. "We understood that you had messages from the Archduke's father."

"Then you understand what we do not," the messenger said, rising again to his feet, as graceful as a cat. "We bear messages from the Untheileneise Court."

Maia said hastily, merely to prevent the altercation from escalating, "Please, explain."

"Your Serenity," the messenger said. "The airship *Wisdom of Choharo* crashed yesterday, sometime between sunrise and noon. The Emperor Varenechibel the Fourth, the Prince Nemolis, the Archduke Nazhira, and the Archduke Ciris were all on board. They were returning from the wedding of the Prince of Thu-Athamar."

"And the *Wisdom of Choharo* crashed," Maia said slowly, carefully.

"Yes, Serenity," said the messenger. "There were no survivors."

For five pounding heartbeats, the words made no sense. Nothing made sense; nothing had made sense since he had woken with Setheris's grip hurting his shoulder. And then it was suddenly, pitilessly clear. As if from a very long distance away, he heard his own voice saying, "What caused the crash?"

"Does it matter?" Setheris said.

"Serenity," said the messenger with a deliberate nod in Maia's direction. "They do not yet know. But the Lord Chancellor has sent Witnesses, and it is being investigated."

"Thank you," said Maia. He knew neither what he felt nor what he ought to feel, but he knew what he ought to do, the next necessary thing. "You said . . . there are messages?"

"Yes, Serenity." The messenger turned and picked up his dispatch case from where it lay on the side table. There was only one letter within, which the messenger held out. Setheris snatched the letter and broke the seal savagely, as if he still believed the messenger to be lying.

He scanned the paper, his customary frown deepening into a black scowl, then flung it at Maia and stalked from the room. Maia grabbed at it ineffectually as it fluttered to the floor.

The messenger knelt to retrieve it before Maia could and handed it to him without a flicker of expression.

Maia felt his face heating, his ears lowering, but he knew better than to try to explain or apologize for Setheris. He bent his attention to the letter. It was from his father's Lord Chancellor, Uleris Chavar:

> To the Archduke Maia Drazhar, heir to the imperial throne of Ethuveraz, greetings in this hour of greatest grief.
>
> Knowing that Your Imperial Serenity will want all honor and respect paid to your late father and brothers, we have ordered arrangements put in train for a full ceremonial funeral in three days' time, that is, on the twenty-third instant. We will notify the five principalities, also Your Imperial Serenity's sister in Ashedro. We have already ordered the courier office to put airships at their disposal, and we have no doubt that they will use all necessary haste to reach the Untheileneise Court in good time for the funeral.
>
> We do not, of course, know what Your Imperial Serenity's plans may be, but we hold ourself ready to implement them.
>
> With true sorrow and
> unswerving loyalty,
> Uleris Chavar

Maia looked up. The messenger was watching him, as impassive as ever; only the angle of his ears betrayed his interest.

"I . . . we must speak with our cousin," he said, the constructions of the formal first person awkward and unaccustomed. "Do you . . . that is, you must be tired. Let us summon a manservant to tend to your needs."

"Your Serenity is very kind," the messenger said, and if he knew that there were only two menservants in the entire household of Edonomee, he gave no sign.

Maia rang the bell, knowing that birdlike Pelchara would be waiting eagerly for a chance to find out what was happening. Haru, who did all the outside work, was probably still asleep; Haru slept like the dead, and the whole household knew it.

Pelchara popped in, his ears up and his eyes bright and inquisitive. "This gentleman," Maia said, mortified to realize that he did not know the messenger's name, "has traveled hard. Please see that he has everything he requires." He faltered before the thought of explaining the news to Pelchara, mumbled, "I will be with my cousin," and hurried out.

He could see light under Setheris's door, and could hear his cousin's brisk, bristling stride. *Let him not have stopped for the metheglin decanter,* Maia thought, a brief, hopeless prayer, and tapped on the door.

"Who is't?" At least he did not *sound* any drunker than he had a quarter hour ago.

"Maia. May I—?"

The door opened with savage abruptness, and Setheris stood in the opening, glaring. "Well? What chews on *thy* tail, boy?"

"Cousin," Maia said, almost whispering, "what must I do?"

"What must thou *do*?" Setheris snorted laughter. "Thou must be *emperor,* boy. Must rule all the Elflands and banish thy kindred as thou seest fit. Why com'st thou whining to me of what thou must do?"

"Because I don't know."

"Moon-witted hobgoblin," Setheris said, but it was contempt by reflex; his expression was abstracted.

"Yes, cousin," Maia said meekly.

After a moment, Setheris's eyes sharpened again, but this time without the burning anger. "Thou wish'st advice?"

"Yes, cousin."

"Come in," Setheris said, and Maia entered his cousin's bedchamber for the first time.

It was as austere as Setheris himself—no mementoes of the Untheileneise Court, no luxuries. Setheris waved Maia to the only chair and himself sat on the bed. "Thou'rt right, boy. The wolves are waiting to devour thee. Hast thou the letter?"

"Yes, cousin." Maia handed Setheris the letter, now rather crumpled and the worse for wear. Setheris read it, frowning again, but this time his ears were cocked thoughtfully. When he had finished, he folded the letter neatly, his long white fingers smoothing the creases. "He presumes much, does Uleris."

"He does?" And then, realizing: "Dost know him?"

"We were enemies for many years," Setheris said, shrugging it aside. "And I see he has not changed."

"What mean'st thou?"

"Uleris has no reason to love thee, boy."

"He says he's loyal."

"Yes. But loyal to *what*? Not to thee, for thou art merely the last and least favored child of his dead master, who wished thee not on the throne, as well thou know'st. Use thy wits, boy—an thou hast any."

"What do you mean?"

"Merciful goddesses, grant me patience," Setheris said ostentatiously to the ceiling. "Consider, boy. Thou art *emperor*. What must thou do first?"

"Cousin, this is not the time for riddles."

"And it is not a riddle I pose thee." Setheris shut his mouth and glared at him, and after a moment, Maia realized.

"The coronation."

"Ha!" Setheris brought his hands together sharply, making Maia jump. "Exactly. So why, I ask thee, does thy coronation not figure largely in Uleris's plans or, indeed, at all?"

"The funeral—"

"No! Thou think'st as a child, not as an emperor. The dead are dead, and they care not for the honor Uleris prates of, as well *he* knows. It is the living power that must concern thee, as it concerns him."

"But . . ."

"*Think,* boy," Setheris said, leaning forward, his cold eyes alight with fervor. "If thou art capable—if thou hast ever thought before in thy life—*think.* Thou com'st to the Untheileneise Court, the funeral is held. What then?"

"I speak to . . . oh."

"Thou seest."

"Yes." Better than Setheris might care to realize, for it was at his cousin's hands that Maia had learned this particular lesson; by waiting, he put himself in the position of a supplicant to Chavar, and supplicants could always be denied. "Then what must I do?"

Setheris said, "Thou must countermand Uleris. Meaning that thou must reach the Untheileneise Court before he has time to entrench himself."

"But how can I?" It took most of a week to reach the court from Edonomee.

"Airship," Setheris said as if it were obvious.

Maia's stomach knotted. "I couldn't."

"Thou *must.* Or thou shalt be a puppet dancing at the end of Uleris's strings, and to a tune of his choosing. And thy nineteenth birthday may very well see thee dead."

Maia bowed his head. "Yes, cousin."

"The airship that brought Chavar's lapdog here can

take us back. They'll be waiting for him. Now, go. Make thyself fit to be seen."

"Yes, cousin," Maia said, and did not contest Setheris's assumption that he would be traveling to the court with the new emperor.

# 2

## The Radiance of Cairado

The airship *Radiance of Cairado* hung ominously beside her mooring mast like an isolated thundercloud against the predawn sky. Maia had not been in an airship since the age of eight, when he had been brought to the Untheileneise Court for his mother's funeral, and his memories of that time were full of darkness. He remembered praying to Ulis to let him die, too.

The crew of the *Radiance* were all very solemn; they knew about the *Wisdom of Choharo*, and he saw grief and fear in their faces.

On impulse, when the captain greeted him with a mumbled "Serenity" at the foot of the mooring mast, Maia stopped and said quietly, "We have nothing but confidence in you and your crew."

The captain was startled into looking up; Maia met his eyes and smiled at him. After a moment, the captain's ears came up, and he bowed again, more deeply. "Serenity," he said in a clear and far stronger voice.

Maia ascended the narrow iron staircase that spiraled around the mooring mast. On the tiny platform at the top, a crewwoman was waiting to steady the emperor into the passenger cabin.

"Serenity," she said stiffly, and offered her arm.

"We thank you," Maia said, accepting help he did not need. The crewwoman seemed almost as startled as the captain had been.

Airships were not primarily intended for passengers, but along with cargo, they transported couriers and other government servants. Maia had refused to allow Setheris to inconvenience the other passengers—four couriers, two missioners, and an elderly maza—by commandeering the ship, and he suffered for his charity now under their wide-eyed, breathlessly silent stares. His translation to emperor had failed to work any comparable miracle on his wardrobe—indeed, he only wished it had worked a miracle on his person—so that while he was correctly dressed in formal mourning, each garment bore betraying signs that black had been at least its third dyeing, and the whole had not been worn in over two years, since the death of the emperor's sister, the Archduchess Ebreneän. The clothes, castoffs of Setheris's, had been too large then; now, they were barely large enough. Lacking tashin sticks or combs, he had had to make do with braiding his hair back neatly and pinning it off his neck, but the style was more suited to a child than to an adult, much less to an emperor.

He took the seat that Setheris and the Lord Chancellor's messenger had left between them. If the messenger recognized in the new emperor's scrambling departure the thwarting of his own master's plans, he gave no sign of it, entering with helpful thoroughness into Setheris's travel arrangements. There was nothing to say he was not as devoted to Maia's service as Setheris was. Maia smiled at the irony.

He and Setheris had disliked each other from the moment they had met, at the funeral of Maia's mother, the Empress Chenelo. The airship that brought her body to the Untheileneise Court from the manor to which her husband had relegated her also brought her grief-sick eight-year-old son. Varenechibel IV took no interest in his youngest child, and immediately after the funeral service, Maia was handed into the care of Setheris Nelar and both of them relegated to the former hunting lodge Edonomee, where they had lived in mutual antipathy ever since.

Maia glanced sideways; Setheris was glowering—insofar as he could tell—at a perfectly innocuous piece of woodwork on the opposite side of the cabin. He had never seen Setheris when he was not angry, save for those times when he had drunk himself into a maudlin stupor. Maia's adolescence had been made a misery by Setheris's anger, and he would bear until his dying day an ugly scrawl of scars on his left forearm, where a blow of Setheris's had knocked him into the elaborate and hideous wrought-iron antlers that adorned the fire screen in Edonomee's main hall.

To do Setheris what justice he deserved, he had been truly horrified, and since that incident, which had enlivened Maia's otherwise utterly unremarkable fifteenth winter, he had been a good deal more circumspect with his fists. But it did not make him like Maia any better, and it was something Maia knew he himself would never be entirely able to forgive.

The crewwoman stepped into the cabin, securing the door behind her. She cleared her throat—out of nervousness, since there was no need to attract the attention of the deathly silent passengers—and said, "Your Serenity, the captain has taken the helm, and we are preparing to cast off."

Setheris's elbow slammed discreetly into Maia's ribs, and he said, "Thank you."

The crewwoman bowed, relief written in every line of her body, and went to the front of the cabin, where there was a speaking tube that communicated with the cockpit. Maia had only a moment to wonder if he would be able to tell when the *Radiance of Cairado* cast off from the mast; then there was the slightest of sideways lurches, and the airship was rising into the dawn sky.

The trip to the Untheileneise Court would take two hours, covering a distance that required four days on the ground, and that given fair weather and swift passage across the Istandaärtha, neither of which could be assumed. He could not help wondering, as the airship's motors cut in, their din ensuring that he would not have to speak to Setheris again until they reached the court, what the final moments of the *Wisdom of Choharo* had been like. Less than a day ago, she had been in the air, carrying the Emperor of the Elflands. He wondered if there had been a moment when they had known, or if death had come as suddenly as an executioner's sword. He tried to imagine his father screaming or crying or even frightened, and could not do it. His memory of his father, the only time he had ever seen him, was of the Emperor Varenechibel IV, tall and distant, with glacial eyes and a face as white and cold as marble. He remembered the white robes stiff with embroidery, the moonstones on his father's hands, braided into his hair, hanging from his ears. He remembered the black bands, the only token of mourning the emperor had deigned to wear for his fourth wife, like smears of ink across the whiteness of his person. He remembered his father's bitter mouth, and his smooth silken voice: *The damned whelp looks just like his mother.* It was as clear and frozen in his mind as the state portrait of the emperor that hung in the receiving room of Edonomee— and now there was no chance for it to change, no hope for it to be replaced.

*Though truly,* he thought, leaning back slightly to lessen the likelihood that he would catch Setheris's eye, *even were it to have been replaced, it would only have*

*been with something worse. Be grateful he cared no
more for thee than "damned whelp."*

His memories of his brothers were nothing more than
wisps of cloud. He had not even been sure which ones
they were in the masses of black-clothed courtiers
around his mother's tomb. It had been the lady charged
with his care during the funeral—a minor noble's wife
whose name he could not now remember—who had
pointed them out. *There your brother Nemolis and his
wife, there your brother Nazhira, there your brother
Ciris.* They had all been adults to his child's eyes, as
white and forbidding as his father. None of them had
ever made overtures, not at the funeral and not since—
whether because they shared the emperor's disdain or
feared his wrath—and Maia had hesitated to make overtures of his own, lest he should anger them. And now it
was too late for that, as well.

He would have liked to rest his head against the back
of the seat and shut his eyes, but he did not need Setheris
to tell him that an emperor could not behave so in public,
and those seven passengers and the nervous crewwoman constituted "public." Despite what had seemed
the overwhelming probability that both of them would
be confined to Edonomee for the rest of their lives,
Setheris had been relentless in maintaining and enforc-
ing court etiquette. Maia had never minded—Chenelo
had taught him carefully—but now it occurred to him
that he ought to be grateful.

He glanced again at Setheris's granite frown. It was
strange in this sleepless dawn to be looking at Setheris
and seeing simply another man instead of the tyrant of
Edonomee, as he had figured in Maia's mind for the past
ten years. Middle-aged, bitter, cunning but perhaps not
wise—Maia had never learned what it was that Setheris
had done to earn Varenechibel's enmity, but he knew it

could not have been anything trivial. Outside Edonomee, Setheris seemed smaller, less dreadful, and it occurred to Maia that if Setheris ever struck him again, it
would mean a death sentence. The idea was dizzying,
and Maia found his hands clutching the arms of the seat,
as if the *Radiance* herself were whirling about, instead
of merely his own mind. He forced himself to relax his
grip before anyone else noticed; it would be unkind in
the extreme to make anyone think him fearful.

Through the windows on the opposite side of the
cabin, he could see great mountains of cloud, stained
with pinks and reds by the approaching dawn. He remembered a Barizheise hymn to Osreian his mother had
taught him and said it to himself, looking at the clouds
and hoping that the goddesses' mercy would extend, not
merely to his father and half brothers, but to everyone
who had died with the *Wisdom of Choharo*.

He was brought back to his immediate surroundings
by the approach of the crewwoman, who came within
arm's length and then went down on one knee. "Your
Serenity."

"Yes?" said Maia, aware of both Setheris and the
Lord Chancellor's messenger coming to full alertness
beside him.

"The captain wonders, Serenity, if you would care to
come forward to watch the sunrise from the cockpit. It
is a very beautiful sight."

"Thank you," Maia said before Setheris could get his
mouth open. "We would like that very much."

He compressed the corners of his mouth against a
smile as he stood up, watching Setheris turn an unflattering shade of red with impotent fury. And following
that thought—and a host of others that had been teasing about the edges of his mind since Setheris's lecture
on dealing with Uleris Chavar—he turned and said to
the messenger, "Would you accompany us, please?"

"Serenity," the messenger said, rising with alacrity, and they left Setheris fuming, unable to invite himself along now that an express invitation had been issued to another than himself. Maia reminded himself that glee was unbefitting an emperor, and thought soberly as the crewwoman opened the narrow door at the front of the cabin, *I must not acquire a taste for this pleasure*. It was heady, but he knew it was also poison.

The door led into a narrow passageway, scarcely broader than the width of Maia's shoulders, and debouched through another door into the cockpit, where captain and first mate shared a wide panorama of clouds and sky.

"Serenity," they said in chorus, though they spared but a glance away from their instruments and the unfurling brightness in the east. The first mate, he saw, was of goblin blood, his skin only a shade lighter than Maia's own.

"Gentlemen, we thank you," Maia said, having to pitch his voice even louder to be heard over the roar of the engines, and allowed the crewwoman to shepherd him into a corner where he could see but would not obstruct anything important. The Lord Chancellor's messenger was likewise shepherded into the opposite corner, and the crewwoman closed the door and braced her back against it.

They stood in silence for fifteen minutes, enrapt and breathless before the glory of Anmura rising from Osreian's embrace. Then the first mate turned, bowing his head, and said, "Serenity, we will be arriving at the Untheileneise Court in approximately an hour."

Interpreting this to mean that they needed their cockpit back, Maia said, "We are most grateful, gentlemen. We will remember this always as the beginning of our reign." Much better this than that confused and frightened awakening in darkness, his own glassy, sharp-edged panic, Setheris's drunken viciousness.

"Serenity," they chorused again, and he could see that he had pleased them.

The crewwoman opened the door and Maia returned to the passenger cabin, to spend the remaining time considering ways and alternatives of greeting his father's Lord Chancellor.

# 3

## The Alcethmeret

The mooring mast of the Untheileneise Court was a jeweled spire in the sunlight. Maia descended the narrow staircase slowly, carefully, aware that the deceptive clearheadedness of fatigue would not extend to coordination, and he would be most unlikely to save himself if he stumbled.

No one knew to await him, and so there was no one at the foot of the mast except the captain, again. Maia was relieved; Chavar caught off balance would be far easier to deal with than Chavar given time to consider and plan.

Maia lengthened his stride past Setheris to catch up to the messenger. "Will you guide us?"

The messenger's eyes flicked from him to Setheris, and then he bowed. "Serenity. We will be honored."

"Thank you. And, if you would—" He lowered his voice and dropped formality: "Tell me your name?"

He at least succeeded in startling the messenger out of his stone face for a second: his eyes widened, and then he smiled. "I am Csevet Aisava, and I am entirely at Your Serenity's service."

"We thank you," Maia said, and followed Csevet toward the long roofed walkway that led to the Untheileneise Court itself.

"Court" was a misleading word. The Untheileneise Court was a palace as large as a small city—larger, in fact, than the city of Cetho that surrounded it—housing not merely the emperor, but also the Judiciate, the Corazhas of Witnesses that advised the emperor, the Parliament, and all the secretaries, couriers, servants, functionaries, and soldiers needed to ensure that those bodies did their work efficiently and well. The court had been designed by Edrethelema III and built during the reigns of his son, grandson, and great-grandson, Edrethelema IV through VI. Thus, for a compound of its vast size, it was remarkably and beautifully homogeneous in architecture; rather than sprawling, it seemed to spiral together into the great minareted dome of the Alcethmeret, the emperor's principal residence.

*My home,* Maia thought, but the phrase meant nothing.

"Serenity," said Csevet, pausing before the tall glass doors at the end of the walkway, "where do you wish to go?"

Maia hesitated a moment. His pressing concern was to find and speak to the Lord Chancellor, but he remembered what Setheris had shown him. The emperor hunting all over the court for his chief minister would look ill and ludicrous, and it would grant Chavar the power he was presuming he had. But, on the other hand, Maia knew nothing of the geography of the court, except for the stories his mother had told him when he was small. And since she herself had lived in the Untheileneise Court for less than a year, he could not rely on her tales for any accuracy of information.

Setheris came up to them. Maia thought, *Thou hast resources, if thou wilt stretch out thy hand to use them.* He said, "Cousin, we require a room where we may have private audience with our father's Lord Chancellor."

There was a flicker of something, some unreadable

emotion, on Setheris's face, gone as soon as noticed, and he said, "The Tortoise Room in the Alcethmeret has always been the emperors' choice for such audiences."

"Thank you, cousin," Maia said, and to Csevet, "Take us there, please."

"Serenity," Csevet said, bowing, and held open the door for Maia to enter the Untheileneise Court.

The court was not as bewildering as he had expected, and his admiration for Edrethelema III increased. Doubtless behind those beautifully paneled walls there were warrens and webs, but the public corridors of the court were straight and broad and clearly designed for an emperor to be able to find his way about his own seat of government. The distances were fatiguing, but about that Maia imagined Edrethelema had been able to do little; the simple fact of the palace's necessary size precluded convenience.

They were seen—as how could they not be?—and he was able, with bitter amusement, to distinguish those who were in the Lord Chancellor's confidence and those who were not, for only those who recognized Csevet and had known his mission looked alarmed. No one recognized the new emperor on his own merits. *In sooth, I look not like my father, and I am pleased at it,* Maia thought defiantly, although he knew that the dark hair and skin he had inherited from his goblin mother would do him no favors in the Untheileneise Court. And, even more grimly: *They will learn to know me soon enough.*

Csevet opened another elaborately wrought door, this one a wicket set in a massive bronze gate, and passing through, Maia found himself standing at the base of the Alcethmeret. Staircases wound in wide spirals around the inside of the tower; the lower levels were disturbingly open, a reminder from one emperor to the next that a private life was something he would not have. But about halfway up the tower's height, the architecture changed, a boundary marked by a pair of floor-to-ceiling iron grilles; those were open now, for there was no emperor in residence, and Maia could see that beyond them the staircase was enclosed and guessed that the rooms would likewise be smaller, more customary. Less exposed.

There were servants everywhere, it seemed; for a moment he could not even sort them out, as they turned and stared and dropped to their knees. Some of them prostrated themselves full-length as Csevet had done, and in that excess of formality, he read their fear. Belatedly, he realized that catching Chavar off guard also meant catching the servants of his household in unreadiness, an unkindness they had done nothing to deserve. Setheris would tell him it was sentimental nonsense to care for the feelings of servants, but in Barizhan servants were family—legally always and often by blood. The Empress Chenelo had raised her child by that principle, and he had clung to it all the harder because of Setheris's opposition.

Csevet said, "The Tortoise Room, Serenity?"

"Yes. And then," arresting Csevet as he turned to lead the way up the nearer staircase, "we would speak with our household steward. And *then* the Lord Chancellor."

"Yes, Serenity," Csevet said.

The Tortoise Room was the first room beyond the iron grilles. It was small, hospitable, appointed in amber-colored silk that was warm without being oppressive. The fires had not yet been lit, but Maia had barely seated himself in the chair by the fireplace when a girl scurried in, her hands shaking so badly she almost dropped the tinderbox before she could get the fire to light.

When she had left—her head lowered so far that, first to last, the only impression Maia gained of her was of her close-cropped, goblin-black hair—Setheris said, "Well, boy?"

Maia tilted his head back to regard his cousin where he leaned, not quite lounging, against the wall. "Do not presume, cousin, when thou hast warned me of presumption so cannily."

A great many things were at that moment made worthwhile, as he watched Setheris gape and splutter like a landed fish. *Remember,* he said to himself, *a poisonous pleasure.*

"I raised thee!" Setheris said, all injury and indignation.

"So you did."

Setheris blinked and then slowly went to his knees. "Serenity," he said.

"Thank you, cousin," Maia said, knowing full well that Setheris offered him only the form of respect, that even now, as at Maia's wave he took the other chair, he was incensed with Maia's arrogance, waiting for the correct moment to reassert his control.

*Thou wilt not,* Maia thought. *If I achieve nothing else in all my reign, thou* wilt not *rule me.*

And then Csevet said from the door, "Your house steward, Serenity. Echelo Esaran."

"We thank you," Maia said. "The Lord Chancellor, please."

"Serenity," Csevet said, and vanished again.

Esaran was a woman in her mid-forties. The sharp, austere bones of her face were suited by a servant's crop, and she wore her livery with an air that would have done justice to an empress's coronation robes. She went to her knees gracefully; her face and ears revealed nothing of her thoughts.

"We apologize for our sudden arrival," Maia said.

"Serenity," she said, the word stiff and precise, unyielding, and he realized, his heart sinking, that here was one who had served his father with her heart as well as her mind.

*I do not want more enemies!* he cried out, but only in his own thoughts. Aloud, he said, "We do not wish to disrupt your work any more than we must. Please convey to the household staff our gratitude and our . . . our sympathy." He could not say he shared their grief when he did not—and when this cold-eyed woman knew he did not.

"Serenity," she said again. "Will that be all?"

"Yes, thank you, Esaran." She rose and departed. Maia pinched the bridge of his nose, reminding himself that, although the first, she would hardly be the last inhabitant of the Untheileneise Court who would hate him for his father's sake. And, moreover, it was foolish and weak to feel hurt at her enmity. *Another luxury thou canst not afford,* he thought, and did not meet Setheris's eyes.

It took some time for Csevet to return with the Lord Chancellor. Maia had been trained, first by his mother, then by Setheris, to disregard boredom, and he had no lack of matters to consider. He kept his back straight, his hands relaxed, his face impassive, his ears neutral, and thought about all the things he did not know, had never been taught because no one had imagined an emperor with three healthy sons and a grandson would ever be succeeded to the throne by his fourth and ill-regarded son.

*I shall need a teacher,* Maia thought, *and Setheris is not my choice.*

If there was a contest waged in the Tortoise Room, it was Setheris who lost it. He broke the silence: "Serenity?"

"Cousin?"

He saw Setheris's throat work and his ears dip, and his attention sharpened. Anything that discomfited Setheris was reflexively a matter of interest. "We . . . we would like to speak to our wife."

"Of course," Maia said. "You are welcome to send Csevet in search of her when he returns."

"Serenity," Setheris said, not meeting Maia's eyes but continuing stubbornly on. "We had hoped to . . . to introduce her to your favor."

Maia considered. He knew little of Setheris's wife, Hesero Nelaran, save that she had worked tirelessly and fruitlessly to get Setheris recalled to the Untheileneise Court and had sent him weekly letters with all the gossip and intrigue she could gather. Maia had assumed— in part because Setheris never spoke of her save, when in a particularly good humor, to relay choice tidbits of scandal over the breakfast table—that theirs was an arranged marriage, as loveless, if not as hate-filled, as his mother's marriage to the emperor. But Setheris's obvious distress argued otherwise.

*Do not make enemies where it needs not,* he thought, remembering Merrem Esaran's enmity, considering the likely course of his upcoming interview with the Lord Chancellor. He said, "We would be pleased. *After* we have spoken to the Lord Chancellor."

"Serenity," Setheris said, acquiescing, and they fell again into silence.

Maia noted when an hour had passed, and wondered if it was that the Lord Chancellor was unusually well hidden—most odd and unadmirable in a man planning a state funeral—or that he was trying to regain the whip hand by a calculated show of disrespect.

*He harms none but himself by such tactics,* Maia thought. *He cannot delay long enough to force me into step with his plans—at least not without risking dismissal on grounds of contempt. Perchance he thinks I would not do it, but he will not rule me, either. And if he has no loyalty to me, it is just as much the case that I have no loyalty to him. I do not even know the man's face.*

Immersed in these grim thoughts, it took him a moment to realize that the approaching tumult on the stairs had to be Chavar. "Has he brought an army with him?" Setheris murmured, and Maia repressed a smile.

Csevet, looking a little winded, appeared in the doorway. "The Lord Chancellor, Serenity."

"We thank you," Maia said, and awaited the entrance of Uleris Chavar.

Without realizing it, Maia had been expecting a copy of his father's state portrait: tall and cold and remote. Chavar proved to be none of these things. He was short and stocky by elven standards, choleric, and he was almost on top of Maia before he bothered to bend a knee.

"Serenity," he said with perfunctory courtesy; Maia had to resist the urge to stand up, to prevent Chavar from looming over him. Instead, he jerked his head at Setheris—tacit permission to send Csevet in search of Osmerrem Nelaran—and, as Setheris crossed eagerly to where Csevet stood, Maia waved Chavar to the empty chair, a sign of favor the Lord Chancellor could not ignore.

Chavar sat down with ill grace and said, "What is Your Serenity's will?"

It was a formula, brusquely uttered; he already had his mouth half-open—doubtless to explain the arrangements he had made for the funeral—when Maia said, as gently as he could, "We wish to discuss our coronation."

Chavar's mouth remained half-open for a moment. He shut it with a click, inhaled deeply, and said, "Your Serenity, surely this is not the time. Your father's funeral—"

"We wish," Maia said, less gently, "to discuss our coronation. When that is arranged to our satisfaction, we will hear you upon the subject of our father's funeral." He caught and held Chavar's gaze, waiting.

Chavar did not look away. "Yes, Serenity," he said, and the hostility was in the air between them like a half-drawn sword. "What are your plans, if we may be so bold?"

Maia saw the trap and skirted it. "How quickly can you arrange our coronation? We do not wish any more delay than is necessary in rendering the proper rites and obsequies to our father and brothers, but we also do not wish to do anything in a slipshod or hasty fashion."

Chavar's expression was, if only for a moment, distinctly pained. It was clear he had not expected an eighteen-year-old emperor, raised in virtual isolation, to provide him with any contest at all. *Sometime, Chavar,* Maia thought, *you must try living for ten years with a man who hates you and whom you hate, and see what it does to sharpen* your *wits.*

Something of this thought must have shown in his eyes, for Chavar said quite promptly, "We can prepare the coronation ceremony for tomorrow afternoon, Your Serenity. It will mean delaying the funeral for another day. . . ." He trailed off, clearly hoping that Maia might still be browbeaten into acceding to his Lord Chancellor's wishes.

But Maia was considering something else. Setheris had been trained as a barrister, before he fell afoul of Varenechibel's temper, and he had passed as much of that training on to Maia as he felt it likely a teenage boy—of whose intelligence he had no great opinion—would comprehend. There had been no kindness in the gesture, merely Setheris's rigid sense of what befitted the son of an emperor, and it did not befit the son of an emperor to reach manhood entirely ignorant. And, Maia supposed, it had been something to *do,* a commodity that Setheris must surely have needed as desperately as he did himself.

But again there was reason for gratitude, although

still he felt none. For at least Setheris had taught him, among other things, the forms and protocols surrounding a coronation. He said, "Will that give the princes time to make the journey?" He knew perfectly well it would not—else Chavar would have scheduled the funeral for that time—but he was not yet prepared to accuse the Lord Chancellor of open contempt. *It would be a rare start to my reign,* he thought, but kept the bitter quirk off his face. He would have to work with Chavar until such time as he was sufficiently familiar with the court to choose his own Lord Chancellor, and he feared that time might be far distant.

And Chavar did a passable job of pretending chagrin. "Serenity, we most humbly beg your pardon for our oversight. The princes, if we send messengers today, cannot arrive before the twenty-third."

*As we know from your letter,* Maia did not say, and he saw acknowledgment of that in Chavar's eyes. The Lord Chancellor said, "Serenity. We will put preparations in train for your coronation at midnight of the twenty-fourth." It was an offer of truce, no matter how obliquely or grudgingly offered, and Maia accepted it as such.

"We thank you," he said, and gestured Chavar to his feet. "And the funeral on the twenty-fifth? Or can preparations be made for the twenty-fourth?"

"Serenity," Chavar said with a half bow. "The twenty-fourth is achievable."

"Then let it be so." Chavar was almost at the door when Maia remembered something else: "What of the other victims?"

"Serenity?"

"The others on board the *Wisdom of Choharo.* What arrangements are being made on their behalf?"

"The emperor's nohecharei will of course be buried with him."

Chavar was not being deliberately obstructive, Maia saw; he genuinely didn't understand.

"And the pilot? The *others*?"

"Crew and servants, Serenity," Chavar said, baffled. "There will be a funeral this afternoon at the Ulimeire."

"We will attend."

That had both Setheris and Chavar staring at him. "They are as much dead as our father," Maia said. "We will attend."

"Serenity," Chavar said with another hasty bow, and left. Maia wondered if he was beginning to suspect his new emperor of insanity.

Setheris, of course, had no doubts; he had aired his views on the perniciousness of Chenelo's influence more than once. But he forbore to speak, merely rolling his eyes.

Csevet had not yet returned, and Maia had a use for this breathing space. "Cousin," he said, "would you have our father's Master of Wardrobe sent to us?"

"Serenity," Setheris said with a bow as perfunctory as Chavar's, and went out. Maia took the opportunity to stand, to try to ease the harp-string tension of his muscles. "Not all hands will be against thee," he whispered to himself, but he feared it for a lie. He rested his elbows on the mantel, his head in his hands, and tried to conjure in his mind the sunrise seen from the *Radiance of Cairado,* but it was blurred and dull, as if seen through a pane of dirty glass.

There was a hesitant tap at the door, an even more hesitant voice saying, "Ser . . . Serenity?"

Maia turned. A middle-aged man, tall and stooped, with the mild, nervous expression of a rabbit. "You are our Master of Wardrobe?"

"Serenity," the man said, bowing deeply. "We . . . we so served your late father, and so will serve you, an it be your pleasure."

"Your name?"

"Clemis Atterezh, Serenity." Maia saw nothing but anxiety to please in his face or stance, heard nothing but diffidence and nerves in his voice.

"We will be crowned at midnight on the twenty-fourth," he said. "Our father and brothers' funeral will be that day. But today there is the funeral for the other victims, which we wish to attend."

"Serenity," Atterezh said politely, uncomprehending.

"What does an uncrowned emperor wear to a public funeral?"

"Oh!" Atterezh advanced slightly into the room. "You cannot wear full imperial white, and court mourning is inappropriate . . . and you certainly can't wear *that*."

At the cost of a savagely bitten lip, Maia did not giggle. Atterezh said, "We will see what can be done, Serenity. Do you know when the funeral is to be held?"

"No," Maia said, and cursed himself for his stupidity.

"We will ascertain," Atterezh said. "And when it is convenient to Your Serenity, we are at your disposal to discuss your new wardrobe."

"Thank you," Maia said. Atterezh bowed and departed. Maia sat down again in bemused wonderment. He had hardly ever had a piece of new clothing before, much less an entire new wardrobe. *Thou'rt emperor now, not a half-witted ragpicker's child,* he said to himself, and felt almost dizzy at the reminder of his own thought from not even twelve hours ago.

A clatter of feet on the stairs. Maia looked up, expecting Setheris, but it was a breathless, frightened-looking child of no more than fourteen, dressed in full court mourning and clutching a black-bordered and elaborately sealed letter.

"Your Imperial Serenity!" the boy gasped, throwing himself full-length on the floor.

Maia had even less idea what to do with the gesture now than he had in the receiving room at Edonomee. At least Csevet had had the grace to get himself back on his feet again. A little desperately, he said, "Please, stand."

The boy did, and then stood goggling, his ears flat against his skull. It couldn't be the effect of being this close to an emperor—the boy wore the Drazhadeise crest and thus was in the service of the emperor's household. Maia knew what Setheris would say: *Cat got your tongue, boy?* He could even hear it, somewhere in the back of his head, and what it would sound like in his own voice. He said patiently, "You have a message for us?"

"Here. Serenity." The boy shoved the paper at him.

Maia took it, and to his own horror heard himself say, "How long have you served in the Untheileneise Court?" He barely managed to bite the "boy" off the end of it.

"F-four years. Serenity."

Maia raised his eyebrows, mirroring the cruel incredulity he had so often seen on Setheris's face; he waited a single beat and saw the boy's face flood red. Then he turned his attention to the letter, as if the boy held no more interest for him. It was addressed, in a clear clerk's hand, to the Archduke Maia Drazhar, a presagement that did not make him any happier.

He broke the seal and then, realizing the boy was still there, raised his head.

"Serenity," the boy said. "I . . . we . . . she wants an answer."

"Does she?" Maia said. He looked pointedly past the boy at the door. "You may wait outside."

"Yes, Serenity," the boy said in a half-choked mumble, and slunk out like a whipped dog.

*Setheris would be proud,* Maia thought bitterly and opened the letter. It was, at least, short:

> To the Archduke Maia Drazhar, heir to the imperial throne of Ethuveraz, greetings.
>     We have need to speak to you regarding the wishes of your late father, our husband, Varenechibel IV. Although we are in deepest mourning, we will receive you this afternoon at two o'clock.
>     With wishes for familial harmony,
>     Csoru Drazharan, Ethuverazhid Zhasan

*I do not doubt that she wants an answer,* Maia thought. The widow empress lacked even the subtlety of the Lord Chancellor. He wondered with an unhappy shiver what Varenechibel had told his fifth wife about her predecessor and her predecessor's child.

The Tortoise Room had a small secretary's desk tucked into the corner behind the door, and no matter the widow empress's rudeness, he owed her a reply in his own hand. Or perhaps more accurately, considering the clerk's hand of her letter, he owed himself a reply in his own hand. He found paper, dip pen, ink, wax—no seal, and he supposed the assumption was that anyone writing a letter would have his own signet. Maia did not; it was one of the many tokens of adulthood he had not received on his sixteenth birthday. A thumbprint would do for now, though it would probably get him accused of following his mother's barbaric customs. *So be it,* he thought, dipped his pen in the ink, and wrote:

> To Csoru Drazharan, Ethuverazhid Zhasanai, greetings and great sympathy.
>     We regret that a prior obligation prevents us from speaking with you this afternoon as you request. We shall, however, be pleased to grant you an audience

*tomorrow morning at ten; we are eager to hear any-*
*thing you can tell us of our late father.*

*Until our coronation, we are using the Tortoise*
*Room as a receiving room.*

*With respectful good wishes,*

And here Maia paused. To sign with his given name
would be to acknowledge that she had been correct in
addressing him in that fashion. But he had not, until that
moment, given any thought to the choosing of a dynas-
tic name, and it was hard to get beyond his first, instinctive reaction: *I will* not *be Varenechibel V.*

*No one forces thee,* he thought as the ink dried
patiently on his pen. *An thou did choose Varenechibel,*
*the court would doubtless construe it an insult.*

He knew from Setheris's impatient tutelage that his
great-great-great-grandfather, Varenechibel I, had chosen to signal his rejection of the policies of his father,
Edrevechelar XVI, by refusing the imperial prefix that
every emperor since Edrevenivar the Conqueror had
used, choosing to become Varenechibel the first of that
name instead of the ninth Edrenechibel. His son and
grandson had followed his lead, being Varenechibel II
and III. His great-grandson (willful, though never particularly imaginative, Setheris had said dryly) had de-
fied burgeoning tradition by becoming Varevesena. And
then had come Varenechibel IV.

And now Maia.

The emperors of what was informally called the
Varedeise dynasty—as if their chosen prefix were a
surname—were noted for their isolationist policies, their
favoring of the wealthy eastern landowners, and their
apparent inability to see anything wrong with bribery,
nepotism, and corruption. Setheris had gone into scath-
ing detail about the Black Mud Scandal of Varenechibel
III's reign (so called because it stained everyone who

came in contact with it), and Varevesena's disgraceful habit of giving munificent but otherwise empty political appointments to his friends' newborn children. "At least he is not *personally* corrupt," Setheris had said grudgingly of Varenechibel IV, but Maia thought that very cold praise.

He did not want to continue *any* of the Varedeise traditions; embracing their traditional hostility to Barizhan seemed self-destructive in a way that he found uncomfortably ambiguous between the symbolic and the literal. Even if he *had* wanted to, the encounter with Chavar demonstrated that he would have a grimly difficult battle winning the trust of his father's ardent supporters.

*Better to build new bridges,* he thought, *than to pine after what's been washed away.* He dipped his pen again and wrote with pointed legibility across the bottom of the page, *Edrehasivar VII Drazhar.* Edrehasivar VI had had a long, peaceful, and prosperous reign some five hundred years ago.

*Let it be an omen,* Maia thought, a quick prayer to Cstheio, the dreaming lady of the stars, and folded and sealed the letter. He had a lowering feeling that he was going to need all the omens of peace he could accumulate.

The boy was lingering nervously on the landing. "Here," said Maia. "Take this to the zhasanai with our compliments."

Wide-eyed, the boy took the letter. He had caught the nuance—"zhasanai," not "zhasan"—and Maia did not doubt that the widow empress would be told. She could style herself a ruling empress all she liked, but she was not one. She was zhasanai, an emperor's widow, and had best remember that she was dependent now upon her unknown stepson's goodwill.

"Serenity," the boy said, bowed, and fled.

*Already I become a tyrant,* Maia thought, and retreated again into the Tortoise Room to wait for Setheris and his wife.

But Setheris did not reappear until after Atterezh had come back bearing a mass of black and plum-colored cloth embroidered in white: mourning colors without the strict formality of court mourning. He also brought the information that the funeral would be held at three o'clock—as sundown was the most correct hour for funerals, it was also the most expensive, so that the families had had to pool their money to get as close as they could—and added that he had advised Esaran of the emperor's intention and obtained her assurance that the emperor's carriage would be ready at half past two. Maia could have wept with gratitude at finding one person who did not resist or resent him, but such an action was unbecoming to an emperor and would frighten and perplex Atterezh very much.

Thus, he stood and allowed Atterezh to take measurements, to drape and fuss with the cloth, and it was in the midst of this, as Atterezh mumbled arcanely to himself, that Setheris appeared in the doorway and demanded, "Has Uleris not sent you a guard?"

"No," Maia said.

"Who is this?"

"Our Master of Wardrobe."

"Then he hasn't sent a maza, either."

"No. Cousin, what—?"

"We will see to it," Setheris said. "And we would advise you to replace your Lord Chancellor as soon as you may. Uleris seems to be growing forgetful in his old age."

Since Setheris and Chavar were of an age, the insult was a pointed one—enough so that Maia realized this was not mere officiousness on Setheris's part, nor angling for Chavar's position. "Cousin, explain."

"Serenity," Setheris said, reminded by the imperative.

"The Emperor of the Elflands has both the right and the obligation to be attended at all times by the nohecharei, the guardian of the body and the guardian of the spirit. And especially if you intend to persist in this lunatic idea . . ." He waved a hand at the cloth draped over Maia's shoulder.

"We do," Maia said. "We are sure the Lord Chancellor has much on his mind. If you would see to the matter, we would be grateful, and when you return, we will be pleased to receive your wife."

"Serenity," Setheris said, bowed, left.

Maia knew—everyone knew—about the emperor's nohecharei, the guardians sworn to die before they would allow harm to come to him: one, the soldier, to guard with his body and the strength of his arm; the other, the maza, to guard with his spirit and the strength of his mind. Edonomee's cook could sometimes be coaxed into telling stories, so Maia even knew about Hanevis Athmaza, nohecharis to Beltanthiar III, who had entered a duel of magic with Orava the Usurper, the only magic-user ever to attempt to take the throne. Hanevis Athmaza had known Orava would kill him, but he had held the usurper off the emperor until the Adremaza, the master of the mazei of the Elflands, had reached them. Orava had been defeated, and Hanevis Athmaza, horribly injured, had died in his emperor's arms. In his early adolescence, Maia had dreamed of becoming a maza, of becoming perhaps his father's nohecharis and earning his love, but he had shown no more aptitude for magic than he showed (Setheris said) for anything else, and that dream, too, had died.

He had never dreamed of becoming emperor.

Atterezh continued with his task, the only sign that he had even noticed the conversation being that his discussion with himself was now inaudible rather than merely under his breath. Maia hoped his father had chosen his household staff for their discretion, for there was no part of that exchange with Setheris that he wished bruited about the court. But to say so would offend Atterezh and shatter the precarious fictions by which servants and nobles protected each other.

"Serenity," said Atterezh, climbing slowly to his feet. "I will have clothes in readiness for you at two o'clock, if that will please?"

"Yes. We thank you, Atterezh."

Atterezh bowed, released Maia from his draperies, and departed. Maia observed gloomily that thus far the life of an emperor seemed chiefly to involve sitting in a small room and watching other people come and go.

*That's more variety than thou hadst at Edonomee, where there was no one either to come or to go,* he thought, and managed a smile at his own foolish self-pity.

He sat down wearily, wondering if there might be time for a nap before he had to dress for the funeral. The clock gave the time as quarter of ten (which seemed either too late or too early, although he could not tell which). Esaran would not love him better if he demanded a bed made ready at ten in the morning.

He rubbed his eyes to keep them from drifting shut, and here was Setheris again, bristling with energy and spite. "Serenity, we have spoken with the Captain of the Untheileneise Guard and the Adremaza, and they will see to the matter. They wished us to convey to you their apologies and contrition. No slight was meant, for they were expecting the Lord Chancellor to inform them of your arrival."

"Do you believe them?"

"Serenity," Setheris said, acknowledging the justice of the question. He considered a moment, his head tilted to one side, his eyes as bright as a raptor's. "We are inclined to believe they speak in good faith. They are men with many other concerns, and we, too, expected Chavar to inform them."

"Thank you, cousin," Maia said; although those words were grimed with years of sullen irony, he said them as lightly, as gently, as he could. "And your wife?"

"Serenity," Setheris said, bowing.

He turned and beckoned. Maia heard the click of shoe heels and rose to his feet. Hesero Nelaran stopped in the doorway to drop a deep and magnificent curtsy, the old-style honor that the Empress Csoru had made unfashionable. "Your Serenity," she said, her voice as smooth as Setheris's was sharp.

She was a year or two younger than her husband, crow's-feet showing behind her maquillage. Her clothes were the black of proper court mourning: a floor-length dress trailing a train like a snake's tail; a quilted and elaborately embroidered jacket, plum on black, frogged with garnet clasps like drops of blood. Her hair was dressed with black lacquer combs and tashin sticks and strands of faceted onyx. She was not beautiful, but through sheer force of elegance she contrived to seem so.

Since his mother's death, Maia's personal acquaintance with women had been limited to Edonomee's stout cook and her two skinny daughters who did the housework. Although he had studied the fashion engravings in the newspapers with great care, there had been nothing that could have prepared him for Hesero Nelaran; he felt his composure shatter and fall to the floor about his feet.

"Osmerrem Nelaran," he managed finally, stumbling over his words like any callow youth, "we are very pleased to make your acquaintance."

"And we are pleased to make yours. We are also more grateful than we can say that you have allowed our husband to return to the Untheileneise Court." She sank again, this time not merely into a curtsy, but into a full-length prostration every bit as graceful as Csevet's. "Serenity, our honor and our loyalty are yours."

He said inadequately as she rose to her feet again, "We thank you, Osmerrem Nelaran."

"May we not count ourself your cousin, Serenity?"

"Cousin Hesero," he amended.

She smiled at him, and he melted in the warmth of it, barely able to keep his wits together sufficiently to realize that she was speaking, asking about his coronation. "Midnight on the twenty-fourth," he said, and she nodded with grave approbation, as if she had been worried that he might choose some other, less suitable time.

"Serenity," Setheris said, "you must not allow us to impose on you."

"We have much to do," Maia said to Hesero, partly out of habitual obedience to Setheris's obliquely worded commands, partly because he did not think he could sustain the audience much longer without making an utter driveling fool out of himself. "But we will hope for an opportunity to speak to you again."

"Serenity," they said. Hesero curtsied again; Setheris made a stiff, jerky little bow like a clockwork toy. She swept out with the same grace with which she had entered; she had one thin milk-white braid falling down her back past her hips, following the line of her spine. Setheris hurried after her, and Maia sank back into his chair, now abruptly breathless as well as fatigued.

*Thou hast no head for dalliance,* he said to himself, and began to laugh. He tried to stop, but it was beyond his power; the laughter seized and shook him like a terrier with a rat. The best he could do was to keep his vocal cords silent, suffering the paroxysm with no more noise than the occasional gasp for breath. It was as painful as choking or the terrible rattling cough of the charcarsa, and when at last it released him, he had to wipe tears off his face.

And then he looked up, straight into the eyes of a sober-faced young man dressed as a soldier and with a soldier's topknot, but wearing the Drazhadeise seal on a baldric across his chest. "Serenity," he said, and knelt. His disapproval was palpable.

Maia wondered in horror how long he had been standing there, waiting for his emperor to be in a fit state to receive him. "Please rise. You are one of our nohecharei?"

"Yes, Serenity," the young man said, standing straight again. "We are Deret Beshelar, Lieutenant of the Untheileneise Guard. Our captain has ordered us to serve as a nohecharis—unless Your Serenity is not pleased to accept our service."

Maia wished he could say, *No, we are not pleased,* and be rid of this disapproving wooden soldier. But he could not offend the Captain of the Untheileneise Guard without giving a reason, and what reason could he give? *He caught me laughing the day after my father's death.* He could not say that, and he read in Lieutenant Beshelar's vast disapproval an equally vast probity, and that, he felt, he would need more than the man's friendship.

"We see no reason to be displeased with the captain's choice," he said, and Beshelar said, "Serenity," in such a flat, withering voice that Maia knew he had heard the phrase as an attempt at flattery.

Before he could decide whether he could say anything to ameliorate the wrong-footedness of the conversation, or whether he would merely dig himself in deeper with the attempt, another voice said, "Oh, damn. We did so hope we would get here first. Serenity."

Maia blinked at this second young man, now kneeling in the doorway. He, too, wore a baldric with the Drazhadeise seal, but it looked almost incongruous over his shabby blue robe. As he stood again, unfolding a remarkable length of bony leg, Maia saw that he was taller than Beshelar, as gawky as a newborn colt. The pale blue eyes behind their thick round-lensed spectacles were myopic, gentle, and the one beauty in a face dominated by a long, high-arched nose. His untidy maza's queue did nothing to flatter him, but he was clearly not the sort of man who would ever care. He said, "We are Cala Athmaza. The Adremaza sent us."

Beshelar let out a slight pained noise, not quite a sigh and not quite a snort. But the maza seemed to find nothing insufficient in his introduction, merely stood blinking benevolently at Maia, and Maia found nothing insufficient in his introduction, either.

"We are pleased," he said. And to both of them, "We are Edrehasivar, to be crowned the seventh of that name at midnight of the twenty-fourth."

"Serenity," they said together, bowing, and then Cala said, "Serenity, there is a young man on the landing who looks as if he does not know whether he ought to stay or leave."

"Show him in," Maia said, and Cala and Beshelar stood aside.

Appearing between them, Csevet said, "We beg your pardon, Serenity. We did not know if you required our services for anything else."

Maia hid a wince. He had forgotten about Csevet, which was thoughtless and arrogant. "Have you other duties?"

"Serenity," Csevet said, bowing. "The Lord Chancellor has been so good as to intimate that he will second us to your service, if it would be pleasing to you."

"That is very kind of the Lord Chancellor," Maia said, meeting Csevet's eyes in a moment of shared, pained amusement. "Then we would be very grateful if you could . . ." He gestured for a word that was not there. "If you could organize our household?"

He heard the plaintive note in his own voice, but Csevet disregarded it. "It shall be as Your Serenity wishes," he said, bowing more deeply. "We will begin with . . ." He consulted his pocket watch. "Luncheon."

# 4

## The Funeral at the Ulimeire

The Ulimeire was on the outskirts of Cetho, the city that circled the Untheileneise Court like a crescent setting for a pearl. Descending from the embarrassingly large imperial carriage after Lieutenant Beshelar and Cala Athmaza, Maia thought unhappily that it might as well have been in another world.

The temple and the wall around the graveyard were made alike of crumbling red brick. The pillars of the temple portico were in need of a coat of whitewash, and their capitals were shaggy with abandoned birds' nests. Weeds thronged the cracks between the paving stones of the walkway from gate to temple, and the grass in the graveyard had grown so tall that the tops of the gravestones appeared like small, barren islands in a tempestuous and brittle sea.

"Serenity," said Beshelar, "are you sure—?"

"Yes," Maia said. "Their deaths weigh no lighter on the earth than our father's."

As Cala opened the gate, a stout black-robed prelate, as shabby as his temple, appeared in the doorway. He stared, mouth agape beneath his dented moon-mask, and then all but threw himself down the stairs. He prostrated himself, and from the dark interior of the temple, there was a great soft rustling as the congregation did the same wherever they happened to be standing.

*Thou must grow accustomed,* Maia said to himself as he followed Beshelar and Cala toward the temple. *Thou art emperor, as Setheris told thee. And at this juncture, truly, thou canst be emperor or thou canst be dead. Which dost thou prefer?*

"His Imperial Serenity, Edrehasivar the Seventh," Beshelar announced; Maia wished he wouldn't.

"Please," Maia said to the prelate, "rise. We wish only to pay our respects to the dead."

The prelate stood up, rubbing his hands anxiously on the skirts of his robe. "Your Imperial Serenity," he said. "We had no idea . . . that is, we weren't informed . . ."

*And someone should have been sent to inform you,* Maia thought wearily. He had imagined somehow that he would be able to slip into the back of the temple and listen to the service without confessing his identity, but that had been a child's wonder-tale, nothing more.

He said, "We are sorry, truly."

"Serenity!" Beshelar hissed out of the corner of his mouth.

"We wished only to acknowledge the loss," Maia continued, raising his voice so that the people inside the temple might hear him clearly, "that all of you have suffered. We did not wish that to be forgotten. We did not wish you to feel that . . . that we did not care."

"Thank you, Serenity," the prelate said after a pause. "We . . . that is, the temple is very small and not what you are used to. But, if you—and these gentlemen— would like to share in our worship, we—" and he used the plural, meaning both himself and the congregation. "—we would be . . ." He trailed off, searching for a word. "It would be an honor."

Maia smiled at him. "Thank you. We also would be

honored." He ignored Beshelar's appalled expression and followed the prelate up the stairs into the temple.

He considered and discarded the idea of telling the prelate that his Ulimeire was preferable by far to the dank and grimy Othasmeire at Edonomee. It was wiser for him to say as little as possible, and he feared besides that the prelate would take it as some sort of joke. But it was true. The Ulimeire was shabby and run-down, but clean, and the whitewash that had not been applied to the pillars had clearly been put to better use on the walls. The shy people, elves and goblins, in their much-mended and ill-fitting blacks—very like the clothes that Maia himself had been wearing when he had left Edonomee centuries ago that morning—were the family and friends and lovers of the crew of the *Wisdom of Choharo,* of the servants whose lives had been lost with their imperial masters. Many of the mourners wore livery; one or two of them were people he thought he had seen in the Alcethmeret earlier in the day. He saw grief and pain on their faces and wished he felt anything of the sort in his heart. He wished he had had a father worthy of mourning.

It took some time to find a place to put an emperor and his nohecharei in the Ulimeire that did not cause great discomfort and embarrassment for all concerned, but between the goodwill of the congregation, the prelate, the emperor, and his maza—and the remarkable and pointed forbearance of his guard—the matter was managed, and the prelate, taking his place before the altar of Ulis, as clean and shabby as the rest of the temple, began the service for the dead.

He spoke the words very simply and honestly, unlike the affected intonations and dramatic pauses of the Archprelate of Cetho who had officiated at the funeral service for the Empress Chenelo. Maia was disturbed to discover how clear and sharp his memories of his mother's funeral were. Ten years might as well have been as many days.

The Empress Chenelo Drazharan had died in the spring of her son's ninth year. She had been ill for as long as he could remember, his gray, stick-thin, beloved mother. Even to a child, it had become clear that winter that she was dying, as her eyes seemed to take up more and more of her face and she became so thin that even a badly judged touch could bruise her. She spent much of that winter and early spring in tears, dying and homesick and desperately afraid for her son.

She had been married very young—barely sixteen—and the marriage her father's idea. The Great Avar of Barizhan wanted to see his daughter an empress. The Elflands, hostile to all foreigners though they were, desperately needed cordial relations with Barizhan, their only access to the rich trade of the Chadevan Sea, and so Varenechibel's Witness for Foreigners had convinced him to agree to the marriage. It had been a bad decision all around, Chenelo told Maia in the days before her death. Her father, bitter in his disappointment that his wife had given him no sons—only two daughters, and one of those ill-favored and half-mad—had cared nothing for Chenelo and everything for the idea of treaties to secure his northern borders against his much larger and more powerful neighbor. The Witness for Foreigners had been an ambitious, greedy man. When Maia had been two years old, the Witness had been caught taking bribes from Pencharneise merchants. Varenechibel had sent Chenelo a gruesomely explicit engraving of the execution.

Varenechibel himself, still mourning for his third wife, the Empress Pazhiro, who had died five years previously, should not have considered marriage at that time, especially not to a girl young enough to be his daughter, a foreigner, a barbarian, a goblin; she had gained the cruel soubriquet "Hobgoblin" among the court before she was even married. Varenechibel found her ugly, boring, unappealing, but his lack of interest in her would not have deepened to hatred had it not been that their wedding night, the necessary legal consummation of their marriage and the only time Varenechibel claimed his marital rights of her, resulted in her pregnancy. Considering the unambiguity of the evidence that she had come a virgin to his bed, he could not even claim the child was not his.

Pazhiro had died in childbirth, and perhaps if Chenelo had done the same, he would have forgiven her. But she survived, and produced a healthy son as dark and ugly as herself; Varenechibel said viciously that if she thought she could replace Pazhiro and Pazhiro's last, dead child, she was very much mistaken. As soon as Chenelo was able to travel, she and her child were sent to Isvaroë, where she would spend the last eight years of her life.

She had died on a gray, windy day in mid-spring, and since a dead empress was marginally more acceptable to Varenechibel than a living one, preparations were immediately put in train for a high ceremonial state funeral. It was also true that the Great Avar, who made no protest about his daughter's treatment while she was alive—and saw nothing to criticize in the idea that a man would want no more congress with his wife than was necessary to beget a son—would have been grossly offended if less than full respect were paid to her corpse. The quiet house at Isvaroë was invaded by secretaries, functionaries, clerics. Most of them, when they noticed Maia at all, looked at him and sighed and shook their heads. He hid in his mother's bedroom as much as he could.

If he could simply have lain down and died of grief,

he would have. His mother had been the world to him, and although she had done her best to prepare him, he had been too young to fully understand what death meant—until she was gone, and the great, raw, gaping hole in his heart could not be filled or patched or mended. He looked for her everywhere, even after he had been shown her body—looked and looked and she could not be found.

He wept only in private, not trusting the strange adults who bustled around him, breaking the peace of Isvaroë with their loud voices and continual racket of packing and planning. And then came the day when they told him he had to leave Isvaroë, and took him in an airship to the Untheileneise Court, in which he had never fully believed, being always half-convinced that it was merely part of his mother's stories.

He sat now, in this clean shabby temple to the moon-god, who was also the god of dreams and death and rebirth, and remembered the cold echoing marble of the Othasmeire of the Untheileneise Court, with its separate satellite shrines for each god. But there was not room in the shrine of Ulis for a full state funeral, and so Chenelo's bier was placed beneath the dome's oculus, as the biers of the Empress Pazhiro and the Empress Leshan had been. Instead of this single prelate, there had been a flock of clerics and canons surrounding the red-robed Archprelate, a miasma of incense, and crowds of white-haired, white-faced elves in elaborate black who stood and listened to the service silently and without emotion. Here, they were *almost* silent, but there were the sounds of sobs choked back; the rustle of cloth against cloth as one mourner comforted another; even, halfway through, the wail of a child realizing loss, and the quick wordless shuffle as people cleared a path for her father to take her out. No one, Maia thought, would have done as much for him.

He remembered standing silent and stony-eyed beside the noblewoman given the thankless task of shepherding him through the funeral. Although the account Chenelo had given him of her marriage had been carefully impartial, carefully judged to what a child could understand, nevertheless his fierce worship of his mother had led him closer to the truth than she had ever wished him to go. It was his father's fault, he understood, and this his father's court, and he imagined that it would please them to see him weep. So he had not wept, not then, although he had wept every night for a week in the cold, musty bedroom he was given at Edonomee. Probably, he thought ruefully, he had frightened that noblewoman very much, and he made a mental note to ask Csevet if she could be found.

The prelate of the Ulimeire used the short form, unlike the interminable ceremony that had been used for Chenelo and would be used for Varenechibel and three of his four sons. The longest single part was the list of the names of the dead and the list of those who survived them. Hesitantly, with a shy glance at Maia, the prelate added at the end, "The Emperor Varenechibel the fourth, Nemolis Drazhar, Nazhira Drazhar, Ciris Drazhar, survived by the Emperor Edrehasivar the Seventh." Blinking back a sudden prickle of tears, Maia bowed to the prelate over his clasped hands as each of the other mourners had done in turn, and cared nothing for the stiff, shocked disapproval of Beshelar at his elbow.

With the service concluded, it was clear to Maia that the prelate and congregation would only be shamed and embarrassed at the spectacle of their emperor picking his way through the tall yellowing grass to the twelve new graves. And there was no difficulty in extricating himself; he simply quit fighting Beshelar for the reins of the situation, and Beshelar with grand pomposity did the rest. Maia smiled at the prelate and the prelate smiled back. Beshelar all but physically strong-armed the emperor into the carriage, crowding Cala and himself in behind. The coachman clucked to the horses and they rattled off.

For ten minutes, no one said anything. Beshelar looked like he was reinventing most of Setheris's favorite epithets—with "moon-witted hobgoblin" at the top of the list—although of course his sense of propriety was too great to allow him to utter them. Cala stared dreamily out the window, as he had on the way to the Ulimeire, and Maia himself clasped his hands in his lap and contemplated their darkness and ugly, lumpish knuckles.

Then Cala turned and said, "Serenity, why did you wish to attend the service?"

He sounded genuinely curious. Maia said, "I don't know." He did know—he knew all too well—but he did not want to discuss his father with his nohecharei, with anyone. *Let that truth be buried with him,* he thought. *It profits no one for Edrehasivar VII to speak of his hatred for Varenechibel IV.* And the worst of it was that he did not even hate his father; he could not hate anyone of whom he knew so little. The thought of Beshelar's shock and disgust was exhausting, like the thought of carrying a massive boulder on his shoulders for the rest of his life.

Then he realized he had forgotten to use the formal first, and Beshelar would be shocked and disgusted anyway. He looked at Cala to avoid looking at Beshelar, and found the vague blue eyes unexpectedly sympathetic. "Nothing can make death easier," Cala said, "but silence can make it harder."

"Speaking helps not," Maia said.

Cala drew back a little, like a cat tapped on the nose, and silence—whether hard or easy—filled the carriage, unbroken, until they reached the Untheileneise Court.

## 5

## *The Emperor's Household*

By the end of dinner that night, Maia was so exhausted he could no longer keep his eyes focused. He had asked Beshelar to see that the grilles of the Alcethmeret were closed as soon as they returned from the Ulimeire and had steadfastly refused to grant an audience to anyone for the rest of the afternoon.

Which did not mean—although he wished it could—that he was either alone or idle. Esaran was lying in wait for him. She would not allow him to return to the Tortoise Room, insisting that it was not suitable to his dignity and dragging him up the next circumference of the stairs to the Rose Room, which was large enough to get lost in and decorated in an oppressive scheme of black and cherry. The wallpaper was an elaborate Pencharneise floral pattern, roses of all shades from deep purple to orange-red, the edges of the petals picked out in gilt.

Esaran had a seemingly endless list of questions he had to answer and decisions he had to make, and just when he thought she might be done, she rounded on him with the reminder that among the victims in the crash of the *Wisdom of Choharo* had been the emperor's edocharei, his gentlemen of the chamber. Her tone indicated without any need of his asking that he would not be allowed to continue to take care of himself as he always had at Edonomee. She added that since Clemis Atterezh was waiting eagerly to fit the emperor for his new wardrobe, it would be as well to take care of the matter promptly.

She did not like him, but it was clear she was not going to let her personal feelings interfere with her efficiency. Possibly she was more keenly aware than Chavar of the emperor's power to remove her from her position if she gave him reason. But her efficiency felt like ruthlessness, and he was so weary already, a headache ticking in his temples, that he said simply, "We are confident that any persons you recommend will be entirely adequate to our needs."

She nodded, despising him for weakness, and whisked herself away. Atterezh came in on a wave of cheerful burbling about cloth and color and pattern of which Maia understood maybe two words in seven. Beshelar and Cala, as befitted the emperor's nohecharei, sat one to either side of the door watching alertly. Maia suspected that this would not be the last time in his life he wished to be able to tell them simply to go away.

And before Atterezh was done, Csevet had appeared, with a list even worse than Esaran's. Word of the new emperor's arrival had spread, and courtiers, the Witnesses of the Corazhas especially, were beginning to gather. Csevet had a towering stack of letters—some delivered through the pneumatic system, others left by various persons with the guards at the grilles when they were not permitted entrance—and he insisted inexorably that every one of them had to be at least *noticed* that evening. He and Maia sat, one on either side of the enormous desk that lurked like a winter-fuddled bear in the back corner of the Rose Room, and went through the letters one by one.

Maia had known that he had been plunged into deep

water by his accession to his father's throne, but it was that stack of letters that showed him just how deep and cold the water was. He recognized some of the names, from gossip Setheris had shared, and knew generally what the Corazhas, the Judiciate, the Parliament were, but the inadequacy of his knowledge became more and more cruelly apparent with each letter, as Csevet read it aloud and paused with his eyebrows raised, and Maia had to ask who the writer was, or what exactly it was that he was writing about. Beshelar and even Cala got dragged into the process of educating the emperor, and Maia sat and listened and hated it.

He had known of the concordat—half cease-fire, half alliance—maintained between Parliament, Corazhas, and Judiciate, supporting the emperor between them like the legs of a fragile and argumentative tripod, but he had never had more than the narrowest crack of a view of them. Now, suddenly, he was surrounded by— almost drowning in—a brilliantly colored panorama: the clamoring House of Commons, the disdainful House of Blood, still resentful all these centuries later that they had to negotiate with men who were merely *elected;* the delicate internecine feuds of the judiciars, no fewer than eleven of whom had sent letters by the pneumatic, each with language more impenetrable than the last; the seven Witnesses of the Corazhas, the advisers of the emperor, none of whom had sent anything in his own person except the most correct and restrained of condolences and good wishes, but whose secretaries had created a deluge of vellum and paper. Then there were the lesser lords and courtiers and merchants and civil servants. . . . And on top of this madness, the emperor was supposed to keep his balance?

The worst was a letter from someone named Eshevis Tethimar, a letter so dense with hints, obscurities, and circumlocutions that Maia could make no sense of it at all, even after Csevet had explained that Eshevis Tethimar was the heir of the Duke Tethimel, one of the wealthiest landowners in southern Thu-Athamar.

"But what does he want?"

"Although we cannot say for certain . . ."

"Please. We beg of you. Guess."

Csevet flicked his ears. "We would guess that Dach'osmer Tethimar is a suitor for the hand of the Archduchess Vedero."

Maia looked doubtfully at the letter, which he still held. "He does not mention our sister."

"Well, he can't," said Cala.

"Beg pardon?"

"Serenity," Csevet said. "After the furor about the Archduchess Nemriän's marriage . . . ?"

"Yes," said Maia. The tempests surrounding the marriage of the elder archduchess, Nemriän, had penetrated even to Isvaroë. He had only been five, but he remembered the breathless gossip of his mother's maid and the housekeeper and the cook, his mother smiling as she pretended not to listen.

"The emperor swore that there would be no public discussion of his second daughter's marriage until the ceremony of signing."

"And?" Maia said.

"And there hasn't been," Csevet said with a helpless shrug. "And everyone who would know was on board the *Wisdom of Choharo*. Except, of course, the archduchess."

"Has our sister written?"

"No, Serenity."

Maia shut his eyes in a wince. He had not expected that someone who had *not* written a letter could be a problem. "And so Dach'osmer Tethimar?"

"Is fishing, Serenity," Csevet said. "He wants to know

how much you know. And he wants to know what you may be willing to concede to him."

"Concede?"

"The Tethimada have been a thorn in the emperor's paw for decades," Csevet said. "They are powerful in their own holdings, and they lead the faction of the eastern lords who are most opposed to the expansion of industry in the west. We know that Varenechibel was most desirous of finding a compromise with them."

"Indeed," Maia said. He felt a bolt of nauseous panic, as if he were a mouse who had stepped on the trigger-plate of a mousetrap and saw his doom in the instant before it broke his neck. He was *emperor* now. Factions and industry and compromises and the war against the barbarians in the north: they were all *his* responsibility, and if he made the wrong choice, hundreds of thousands of people might suffer. People might even die, and all because their emperor was too young and stupid to know how to save them.

"Serenity," Csevet said, sounding cautious. "It is very encroaching of Dach'osmer Tethimar to write you such a letter at this time. We can write back, at just as great a length as he, and give him no information at all."

In his own ears, Maia's laugh sounded like the choke of a dying mouse, but it was a laugh and not a scream, so he supposed he should count it a victory. "Yes, please, Csevet. We should appreciate it."

And then, when at last they had reached the bottom of the stack, Esaran returned with three nervous young men in tow. One of them was about Csevet's age, the other two about Beshelar's age—four or five years older—and Maia felt oppressed by the irony of being the youngest person in the room, and yet the person to whom all the others were bowing.

The three young men were Esha, Nemer, and Avris.

Esha and Nemer were goblin-dark, like Maia himself; Avris was pale. Esaran did not think their surnames worthy of mention. They were to be Maia's edocharei, "unless Your Serenity is pleased to indicate otherwise," Esaran said with her eyebrows lifted, and Maia had to disclaim hastily before Nemer, the youngest, burst into tears. On her way out, Esaran delivered a vicious parting shot: "Tomorrow, of course, Your Serenity, you will wish to discuss with the kitchen master the meals for the coming week, but for tonight we thought it right to tell him he could prepare something simple."

One more duty landed across Maia's shoulders. He said, "Thank you, Esaran," because he had to.

Csevet suggested firmly to the edocharei that they should go up and familiarize themselves with the emperor's private chambers and that moreover they could make themselves useful by preparing the rooms for use. Maia could only watch in hopeless admiration as this tactic cleared the room of his newest anxious dependents, and then Csevet turned back and said, "Serenity, there is one other matter."

"There is?"

"We do not like to bring it up, but we cannot . . ."

Back straight, hands folded in lap, face controlled. "Tell us," Maia said.

"It is the letter from Dach'osmer Tethimar that made us think of it," Csevet said. "Serenity, you must begin to consider your own marriage."

"*Marriage?* But I'm not even emperor yet! I mean—" And then he realized he had broken formality into seventy embarrassing pieces and bit his tongue.

"It will be the first thing on the minds of many of the court," Csevet said.

"All of those with marriageable daughters," Beshelar put in cynically.

"But we don't wish to marry anyone," Maia protested, and at least it was the correct level of formality, even if the tone was perilously near whining.

"You will have to sooner or later, unless you intend to let Idra Drazhar succeed you, which we would not recommend."

"Know you something to the discredit of our nephew?"

"How could we? He is a child still. We were thinking, Serenity, of the example of Belmaliven the Fifth."

Maia took his point. Belmaliven V, coming to the throne after the sudden death of his brother Belmaliven IV, had felt the succession amply secured by his two nephews, so he had not divorced his beloved but barren wife. In the second year of his reign, he was deposed and murdered by "supporters" of his elder nephew, who was crowned as Belvesena XI and survived as a sickly puppet for six years before he in turn was ousted by his brother, Belmaliven VI. The exact manner and date of Belvesena's death were not known, but it was generally assumed that he had not long survived his brother's coronation and that his death had not been an accident.

"You think it necessary for us to move this quickly?" Maia asked unhappily.

"Serenity," said Csevet, "we think that you should be prepared for the matter to arise. And we think that you should be well enough informed to make a decision, rather than being pushed into marriage as the late emperor was on more than one occasion."

Maia winced.

Csevet's eyes widened. "Serenity, we beg your pardon. We did not mean——"

"No, we understand. And you are perfectly correct." Panic was back, knocking against his ribs, tightening clammy fingers around his throat. He swallowed hard. "How would you suggest we proceed?"

"Let us gather information for you," Csevet said. "That is, if you will trust us to do so?"

*I must trust someone,* Maia thought. "Yes, please."

"We will see to it."

The headache was getting worse; Maia was cravenly grateful that one of Esaran's underlings appeared at that moment to announce dinner, before Csevet could come up with another "one other matter."

Csevet excused himself gracefully, sparing Maia the necessity of determining how many people Esaran had told the kitchen master to prepare for. The emperor ate in solitary splendor, with his nohecharei again seated one to either side of the dining room door.

Egg-and-broth soup, an eel casserole, seared colewort: Maia ate without tasting any of it, from some unknown reserve dredging up a smile for the timid server—another one with goblin blood—and praise to be relayed to the kitchen master and chefs. Dessert was a sorbet; it tasted like winter, and Maia only wished he could transfer the blissful cold to his throbbing temples. The server presented him with a cordial before he could tell her not to, and after the first sip, he said abruptly to his nohecharei, "When will you eat?"

"Serenity?" said Beshelar, startled. Cala seemed to focus his eyes as if from a very great distance away.

"You must eat," Maia said. "When?"

"When you are in bed, Serenity," Cala said. "We will trade off, one to guard while the other eats. You must not worry about us."

"Could you not—after tonight—eat with us?"

Beshelar's expression was, predictably, scandalized. Cala smiled. "After tonight, Your Serenity, you will not be eating alone."

"Oh, yes," Maia said, and drained the rest of the cordial in one swallow. "How stupid of us to forget."

Cala coughed discreetly. "We understand from Mer Aisava that Your Serenity got no sleep last night."

"Very little," Maia said, resisting the urge to rub his blurred and aching eyes.

"Then we suggest Your Serenity retire to bed. Your edocharei will be waiting to care for you, and you may with good conscience and peaceful soul imagine us dining as well as you just have."

"Serenity," said Beshelar, "Cala Athmaza is frivolous, but his suggestion is a wise one."

The effort not to laugh was almost too much for him. Maia bit his lip and got to his feet. His bones ached and his muscles seemed made of lead, but he was satisfied that his legs would hold him. "We thank you," he said to both of them.

It was embarrassing how close they stayed to him, one to either side, on the way up the stairs. Two full turns around the Alcethmeret to the doors of the emperor's bedchambers, where Esha and Avris were waiting. They paused there, nohecharei and edocharei eyeing each other uncertainly. Maia, too tired to be politic, said, "Cala, will you stay?"

"Yes, Serenity," Cala said; Beshelar offered a stiff salute and stalked back down the stairs.

Young and nervous they might be, but his edocharei knew their job. They unpinned his hair, unfastened his clothing, so smooth and swift and silent about their work that he was naked in front of them before he remembered to be self-conscious about his skinny frame or the ugly color of his skin. In mere moments more they had him clad again, this time in a nightshirt as soft as a cloud, and were braiding his hair for the night.

One of them—Esha, he thought, although he was no

longer sure of anything—assured him that they had changed all the bedding and it was clean and well aired, and he was aware of lying down, of gentle hands helping with the covers, and then he remembered nothing more.

He woke once in the night, from a confused nightmare of Setheris telling him that his mother was in the burning wreckage of the *Wisdom of Choharo*, and a voice said softly in the darkness, "Serenity?"

"Who?" Maia said thickly.

"It's I, Cala. You had a bad dream, it sounds like. It's all right."

"Cala," Maia said, remembering kind blue eyes. "Thank you." And then he fell into sleep again, as helplessly heavy as the *Wisdom of Choharo* crashing to the earth.

# PART TWO

# The Coronation of
# Edrehasivar VII

# 6

## The Widow Empress

Maia opened his eyes to glowing sunlight and lay blinking in puzzlement. This was not his room in Edonomee; it was not his barely remembered room in Isvaroë. The bed-hangings were far too sumptuous for either, and the wrestling cats of the Drazhada worked into the brocade suggested he must be in one of his father's households, but . . .

When he remembered where he was and what had happened, he was convinced that he was dreaming.

The thought was a tremendous relief.

Soon he would awaken in his own narrow, sagging bed in Edonomee, and he might not even remember having had such a ridiculous dream. An he did, it would remind him to be satisfied with what he had rather than pining after what he did not.

*A sound and valuable moral lesson,* Maia thought with sleepy satisfaction, and then the sound of a door opening brought him up on one elbow, confusedly fearing that it would be Setheris coming to tell him a messenger had arrived from his father.

But it was a stocky, dark boy in Drazhadeise livery—Nemer, Maia remembered—who seemed slightly alarmed to find Maia awake, but blinked and said timidly that he had been sent to discover what kind of tea His Imperial Serenity favored with breakfast.

*Merciful goddesses,* let *this be a dream*—but it was not.

"Chamomile," which his mother had loved and Setheris hated. "Thank you."

"Serenity," Nemer answered, bowing. "Do you wish to breakfast in bed or . . ."

"No," Maia said. He felt vulnerable in this enormous expanse of bed, dressed only in a nightshirt. "We will rise, thank you."

"Serenity," Nemer said, bowing again, and effaced himself.

"Serenity," another voice said from the opposite corner of the room, startling Maia into a yelp and very nearly into falling off the bed.

It was Beshelar. He had clearly chosen his position so that he could watch every corner of the oddly shaped room, and of course it was Beshelar, whose great talent seemed to be for making his emperor feel like a gauche and grubby boy.

"Don't you *sleep?*" Maia said, more waspishly than he had intended.

"Serenity," said Beshelar. "There was not time yesterday, but today it is hoped the Adremaza and Captain Orthema will be able to choose seconds for Cala Athmaza and ourself. Assuming they are acceptable to Your Serenity, we will then be able to guard you in shifts. But we," with a sudden access of ferocity and the plural to include Cala, "are your First Nohecharei."

Maia could have lowered his head into his hands and wept. Here he had been resenting Beshelar, while Beshelar had been shouldering a burden he, Maia, had not even had the wit to recognize. *Thou grow'st arrogant already,* he said to himself. *Accepting it as ordinary that those who guard thee should be on duty constantly.* A smaller, darker voice added: *As thou art.* Maia moved with sudden decisiveness to get out of bed.

As if they had only been waiting for their cue, Esha and Avris came in, telling him that his bath had been drawn, that Dachensol Atterezh and his apprentices had labored all night and sent several sets of garments with assurances that His Serenity's coronation robes would not be delayed in the slightest. There was no comfort in their words or their ministrations, but Maia followed where he was led, noticing with bitter amusement what he had been too fatigued to see the night before: the emperor was granted the illusion of privacy by certain cunningly placed panels of frosted glass; he bathed, dressed, allowed Avris to dress his hair—although he dismayed his edocharei greatly by refusing all jewelry. "Not until we are crowned," he said. In truth he would have preferred to wear no jewels at all. They reminded him of his father.

He sat down to breakfast with both nohecharei in attendance and the same shy server he had had the night before. With his first sip of tea, the door opened to admit Csevet, burdened with another great stack of letters, and Maia, whose mind had been running moodily on jewelry, forestalled whatever Csevet might have said by asking, "To whom do we speak about our imperial signet?"

"Serenity," Csevet said, setting down the stack of letters at the end of the table; the server fetched another cup. "That is traditionally the purview of the Lord Chancellor."

"Is it?" Maia said thoughtfully.

"The Lord Chancellor is the Master of Seals," Csevet said carefully, almost uneasily.

"What did you use to seal our letters yesterday?"

"The Drazhadeise house seal," Csevet said. "We think it unlikely that anyone will claim they are forgeries."

"Most unlikely," Maia agreed, and Csevet seemed to relax slightly. "But Lord Chavar surely does not design signets himself."

"Oh! No, of course not. That is the work of Dachensol Habrobar."

"Can you . . . that is, do we summon Dachensol Habrobar to our presence, or . . . ?"

"We will take care of it, Serenity."

"Thank you," Maia said. "We see you have brought us more letters."

"Yes," Csevet said. "The Corazhas are not the only ones made uneasy by an emperor who does not parade himself before them."

"Ought we to?" Maia said. "Parade ourself?"

"No, Serenity," Csevet said. "It does your courtiers no harm to be a little unsettled. They will see you soon enough." He coughed politely and said, "There *is* a message from the widow empress."

Maia had almost forgotten about the widow empress in the press of other concerns, but a glance at the clock showed him he would have to face her in an hour. "We have agreed to give her an audience at ten o'clock," he said. "She wrote yesterday."

"Your Serenity is very kind," Csevet murmured, and passed him the widow empress's letter.

Maia broke the seal and read:

*To the Archduke Maia Drazhar, heir to the imperial throne of Ethuveraz, greetings.*

*We are greatly disappointed with your coldness and fear that much of what the late emperor your father said of your character, which we dismissed as an old man's prejudices, must indeed be true.*

*We will come to the Tortoise Room at ten o'clock.*
*With great hope and compassion,*
*Csoru Drazharan, Ethuverazhid Zhasan*

Maia considered this missive carefully, and then said, "What sort of lady is the widow empress?"

"Serenity," Csevet said with another polite little cough. "She is a very young lady and somewhat . . . wild."

"Csevet, we beg of you, speak plainly."

Csevet bowed. "She is spoilt, Serenity. She is young and very beautiful, and the late emperor treated her as a doll. She got her way with tears and tantrums, and when those palled, as they would on a man who was tired and old and had buried three wives, she turned to illnesses—fainting spells, dizziness, nervous prostration. She wished for power, but he was too wise to give her any."

"Then it is probable that power is what she seeks now?"

"Yes, Serenity, very probable."

A silence, cold and hard like a granule of ice. Maia took a deep breath and said, "What did our late father say of us?"

He saw Csevet's appalled glance cross Beshelar's and knew he did not wish this knowledge. But . . . "We must know. We cannot face those who have heard his opinions an we do not know them ourself."

"Serenity," Csevet said unhappily, and bowed his head. "He loved not your mother, as you know."

"Yes," Maia said, all but under his breath. "We know."

"He did not discuss her—or yourself, Serenity—in public, but there was always gossip. Some of it from servants. Some of it, we fear, spread by the Empress Csoru herself."

"Why?"

"Boredom. Petty malice. The joy of scandal. Most of the stories were not credible, and we most earnestly beg Your Serenity to dismiss them utterly from your mind."

"But the others?"

He was backing Csevet into a corner, and he was sorry for it. *This is what it is to be emperor,* he thought. *Do not forget it.*

And Csevet capitulated as gracefully as he did everything else. "The late emperor said—and this occasionally in public—that the Barizheisei were degenerate, given to inbreeding. In private, so the rumors go, he said that the Empress Chenelo was mad, and that you had inherited her bad blood. He frequently used the word 'unnatural,' although the stories differed on what he meant by it."

"How much credence has been give to these stories?"

"Serenity, everyone knows how much the late emperor loved the Empress Pazhiro. And it is common knowledge that marriage with the Empress Chenelo was pressed upon him by the Corazhas and was not of his own choosing. But it is also true that your . . . isolation at Edonomee has caused comment, and more so in recent years."

"For all the Untheileneise Court knows, we *are* an inbred lunatic cretin." He could not bite back a laugh bitter enough to make Csevet wince.

"Serenity, they have only to look at you to see that you are not."

"The question being," Cala murmured, "how many of them will look."

Beshelar glared at him, but the apologetic look Csevet gave Maia told him that Cala's remark was honesty, not cynicism.

Continuing this conversation as matters stood would only make him despondent to no purpose and possibly cause Csevet and his nohecharei to feel put-upon and ill used. He said with a note of briskness he did not feel, "Are there any of those letters which we ought to read before our audience with Csoru Zhasanai?"

There were, of course; he bade Csevet come down to

the Tortoise Room with him, and there Csevet ensconced himself at the secretary's desk while Maia sat by the fire and Cala and Beshelar patiently guarded the door against nothing.

It was easier to deal with the letters today. He felt that the depths of his ignorance had already been revealed and so had no compunction about asking for information. And with Csevet's guidance—Csevet who had been an imperial courier (he admitted when asked) since he turned thirteen—Maia was learning to decipher the elaborate flatteries and circumlocutions and how to answer in kind. And to recognize when not to. It was a little hard not to resent Csevet's easy familiarity with names and factions and cherished causes, but Csevet put that knowledge unreservedly at Maia's disposal, and if he wished to be angry at someone, it was not Csevet who deserved his anger.

The most important of the letters, its significance apparent to Maia even without coaching, was that from the Barizheise ambassador. It stood out among the neat stack of correspondence, not merely because it was written on vellum—many of the older courtiers still preferred parchment to paper—but because it was rolled rather than folded. The cord that held it was plum-colored silk, threaded through an ivory toggle and elaborately knotted. Csevet regarded it a little helplessly.

"Your Serenity must know more of Barizheise customs than we do," he said.

Maia shook his head, wincing at Csevet's raised eyebrows. "Our mother died when we were eight. She did not speak Barizhin with us, nor did she tell us much of her homeland. We think she had been forbidden to." He remembered with perfect clarity every tiny moment of rebellion, but there had been too few of them.

Csevet frowned, his ears dipping. "We know that the use of a nesecho"—and he flicked the ivory toggle with a plain-lacquered fingernail—"is of great meaning to goblins, but we know not what that meaning is. Nor do we know anything about goblin knots."

"Is there anyone in our household who might?" Maia asked, thinking of the number of dark-skinned servants he had seen in the Alcethmeret.

"Serenity," Csevet said, rising with a bow that, Maia thought, expressed appreciation of a helpful idea. "We will ask."

He returned a few minutes later, bringing a middle-aged man in his wake. "This is Oshet, Serenity," said Csevet, as triumphant as a retriever presenting his master with a dead duck. "He is one of your gardeners. He came to the Untheileneise Court with the ambassador five years ago, and his service was presented to your imperial father because of his gift for rose-growing."

"Serenity," murmured Oshet, going to his knees and bowing his head. His skin was almost perfect black; he wore his hair shaved rather than merely cropped, which made the steel rings in his ears—steel, as even Maia knew, being the mark of a sailor—impossible to miss.

"Please," Maia said. "Stand." Oshet rose obediently; he was a full head shorter than Csevet, stocky and densely muscled. His forearms were crisscrossed with scratches old and new, his fingernails rimmed with dirt. He had the heavy underslung jaw and protuberant eyes typical of goblins; Setheris had always been very pointed in his comments about Maia's luck in inheriting his father's elvish bones.

"Did Mer Aisava explain our question?" Maia asked.

"Yes, Serenity." Oshet's eyes were a vivid orange-red, disconcerting against the blackness of his skin. Maia knew his own eyes, the pale Drazhadeise gray, were just as bad. "Is nesecho, yes?"

"Yes." Maia took the roll of vellum, with its adornments, from the table and handed it to Csevet, who handed it to Oshet. The gardener's thick-fingered hands were delicate of touch; he traced the lines of the knot, then the lines of the nesecho, lingering over the tiny pointed face of the animal carved into it. Then he handed the vellum back to Csevet and clasped his hands together behind his back.

"Well?" Csevet said.

"Is suncat," said Oshet.

"We beg your pardon?" Maia said.

"Little animal. Is suncat. Live along southern coast. Friendly. Always curious. Kill snakes and rats. Many ships have suncat. Is very good luck."

Maia held his hand out, and Csevet gave him the roll of vellum. He looked carefully at the nesecho, seeing the way the suncat had been carved to appear as if it were playing with the cords, seeing the bright happiness the carver had put into its face.

"What does it mean?" Csevet said impatiently.

Oshet's massive shoulders rose and fell in a shrug. "Is good luck," he said. "Is friends. We have nesecho, given by closest friend on ship when we left." He tugged a cord bound around his belt and pulled a nesecho out of his pocket. It was a little larger than the suncat, and Maia recognized it by the scales carved on the rounded back, even before Oshet turned it so he could see the squared, smiling, tongue-lolling face of a tangrisha. "Tangrisha is protection," Oshet said. "Suncat is . . ." His face screwed up into a scowl as he tried to find the right words. "Is wish for great happiness."

Maia wanted to ask more questions, about nesechos and about Oshet's ship and about why the ambassador would be sending him a wish for "great happiness," but Csevet pursued, single-minded, "And the knot?"

"Is knot for important message," said Oshet, tucking his tangrisha back in his pocket. "But is message to emperor."

"Are there protocols?" Maia asked hesitantly. "Is it wrong to cut the knot?"

Oshet's eyebrows shot up, and the twitch of his ears made his earrings jangle. "Is no need, Serenity. Pull gold bead. Knot will untie itself." He paused, then added, "Nesecho is gift, always."

One of the strands of cord had a gold bead knotted at its end. Maia had assumed it was only decoration. *It is but one more chance to feel ignorant,* he told himself, and tugged the cord, surprised despite himself at how swiftly the knot unraveled. He freed the vellum from the cord and quickly tucked cord and nesecho in his pocket before anyone could tell him he ought not to.

"Thank you," Csevet said to the gardener. "You may go."

Oshet nodded to Csevet and bowed deeply to Maia. "Serenity."

"Thank you, Oshet," Maia said, remembering to smile, and only then turned his attention to unrolling the vellum.

The letter was written in a strong hand, the letters small and well formed, with elaborately swooping heads and tails. Not a secretary's hand. The salutation was, *To our most serene imperial kinsman, Edrehasivar VII,* and Maia got no farther, looking up at Csevet in a certain amount of shock. "Kinsman?"

For once, Csevet was also at a loss. "The ambassador is not a blood relative of the Avar."

"He must mean our mother's mother," Maia said. "But we know not her name, nor her family."

"He's certainly never mentioned it before," Csevet said, very dryly.

"It would scarcely have been a political asset," Maia said. He meant to sound dry, too, but his voice was merely weary. "Well, let us see what our kinsman wants."

The letter was brief:

> *To our most serene imperial kinsman, Edrehasivar VII, greetings.*
>
> *We extend our deepest condolences on your loss and wish to assure you that Barizhan will not hold you to the trade agreement which we were negotiating with your late father. It is our greatest and most cherished hope that relations between Barizhan and the Ethuveraz will move beyond peace to friendship, and in that hope we sign ourself yours most obediently to command,*
>
> *Vorzhis Gormened,*
> *Ambassador of the Great Avar to the court*
> *of the Emperor of the Ethuveraz*

Maia looked helplessly at Csevet. He could identify the presence of a hidden agenda in those very careful words, but he had not the least idea what it might be.

Csevet, frowning thoughtfully, read the letter over again and said, "We wonder if Ambassador Gormened has the approval of his government for the contents of this letter."

"There's hardly been time," Maia protested.

"Yes," said Csevet. "We know."

"Then you think . . ."

"The Great Avar is well known to reward initiative and audacity—when they succeed. We would suggest, Serenity, that you respond to the ambassador so that his relinquishment of the trade agreement becomes a matter of record."

Everything the emperor said, as Maia had already learned, was a matter of record.

"Was the trade agreement so disadvantageous?"

"If Gormened thinks that you will be grateful to be released from it, yes," Csevet said bluntly. "We will query the office of the Witness for Foreigners and request the details."

"Yes, please do. And tell us how to answer our . . . kinsman."

"Serenity," murmured Csevet, and began a crisp dissection of the ambassador's letter.

Five minutes before ten o'clock, Beshelar started up from his chair and said, "Serenity, our seconds are approaching."

"Oh, thank goodness," Cala said, and stifled a yawn.

The Second Nohecharei proved to be in many ways indistinguishable from the First. A lieutenant and an athmaza, about the same age as Beshelar and Cala, the one starched and polished, the other shabby and unworldly—although this maza's robe was of a newer, brighter blue, and his hair held a braid better than Cala's. But Maia noticed that the new lieutenant, Telimezh, seemed nervous of Beshelar as well as of his emperor, while the maza Dazhis seemed anxious only that Cala should not forget to go to sleep.

"No fear," Cala said, stifling another yawn. "I may be absentminded, Dazhis, but I'm not made of stone. Serenity."

He and Beshelar bowed, and Maia dismissed them, quashing a ridiculous impulse to beg them to stay. Beshelar and Cala needed and deserved their rest, and there was no reason to feel like an abandoned child, nor to feel frightened of his Second Nohecharei.

*Thou shouldst be pleased to be rid of Beshelar for a while,* he chided himself, and turned back to Csevet.

They dealt with another two letters before a great tumult on the stairs heralded the tardy appearance of the widow empress, Csoru Drazharan.

Thanks to Csevet, Maia had some idea of what to expect and thus was not completely overwhelmed by the vision that posed in the doorway between Telimezh and Dazhis, putting back her veil with deliberation worthy of an opera singer. The widow empress was a small woman—doll-like as Csevet had called her—with a heart-shaped face and eyes of a remarkable, lush deep blue. She was also no more than three years older than Maia himself.

With the example of Hesero Nelaran as a guide, Maia could see that Csoru was overdressed, flaunting her status as she had in her letters to him. The silver bullion embroidery of her jacket was coming very close to the imperial white, which she only dubiously had the right to wear. And her hair, piled in an elaborate edifice of buns and twining braids, would have looked better without the adornment of glittering black beads, each as big as Maia's thumbnail, that looked uncomfortably like beetles.

It was also, he discovered, easier to cope with the out-and-out beauty of a woman he already disliked than it was the grace of a woman like Hesero.

He rose unhurriedly to greet his father's widow, and she made him a small, stiff bow. She did not otherwise acknowledge his rank, and he was heartened to notice both Telimezh and Dazhis Athmaza glowering disapprovingly at her back.

Csoru's gaze darted around the room and came to rest on Csevet. "Who is this?"

"Our secretary," Maia said.

"Oh." She dismissed Csevet from her attention entirely—at which Csevet looked affronted—and stood, staring at Maia with a slight frown of displeasure.

Finally, Maia said, "Csoru Zhasanai, *you* wished to see *us*."

She said, "We hoped that you would be receptive to advice," her tone indicating that her hopes had been cruelly disappointed.

"What advice would you give us?"

"We do not think you will listen," she said with a toss of her head that looked ill on an empress.

He waited a few courteous moments, then said, "As it happens, we have a matter about which we wish to speak to you, for it concerns our honor and our sovereignty." Csoru looked hopeful, Csevet alarmed. "Namely, merrem, you are not Ethuverazhid Zhasan, and having no child you cannot hope to be. Unless, perchance, there is that afoot which we know not?"

Csevet coughed in a strangled sort of way. Csoru said furiously, "We are the wife of the emperor."

"You are the *widow* of the emperor. Unless you have conceived his child, that title must pass from you."

"No," she said sullenly. "But you have no empress."

"That does not mean the position is yours for the taking," Maia said. "Be content, merrem, to style yourself Zhasanai. For such you are. And we are Edrehasivar Zhas and will have that honor from you if you intend to remain at the Untheileneise Court."

He could see her recalculating her position and her strategy. She bowed her head and said in a softer, meeker voice than any he had yet heard from her, "Edrehasivar Zhas, you must forgive a widow her grief."

"And we do, so long as it does not lead her to behave in ways embarrassing to either the emperor or the House Drazhada. If you are overset, Csoru Zhasanai, perhaps you should retire to the country for a time. We have many manors which we would be most pleased to grant to your use."

Her eyes went wide and her ears lowered; she heard the threat, and doubtless the examples of Arbelan Drazharan, Varenechibel's first wife, and Chenelo Drazharan, his fourth, were present to her mind. "Serenity," she said, bowing more deeply. "We thank you for your consideration, but we feel it unworthy of a widow empress to give way to her grief."

"Even so," Maia said. "We are busy, Csoru Zhasanai. Was there another matter on which you wished to speak to us?"

"No, Serenity," she said. "We thank you." She did not flee the room, but she left far less ostentatiously than she had entered. They listened as the sharp, hard sound of her feet on the stairs receded into nothing.

"Csevet," Maia said thoughtfully, "will you write to Arbelan Drazharan at Cethoree and invite her to attend our coronation?"

"Yes, Serenity," Csevet said, and added it to his list.

# 7

## The Tomb of the Empress Chenelo

Csevet and Maia spent the rest of the morning and half the afternoon going through the latest batch of correspondence. They agreed that many of the problems, questions, and concerns were better dealt with after the coronation, when there would no longer be the slightest ambiguity in the emperor's position. There was another letter from Eshevis Tethimar, which Csevet frowned at and muttered, "Encroaching!" loud enough for Maia to hear. There was a letter from Setheris complaining of being denied admittance to the Alcethmeret; Maia thought wearily, *Thou wilt be obliged to deal with him sometime*. But Csevet assured him that he could without impoliteness defer that meeting until after the coronation, and Maia wrote a message to Setheris in his own hand to promise an audience after he was crowned and properly out of seclusion.

Then Csevet sat down to write another round of soothing and uninformative letters to the Corazhas, while Maia, Telimezh and Dazhis in tow, set out to deal with what matters he could.

The first was a full inspection of the Alcethmeret, top to bottom, and introductions to all the staff. Esaran looked incredulous and offended when Maia mentioned the latter, but he set his jaw and insisted.

"The emperor your father," she began, but he cut her off.

"We want to know who serves us," he said. Esaran acquiesced, but he knew she was not pleased. It was worth it, though, to learn that the shy little server in the dining room was named Isheian, to know the names of the laundresses and charwomen, the grooms and scullions and gardeners—for the Alcethmeret, Maia learned, had its own garden, separate from the gardens of the Untheileneise Court, where the gardeners grew roses that in the spring and summer would fill the tower with color and scent. Oshet might have been guilty of the impropriety of winking at his emperor. The kitchen master was not nearly so alarming as Maia had imagined; he was a grandfatherly gentleman with a tremendous white mustache. His name was Ebremis, and he questioned Maia closely and respectfully about his likes and dislikes. Maia tried not to explain about the household at Edonomee, which was ruled both by parsimony and by Setheris's tastes, but he sensed uneasily that Ebremis guessed much of what he did not say.

Beneath the Alcethmeret, he met the girls who sat in the center of the spiderweb of pneumatic tubes that ran throughout the Untheileneise Court, and watched raptly for several minutes as they did their job. Back in the Tortoise Room, remembering Csoru's flustered page boy, he asked Csevet what the use of a personal messenger meant.

Csevet's eyebrows went up. "It might mean any of several things, Serenity. Such as the desire for secrecy."

"Ah. No. The message was from Csoru Zhasanai."

"Well," said Csevet, "it indicates the desire to be certain that the message is delivered directly into the hands of the intended recipient. Also, of course, the insistence on an immediate reply. It may also indicate that one feels one's message to be too important and too urgent to wait."

"Of course," said Maia, and Csevet almost grinned before he caught himself.

That night at dinner when Maia smiled at Isheian, she smiled back.

The plates had scarcely been cleared when the Lord Chancellor was announced. He came in like a storm; before Maia could so much as offer him a seat or a glass of liqueur, he had begun to explain, in a hectoring voice and excruciating detail, the rituals surrounding an emperor's coronation. The fasting, the hours spent in meditation: "The emperor's daylong meditation takes place in a vigil chapel beneath the palace itself. The Archprelate will take you, and it is traditional for the emperor to choose two close friends to accompany him on the journey to and from the chapel. Since you have no friends at court, you will of course choose your nearest male relatives who are of age. We make those out to be the Marquess Imel, your sister Nemriän's husband, and Setheris Nelar."

"We—," Maia began, but Chavar continued over top of him: "At sundown begin the rituals of coronation itself," and he was launched on a flood of archaic formulas and significant gestures, leaving Maia without a chance to say that he would under no circumstances allow Setheris Nelar to play a role of any ritual importance whatsoever in the process of his coronation. And Chavar's smug and patronizing air, his condescension—*of course you have no friends, you ugly hobgoblin*—was enough to make Maia not merely resentful, but actually rebellious. *Chavar is not my cousin*, he thought, *and this is not Edonomee. I can make my decision as it pleases me, and he cannot stop me*. He heard Chavar out in patient silence, without giving any indication that his own plans were already diverging from the Lord Chancellor's ideas.

When Chavar finally left, Maia turned his attention to the other matter with which he could deal before being crowned Edrehasivar VII; this matter was a personal one, and it took some arguing before Csevet and his nohecharei would let him attend to it. It was not—as Telimezh said earnestly, having found himself somehow saddled with the job of spokesman—that they did not approve of His Serenity's sentiments, but that as an uncrowned emperor in full mourning, he ought not to be seen wandering the halls.

"We do not wish to wander the halls," Maia said crossly. "We wish to visit our mother's tomb, which we have not been able to do since her funeral ten years ago. We personally would find far more shocking an emperor who did *not* visit his mother's tomb than one who did."

To his exasperation, Csevet insisted on calling the edocharei in to consult on the matter, but they were an unexpected source of support. Nemer said, "Of *course* Your Serenity should visit the empress's tomb," and then retreated under a quelling stare from Avris. But Avris and Esha, in whose rectitude he also detected something of Nemer's partisanship, said there was no impropriety in it, so long as the emperor agreed to go veiled. "You should not have gone to the Ulimeire unveiled, Serenity," Esha said sternly. "We have spoken with Atterezh about it already."

"We will agree to anything," Maia said, "an it permits us this one thing which we so greatly desire."

"Serenity," Csevet murmured, giving way.

Maia had last worn a mourning veil also ten years ago. It had reeked of cedar and been scratchy against his face. The veil Esha produced was as light as a cobweb and smelled only of the sage and lavender that the edocharei used to perfume the emperor's wardrobes and cupboards. There were bronze pins to hold it, their black enameled heads worked with the Drazhadeise device, and Maia felt strangely peaceful when Avris at last lowered the veil over his face.

With the entire Untheileneise Court in mourning, the halls were nearly deserted, though normally, Telimezh told Maia, the courtiers would be promenading in favored corridors until midnight at least. Those few whom they encountered bowed hastily and profoundly. They would not look Maia in the face, but he was aware of their eyes on his back until he had passed out of sight.

The Othasmeire of the Untheileneise Court, the Untheileneise'meire, was a vast white edifice, a dome supported on pillars like the trunks of ancient trees. The gaslights, in their antique faceted globes, cast strange shadows among the pillars. It was cold, colder even than the frigid open rooms of the Alcethmeret.

The tombs of the Drazhada circled the walls outside the ring of pillars, a wide double-row of sarcophagi, too many to count and yet not enough to complete the circle around the dome. The location where Varenechibel's tomb would be built had already been marked off, although the marble was still in a quarry among the islands of the Chadevan Sea, and the space was heaped with flowers—mostly silk at this time of year, but there were a few bouquets of chrysanthemums gently shedding their petals among the artificial roses and lilies.

The tombs of Varenechibel's second, third, and fourth wives were in the outer ring: the Empress Leshan, the Empress Pazhiro, the Empress Chenelo, each of them dead before her thirtieth birthday. The stylized bas-reliefs on the lids of the sarcophagi gave no real impression of what the empresses had looked like, much less what kind of people they had been. Maia ran his fingers over the white marble nose and cheek of the figure on his mother's tomb, a gesture as symbolic and meaningless as the figure itself.

He knelt then, putting his veil back, aware of but ignoring Telimezh and Dazhis, who were standing stiffly by the nearest column. He had nothing to say, no offering to make, only the feeling, deeper than words, that he had to pay honor to his mother before the great public honor that would be paid to his father. He wondered if his mother would have been proud or sorrowful at his sudden elevation. Sorrowful, he thought; exalted rank had brought her nothing but grief and pain.

Finally, he whispered, "I am here." It seemed the only thing worth saying. She was ten years dead, and all the things he had wished to say to her, all the things he had dreamed of saying during the cold years at Edonomee, seemed now like the pitiful whining of a child. *Even an she heard,* he thought, *it would but grieve her.* He clasped his hands and bowed to the tomb, determined even in this desolation of white marble to do her honor.

He stood, lowered his veil, realized there was one thing still to say. He touched the incised strokes of her name and said, low but clear, "I love thee still."

He turned then and left his mother's tomb, walking back toward where his nohecharei waited for him in the light.

# 8

## *The Coronation of Edrehasivar VII*

The preparations for the crowning of the Emperor Edrehasivar VII began at six o'clock on the morning of the twenty-third. He did not break his fast, and would not until after he had been crowned. He bathed in water steeped with herbs; the scent of the herbs caught in the back of his throat and made his eyes sting. While Dazhis observed, Esha and Nemer dressed Maia in a long, white, sleeveless and shapeless garment called a keb, an archaic piece of clothing used now only for initiations among the mazei and clergy, and for coronations. Maia, used to tight-fitting trousers and padded jackets, found it unnerving; the rituals proscribed wearing anything beneath it, and he felt rather less clothed than he would have in a nightshirt.

Then Avris combed his hair patiently and thoroughly, teasing all the tangles out of his unruly curls until they hung sleek and dark and wet down his back. Esha opened a secret panel in the wall of the dressing room and brought out a heavy oak casket, which held the imperial court jewels. Some pieces had been lost with the late emperor, he said sadly, and new would have to be commissioned, but those were only the Lesser Jewels, the Michen Mura. The Greater Jewels, the Dachen Mura, never left the Untheileneise Court.

Maia suffered himself to be adorned. Rings for his fingers, silver set with jade and moonstones; bracelets like manacles, silver set with dull cabochon emeralds; a series of rings for his ears, more pale-green jade; a necklace of moonstones and cabochon emeralds that clasped tight around his throat; a silver and moonstone diadem. He declined when Nemer offered him a mirror; he would not recognize himself, and he did not want to see what he was becoming. He was afraid he would recognize his father.

In the outer chamber, Cala, Beshelar, Telimezh, Csevet, and Chavar were waiting, along with the Archprelate of Cetho, the Adremaza, and the Captain of the Untheileneise Guard. They all knelt at Maia's entrance. Then they stood again as Dazhis crossed the room to stand beside Telimezh, and Chavar and Maia clasped hands, right to right and left to left; Chavar asked the three ritual questions, the truth of Maia's answers to be witnessed by the Adremaza and the captain.

Chavar asked the questions: the time of his birth; the true name of his father; the augury of favor. Maia answered them: the Winter Solstice; Nemera Drazhar; Cstheio Caireizhasan, the Lady of Stars. He felt like a prince in a wonder-tale; he could remember his mother telling him countless stories in which the hero had to answer those same questions, although in wonder-tales, the augury of favor was framed differently. He could hear his mother's soft Barizheise voice saying, *Whose child art thou?* and his own voice, answering delightedly, *The star's child.*

He shook himself back to the present as Chavar asked a question not in the wonder-tales: "By what name will you be known?"

"Edrehasivar," Maia said. "Seventh of that name."

Chavar had never asked him what name he intended to take, and although it had been no secret, clearly the

Lord Chancellor had not bothered to keep himself informed. Or perhaps he had not believed Maia would go through with it. The ritual stumbled to a halt as Chavar stared at Maia, the words visibly forming: *Are you quite sure?* Maia met Chavar's eyes levelly and repeated, as if he thought only that Chavar had not heard him, "Edrehasivar. Seventh of that name."

This time, Chavar made the correct response, and the Adremaza and the Captain of the Untheileneise Guard spoke the words of witnessing. Chavar released Maia's hands.

The next part of the ritual belonged to the Archprelate. He was not the same Archprelate who had officiated at Chenelo's funeral, for the old Archprelate had died two winters ago, the coldest winter in living memory. The new Archprelate was named Teru Tethimar; for this part of the ceremony, he was not masked—a gesture of equality between archprelate and emperor—and Maia saw that he was young for his position with an ascetic's face and a stubborn jaw. He had a beautiful voice, a tenor as clear as spring water, and he spoke the words of the cleansing and releasing as if he meant them.

The ritual released Maia from his old life, leaving him free to take up the strands of the new. For now, he was in between worlds. It was a time, as the Archprelate said, for purification and tranquillity, and he asked Maia, the words heavy with their freight of ritual, whom he would choose to serve as his guides to and from the vigil chapel where he would spend these hours between casting off his former self and garbing himself to greet his new being.

Maia did not hesitate. "Cala Athmaza and Deret Beshelar," he said.

The Archprelate stopped with his mouth half open.

This time, Chavar exploded, "Serenity, you cannot—!"

Maia said, "You will not tell us what we can and cannot do, Chavar."

The silence was thick with consternation, a roomful of men suddenly afraid to move. Maia continued, quiet but stubborn, "I trust them." They had gone with him to the Ulimeire; it felt necessary that they should join him on this pilgrimage as well.

Tethimar, quicker-witted than the still spluttering Chavar, collected himself and bowed agreement. Cala and Beshelar came to stand by Maia, one on each side, almost their normal positions except that now they stood even with him, rather than one pace behind. Tethimar said simply, "Follow me," and Maia, Cala, and Beshelar followed him, leaving the others standing like actors bereft of a play.

The Archprelate led them silently down the stairs of the Alcethmeret and across its inlaid marble floor to the pair of pilasters, three sets off from being exactly opposite the doors to the rest of the Untheileneise Court, where there was a candlestick, already lit, waiting prosaically on the floor. Maia did not see exactly what Tethimar did, where exactly he pressed, but one of the pilasters gracefully fell into the wall, revealing a narrow, dark passage, to which the pilaster itself served as a bridge. Tethimar went first, then Beshelar, then Maia, and Cala brought up the rear. The painted wood was cool and slightly gritty under Maia's bare feet, the stone of the passageway shockingly cold.

The passage bent sharply back and forth; Maia guessed it followed the walls of the palace rooms. They had not gone far, however, before the passage ended in a staircase, a tight, steeply descending spiral, its central pillar so narrow that Maia could almost join his hands around it. The Archprelate's candle cast only barely enough light, and there was no banister, nor any hand grips. Maia braced his hands against the pillar on one side and the wall on the other and proceeded with vertiginous caution. The heavy jewelry fretted him; it made his hands feel strange and clumsy, and he wished he could just take it off and leave it here on the stairs for the ghosts and spiders. He curled his toes so hard against the worn, slick edges of the steps that his feet began to ache. Neither Tethimar and Beshelar ahead of him nor Cala behind him seemed to be having any particular trouble, and he resented them for it in a tired, childish way.

They reached the bottom of the staircase, passed through an antechamber no larger than a broom cupboard, and entered the vigil chapel. It had a pointed vault, unlike the domes that Maia was used to, and on the walls were painted the devices of the gods, both the seven with which he was familiar and many with which he was not. The cold, bare, stone floor was so freshly scrubbed that it was still damp in places. A small spring bubbled up in a niche beside the arched opening to the antechamber; it tumbled over the edge of its natural bowl and disappeared into a hole in the floor. Maia could faintly hear it becoming a river somewhere in the dark below.

A lantern hung in the tall arch of the doorway; Tethimar reached up and lit it with his candle. He said, his beautiful voice quiet and grave, "The water is sanctified. You may drink it. We will return at sundown." And he, with Cala and Beshelar following, turned and began to climb the stairs back to the world above. Maia locked his throat against the impulse to call them back, to beg them to stay, not to leave him down here alone in the dark. The lantern light mocked him, a taunting reminder of the light of the world. He shut his eyes so that he would not have to watch the light of the candle recede, and counted slowly to one hundred. When he opened his eyes, he looked around at the cool darkness, this well of silence, the weight of rock and loneliness, and thought, *This is what it is to be emperor.*

He drank a little water, mostly to wash the taste of panic out of his mouth, then sat cross-legged in the middle of the floor and began patiently and without emphasis to think about his breathing.

He had been too young when his mother died to inherit much of her Barizheise mysticism, but she had taught him the few small, simple things that a child's bright butterfly mind would hold to. Setheris, who professed the fashionable agnosticism, had no patience for what he called "flummery"; Maia had clung to the fragments of his mother's teachings mostly out of defiance. As he grew older, he discovered that he could use the breathing exercises she had taught him to calm himself, or to combat his fear and boredom when he was being punished for infractions of Setheris's rigid rules. He had missed the habit over the past two days, but there had never been—

He lost his rhythm, almost choked, realizing in a new and heavily visceral way that his privacy was gone, not merely for a day or two, but for the rest of his life. He assumed—desperately hoped—that there was some compromise allowed for sexual activities, but emperors did not have privacy. Even behind the grilles of the Alcethmeret, the servants would be there, and if not the servants, the nohecharei, and although their function was largely symbolic in this day and age, their presence was not. He imagined losing his virginity under Beshelar's critical eye and was seized by a lunatic fit of shrill, painful laughter. But even when he calmed again, that cold lump of truth was still lodged in his throat: he could not get privacy without demanding it, and he could not demand it without explaining his purpose. The court would not care for a mystically minded emperor; they might well take it as proof that Varenechibel's bitter calumnies had been true.

*Perhaps canst meditate with one other in the room?* he offered, aware of his own doubtful tone, like a man offering a screaming child a sweet. *Cala would not laugh, nor would scorn thee nor bear tales.* But he could not imagine it.

He settled himself, inhaled deeply, exhaled, and began again the patient contemplation of his breathing. His mother had taught him a prayer that could be used as a mantra: *Cstheio Caireizhasan, hear me. Cstheio Caireizhasan, see me. Cstheio Caireizhasan, know me.* One did not ask for more than awareness from the Lady of the Stars; hers was the gift of clear sight, not of mercy or protection.

He let himself sink into the mantra's rhythm. As a child, he had recited it faster and faster until it degenerated into a gibber of nonsense. Chenelo had giggled with him over it, but then said gently that the point of the mantra was not to finish it, nor to say it as many times as he could in five minutes. "The point is to *be* in it," she had said, and although he had not understood her then, he did now. He let go of all the things that were not himself and the mantra and the cold silence of the vigil chapel. Periodically, he got up to pace the circuit of the room, touching the wall gently beneath each god's device, and to drink a handful of the water, which, cold and slightly metallic, began to taste to him like the tranquillity the Archprelate had said he should seek.

After a time, he felt a deeper rhythm, the rhythm of the stone and water, not the rhythm of his words and heartbeat. He breathed into this deeper rhythm, let it teach him a new mantra, a wordless mantra that waxed and waned, ebbed and flowed, moon and stars and clouds, river and sun, the wordless singing of the earth beneath it all like the world's own heartbeat. He laid his palms flat on the stone beneath him and listened in quiet rapture to the mantra of the world's praying.

It drained away from him gradually, until he was again aware of his body, stiff and cold and cramped and thirsty. He got up, almost falling when his numb legs would not support him. He staggered, stretched first one leg, then the other, then hobbled to the niche in the wall, where he drank another handful of water and then plunged both hands into the bowl, gasping a little with the icy shock of it. But it grounded him, cleared his head. He walked a slow circle around the chapel, then another, flexing his feet against the cold stone.

He was on his third circuit when he realized the chapel was getting brighter. For a moment, he was simply bewildered, as if he were watching a second sun rising in the sky; then he realized the light came from the Archprelate's candle, and the weight of stone and obligation above him all but forced him to the ground. At least the light had given him warning of their approach. He straightened his shoulders, forced his ears up, composed his face. When the Archprelate appeared beneath the lantern, Maia was standing calmly in the middle of the floor, spine straight, chin up, and the sick thud of his heartbeat audible only to himself.

The Archprelate bowed; Maia bowed in return. Behind Tethimar he could see Beshelar and Cala, reminders that not everything that awaited him was threatening or onerous. Maia's heart lifted, and he knew he had been right to choose his First Nohecharei as his guides.

They returned as silently as they had come; this time Cala followed Tethimar, and Beshelar was in the rear. Maia stumbled once, near the top of the stairs, but Beshelar steadied him before he fell.

After Tethimar had closed the pilaster, he bowed and left them to prepare for his own part in the coming ceremony. Cala and Beshelar escorted Maia up to his chambers, where the edocharei waited to take him in hand, Telimezh standing watchful behind them.

Cala and Beshelar bowed and effaced themselves, but Maia barely noticed them leave, the edocharei clustering around him like black-liveried butterflies. They divested him of the jewelry and the keb and shepherded him in to take another bath, this one less ritual and more comforting. Maia relaxed into the hot water, which seemed both to wash away and to deepen his experience in the living rock of the vigil chapel. His time sense remained suspended, like the remission of a tertian ague, but the water was tepid when he opened his eyes and found Nemer saying apologetically, "Serenity, it is time."

They dried him and dressed him: snow-white linen; white stockings and white court slippers; white velvet trousers; a white silk shirt; and over it not the ordinary quilted jacket but a long white robe, quilted and brocaded and by far the most beautiful item of clothing Maia had ever worn.

*I shall grow weary of white before long,* he acknowledged ruefully, but for now he was entranced.

Avris combed his hair as before, but this time braided it into a great knot at the base of his skull, with long thin plaits, braided with white ribbons and strands of pearls, hanging down his back. Then the Dachen Mura were brought out again, and this time Maia was arrayed entirely in opals and pearls: rings, bracelets, earrings, necklace. He was spared the diadem, because the Ethuverazhid Mura, the imperial crown, awaited him like some monstrous bridegroom.

The edocharei did not hurry. When they released him, and he returned to the outer chamber, the clock on the mantel read nine o'clock.

*Three hours,* Maia thought, but Chavar demanded his attention before he could decide whether that was too much time or not enough.

Now began another set of rituals, the oath-takings. First were his nohecharei: Cala, Beshelar, Dazhis, Telimezh. They were now bound to him until their deaths, and past, for they would be buried with him— as his father's nohecharei would be buried with their emperor tomorrow.

Then came the Corazhas. Maia had, he felt, the easy part; he had only to sit in a heavy and uncomfortable chair in the audience chamber that was the first floor of the Alcethmeret, and accept the hands that were held out to him. It was the Corazhas, the Witnesses, who had to remember the long, archaic formulas of the oaths and repeat them without stumbling. Given the length of Varenechibel's reign, none of them was old enough to have given the oath more than once before.

Nine Witnesses made up the Corazhas, each of them ruler of his own small empire. The Witnesses knelt, and Maia received their oaths, wondering how many of them meant the loyalty they professed, how many of them, like Chavar, were loyal still to Varenechibel's memory. After them, the Adremaza and the Captain of the Untheileneise Guard swore; the captain, robed and masked and armored as both prelate and knight of Anmura, frightened Maia slightly with his ferocity.

The five princes entered next, and Maia, growing light-headed from nervousness and lack of food, remembered of them only the haunted eyes of the Prince of Thu-Athamar. Maia leaned forward when the prince had given his vow and said, very low, "Neither blame nor guilt belongs to you, so do not hold them so closely." The prince seemed more startled than reassured, but his look quickly became thoughtful, and he was still frowning slightly, his eyes distant, when the princes filed out.

Maia had been dreading the oaths of the Drazhada only slightly less than the coronation itself. The widow empress; his half sisters Nemriän and Vedero; his half brother Nemolis's widow and three children; his half brother Ciris's fiancée; and last in line, Arbelan Drazharan, Varenechibel's first wife, put aside for barrenness thirty years ago, but never released from her ties to the House Drazhada. Both Csoru and Sheveän, the Princess of the Untheileneise Court, were giving her offended sidelong glances, which Arbelan affected not to see.

Arbelan was in her mid-sixties, a tall, proud woman still, with brilliant blue eyes. Beside her, Csoru looked even more doll-like, while Nemriän and Sheveän seemed callow, petulant girls. Stano Bazhevin, Ciris's fiancée, was a nonentity, just another white-faced woman in black. Only Vedero held her own.

The Archduchess Vedero Drazhin was a big woman, two inches taller than Maia himself, broad in the shoulder and hip. Her hair was smooth white silk, her eyes the Drazhadeise gray. Her features were strong but good and her presence one of tremendous dignity. Black did not become her, and he could see by the grayness of her face and her red-rimmed eyes that she had been weeping and had scorned to hide the evidence. He liked her the better for it, though he feared from the look she gave him that she did not like him and would not care whether he liked her or not.

The oaths were properly given, and Maia heaved a small, inward sigh of relief. The oaths were no more than a formal deterrent to troublemaking, but they were better than no deterrent at all. Fourteen-year-old Idra, the new Prince of the Untheileneise Court and Maia's own heir, seemed to mean them sincerely, and Maia dared to smile at him. Idra did not quite smile back, but his eyes lightened. Idra's sisters, Ino and Mireän, were too young to understand fully what they did, but they placed their small hands in Maia's confidently and without hesitation.

The women were a different matter; Nemriän, Csoru, and Shevëan clearly disdained him. Stano was frightened of him. Vedero he could not read; her face was as impassive as marble. Arbelan seemed amused, if anything, although that might have been aimed more at Csoru's territorial bristling than at Maia himself.

Chavar was the last person to take a private oath to the new emperor, having been up to this point acting as the representative of the dead. Chavar's broad hands were hot in Maia's, and he swore the oath in a perfunctory growl, as if he neither respected nor believed the words he spoke.

*We will have conference of this,* Maia thought, but this was neither the time nor the place for those words. He watched Chavar broodingly as the Lord Chancellor organized the procession to the heart of the Untheileneise Court: Maia and his nohecharei, both First and Second; the princes; the Witnesses; the Drazhada of Varenechibel's line: all herded into line with the Captain of the Untheileneise Guard and the Adremaza, and Chavar in the lead.

*I like this symbolism not,* Maia thought, walking in a square formed by the nohecharei. *It says that the emperor follows where the Lord Chancellor leads. I do not, nor do I intend to.* He knew that Chavar was in fact representing the old emperor, guiding his successor to crown and throne—*but then, I do not wish to follow my father, either,* he thought and had to repress a smile.

The procession wound its stately way through the Untheileneise Court; the courtiers were already in the Untheileian, the hall of the Ethuverazhid Zhas, but servants and secretaries lined the corridors, watching, and when they passed through the great public courtyard, it was packed with people from Cetho and the surrounding countryside, come to catch a glimpse of their new emperor.

It was also bitterly cold; at first, Maia thought the spots in front of his eyes meant he was about to faint, but then he realized it was snowing. He managed to lean close enough to Telimezh to whisper, "Isn't it early in the season for snow?" and to hear Telimezh's whispered response, "Yes, Serenity." And then they were back inside and approaching the doors of the Untheileian. It was midnight.

The Untheileian was a long, tall-windowed room with magnificent stained glass, visible now only as brighter splotches of color along the walls. The courtiers filled it in well-disciplined rows, all of them dressed in full court mourning, faces white and eyes glittering in the gaslight. Maia suffered an uneasy fancy that they, like a pack of wolves, would descend on him and tear him limb from limb. But they only watched.

Out of the corner of his eye, he saw a pair of dark faces in that pale, gleaming sea, and he knew they must be Ambassador Gormened, who claimed kinship, and his wife. He could not turn his head to look, but he found himself comforted—not for any trust he placed in the ambassador, or in Barizhan behind him, but for the much-needed reminder that there was, in fact, a world beyond the Untheileneise Court. He walked steadily up the hall, and the procession dispersed behind him as Drazhada, princes, Witnesses, Adremaza, and captain all found their appointed places. The Archprelate waited on the dais, standing in front of the tall ivory throne, with the Ethuverazhid Mura cradled in his hands. The nohecharei took their positions at the two great torchières that flanked the dais, and Maia walked the last ten feet on his own, more aware than ever of being eighteen, skinny, dark, and never the heir that Varenechibel had intended.

He climbed the five steps of the dais and bowed to the Archprelate. The Archprelate bowed in return; what

Maia could see of his face behind his mask was at least not judgmental. He asked the binding questions, and Maia swore his answers. "Then kneel for the last time, Edrehasivar Drazhar," the Archprelate said, allowing his voice to rise to a shout, "and accept the crown of the Elflands!"

Maia knelt. The Ethuverazhid Mura, a heavy, archaic circle of silver set with opals, pressed down upon his head. He stood again, trying not to let his knees shake, and turned to face the Untheileian.

En masse, and beautifully, the assembled courtiers bowed; some of the women curtsied, and he wished he could see their faces clearly enough to mark them, for they would be enemies of Csoru Zhasanai and he desired to know them better. But the court blurred before his eyes, and the first half hour of Edrehasivar VII's reign was a stubborn struggle not to faint.

Then his nohecharei surrounded him again, and he was able to return by a much shorter route to the Alcethmeret, where the edocharei made a fuss and insisted on feeding him soup before they would allow him to crawl into bed.

Maia lay in the great canopied bed of the Emperors of the Elflands, staring up into the darkness at the Drazhadeise cats he knew were there, although he could not see them. Cala sat in the corner, he knew, peacefully guarding him. He was exhausted, feeling pressed against the bed by the weight of his own body, and yet sleep would not come. When he closed his eyes, the day jumbled behind them in such a confusion of images that he had to open them again. He remembered the tranquillity he had felt in the vigil chapel, but it was as elusive and chimerical as the sleep he could not find.

He lay and stared up into the darkness, and when at last sleep found him, he did not even know it, for his dreams were as dark and silent as his bedchamber.

# 9

## The Report of the Witnesses
## for the Wisdom of Choharo

In the morning when Maia looked out, the roofs of the Untheileneise Court were dusted with snow. "Most unseasonable," Esha said primly when he noticed the direction of Maia's gaze.

Now that he was crowned, no longer merely the emperor-apparent, Maia could not stay in what he had come to think of as the safety of the Alcethmeret. He did not, Csevet assured him, have to use the Untheileian except on state occasions, but it was customary for the emperor to grant audiences in the Michen'theileian, and despite the funeral of Varenechibel IV that would be held that evening, audiences (Csevet said firmly) the new emperor must grant.

"The government has ground to a halt," he said, seated at the foot of the dining table, immaculate and poised as always. "It must be pushed into motion again, Serenity, and you are the only person who can do that."

"I suppose I am," Maia said under his breath.

"Serenity?"

"Nothing. To whom do we grant audiences today?" The words came out in a snarl, and Csevet drew back, his ears flattening.

"Serenity, we did not mean to offend you. We thought only to help."

Maia set his cup do... h hard, slopping tea into the
saucer, his entire body h hard, slopping tea into the
he said. "We spoke ungra shame. "We apologize,"
which we should not have ly and out of ill temper
not have disparaged your se... on you. We should
truly grateful. We are sorry."        for which we are so

"Serenity," Csevet said uncom... bly, "you should
not speak so to us."

"Why not?"

Csevet opened his mouth and clos.d it again. Then,
deliberately, he set down his cup, stood up, and with
infinite grace prostrated himself beside the table. Isheian watched him with alarm.

Csevet stood up again, unruffled and perfect, and said,
"The Emperor of the Elflands does not apologize to his
secretary. And yet, we thank you for doing that which
the emperor does not." He smiled, a warm beautiful
smile that made his face suddenly, momentarily alive,
and sat down again. "Serenity."

Wordlessly, Isheian presented Maia with a clean
saucer. Wordlessly, he picked up his cup and let the
chamomile scour away the thick taste of sleep. Then he
asked, "Who petitions for an audience this morning?"

"Serenity. The most important are the Imperial Witnesses for the *Wisdom of Choharo.*"

Maia went cold. He set the teacup down, carefully
this time, and picked up a buttered crumpet, as being
neither spillable nor breakable. "When do they wish to
be heard?"

"They ask for the earliest time convenient for Your
Serenity."

"Oh." He took a bite, chewed, swallowed, all without tasting. "Then by all means let them have it."

Csevet glanced at the clock. "Nine o'clock," he said,
with perhaps a quarter twist of question.

"Yes," Maia said.

"Serenity. We will wwish to read this letter from meantime, you may pe... necessary reply. In the Setheris Nelar."

The studied neut... of Csevet's tone told Maia that there was probabl... thing in the world he wished less, but he accepted ... letter that Csevet held out to him.

Setheris's fam... ar handwriting struck him like one of Setheris's rem... bered blows. He picked up the crumpet again, to give himself a moment's respite, and forced himself to eat it. He was even able to notice how good it was, although it was almost impossible to swallow past the dryness in his throat.

He could stall no longer. Grimly, he picked up the letter (taking a sullen, childish pleasure in getting butter on the edges) and set himself to read:

*To his Imperial Serenity, Edrehasivar VII, greetings.*

*It is a matter of great concern to us—and also to our wife, who asks to be remembered to you—to discover what Your Serenity intends for us now that the household of Edonomee is disbanded. We dare to hope that our relegation is ended, for which we thank Your Serenity most profoundly and sincerely, and we profess our utmost ability and desire to serve Your Serenity in any capacity we may.*

*With great loyalty and familial affection,*
*Setheris Nelar*

*Hesero wrote that,* Maia thought. He knew Setheris's turn of phrase, knew his mind, and while the handwriting was his, the sentiments and careful phrasing were not. He could imagine Hesero standing beside the desk, watching closely to be sure Setheris used the words she specified.

Hesero wrote it, but how was he, Maia, to answer it? He did not want Setheris in his household, but the letter was as much a request for a job as it was a plea for reassurance, and to refuse Setheris a post, no matter how satisfying the gesture would be, would spark exactly the kind of gossip he most wished to avoid.

Csevet finished the message to the Witnesses for the *Wisdom of Choharo* and rang for a page boy to deliver it. After the boy had gone, Maia said, "Csevet, we must speak with you."

He felt the other four people in the room freeze into alertness. He had failed to keep his distress out of his voice. He might as well, he thought defiantly, make the experiment now, and added, *"Alone."*

Telimezh and Dazhis exchanged a look rich with consternation, and Telimezh said, "Serenity, we cannot—"

"Why not?" Maia demanded. "What attack do you fear?"

"Serenity, it is our oath. We are sworn to guard you, just as we are sworn to silence about anything we may witness. We will not betray you."

*Truly,* Maia thought, *that is not my fear. Shall betray myself, but I would not have it be to you.* He said, "Can you not guard us just as well from the other side of the door?"

"Serenity," Telimezh said; his ears were flat against his head with unhappiness.

"An we command it?"

"Serenity," Dazhis said, bowing. "If you were to die in our dereliction, know that we would kill ourselves at the feet of your corpse. Do you wish that?"

He felt frustration like a black weight pressing against his chest. But if he could win only by wronging his nohecharei, then he could not win at all. "No, of course not," Maia said wearily. "Isheian, would you?"

"Serenity," she said, bowing, and left by the servants' door.

He looked at the three of them, Csevet, Telimezh,

Dazhis. He wished dully that it were Beshelar and Cala instead; they had already seen him at his worst.

"Know then," he said, dropping his gaze to the table-cloth, "that Setheris Nelar served as our guardian these past ten years since the death of our mother, and he . . ." He could not say it, and finished hastily and lamely, "We love him not."

Into the puzzled silence, Telimezh said, "No reason you should, Serenity. He is not a cousin of your house, and—"

"No! We mean—" He stopped, gripping his hands tightly together in his lap. "Plainly, I hate him, and I will not have him near me."

He looked up. Telimezh and Dazhis seemed simply shocked; Csevet, who had seen the household at Edonomee, however briefly, allowed his eyebrows to rise in token of enlightenment. He said, "You have not told us this for your pleasure, Serenity. What is your wish?"

"We wish a post for him so that he may live honorably and comfortably, and we need neither see him nor receive his importuning letters."

"Serenity," Csevet said very gently, "if you wish not to be troubled with this man, you have only to say so."

"No, that is not what we mean. He has done no wrong." The memories of a thousand separate cruelties mocked him, but no one save Maia himself had ever counted those as wrongs, and it was unjust to have them declared wrongs now, merely because he could. "We do not wish him unhappy or ill-used. Merely *away*."

"Serenity, we will see what can be done." Csevet paused and added, as one who did not wish to speak and suspected that he would make trouble for himself thereby: "You know that such is properly the Lord Chancellor's concern."

"Then take it up with him. We care not, an it be done."

"Serenity," Csevet said, bowing. He glanced at the clock. "Nine o'clock approaches."

"Then we must go," Maia said, nothing loath to be released from this uncomfortable interview. "We thank you all."

"Serenity," they replied, bowing, and Telimezh turned to open the door.

The Michen'theileian proved not to be the copy in miniature of the Untheileian that Maia had feared. It was more lavishly appointed than he cared for, in ivory and gold, which would emphasize his dark coloring, but it was sensibly furnished with a long table and massive padded chairs, was well heated, and was not, withal, a bad room in which to do business.

The Witnesses for the *Wisdom of Choharo* were there when he and his nohecharei and secretary arrived: two men and a woman, all dressed with shabby respectability and all wearing scholars' keys around their necks. Although, unlike the prelacy and the mazei, scholars did not swear oaths of poverty, it was rare for one to attain great wealth. Setheris had said this was because they were fools, but Maia looked at the tired, drawn faces of the Witnesses and saw no foolishness.

They had gotten only as far as introducing themselves—Pelar, Aizheveth, Sevesar, all scholars of the second rank—when Chavar arrived, indignant, slightly out of breath, and trailing secretaries as a peacock does his tail. There was a lengthy delay while Chavar settled himself and sent his secretaries on unnecessary errands to demonstrate his own importance. Maia wondered if he had behaved so in Varenechibel's service, and was inclined to doubt it. But at last the Lord Chancellor pronounced himself ready, and Maia nodded permission for Mer Sevesar, the seniormost scholar, to begin.

Mer Sevesar wasted neither time nor breath in

equivocations. He stood, bowed to emperor and Lord Chancellor, and said, "Serenity, the wreck of the *Wisdom of Choharo* was caused by sabotage."

"Preposterous!" Chavar cried, but Maia raised a hand to silence him.

"How do you know?" he asked Sevesar. "And what did they do?"

The answer was lengthy and sometimes difficult to follow, but Maia grasped the gist of it. The Witnesses, in examining the wreckage, had found the charred and partially melted remains of an object that, Sevesar said emphatically, was no part of the construction of any airship in the Elflands. He referred to it as an "incendiary device," though neither Maia nor Chavar fully grasped what that term meant. After some futile back-and-forth that made things, if anything, more obscure, Min Aizheveth spoke up suddenly, impatience in her tone, "It ignited the hydrogen."

"Merciful goddesses," someone said faintly.

"It could not be . . . accident?" Chavar said, for once sounding neither pugnacious nor contemptuous.

"No," Sevesar said. He bowed to Maia. "Serenity, we are most sorry, but we thought it best that you should know immediately."

"No, you were right," Maia said. He was hollow, cold; the emotions he should have felt were not there, their absence crippling. It was an effort to think of the right words to say. "We commend you on your dedication and your patient zeal. And we thank you for finding the truth."

"We have found only a small part of the truth, Serenity," Sevesar said. "We do not know who did this thing, or why. We know only that it has been done."

"Yes," Maia said. "But those questions are not within the purview of your witnessing, and we cannot ask you to answer them. You have witnessed for the *Wisdom of*

*Choharo,* and you have witnessed truthfully and with honor."

"Serenity," the three scholars said, bowing. He thought they seemed grateful to escape, and he did not fault them for that. They must have been expecting to be blamed, or to be asked questions to which they could not possibly have the answers. He wished only, unworthily, that he could escape with them. The silence in the Michen'theileian when they had gone was as heavy as a velvet pall. Everyone had become unnaturally careful not to catch anyone else's eye.

Maia said, "What must we do?" and thought of Setheris standing drunken in the door of his room in Edonomee. But he had used the plural this time; this was a decision he neither could nor should make on his own. He looked at Chavar.

Chavar was splenetic again, which was no comfort. "We must find out who perpetrated this vile and contemptible crime."

"Yes," Maia said, "but how?"

Chavar sputtered, his fine rhetoric deflated. Maia looked around the table at all those secretaries he did not know, and said, "We do not know how to go about this. We know that when there is a murder, one asks the judiciar to send a Witness for the Dead, but to which judiciar's sovereignty does this belong? The place where the *Wisdom of Choharo* crashed? The place from which she left? The place to which she was going?"

It was not a trivial question. Maia knew, from Setheris and from newspapers, how jealous judiciars were of their sovereignty, and for the death of an emperor . . . no matter which judiciar was chosen, the others would be offended, and doubtless the Judiciate of the Court would be offended along with them.

Chavar said, "And what will happen if the inquiry should need to cross jurisdictional boundaries? We have seen that happen occasionally—there was a case of theft in which the guilty party was a bargeman, for instance—and it was . . . badly handled. There were satires"—which he said in the tone another man would have used for the word "cockroaches"—"and we only wish we thought matters would have improved since then."

"We do not wish our father to be the target of satires," Maia said firmly.

Chavar gave him a look that was almost approving.

"Perhaps," Csevet said hesitantly. Chavar glared, but Maia made an encouraging gesture, and Csevet continued, "Perhaps the answer is not to try to choose *one* Witness for the Dead. After all, Varenechibel was the emperor of all the Elflands."

Chavar went from anger to approbation in no more than the space of time it took for him to comprehend Csevet's idea. Maia watched, in something less comfortable than amazement, as Csevet's suggestion was seized, gutted, and remounted at a vastly inflated size. Chavar was creating a pageant of investigation, involving all the highest ranked Witnesses in the Judiciate of the Court. He sent secretaries scurrying to arrange for the Witnesses to view the bodies of the emperor and his sons before the funeral. Maia nerved himself to mention that the bodies of the airship crew and Varenechibel's servants were already buried, but Chavar just said, "Leave it to the Witnesses, Serenity," and swept himself and his secretaries out on a tide of barked orders and demands for information.

For the moment, Maia and Csevet (and Maia's stone-silent nohecharei) were alone in the Michen'theileian. Maia noticed the way in which the investigation had become Chavar's property, to be managed and controlled as he saw fit. The emperor would be reduced to petitioning for information—or simply leaving it entirely in the Lord Chancellor's hands, which was surely what Chavar expected and desired.

Maia said, "Was that your intent?"

Csevet froze in the middle of tidying a stack of papers, his white, ringless hands suddenly tense. "Serenity?"

"You worked for Lord Chavar for many years. You have already showed that you know how to . . . to manage him. Did you intend for him to take over as he did?"

"Serenity," Csevet said, setting down the papers as carefully as if they were spun of glass. "It is true that we knew Lord Chavar would approve of any suggestion that would make the investigation larger and more . . ." He hesitated while Maia silently willed him to be candid, and finally Csevet said, "More ostentatious. But we did not expect him to become quite so *enamored* of the idea. We wonder if our notion has dovetailed with one of the Lord Chancellor's other enthusiasms. We know that he is at variance with the Witness for the Judiciate. Perhaps he sees a way in which he can turn this investigation to his advantage."

"Perhaps," said Maia. "Do you think the investigation will succeed?"

"We know the Witnesses will do their best. And we know that Lord Chavar is entirely sincere in his desire to see the murderer caught."

"Yes," Maia agreed dismally.

"Serenity?"

Maia didn't know how to articulate his concerns—nor was he even certain that they were anything more than pique at being so deftly excluded—and he'd caused Csevet more than enough bother for one day. He shook his head, and was going to ask what horrible thing he had to face next, when Csevet said, watching him closely,

"We admit, we could wish that Lord Chavar were not focused so exclusively on *judicial* Witnesses."

"What do you mean?"

"As we are sure Your Serenity knows," Csevet said, even though he had to know Maia didn't, "there have always been two classes of Witnesses, the judicial and the clerical. It has become unfashionable to call clerical Witnesses, just as it has become unfashionable to believe that the gods might grant extraordinary powers to them."

"So you are suggesting we consult a clerical Witness for the Dead? But how are we to find such a person?" *Without alerting Chavar,* he did not add.

"Actually," Csevet said, and cleared his throat, "there is a clerical Witness for the Dead, an unbeneficed prelate of Ulis as it happens, here in the Untheileneise Court."

"How comes he here?" asked Maia.

"We do not know his story," Csevet said. "We know only that he abdicated his prelacy and traveled to the court to live."

Maia could feel the missing information in what Csevet had said and prodded for it: "Why here?"

"The charity of his kinswoman," Csevet said with marked reluctance. "The widow empress."

# 10

## The Witness for the Dead

With more relief than compunction, Maia instructed Csevet to inform Setheris that he would have to wait for the next day to have his audience. He spent most of the day dealing with items of business that had been unresolved at the time of his father's death. They were many and tedious, and each seemed to require a suffocating amount of explanation. It was late in the afternoon before he could grant an audience to the Witness for the Dead.

He had managed to divest himself of the secretaries who had rushed in and out like swarming bees all day. The only people in the fading winter sunlight of the Michen'theileian were the emperor, his nohecharei, his secretary, and Thara Celehar.

He was younger than Maia had expected, no more than ten years older than his imperial patroness. But Maia had never seen a man who looked so ill and tired. He was slight-boned—in that way like Csoru—but with so little flesh over his bones that Maia could see every separate knob of his wrists. His eyes, in dark hollows of sleeplessness, were vivid blue; he had cut off the long braid his prelate's rank had entitled him to, and his fine milk-white curls were barely jaw length. He did not wear prelate's robes, being dressed in unexceptionable mourning. Maia noted the worn patches at the cuffs of the jacket and the turned-up cuffs of the trousers and surmised that the limits of the widow empress's charity were very straitly defined.

"Serenity," Celehar murmured, bowing. His voice was rough, gravelly, strangely at odds with his fastidious and respectable appearance.

"We hope that you were told why we wished to speak to you," Maia said tentatively, for there was something in Celehar's gaze that made him wary.

"Serenity," Celehar said, bowing again.

"Yes or no, Mer Celehar."

"Yes, Serenity."

Maia waited. Celehar did not speak. "And?"

Celehar seemed only wearily perplexed.

Maia said, "Will you act as our private Witness for the Dead?"

"Beg pardon, Serenity," Celehar said, bowing. "We were not aware that we had a choice in the matter."

The words hovered on the brink of insolence, as Maia saw reflected in Dazhis and Telimezh's bristling and the very deliberate way Csevet set down his pen, but the tone held nothing but exhaustion.

He said gently, "Mer Celehar, you are free to decline."

He thought later that Celehar would have been less surprised if Maia had ordered Telimezh to run him through. For a moment, his eyes were shocked wide. Then the shutters of a well-bred man flipped back into place, and he was regarding Maia with nothing more showing than weary bemusement. "Your Serenity is most kind. We thank you."

"You may thank us by giving us your answer, Mer Celehar."

"Serenity," Celehar said with a deep bow that Maia suspected was more to hide his face than to show respect. "We will be honored to witness for your dead."

"Thank you." Maia waited until Celehar was standing straight again, then said, "We know nothing of the workings of your witnessing. Tell us what you need."

"Serenity." Celehar hesitated. "We need . . . we need to see and touch the bodies. And it helps if one whose living blood calls to theirs can be present."

Maia understood Celehar's hesitation; he hesitated himself. But if he did not grieve for his father, yet he was horrified at the cruelty and injustice of his death, and fearful of what the murderer—or murderers—might do next if not apprehended. He said, "We will accompany you. But we must go now. The funeral is to begin at sundown."

"Serenity, we assure you," Celehar said, with the faintest lift of wryness in his voice, "we had no other plans."

Predictably, the nohecharei objected. Maia smiled at them and said, "We pity you that so much of your post lies in trying to prevent us from doing what we must." Beshelar would have had an apoplexy; Telimezh and Dazhis subsided in abashed confusion. Cala, he thought, would not have tried to talk him out of it in the first place.

There were only two hours before the funeral, and the Untheileneise'meire was clustered with clerics: black robes and green robes, brown and gray and the deep marigold robes of the devouts of Anmura. Five clerics of Ulis, black-robed and black-veiled, though not masked, bowed as they passed, their arms incongruously full of color as they moved the floral offerings to make way for the coffin, which would remain lying in state, guarded and prayed over by the canons of the Untheileneise'meire, until the sarcophagus was built around it. Varenechibel's four nohecharei had already been cremated; their remains, each in its own gold-inlaid jar, were set in holders at the four corners of the coffin, his First Nohecharei at his head (soldier to the right, maza to the left) and his Second Nohecharei at his feet (maza to the right, soldier to the left). They defended the emperor in death as they had defended him in life—from everything until the thing, the *incendiary device*, that had killed them all.

The bodies of the Emperor Varenechibel IV and his three eldest sons were currently lying directly beneath the dome of the Untheileneise'meire. In closed coffins. That aspect of the crash of the *Wisdom of Choharo* had not forced itself on Maia's attention before; he felt now both stupid and sick. He wanted, badly, to look away—even to leave. But it was clear that Celehar was encountering some opposition from the senior canon, and it only seemed to be getting worse. Maia had let Telimezh and Dazhis and Csevet herd him subtly into a pocket of clear space, but now he stepped forward (unhappily amused by the way Celehar and the canon both involuntarily stepped back) and said, "Mer Celehar? Is there a difficulty?"

Celehar bowed his head slightly and said, "Serenity, Canon Orseva is explaining to us that a number of Witnesses for the Dead have already been allowed to examine the bodies at the cost of a significant delay to the funeral preparations. Canon Orseva fears that there is not time for another examination and does not see what good it can do."

Canon Orseva did not look entirely happy at this summation of his words, but he did not repudiate any of it. In truth, Maia wasn't sure what good it would do, either; he was only certain that he could not leave the matter blindly in Chavar's hands.

While he was still trying to find some compromise between a blunt truth and a political lie, Csevet cleared his throat and announced in an unexpectedly carrying voice, "The emperor would like a few minutes alone with the bodies of his family."

Within moments, miraculously, the Untheileneise'meire was empty save for one junior canon, her ears flat with unhappy obstinacy, who would not leave her post of vigil-keeper over the bodies.

"Csevet!" Maia said in a shocked whisper.

Csevet smiled at him, unrepentant. "You *are* emperor, Serenity. It is not Canon Orseva's place to dictate to you."

Celehar said, "Canon Thorchelezhen does not object to helping us," and Maia managed to smile at the junior canon. It was not a very good smile, and Celehar, surprising him with his understanding, said, "You don't have to look, Serenity. You can stay where you are."

And truly Maia did not wish to look, nor go any closer to those four lacquered black coffins. But something—not desire, but something else, duty or guilt—drove him forward. When Celehar and the canon lifted the lid off Varenechibel's coffin, Maia was standing beside them.

The votaries of Ulis who had laid out the body had done their best, straightening the limbs, muffling the worst brokennesses in linen and silk. But the only thing they had been able to do for the dead emperor's seared and twisted features was to veil the head in white lace. Celehar gently lifted the veil, and Maia had to turn away.

Celehar began to say the prayer of compassion for the dead in his rasping, broken voice, and Maia stood looking at the white columns and struggled with the pity and disgust and hatred and sorrow in his heart, all for Varenechibel, his father.

Presently, Celehar fell silent. Maia did not turn around; he did not want to watch the communion between the dead and the Witness, whatever it might consist of. After a while, he heard Celehar and the canon replacing the lid of the coffin and said, still not turning, "Do you need to see the . . . the others?"

"Serenity," Celehar said apologetically. "It would help."

"Very well," Maia said, although he longed to order Celehar to leave the bodies, leave the Untheileneise'meire, allow him to leave as well. "Let us continue."

He stayed where he was, not turning, while Celehar and the canon repeated their grisly ritual three more times. He noticed that the kindness and patience in Celehar's ugly voice never faltered, that he said the prayer of compassion for the fourth time with the same focused attention he had said it the first. He had not renounced his prelacy for lack of belief or calling, then. Maia knew he would not ask after the real reason; he did not have the right. But he could not help wondering what had happened.

In time, Celehar said, "Serenity, we have finished."

Maia turned. The Witness for the Dead was standing quietly among the coffins; he looked, at least, no worse than he had in the Michen'theileian. "What do you do now?" Maia asked him.

"Serenity. Your dead do not have answers. They died in fear and confusion and will not find clarity until Ulis grants it to them. But there are other places to look for answers. There are other dead."

"The graves at the Ulimeire," Maia said.

"Serenity. If it does not displease you, we will begin our searching there tomorrow."

"It pleases us, Mer Celehar. And we thank you."

"Serenity," Celehar said, bowing, his tone so neutral that it was itself a judgment. He came out from between the coffins. He was several inches shorter than Maia, but seemed not in the slightest discomposed by having to tilt his head back to look his emperor in the face. "Do not thank us when you know not what we will find."

"It matters not what you find. We thank you for seeking the truth, and we thank you for doing this thing although you did not wish to."

"We have found truth before, Serenity, and it profits us not. We would give much to have some truths remain lost, and we do not think you will find this truth to be any different."

"It matters not," Maia said again. "We do not ask this truth for ourself. We ask it for . . ." He hesitated, uncertain. He did not want the truth on his father's behalf, or on his half brothers'. Finally, he said slowly, "We ask it for those who died because they were near our father. We ask it for those who are afraid, now, because their emperor fell from the sky and lay burning in a field. We ask it for those who did not want their emperor murdered. For without the truth, how can they trust that their emperor will not be murdered again?"

He could not read Celehar's expression. The Witness for the Dead bowed, murmuring, "Serenity," and then stepped past him and walked out of the Untheileneise'meire.

Maia stood, staring at the coffins, at the columns and tombs and up at the oculus at the apex of the dome, his head thick with half-understood emotions, his throat tight with words he could not speak, until his nohecharei advanced to remind him that the funeral was supposed to begin at sundown, and there was very little time left.

# 11

## The Funeral and the Wake

He could not help remembering, as the sun sank into a bank of violent red clouds in the western sky, that the only time he had ever seen his father in life had been at his mother's funeral. And he could not help remembering the disrespect the emperor had chosen to show his fourth empress, that single black stole against the imperial white.

It would be no more than justice were he to slight his father as his father had slighted his mother. Maia toyed vengefully with this fantasy, then acknowledged with a sigh that it was not in him to carry it through. He was too aware of the distress it would cause the court, the surviving family, his own household. He remembered too vividly his own distress and the deeper bitterness it had given a grief already deep enough to drown in.

Therefore, he stood patiently and allowed his edocharei to encase him in the immobilizing regalia of full imperial mourning, layers of black-on-black brocade oversewn with pearls; silver rings set with strange, dark, clouded jewels; pearls for his ears and neck and wound in the braids of his hair; the Ethuverazhid Mura; and over it all, yards of black veiling that made the opals of the Ethuverazhid Mura as eerie as the moon seen through clouds. Maia looked at himself in the mirror and shivered.

Sometime in the midst of the preparations, his nohecharei had changed shifts, so that when he turned away from the mirror it was Beshelar who was waiting for him, who bowed his head as if he did not want to meet Maia's eyes and growled, "Your Serenity."

"Lieutenant," Maia said, amused at the sudden resurgence of Beshelar's stiff formality. But Beshelar merely opened the door and stood aside.

Cala was waiting in the outer chamber. He bowed solemnly and said, "Serenity, it is probably best if we go now. The Archprelate suggested . . . that is, the funeral is already late, and it will look well if you are there first. To pray for . . . that is, to pray."

Cala, too, seemed unusually flustered, but this was not the moment to attempt to discover what was wrong. Maia merely said, "Very well," and returned to the Untheileneise'meire, this time ascending a narrow staircase to the emperor's balcony, which hung between the pillars like a spider's egg sac anchored in its web.

He had a moment of vertigo, looking down at the coffins, remembering being a child looking up at the white and distant figure, the emperor. "Serenity?" Cala said anxiously, but Maia waved him away.

He rested his hands on the balustrade and took a deep breath to steady himself; he began to pray, repeating silently the prayer of compassion for the dead he had heard Mer Celehar say that afternoon, trying to say it each time as patiently and sincerely as Celehar had. Compassion was all that he could hope for. He could not pray for love or forgiveness; both were out of reach. He could not forgive his father, and he could not love his brothers whom he had never met. But he could feel compassion for them, as he did for the other victims, and it was that he sought more than anything else: to mourn their deaths rather than holding on to his anger at their lives.

Below him, the courtiers began to file in. He caught several glances up at him and then quickly away, and thought with sudden, inexpressible weariness that he had to reawaken the court as well as the government. He would have to ask someone—Csevet would know—what the court functions were and what the emperor had to do when he attended them. And did he have to order them, or did they somehow take care of themselves?

*I was not meant for this,* he thought, his neck and shoulders tensing with the effort of keeping his chin up, and the scholar's quiet voice said in his mind, *Serenity, the wreck of the* Wisdom of Choharo *was caused by sabotage.*

It was a relief when the Archprelate emerged to begin the ceremony, even though Maia was guiltily aware that they were starting late. There was nothing inauspicious about beginning a funeral after sundown, so long as it was before moonrise, but there would be plenty of sticklers in the court who would consider it sloppy and disrespectful. And there could be no doubt that Canon Orseva would let them know who was to blame.

He set himself to listen to the Archprelate's beautiful voice, grateful that between the veil and the balcony, none of the court would be able to see his face. He found his sisters, Nemriän and Vedero, in the crowd; Arbelan Drazharan and the widow empress (standing at a careful remove from each other); Ciris's fiancée, Stano Bazhevin, standing awkwardly alone; the Princess of the Untheileneise Court and her children. The little girls were about the age he had been when his mother had died; he looked anxiously but saw nothing more than wide-eyed solemnity behind their veils. He wondered if his brother Nemolis had been a kind father, if his children had been given the chance to love him. Idra was standing very straight and dignified beside his mother; he was Prince of the Untheileneise Court now, and he seemed to feel the responsibility as much as Maia felt his own.

The Drazhada did not look up at him, except once. When the Archprelate began to speak over Nemolis's coffin, his widow Shevëan turned her head; even through the veil, the hostility in her gaze was nearly enough to make Maia step back. She looked away, dismissing him from her attention, and Maia, his fingers tightening on the balustrade, wondered what had happened. She had not liked him at the oath-taking, but she had not *hated* him.

Compassion, he thought, fixing his eyes on the Archprelate, and sank himself again in the prayer of compassion for the dead. It saved him from thinking.

The wake, which as emperor he had both to open and to close, was held in the Untheileian. He had not been allowed to attend his mother's wake and so had not known what to expect, but he was still discomfited to discover the laden sideboards and the center of the great hall cleared for dancing. "What must I do?" he hissed in Cala's ear. "I can't dance!"

"You need not, Serenity," Cala said. "You ask the court to dance the dead to peace, and then you may sit or stand or dance as it pleases you."

"Thank you," Maia said, although he was not greatly comforted.

He put his veil back before ascending the dais; its obscurity felt now like blindness instead of safety. He spoke as Cala had told him, although the words felt clumsy, stilted, and he could not judge the tone of his own voice, whether he sounded sincere or petulant or bored. The court watched him with glittering, predatory eyes, but when he gestured to the musicians, they formed obediently into couples and traced swirling, sparkling patterns across the floor, patterns too elaborate for Maia to follow.

*Thou must learn to dance,* he said to himself, and sank wearily onto the throne. It was not comfortable, but at least it was a seat. Beshelar and Cala took position, one at either side of the throne. He tilted his head back to ask Cala, "May you not sit?"

There was a strangled noise from Beshelar's direction. Cala said, "Thank you, Serenity, but no. We are well."

"What if you wished to dance?"

"Serenity, *please,*" Beshelar hissed.

"We are not, strictly speaking, members of Your Serenity's court," Cala said. "Were we not your nohecharei, we would not be here to begin with. So it would be the grossest impropriety for us to dance, even were there a lady in the hall who would accept us as partners."

"Oh," Maia said, feeling very young and stupid, and Beshelar said, sounding almost relieved, "Serenity, the Lord Chancellor approaches."

Maia looked and there was the choleric Lord Chancellor heading for the dais, and with him was a young man, short and stocky like Chavar himself, but dressed in what even Maia could tell was the extreme of elegance, and with a brightness about him his father lacked.

They stopped at the foot of the dais. Maia beckoned them closer, resisting the impulse to make Chavar wait.

"Serenity," Chavar said, kneeling, "may we commend to your attention our son, Nurevis?"

"Serenity," the young man said, sinking to one knee as gracefully as he had crossed the hall.

"We are pleased," Maia said, a meaningless phrase, but one that seemed to satisfy Chavar and his son.

They stood again, and Chavar said, "We realize that

it is difficult for you, Serenity, to be thrust into the court so suddenly and with no one about you of your own age."

Behind Chavar, Nurevis rolled his eyes and winked at Maia. Maia felt suddenly and inexpressibly lighter. He said dryly, "We appreciate your thoughtfulness, Lord Chancellor," but did not, as he otherwise might have, remark that it would be even more appreciated were the Lord Chancellor to bend that thoughtfulness to the performance of his office.

Chavar, beaming widely and unappealingly, bowed himself out of the way, and Nurevis, coming closer, murmured, "Serenity, we *do* apologize. When Father gets an idea into his head like that, we have learned from long experience not to argue with him."

"Not at all," Maia said. "We are grateful. We have not . . . that is, there has not been a chance for us to become familiar with our court."

"No, it's all happened so fast, hasn't it? Well, we can hardly go about introducing the emperor to all our closest friends, but if Your Serenity would like . . ." He trailed off, one eyebrow raised in friendly mockery.

"Yes?"

"We would be happy to identify people for you. We do know almost everyone at court."

"You are very kind," Maia said. "Please."

Nurevis stood by the throne for the next quarter hour, providing Maia with names and bits of mild gossip. Maia listened and watched and tried to remember, although he was afraid his memory for names and faces was not as good as it needed to be. Then Nurevis excused himself, smiling, saying that it would hardly do for the emperor to choose favorites before he'd had a chance to meet everyone, and sauntered off to find a partner for the next dance.

The dais felt three times as lonely as it had before.

Somehow, having been introduced to one person, Maia no longer felt that he could turn to talk to his nohecharei; Nurevis's comment about favorites made him uneasy, and he wondered if he was already being perceived that way, having stuck so closely to his own household in the days since Varenechibel's death.

Another reason to arrange court functions, he thought. *And* learn to dance. He was burningly aware of the glances of the young women as they swept by in their partners' arms, unable to keep himself from imagining what it would be like to dance with one of them, to touch them as the young men of the court did.

*Must* learn *to dance,* he said wryly to himself.

He was almost relieved when a page boy approached the dais, although it took him a blank moment to identify the livery as that of the Tethimada. The boy knelt at the bottom of the stairs, holding out a sealed envelope.

Beshelar said, "Shall we, Serenity?"

"Yes, please," Maia said, and Beshelar descended the steps to take the envelope.

Given Dach'osmer Tethimar's previous letter, Maia was gratefully surprised to find this one both short and comprehensible. It said merely, *Serenity, we fear we have offended you. Please allow us to approach and apologize?*

He looked up and saw Eshevis Tethimar immediately, a tall, broad-shouldered man, in perfect court mourning down to the row of onyx beads hanging along the curve of each ear, who had placed himself carefully to be in the emperor's line of sight. He was extremely good-looking, and something in his bearing suggested he knew it. He did not, Maia noted grimly, look in the least like a man who was worried that he had offended his emperor.

Maia saw, quite clearly, that Tethimar had pinned him

in a fork as Haru the gardener pinned marsh vipers. If he refused this very reasonable request, he put himself in the wrong and Tethimar had another to add to the list of grievances the eastern lords held against the emperor. On the other hand, if he granted Tethimar's request, Tethimar gained the advantage of appearing to be in the emperor's favor, as being the second person to be granted an audience with him publicly. It took no great intelligence to see that if Tethimar had had any true concerns, he would not have made the request now, and he most certainly would not have asked to be allowed to approach here at the wake.

*I do not like thee, Eshevis Tethimar,* Maia thought. But as best he could tell—and he wished for Csevet to advise him—he would do less damage by granting Tethimar's request than by snubbing him. He tucked the note in his pocket and said to the page boy, "Tell your master he may approach us." It was more formal and tedious than simply beckoning Tethimar over, but by the same token, he hoped it reduced the appearance of familiarity between himself and Tethimar.

He thought of the marshes around Edonomee: the Edonara the locals called them, although they had no name on the imperial maps, with their vipers and quicksands and endless rising mists. He thought of Haru saying—one of the few times Haru had spoken to him directly—*I hope Your Lordship never finds yourself out in the marshes, but if you do, you test every step before you take it. Don't trust it just because it looks all right, or because it was all right the last time you stepped on it. Because it won't be the same. And because the Edonara takes its own sacrifices.* And then he'd stopped and ducked his head and mumbled something that might have been an apology and lumbered off. And Maia hadn't known how to tell him not to.

The Untheileneise Court, for all its beauty, was just another version of the Edonara. *Test every step before you take it, and trust nothing*. He thought of the boy emperors lying entombed in the Untheileneise'meire, thought of his father's wives. The Untheileneise Court took its own sacrifices, as well.

But now Dach'osmer Tethimar was climbing the steps of the dais. He stopped in exactly the right place, knelt, murmured, "Serenity," in a beautifully modulated baritone.

"Rise, please, Dach'osmer Tethimar," Maia said, feeling more than ever like a loose-jointed doll swaddled and draped in the robes of an emperor. His voice sounded thin, childish, painfully hesitant in contrast to Tethimar's.

Tethimar's eyes were a very dark blue, almost black against the whiteness of his face, and he clearly knew their effect: as he stood, he caught and held Maia's gaze, and although what he said was, "We thank you, Serenity, for granting us our request," the dark intensity of his eyes added, *You were wise to do so*.

It was almost comforting, though, to deal with intimidation; it was so very familiar, and Tethimar did not have Setheris's advantages. Maia smiled pleasantly and said, "We confess, Dach'osmer Tethimar, that we were very puzzled by your letter."

And there was a moment, before Tethimar managed to look equally pleasant and puzzled, when Maia saw that he was actually taken aback. It felt like a tiny victory. "But, Serenity," said Tethimar, "you know, of course, that we aspire to marry your sister."

Maia had learned to play dumb from watching the staff at Edonomee deal with Setheris. "Do you?" he said.

"We had entered into negotiations with the late emperor your father," said Tethimar, his voice rising just slightly.

"Had you indeed? No betrothal has been announced that we are aware of."

Tethimar stared at him, and if he had been taken aback before, he was now nearly horrified. "But, Serenity—"

Maia cut him off with an upraised hand. "We think, Dach'osmer Tethimar, that our father's wake is not a suitable place to discuss this or any other matter of import." And he met Tethimar's eyes squarely, knowing that his own eyes were just as disconcerting and knowing how little that actually meant.

Tethimar looked down first. "Of course, Serenity. We beg your pardon. Again." And he managed a rueful quirk of a smile that made Maia almost like him.

Tethimar left the dais and Maia was about to relax—inwardly, for of course the emperor could no more show that he was relieved by Dach'osmer Tethimar's departure than he could show he had been alarmed by his approach—when, his eye caught by darkness that was not mourning colors, he realized that Ambassador Gormened, his wife beside him, was approaching the throne.

He wished, again and even more desperately, that Csevet were here. He could not ignore the ambassador of Barizhan, nor refuse to speak to him, but he could imagine all too clearly what Setheris and his ilk would say about the goblin emperor—and if they were not calling him that yet, it was only a matter of time—chatting publicly with the Great Avar's representative. Yet (he thought, his mind racing), it would counter any favor Dach'osmer Tethimar might be perceived to have gained. And there was the nesecho, tucked safely in one of his inner pockets. Avris had threaded it on a fine gold chain for him, so that it could be secured unnoticeably through a buttonhole or a belt loop, and Maia had been so overwhelmed by this kindness (for which he would never have thought to ask) that he had barely been able to stammer a thank-you. But it had been Gormened's gift to begin with.

Initiative and audacity, Csevet had said. As Gormened stopped at the foot of the dais, Maia could see that he was a young man, goblin-stocky, with a dueling scar on one broad cheekbone. He wondered if Ambassador to the Ethuveraz was a prestigious post or a punishment.

Maia gestured to the ambassador to approach.

"Serenity," said the ambassador, kneeling, while at his side, his wife sank into, and held, a curtsy so deep that Maia was amazed she didn't fall over. "We are Vorzhis Gormened, Ambassador of Barizhan, and this our wife, Nadaro." He pronounced her name goblin-fashion, with the accent on the first syllable, and Maia was ambushed by grief for his mother; she had taught him how to say her name—*CHE-ne-lo*, not *che-NE-lo*—so that there would be one person she knew who said it correctly.

"Stand, please," he said, and watched Nadaro rise with that same iron grace. He realized he had been presented with an opportunity for a petty revenge, and he was not strong enough not to take it. "We are gratified to meet a kinsman of our mother at last. Were you close to her?"

The words were regretted as soon as spoken, but it was not the ambassador who answered. His wife said, "Her mother was our aunt, our father's sister. We were allowed to see Chenelo occasionally as girls, as the Great Avar and our father were allies. It was not so later."

Maia's knowledge of the internal politics of Barizhan was sketchy, and based largely on the cheap blue-backed novels beloved of Pelchara and Kevo back at Edonomee. He did know that the Great Avar was the ruler of the country only because he held the allegiances of the avarsin, the myriad lesser rulers—more numerous than princes, but far more powerful than even the Ethuverazheise dukes—who made up the practical government of Barizhan. The shifting alliance of which Osmerrem Gormened spoke was no trivial matter.

Nadaro Gormened said, "We lit candles for her when we heard of her death. It was all we could do." There might have been the faintest of rebukes in her words, aimed at her husband, for like any elvish woman, when she said, *all we could do*, she meant, *all we were allowed*.

"Candles would have meant much to her," Maia said. "Thank you, Osmerrem Gormened."

She curtsied again, and the ambassador, accepting with unlooked-for tact that the audience was over, bowed and escorted her away. Maia noticed only because he forced himself to, largely consumed with fighting a stinging rush of tears. Chenelo had been dead for ten years; it was pointless, childish, to miss her so terribly. He forced his face to stay still and his ears to stay up, forced his breathing to stay even, and after a stretch of unreckoned time, the pain ebbed, and he was able to ease the interlocked grip of his fingers on each other. Able to breathe, able to look again beyond the limits of the dais, able to lose himself for a time in the swirling patterns of the dance and the arching darkness of the night outside the windows.

And then Cala hissed, "Serenity, the princess!"

Maia turned his head and saw the Princess of the Untheileneise Court making her way up the hall, Stano Bazhevin trotting behind her. Sheveän had not raised her veil, and there was no hint of peace in her carriage. The courtiers moved out of her way, most of them gracefully, so that it looked merely polite, but a few of the youngest girls almost scurried to the side of the hall, and long before he could see her face, Maia knew that the Princess Sheveän was in the same mood she had been in beside her husband's coffin.

She did stop at the foot of the dais, her blue eyes

almost seeming to burn through her veil. Maia did not hesitate in gesturing her closer, knowing that everyone in the Untheileian was watching them, whether openly or otherwise. Stano Bazhevin, awkward and hesitant again, stayed behind, her hands clenched tightly together before her breast. Maia knew that trick, although Setheris had broken him of it: hands clenched together were hands that could not fidget. Osmin Bazhevin was frightened, as she had been at the oath-taking, but this time he thought it was Shevëan she feared. Or Shevëan's errand.

Shevëan swept a low obeisance that might have been a full genuflection or might merely have been a very low curtsy; Maia was not inclined to inquire. "Serenity," she said, her voice low, controlled, and as frigid as the wind in winter.

"Princess," Maia said. Back straight, hands folded, chin and ears up. No outward sign that she was frightening him.

She stood straight again and put back her veil, though only to be better able to glare at him. "We have heard things—shocking, scandalous rumors—and we have come to you that you may assure us that we have been most dreadfully lied to."

"Princess, we do not know what you—"

"We have been told," she said, low and poisonous, "that you allowed—encouraged!—the desecration of our husband's body this afternoon."

"Desecration?" Baffled, Maia had to scramble for something to say. "Princess, we assure you that no desecration has been committed."

"Then it is *not* true that you ordered the prince's coffin opened?"

He did not allow himself to wince. "Princess, you have been given a very imperfect understanding of our purpose."

"You *did* open the coffin!" The gasp was half shock, half wrath, and he thought entirely theatrical.

"Princess," he said firmly, not allowing his voice to rise, "all four coffins were opened in our presence by a canon and a Witness for the Dead. They were treated reverently. Prayers were said. There was no—"

"A Witness for the Dead?" Her voice was louder, and he knew she was playing for the avidly watching court. "What possible need could there be for *that*?"

"Princess Sheveän, moderate your voice."

"We will not! We demand to know—"

"Princess," Maia said sharply, and succeeded in cutting her off. He said in a lower voice, "There are reasons, but we do not intend to discuss them at our father's wake. We will grant you an audience as soon as we may, and you will have the full and open truth."

"Your Serenity is too kind," she said, bitterly ironic.

"Sheveän, we are not your enemy. We respect your grief—"

"Respect! Have you wept at all? Do you mourn your family, Edrehasivar, or are you too busy gloating?"

Maia stared at her, bereft of an answer, an evasion, a deflection. He had forgotten the nohecharei, and started violently when Beshelar said, "Princess, we fear you are becoming overwrought. May we call one of your ladies to you?"

Sheveän shot him a murderous look, then curtsied stiffly. "Serenity, forgive us. We are not ourself."

"We understand," Maia said, and did not know if he was lying or not. "Come to us tomorrow, Sheveän, and we will talk."

"Serenity," she said, still unyielding, and swept away, collecting Osmin Bazhevin as she went. Osmin Bazhevin glanced apologetically at Maia over her shoulder; it was notable that the Princess Sheveän, in her dramatics, had forgotten to mention Osmin Bazhevin or Osmin Bazhevin's (presumable) concerns for her fiancé's body.

Maia had to take several deep breaths before he could say, in a quiet, even voice, "Thank you, Beshelar."

"Serenity," Beshelar said gruffly. "It is our job."

# 12

## The Princess and the Witness

He was in the Untheileneise'meire again, although he did not know why. He had forgotten something, he thought, something precious. He had left it by his mother's tomb, and if the morning sunlight touched it, it would disintegrate and be gone.

So here he was in the Untheileneise'meire in the dark. There was a shaft of moonlight streaming through the oculus, and in the moonlight he could see snow falling, collecting on the lacquered coffin that stood alone in the center of the ring of columns.

To reach his mother's tomb and the precious thing he had left there, he had to pass the coffin.

His heart beating too fast, he began to cross the Untheileneise'meire.

As he approached it, the coffin seemed to swell, until it stood taller than himself and completely blocking the diameter of the circle. He would have to climb over it, although he was weighed down by his robes and encumbered by yards and yards of billowing veil. He struggled up the side of the coffin, dragged backwards by his robes, half-strangled by the masses of veiling, and when he finally reached the top, he discovered that the lid had been removed.

*Mer Celehar must be here somewhere,* he thought,

and he wanted to call out to him, but his voice would not work.

The corpse lay as he had seen it, hands folded, head muffled in white lace. He would have to climb over it, but he could do that. "I mean no disrespect," he whispered to it, and stretched one hand across to get a grip on the opposite side of the coffin.

The corpse's hands fastened around his wrist with an iron-cruel grip. "Disrespect?" it said, its voice muffled and wet. He could see, behind the veil, the dark, ragged hole of its mouth. "Hast thou wept at all? Dost thou mourn thy family, Maia?" It dragged itself upright with its leverage on his arm. "Dost weep for *me*?"

The muffled head was coming closer; he leaned back, back, was falling, flailing, and then he was running, stumbling, through the dark and narrow corridors of Edonomee, sobs caught in his throat, and the corpse dragging itself along behind him, calling in its terrible voice, "Weep for me! Weep for thy father!"

The veil caught around his feet; he fell and the harder he struggled to get up again, the more entangling and heavy his robes became. He was thrashing helplessly, hands scrabbling for purchase on the floorboards, mouth filled with veiling. His father's dead hand closed around his ankle.

Maia screamed and woke.

"Serenity?" Cala's voice, Cala's angular shape outlined against the window.

"'Tis an ironic title, in sooth," Maia said feebly, realizing that the entangling garments of the nightmare were merely his bedsheets. His heart was hammering, and he was clammy with sweat.

"Serenity, are you well?"

The door was flung open; Maia put his arm up in a futile, instinctive attempt to shield himself from view.

"I thought I heard . . ." Beshelar, sounding anxious.

"He's all right, I think," Cala said. "I think it was just a dream. Serenity, are you well?"

"We are fine," Maia said. "We beg pardon for alarming you."

"Serenity," Beshelar said, and shut the door, not quite slamming it.

"What's the clock?" Maia said, squinting past Cala at the window.

"Half past six, Serenity. You've not been asleep but three-quarters of an hour."

"No wonder I feel as if I've been kicked by a horse. I'm sorry, Cala. I really didn't mean to frighten you."

"It harms us not," Cala said. "You should sleep, Serenity."

Maia felt the rebuff like a drench of icy water. He sat up, reaching out a hand impulsively. "Cala, have I offended you?"

Cala was standing by the window, his hands folded in the sleeves of his robe. There was a silence, all the uglier for its unexpectedness. Then Cala said, the words blurted, stark and hard, "Serenity, we cannot be your friend."

"Friend? Cala, I—if we have been overfamiliar, we apologize."

"It isn't that." Cala did not sound happy, and his ears were flat, but he had carefully turned to look out the window so that Maia could not see his face. "It has been noticed, Serenity, that you treat your nohecharei more as equals than as servants."

"But you are not my servants."

"We are not your equals, Serenity. We have obligations to you which we must fulfill, and in the fulfillment of those obligations must lie the extent of our relationship."

Now Maia felt as if he were drowning. "Cala," he tried to say, but his voice stuck in his throat.

"It *must*, Serenity. The Adremaza spoke to us before the funeral. There have been murmurs already that you act not as the late emperor did and that he would not approve. It looks not well to the court that you chose Beshelar and us to be your guides—"

"Who else was I supposed to choose?" Too late, he heard the rawness in his own voice. He shut his eyes, lowered his face into his hands. His eyes were burning; he told himself it was just tiredness.

"Serenity," Cala said, his voice gentle, "we did not see the evil, either. We—*I*—I was pleased and proud, and so I always shall be. But the Adremaza is right. We are here to guard you. We are your nohecharis. We cannot be aught else."

"We understand," Maia said, forcing the words past the ache in his throat. He threw himself down with his back to Cala. "You are right. We should sleep."

"Serenity," Cala murmured.

Maia lay with his eyes tight shut, forcing his breathing to stay slow and even despite what felt like rocks in his throat and chest, and although eventually he slept, his sleep was not restful.

When he woke again, it was half past nine, the sun was streaming in the window, and Esha was leaning over him, saying, "Serenity? Serenity, your secretary is without and says he must speak to you urgently."

Maia struggled up out of bed, sleep, and sullen hurt. "Did he say what matter?"

"No, Serenity." Esha helped him into a quilted dressing gown with shagged velvet cuffs and collar. "Only that it was important and that it would not wait."

"Thank you," Maia said, lifting his night-braided hair free of the collar and letting it flop down his back. And he went out to see what was agitating his secretary.

Csevet, because he was Csevet, made a proper formal bow, but he was clearly distressed, his ears twitching despite his best efforts to maintain his poise. Maia stifled a yawn and said, "What's toward?"

"Serenity, *what* did you say to the Princess Sheveän?"

"That we would speak to her today regarding her concerns about the body of her husband. Why?"

"She waits in the receiving room, breathing fire. She says if you will not see her, she will seek redress from the Lord Chancellor."

Cursing was for commoners, both Chenelo and Setheris had said, the recourse of those with neither breeding nor education. Maia clenched his teeth against a number of words he'd learned from Haru, and said, "She wishes to stampede us."

"Serenity?"

Briefly, Maia told Csevet of his interview with the Princess of the Untheileneise Court the night before. "We see," he finished, "that we were unwise not to specify a time, but we did not think . . ."

"That the princess would stoop to such low tactics?" Csevet said, an eyebrow quirked.

"We were perhaps naïve," Maia said, and Csevet murmured, "Serenity!" in mock horror.

*He cannot be thy friend, either,* Maia thought, and pulled his dressing gown closer against a chill that was not in the air. He said, "We do not think any good will come of the princess accosting the Lord Chancellor."

"No," Csevet said. "We are inclined to agree."

"Can you . . . detain her? We cannot grant an audience to the Princess of the Untheileneise Court in our dressing gown."

"Serenity," Csevet said, bowing deeply. "We will do our best."

He departed, and Maia returned to his bedchamber to tell Esha he needed to dress in a hurry.

The edocharei were, he thought, a little miffed at his impatience, though he made the deduction only from the tight-lipped, low-eared silence in which they went about their work. Their efficiency and care abated not in the slightest; although he was dressed very simply (for an emperor) when he descended the stairs of the Alcethmeret to the receiving room, he was immaculate, every hair and crease in place.

The Princess of the Untheileneise Court stood in the center of the vast room, still dressed in full mourning. She was alone; she had not bothered with Osmin Bazhevin's negligible support. She put her veil back at his approach and curtsied, though not deeply. "Serenity."

"Sheveän. We trust you slept well."

"We have not slept," she said, as if only a heartless monster would imagine she could have.

Maia allowed a pause, an acknowledgment of the rudeness of her response, then said, "Please. Sit down."

She sat, her back stiff as a poker, her eyes fixed on him with unwavering suspicion. Maia sat as well and, seeing no way around it, said simply, "The *Wisdom of Choharo* was sabotaged."

He thought at first she had not understood him; then she said, "Yes?" and he realized that she did not in any way consider that relevant to her complaint.

"We must find out who murdered our father and brothers," he said. "For that, we need a Witness for the Dead."

"Yes," she said with the impatience of a woman speaking to an idiot. "And Lord Chavar himself assured us that the Witnesses had viewed the bodies with due reverence and that the funeral would be in no way impeded. And *then* we learn that Edrehasivar has interfered, delaying the ceremony and inconveniencing everyone—not to mention showing disrespect to his father—by bringing in Csoru's *cousin*!" Her fury overcame her, and Maia wondered, in that cold, snide corner of his mind that sounded like Setheris, whether she was angry because of the disruption to the funeral or because of the perceived favor to the widow empress's kinsman.

His heart was hammering in his throat; he felt as small and sick as he had ever felt before Setheris's wrath. But he remembered Csevet saying, *It is not Canon Orseva's place to dictate to you,* his own determination not to let Setheris rule him. It was the same thing, the same necessity.

"Princess, we can only assure you, again, that there was no desecration. You may speak to the Witness, if you wish." He heard the shake in his voice and could only hope she didn't.

"Yes," she said, flat and cold, and Maia had no choice but to summon a page boy and ask him to request Thara Celehar to attend upon the emperor.

The stony silence between them was unbroken while they waited. To Maia's great relief, Celehar was prompt; he realized he did not know where the Witness had his rooms. Celehar was dressed in shabby mourning, as he had been the day before. He and Shevän were strangely well matched, with their white masklike faces and eyes like cinders. *Whom has he lost?* Maia wondered even as he was gesturing Celehar back to his feet and trying to think of a way to explain the situation that would not come out sounding like: *The Princess of the Untheileneise Court has all but accused us of grave-robbing.*

He said, "Mer Celehar, the princess desires assurance that her husband's body was treated respectfully in your . . ."

Celehar might be acting as Witness against his inclination, but he was not cruel. He bowed to Shevän and said, "Princess, we offer our most sincere condolences."

"We thank you," she said coldly.

"We are both a prelate of Ulis and a Witness for the Dead," Celehar said. "Though we have renounced our prelacy, we are still sanctified. We alone placed our hands on your husband's body, and we assure you we did so reverently and with prayers. Please, speak to the Archprelate if you are in the least doubtful."

"*You* are a Witness for the Dead."

"We are." He did not react to the scorn in her voice; Maia wasn't even sure he heard it.

"Then why were you not asked to be part of the Lord Chancellor's investigation?"

"We understand that the Lord Chancellor prefers judicial Witnesses," Celehar said.

"We see," said Shevëan. "We suppose we should have expected as much from Edrehasivar." Her glance at Maia was pure poison, and he understood perfectly that she had just called him a superstitious lout.

He did not care; he merely wished this confrontation to be over. He rose and said, "Shevëan, if you have no more questions for Mer Celehar, we are busy this morning."

She stood, obedient to etiquette if not necessarily to the emperor. "Yes, so we had heard. Serenity." She swept him a curtsy without an ounce of genuine respect in it, and left.

"Serenity," Celehar said, "did we say the wrong thing?" He even sounded worried.

"No. No, Mer Celehar, we fear we had taken care of that long before you arrived. It is no concern of yours, and if the princess should . . . should harry you in your searching, you must tell her to come speak to us. She is our problem."

"Serenity," Celehar said. He hesitated, then said, "We wish, as we said, to visit the Ulimeire of Cetho. We would be grateful if you could write a letter of introduction for us."

"To the prelate? But you . . ." Maia faltered before the glare Celehar gave him, like the snarl of a wounded animal. "We will be pleased to write you such a letter, Mer Celehar."

"Thank you, Serenity," Celehar said, bowing.

"Will you wait? We will write it now if that suits."

"You do us undeserved honor," Celehar said, too blandly. Maia was glad to leave him in the receiving room while he ducked into the Tortoise Room to write the letter.

Given Celehar's apparent objections to identifying himself as a fellow prelate, Maia kept the terms of the letter as general as he could, merely asking the prelate of the Ulimeire to give all reasonable aid and assistance to the bearer, one Thara Celehar, who was acting as an agent of the emperor. It was not elegantly worded, but it was functional, and he was naggingly aware that somewhere in the Alcethmeret, Csevet was lurking with a list of things the emperor had to attend to, and that that list would not be getting shorter for the delay.

He returned to the receiving room, gave Celehar the sealed letter. Celehar bowed his thanks and departed, leaving Maia alone with Cala and Beshelar. He hovered for a moment on the brink of saying something to them, as he would have the day before, but remembered Cala saying flatly, *We cannot be your friend.* He walked past them, not meeting their eyes, and ascended again into the private section of the Alcethmeret, his nohecharei following dutifully behind.

# 13

## *Bargaining*

In the event, the duty with which Csevet waylaid him was the first meeting of the Corazhas of the reign of Edrehasivar VII. The Corazhas met in a long, southern-facing room called the Verven'theileian, the Hall of Consultation; Maia went and sat and watched the snow through the arched windows, while Csevet, positioned at his elbow, took frenetic and copious notes. He felt helplessly, hopelessly out of his depth; the Corazhas might as well have been speaking a foreign tongue most of the time, and their brisk, efficient tones made it clear that interruptions from an ignorant emperor would not be welcome.

*Thou must learn to rule,* he said to himself. *Thou must learn these things.* But he could not pry his teeth apart, too aware of what the Corazhas would think of him, too aware of Cala and Beshelar standing like statues.

*I will ask Csevet later,* he promised himself, and continued to feign attention to the workings of his government. The Corazhas asked him no questions, seemed to have no interest in his opinions or ideas. *They know thou hast none,* he thought scathingly. Certainly, he had no opinions about the principal matter under debate this morning. He had never heard anyone suggest bridging the Istandaärtha before; he had a hard time believing it was possible.

In fact, that was one of the points of contention: the Witness for the Judiciate flatly refused to believe that the Istandaärtha could be bridged at all, and certainly not above Cairado. The Witness for the Parliament was at a disadvantage, for while he staunchly asserted that the proposal was feasible, it was clear that he himself did not understand the mechanics of how the widest and fastest river in the Ethuveraz was to be bridged.

"And what about river trade?" demanded the Witness for the Treasury. "What are the barges from Ezho supposed to do? Leap this marvelous bridge like frogs?"

"It is to be a sort of drawbridge," said the Witness for the Parliament, and went red at the disbelieving snort from the Witness for the Judiciate.

"A drawbridge two miles long?" said the Witness for the Treasuries. "Deshehar, we fear you have been gulled."

"We assure you," the Witness for the Parliament said stiffly, "there is no doubt of the honesty and earnest good faith of those who brought this proposal to the Parliament. We do not do their ideas justice, and indeed all they asked was the opportunity to appear before the Corazhas."

"But why should they bring it before the Corazhas?" asked one of the Witnesses whom Maia had not been able to keep straight. "Should it not properly go to the Universities?"

"We have wasted enough time on this nonsense already," said the Witness for the Judiciate, forestalling what looked like an imminent explosion from the Witness for the Universities. Another witness said, "Hear hear." Maia bit his tongue and tried not to look as if he would have liked to ask other questions. *Thou wouldst only make a greater fool of thyself,* he thought, and waited in dismal silence for the meeting of the Corazhas finally, *finally* to come to an end.

And even when he escaped the Corazhas, it was merely to be ambushed by another obligation. Setheris was waiting for him in the hall.

"Cousin Setheris," Maia said, stopping short.

"Serenity," Setheris said, bowing. It was only with a great effort that Maia kept himself from backing away. His rational knowledge that he had nothing to fear from Setheris now, and never would again, was swamped by ten years' accumulation of blows and jeers, the old burning pain in his left forearm, the instinctive duck of the chin to avoid looking Setheris in the eyes.

"Serenity," Setheris said, straightening, "we have been seeking an audience with you for some days."

Maia caught himself, lifted his chin—and the flattened ears might be taken for irritation rather than fear. "We have been busy, cousin."

"We understand that, Serenity, but the matter is pressing, and—"

At that moment, Csevet emerged into the hall. He moved at once to interpose himself between Maia and Setheris. Maia was able, gratefully, to move back and to take a proper breath. Csevet and Setheris bristled at each other like fighting dogs, and although Maia wanted nothing more than to run—he was the emperor, after all, and who would stop him?—he said, "Csevet, please arrange an audience for our cousin at the earliest convenient time. We are returning to the Alcethmeret."

"Yes, Serenity," Csevet said.

"Thank you, Serenity," Setheris said. Maia read the unspoken rider in his eyes, *It is good to see thou hast not forgotten* everything *about Edonomee.* Then Setheris turned to Csevet, his polished court mask back in place. Maia had to make a conscious and deliberate action of turning his back on Setheris. It was even harder to walk rather than run away from him. *He cannot hurt me now,* Maia said to himself, but the words had no conviction and scarcely any meaning. His forearm burned, and he forbade himself to rub at it.

He was walking faster than normal, but he could not force himself to slow down. And he was not sorry to get quickly out of the public halls of the Untheileneise Court.

As they approached the doors of the Alcethmeret, Cala said, breaking a long silence, "Serenity, are you well?"

"We are, thank you," Maia said politely, distantly.

Cala did not try again.

There was a letter waiting for Maia, but this time it was a private one, an invitation from Nurevis Chavar to an entertainment he had arranged for that evening: a soprano from the great Opera House of Zhaö, singing arias from a number of famous operas. Maia had never been to an opera, although he had read about them in the newspapers that from time to time infiltrated Edonomee, and he was too pleased by Nurevis's overture to dream of rejecting it. As soon as Csevet returned—as bland-faced as ever, although Maia thought he caught an eartip twitching with irritation—Maia directed him to send an acceptance.

There was also a letter from Thara Celehar:

*To his Imperial Serenity, Edrehasivar VII, greetings.*

*In obedience to Your Serenity's wishes, we went this morning to the Ulimeire of Cetho. As we do not know when Your Serenity will next be able or inclined to grant us an audience, we thought it best to send Your Serenity this report.*

*We presented your letter to the prelate of the Ulimeire, who was most gratified and eager to be of assistance. He told us everything he knew about the victims—not a great deal, as of course the nature of his prelacy precludes a faithful congregation of the living—and then showed us their graves. Their families, he told us, are pooling their money for a gravestone.*

Maia had to set the letter down. He wondered dismally, turning so that Csevet would not notice and be alarmed by the tears in his eyes, how many more moments like this he would have to go through, how many more times the reality of the tragedy would bludgeon him to the floor. Each time he thought, *Surely* this *is enough to bring it home,* but then he would turn some other unexpected corner, and there it would be again, cruel and stark and pitiless. This time, he thought of the crew and captain of the *Radiance of Cairado,* their anxiety and kindness, and wondered who would have mourned them if it had been their airship that had been sabotaged.

"Csevet."

"Serenity?"

"We wish gifts to be made to the families of those who died with the *Wisdom of Choharo.*"

"Serenity?"

He turned. "Did we not speak clearly enough?"

"But, what sort of gift, Serenity?"

"We do not know. We know not what would be appreciated. Can we give them money?"

"Your Serenity may do anything that pleases you."

"If we give them money," Maia said, slowly and distinctly, "will it cause offense? We are tired of causing offense with everything we do."

"Serenity, we do not understand—"

"Yes or no."

"Serenity," Csevet said. He paused, toying unhappily

with his pen. "It will be considered more gracious if the gift has some . . . some *meaning*."

"Very well." He picked up the letter again, to gesture with it at Csevet. "Mer Celehar tells us that the families wish to purchase a gravestone. Would that be a gift with suitable meaning?"

"Yes, Serenity."

"See to it, please."

"Yes, Serenity."

Maia returned to the letter.

*We have meditated among the graves and, having obtained from the prelate the names of those who survive the crew of the airship, shall interview them as we are able to arrange meetings. These persons, having only the connection of death with the late emperor—what the teachings of our order call* stathan—*are those whose lives and deaths may show most clearly the break in the pattern which we seek. Such is not always the case, but it is true often enough to be worth pursuing.*

*We would note also that the prelate of the Ulimeire has been warned to hold himself available for the Witnesses of the Lord Chancellor's investigation, so Your Serenity need not fear that their investigation will be anything but rigorous. But as Your Serenity seems to wish it, we will continue our own search for the truth.*

> *Hoping that Your Serenity approves of our actions and intentions,*
> *Thara Celehar*

*I don't know enough to disapprove*, Maia thought. He was not so naïve that he could not see what Celehar's strategy of letter-writing was designed to do, but neither was he so naïve that he thought his management of the affair would be in any way an improvement.

Celehar was trained for this, and although Maia worried about his disaffection, he did not believe that Celehar would shirk a duty once he had accepted it.

Csevet gave a polite and slightly nervous cough. Maia set Celehar's letter down and turned toward him, eyebrows raised.

"Serenity. It is the matter of the Archduchess Vedero's marriage."

It took a moment for Maia to remember what Csevet meant. "Yes. Has Dach'osmer Tethimar spoken to you yet? We told him he should."

"No, Serenity. That is, yes, Serenity, there is a letter from Dach'osmer Tethimar asking for an audience, but that is not what we meant. There is . . . a new complication."

"Of course there is," Maia said, biting back a laugh. "Tell us the worst at once."

"Serenity." Csevet sounded happier now. "You are aware, of course, that the Archduke Ciris was engaged to be married."

"It had reached our attention," Maia said, remembering a slanderous comment or two that Setheris had allowed himself at the breakfast table, remembering Stano Bazhevin, the scared nonentity scurrying in Shevelän's shadow.

"Count Bazhevel, the father of the intended bride, has written, and the Lord Chancellor's office has seen fit to pass the matter on to you."

"Should they not?"

"Serenity." Csevet made an ambivalent, dissatisfied gesture with his pen. "Essentially, yes, but we would have expected them to do a certain amount of the necessary work first."

"'Necessary work'?" He felt stupid for asking when Csevet clearly expected him to understand, but he trusted Csevet, unlike the Corazhas, not to hold—or use—his stupidity against him.

"Serenity, what Bazhevel proposes is a marriage to replace the chance for union lost with the archduke."

"He *can't* expect our sister to marry his daughter."

Csevet smiled slightly in acknowledgment of the joke. "No, Serenity. But he seems rather to expect that *you* will."

Maia stared at him. "But we can't marry her! She's Drazhadeise!"

Csevet made a dissatisfied noise. "This is why we are displeased with the Lord Chancellor's office. The Count Bazhevel argues that since the marriage was neither sworn nor consummated, it ought to be regarded as null and Osmin Bazhevin still Bazhevadeise."

"They signed the contract," Maia said—and was a little amused at the outrage plainly audible in his own voice.

"The Count Bazhevel is ingenious," said Csevet, "but we suspect that he does not intend his argument to be taken very seriously, for he immediately proposes an alternative. Though he has no marriageable sons himself, he says he and the honor of his house would be satisfied if the archduchess were to marry his brother's eldest son, Osmer Dalera Bazhevar."

"So his first suggestion is merely a feint," Maia said, but most of his attention was on something else. He quoted thoughtfully, "'The honor of his house.' Is he implying that the death of the archduke was intended by the Drazhada as an insult to the Bazhevada?"

"We think, Serenity, that he hopes the threat of such an implication will . . . encourage you to comply with his scheme, just as the suggestion of your marriage to Osmin Bazhevin will make you regard his second suggestion with relief."

"Either he is very stupid or he thinks we are."

"Serenity," Csevet murmured noncommittally.

Maia sighed. "We must speak with our sister, it seems. In sooth, we find it a little disturbing that she has not attempted to speak to us."

Beshelar said unexpectedly, "The archduchess is well known not to favor marriage. Perhaps she hoped the matter might be lost in the confusion."

"Perhaps," Csevet said dubiously.

Maia looked at the clock. Half past three. "We dine with the court, yes?"

"It is expected, Serenity."

"At eight, we believe Esha told us?"

"Yes, Serenity."

"Have we other matters to which we must attend before that?"

"None that cannot be deferred, Serenity. We would not grant Osmer Nelar the satisfaction of an audience this afternoon."

"We thank you. Will you, then, send a page boy to see if the Archduchess Vedero can attend on us?"

"Yes, Serenity," Csevet said, and pulled the bell-rope.

The archduchess appeared promptly in response to the summons. She still wore full mourning, and unlike most court ladies, she made no effort at ornamentation. Black on black quilting, black ribbons in her hair, and no jewelry at all, save the unadorned rings in her ears. Maia, whose hands ached from the weight of his rings, envied her that.

She curtsied with a murmured "Serenity," sat down at his invitation, and once seated seemed almost to transmute to marble. Face impassive, posture perfect, she evinced no curiosity about why he had wished to see her, and offered not so much as a conversational gambit of her own. Maia realized very quickly that she would win any game of waiting, and said, "We must speak to you about your marriage."

Vedero considered this statement and said, "We do not wish to be married." Her voice was devoid of passion, or even interest.

"We understand that our late father was negotiating your marriage."

"Yes."

He began to wonder if she was goading him deliberately, but if she was or if she wasn't, nothing would be gained by losing his temper. He said patiently, "With whom?"

At least she did not pretend not to understand him. "With the Duke Tethimel, on behalf of his son Eshevis." There was nothing in her tone to indicate whether she liked, loathed, or indeed had ever even met Eshevis Tethimar. Such perfect disengagement itself suggested, unhappily, what Vedero's true opinion might be.

"How far had negotiations proceeded?"

"We do not know, Serenity."

If she was lying—and he thought she might be—she did it well. Maia thought of Eshevis Tethimar, encroaching every inch he thought he could get away with, trying to bully the negotiations through—thought of the Count Bazhevel trying to swap one marriage for another as if Vedero and his own daughter were no more than dairy cows. He said abruptly, "Were you not to marry, what would you do?"

"Serenity?"

He was perversely pleased to see that it was possible to startle her. "If you did not marry. What would you do instead?"

"We thank you, Serenity, but we do not expect you to be interested in our foolish, daydreaming ambitions."

It was the most words he'd gotten out of her at one

time. Maia smiled gently and, taking a leaf from her book, simply waited in silence.

She gave him a bitter look when she realized he would neither speak until she did nor dismiss her from his presence, then said in a small, defiant voice, a unexpected hint of what she would have been like as a child, "We would study the stars."

"The stars?"

"Yes, Serenity," she said, and it suddenly struck him as ludicrous and demeaning that a woman of twenty-eight should be subject to the judgment of a half brother ten years younger than herself.

He said, "Then you should."

From the stricken way they all stared at him—Vedero, Csevet, Cala, Beshelar—he realized that he had said the wrong thing again. There was a painful silence; Maia felt his face heating. It was Vedero who squared her shoulders and said, "Serenity, you need our marriage."

"But if it is not what you wish . . ."

"Serenity, your bargaining position is weak enough as it is. You cannot afford to wait until Ino and Mireän are of age."

"But with whom are we bargaining?"

"The world, Serenity," Vedero said sadly.

By her voice, her bearing, he was reminded that she had been at court since her earliest childhood. He wished that he could ask her advice, but despite her sudden access of honesty, he was afraid she still hated him, and knowing that his ignorance was weakness, he was loath to make it any more explicit to her than it already was.

He stood up, signaling the end of the audience. "We thank you, Vedero. We will think on what you have said."

"Serenity," she said, rising and curtsying. "You must not regard us in making your decision. Our late father did not."

She had given advice without being asked. The trouble was—Maia thought as he watched her leave, her dignity like armor around her—he was not sure it was advice he wanted to follow.

Csevet cleared his throat; Maia turned and found him looking both apprehensive and obstinate. "You wish to say something we will not like," Maia said.

"We fear it, Serenity. For the archduchess is correct. You must bargain with the world, and you cannot afford to wait until your nieces are of marriageable age."

"You are talking about *our* marriage again."

"Yes, Serenity. But perhaps . . . Your Serenity asked us about signets, and we have had a pneumatic from Dachensol Habrobar to say that he holds himself at Your Serenity's disposal. It will take us perhaps a quarter of an hour to reach his workshop from here, and we may discuss matters as we go."

"The emperor attends upon Dachensol Habrobar?" Maia said, not offended—he had not yet grown so vast in his own conceit—but amused.

"Serenity. We understand that, in order to decide which design will best suit any individual, Dachensol Habrobar must be able to consult his collection of signets, of which he has several thousand."

"Quite," Maia said—and realized that Csevet had succeeded in making him eager to visit Dachensol Habrobar and thus without ground to resist discussion of his hypothetical wife. *There is more than one kind of bargaining,* Maia thought, and set himself to uphold his end of the bargain by listening carefully to what Csevet had to say.

He was not surprised to discover that Csevet had a list. "We thought, Serenity, it might be best to tell you something about the women who are currently at court, so that you may decide as you meet and speak to them which of them you like. For while this is certainly an *important* matter and one which you should not neglect, it is not something we think you should *rush*."

"No," Maia said. "We do not wish to emulate our father in his approach to marriage."

Csevet's ears twitched and flattened a little. "Serenity, we feel that we must point out that, to a great degree, the late emperor's numerous marriages were not his fault."

"Perhaps," Maia said. He did not want to argue with Csevet. "Tell us of our potential empresses."

Csevet consulted his list. "We understand, first of all, that Eshevis Tethimar has brought his oldest unmarried sister, Paru Tethimin, to the Untheileneise Court, although we have not seen her. She is fourteen, and Dach'osmer Tethimar is probably cursing his luck that he squandered his sister Uleviän on the Prince of Thu-Athamar, for she is of an age with you."

"You do not like Dach'osmer Tethimar," Maia said, a little surprised that Csevet would let any kind of bias show, positive or negative.

"We apologize, Serenity," Csevet said, the tips of his ears turning pink. "We allowed our tongue to run away with us."

"No," Maia said, "we are not offended. And we value your opinion. We have not found Dach'osmer Tethimar congenial ourself."

"There was an incident," Csevet said, the blush spreading from his ears to his face, "when we were first a courier. We would prefer not to discuss it, but . . ." He cleared his throat and twitched his ears straight. "It is perhaps the case that we bear a grudge against Dach'osmer Tethimar."

"We will remember," Maia said. "And we think fourteen is very young to be married."

"Yes, Serenity," Csevet said. "Also at court is Osmin

Loran Duchenin. She is twenty, the second daughter of the Count Duchenel. She is also the niece, in his mother's line, of Lord Chavar."

"We thank you," Maia said, "for we would not have known that."

"How could you, Serenity?" Csevet said mildly, as if there were nothing unusual or tedious in having to educate an emperor in matters he should have known unthinking, as he knew how to breathe. "Osmin Duchenin is a very accomplished and beautiful young lady; she is something of a rival to the widow empress. On the other hand, Dach'osmin Csethiro Ceredin, who is the greatniece of Arbelan Drazharan, is equally accomplished, but of a more scholarly bent." He paused, eyebrows raised, as if expecting Maia to have an opinion about the desirability—or lack thereof—of a *scholarly bent*. Maia had none. Perceiving this, Csevet continued, "Dach'osmin Ceredin and Osmin Duchenin are the most established courtiers of the women who are close to Your Serenity in age—which means that both they and their houses are ambitious and therefore very likely to pursue a marriage."

"Yes, of course," Maia said, feeling a combination of unhappiness and unreality with which he had become familiar since arriving at the Untheileneise Court. "We imagine they are not the only ones."

"There are several families of great ambition," Csevet said, "but of course they have not been grooming their daughters as potential empresses, and there is likely to be a certain amount of scrambling—as with Dach'osmin Tethimin, who probably will not be allowed to appear publicly until she has been properly coached. However, Your Serenity is correct, and we have no doubt that the Ubezhada, the Erimada, the Shulihada—" He scanned down his list. "—also, the Virenada and the Olchevada will be putting their daughters forward. And perhaps Your Serenity will prefer one of the less polished young women."

He raised his eyebrows at Maia, who said helplessly, "We do not know." He had never thought of marriage, never in his wildest fantasies imagined that young women might be competing for *his* favor. When presented with it in reality, it was not a comfortable prospect.

"There is time, Serenity," Csevet said reassuringly, "and this is Dachensol Habrobar's workroom."

The workroom was less a workroom than a vault, a great echoing dark space with every wall showing row after row of small square drawers. In the middle, there was a table, lit by a modern gaslight chandelier, and at the table was Dachensol Habrobar.

He was a small man—less than five feet tall when he leaped up to greet the emperor—with silver gray skin and silver gray eyes. He was perfectly, gleamingly bald. He spoke with an accent Maia did not know, which seemed to chip the edges off all the words in its rush and tumble, for Dachensol Habrobar used five words in the time it took Maia to say one. He had brought out from the depths of the vault a box like an oversized jewelry box, containing padded wells, each of which held what he called the "type" of a signet. "So that if you are careless, yes? If you are careless and you are walking in the Duchess Pashavel Gardens and perhaps you are tossing your signet idly from hand to hand, though it is not what we recommend, Serenity. And as you toss it—oops!—there it goes into the ornamental pond and before you can even think to wade in after it, there it is eaten by an ornamental carp, which the Pashavada import at great expense from somewhere in the west and how they keep them alive we often wonder. So you come to us in despair and embarrassment, and yet all is not lost, for we have kept the type." And he reached into one of the padded wells with small deft fingers. "You see, Serenity, it is not the signet, but the impression from which the signet is made. We keep all of them that we make. This is the type for the signet of Dach'osmin Lisethu Pevennin. She was the last of her family, poor lady, and she died before she'd used her signet more than five times."

Maia looked at the signet, a delicately rendered swan with a tiara, and tried to place the name Pevenn-. Pevennar, Pevennada, Pevennel . . . it was an odd name, archaic. . . .

"Dach'osmin Pevennin died almost five hundred years ago," Csevet said, "at the command of Edrethelema the Fifth."

"She was a very *unrestful* lady," Dachensol Habrobar said sadly.

And of course the reason Pevenn had sounded familiar was that the Pevennada had led the last great rebellion against the Drazhada.

"We beg your pardon," Maia said to Dachensol Habrobar. "But *you* made her signet?"

"Our people are very long-lived," Dachensol Habrobar said. "We are old, but we will most likely live to make signets for your grandchildren, Serenity."

*An I have any,* Maia thought. He hoped he controlled his flinch, but it was probably not coincidence that Habrobar immediately said, "We have brought out a selection of Drazhadeise signets, so that you may see the range of options before you." He laid them out neatly and quickly, identifying each by the name of the emperor, empress, archduke, archduchess, or lesser scion of the House Drazhada to whom it had belonged. Cats everywhere: couchant, rampant, curled in realistic sleep, pouncing on a mouse, holding a rose, holding a sword; a black cat and a white cat coiled around each other; a snarling cat's face with exquisitely rendered whiskers and teeth; a cat's paw with hooked claws. "The late emperor your father," Habrobar murmured, "chose this design." He put down on the table a type with a cat resting one paw upon a crown. The crown was recognizably the Ethuverazhid Mura, and Maia was impressed by Habrobar's craftsmanship at the same time he was repelled by the design. "Edrehasivar the Sixth," Habrobar said, setting down a type of a cat seated with its tail curled about its paws, looking solemnly outward. "We will be glad to show Your Serenity any other type you should wish to see in order to help you decide."

Maia stared blankly at the types laid out before him. There was something missing, but it took him a long time to see what it was. "Did you make a signet for—that is, did the Empress Chenelo our mother have a signet?"

"Of course, Serenity," said Habrobar. "We weren't sure . . ." Whether from fear of offending the emperor or simple tact, he did not finish the sentence. "Just a moment." He lifted out the top layer of padded squares and picked a type unhesitatingly out of the layer beneath. "The Barizheise do not use signets, but each avar has a device which he uses on his war banners. That of the current Great Avar is the sea serpent the Barizheise call the *Corat' Arhos*, the 'Cruelty of Water.' Thus, for the Empress Chenelo, we made this." He set it down: a delicate picture of a creature half cat and half twining serpent. It was grotesque, but it was also oddly, inexplicably hopeful, and Maia had to blink hard against the heat of tears.

"We regret," Habrobar said in that same mild, rapid voice, "that she was never able to use it. The emperor found it unsuitable and insisted that she use the Drazhada's cats instead. But we kept it, as we keep every type we make. We did not know if you would wish to see it." His gray-silver eyes met Maia's. "Serenity, if you should wish to use it, we think it would not be unfitting. It was never even made into a ring for her."

"Yes," Maia said, and everyone pretended his voice hadn't cracked. "Yes, we thank you."

"It should take us no more than a week," Habrobar said. "Now, if you will permit us . . ." There was a rapid flurry of measurements and questions, and by the time Maia left Dachensol Habrobar's vaulted workshop, he was almost able to forget he had embarrassed himself. But he did not forget, and told himself he *would* not forget, that it was possible for people to be kind without ulterior motive, that sometimes bargaining was not necessary.

*Sometimes,* said that cold Setheris-like voice in his head. *But not often.*

# 14

## *Min Nedaö Vechin*

Dining with the court was an experience hated as soon as embarked upon. Thanks to the combined efforts of Chenelo and Setheris, Maia's etiquette was perfect and unthinking—which he recognized as the boon it was—but what they had neglected, Chenelo because Maia was too young, Setheris because it would never have occurred to him to bother, was the art of conversation. Maia sat with his half sister Nemriän at his left hand and Lord Deshehar, the Witness for the Parliament, at his right, and had not a word to say to either of them.

Nemriän, who clearly would not have wished to talk to him in any event, focused her attention without apology on her other dinner partner, the elderly but sharp-witted Witness for the Judiciate; Deshehar, either naturally better mannered or more sensitive to the dangers of slighting an emperor, made a number of forays. He had the tact to stay away from politics, but since he fell back on literature, most of which Setheris had forbidden Maia to read and the rest of which had not appeared in Edonomee's barren library, his efforts were not successful and left Maia feeling ill mannered, ignorant, and incomparably loutish. It was a relief to escape the table, an even greater relief to find Nurevis waiting for him, smiling and immediately taking the entire burden of the conversation on himself.

Maia could not tell whether it was deliberate or not that Nurevis's seemingly artless chatter in fact provided him with a great deal of information. He learned about the Opera House of Zhaö—"the oldest in the Elflands, you know, and every composer worth anything premieres there"—and then Nurevis came to the topic of the soprano who was singing that evening and waxed rhapsodic, seeming to forget his companion entirely.

Her name was Nedaö Vechin. She was the youngest prima soprano in the history of the Zhaö Opera, and the power of her voice was not merely remarkable but (some said) divine. She was beautiful and intelligent, and although she was not of good family, Nurevis said her manners and speaking voice were beyond reproach. "You've never seen anything like her in your life, Serenity," he said, and Maia did not tell him just how little that meant.

The Lord Chancellor's apartments, though of course not comparable to the Alcethmeret for size or grandeur, were spacious, well appointed, and eloquent to Maia's eyes—trained by the shabby semi-poverty of Isvaroë and Edonomee—of wealth carefully used but not stinted. He wondered, not quite idly, where the wealth of the House Chavada came from, and made a mental note to ask Csevet. Was the Lord Chancellor's a salaried position? Another in the ever and infinitely expanding list of things he did not know.

The salon was already thronged with brightly dressed courtiers. The period of official court mourning had ended with the wake; those who continued to wear black, as Vedero did, did so because they felt some closer, more personal connection with the dead. Maia himself, torn between honesty and tact, wore the dark-jeweled rings appropriate to mourning but had otherwise reverted to imperial white. He was sure there were many whom he offended by refusing to acknowledge a grief that he did not in fact feel, but the dishonesty would be an insult to himself, to the dead whom he had not loved, and to his mother, for whom he had not been allowed to wear mourning after the funeral because Setheris considered it unseemly. But he still felt the judgment in the court's eyes.

Nurevis, fussing amiably, cleared a path through the crowd for Maia and his nohecharei to the place where he intended the emperor to sit. Maia found it embarrassingly prominent, with a gleaming expanse of floor like a moat between it and the decorous rows of chairs for the rest of the audience. Even here, he was forced to be the emperor. *Wouldst liefer sulk in thy tower?* he asked himself, and felt better for being able to mock his own discontent.

The arrival of the emperor was the signal for the evening's entertainment to start. The courtiers disposed themselves on the chairs, and the soprano, who had been surrounded by admiring men in a corner of the room, advanced to the place meant for her, flanked by two tall candelabra. Maia forgot himself and became still with wonder.

Nedaö Vechin was not merely beautiful. Small, slender, with eyes of an extraordinary jade-pale green, she was perfect, her skin like porcelain over the exquisite fineness of her bones. She was dressed with elegant simplicity in a tulip-hemmed dress of a deep rose color with a long, trailing train. Her moonlight hair, piled and braided, was held with tortoiseshell combs and rose-colored ribbons, and her only jewelry was a series of tiny gold-beaded hoops in her ears. She could not have made a more stunning impression if she had been covered in rubies from head to foot.

Maia guessed she was maybe three or four years older

than he was, and he marveled at her composure. Effortlessly, she collected the attention of her audience, gave them a brilliant smile, and without any further fanfare began to sing.

Her voice was rich and pure and to Maia astonishingly clean. The best singing he had ever heard before had been one of the Edonomee cook's daughters, and the power of Min Vechin's voice was showing him exactly what the difference was between Aäno's sweet voice singing old ballads and a real singer. Chills were running along his spine, and he was almost afraid to breathe, afraid that somehow he would destroy the beauty she was spinning out of thin air.

He knew none of the songs, knew nothing about the operas they were from. But it did not matter; he listened to Min Vechin and felt almost as if he were flying, carried by her voice. When she stopped, it was a moment before he could collect his wits sufficiently to realize there was something he was supposed to do. The expectant silence said as much, the courtiers' ears cocking toward him, Min Vechin's bright, hopeful face and the beginnings of something that might be fear in the back of her eyes.

"Applaud, Serenity," Telimezh said in an urgent mutter, and in relief and embarrassment, Maia applauded fervently. The courtiers added their applause at once, and Min Vechin curtsied deeply to her emperor before curtsying to the rest of her audience.

He had to rise, to release the courtiers from the bonds of etiquette; but when they began to converse and mingle again, Maia stayed where he was, thinking that now all those stories about emperors who went out among the common people in disguise made a great deal more sense than they ever had in the shabby confines of his bedroom at Edonomee. He looked around at the crowd enthusiastically discussing and dissecting Min Vechin's performance and wished he could simply have walked over and joined one of those conversations, wished with all his heart that his father had seen fit to have him raised at court—or even in one of the empire's lesser cities, where at least he could have learned how to conduct himself in society and not been left standing here paralyzed by his knowledge of his own ignorance and ineptitude.

*I should leave,* he thought, and was on the verge of turning to indicate as much to his nohecharei when he saw Nurevis plowing determinedly through the crowd toward him, Min Vechin stepping as delicately as a fawn in his wake.

She stopped politely just out of earshot, and Nurevis came up to Maia alone.

"Serenity," he murmured, "Min Vechin has expressed a great desire to be presented to you. Will you permit us . . . ?"

Maia looked incredulously from Nurevis to Min Vechin and back again. "To . . . to *us?*"

"You *are* the emperor," Nurevis pointed out with a smile.

"Yes. Yes, of course . . . that is, we would be delighted to make the acquaintance of Min Vechin." It felt as if his face were about to catch on fire.

"Splendid!" Nurevis said, politely ignoring his emperor's flusterment. He turned and beckoned to Min Vechin, who advanced and made her deepest curtsy yet. "Serenity," she said, and her voice was as beautiful and clear speaking as it was singing.

Maia felt anything but serene. She was even more dazzling up close, and the scent she wore was delicate and subtly spicy and completely unlike anything Maia had ever encountered before. His heart was hammering.

"We are very pleased to meet you, Min Vechin." And,

scrambling for something to say, he added, "Your voice is very beautiful."

"Thank you, Serenity," she said as Maia cursed himself for the moon-witted hobgoblin Setheris had always called him. To his horror, he heard himself continuing, "We know very little about opera, but we enjoyed your singing very much."

"Your Serenity is most kind," she said. Her politeness was perfect, but he could feel her retreating behind it, disappointed by the dullness of his response.

"No, I—" He caught himself and said carefully, "We meant that we cannot offer you educated praise, only sincere admiration."

His slip had at least refocused her attention. Her green eyes, their color made even more dramatic by the kohl darkening her lids, considered him carefully. Some rawly oversensitive part of him noticed that the courtiers were observing the encounter, even while continuing their own conversations.

Then Nedaö Vechin smiled, and the rest of the world dropped away. "We shall treasure Your Serenity's good opinion all the more, knowing that it is entirely honest."

She had a slight, unfamiliar accent, the faintest hint of a lisp brushing her sibilants. But the deeper clarity of her voice smoothed her speech into art as radiant as blown glass. Maia realized he had become entranced again and said hastily, "How long have you been with the Zhaö Opera?"

It was a crushingly banal question, but Min Vechin forgave him that, too. "Since we came of age," she said. "We have wanted to sing since we were very small, but the company will not take underage apprentices. But we sang in their Children's Choir before that."

"What does an opera company have to do with a children's choir?"

She laughed, and he knew he had said something else that betrayed his ignorance. But her smile was still warm. "We see that you have indeed been kept apart from the world of opera, Serenity. Many great operas use a chorus of children. We sang as a tree frog in *The Dream of the Empress Corivero* when we were eleven. And, of course, there are the Michen-operas."

"Beg pardon?"

"The little operas?" She seemed baffled, but he truly had no idea what she was talking about. "Did Your Serenity never go to a Michen-opera when you were a little boy?"

"No," he said, and struggled futilely with the idea of explaining how utterly Setheris would have condemned the notion, had it ever arisen. He settled for, "We have always lived far from any but the smallest villages."

She looked appalled for a flicker of a second, then recovered her manners. "We hope that your first experience will incline you to seek out more opportunities hereafter."

"Yes," Maia said, and then Nurevis was at his elbow again, murmuring about someone else who wished to be presented to the emperor.

Min Vechin curtsied deeply, with another brilliant smile, and moved away into the crowd.

Maia, still breathless, watched her go.

It took a considerable, and very deliberate, effort to refocus his attention and be courteous to the person Nurevis was introducing. And the next person. And the next. Everyone wished to be presented to the emperor, and all Maia could do was smile and say neutral, meaningless phrases like, "Thank you," and "We are very pleased," and try desperately to remember names and faces. He abandoned as hopeless the deciphering of the intricate connections between House and House until, much later, Nurevis murmured, "And this, Serenity, is Osmin Loran Duchenin."

Tired and overwhelmed though he was, Maia recognized that name, remembered Csevet saying she was Chavar's niece: accomplished, ambitious, a rival of Csoru's. A woman who would want to be empress. He blinked, forcing himself to attend to the woman in green silk who was sweeping a curtsy before him.

As she rose, he saw that she was taller than Csoru, though just as fine-boned. Her eyes were a darker green than Min Vechin's, and she set them off with peridots. She smiled at him and said, "We hope Your Serenity enjoyed the concert."

"Very much," Maia said.

There was a pause in which he knew he should be saying something, but he had no idea what. Osmin Duchenin's perfect eyebrows drew together in a very slight frown. Then the smile reappeared, and she said, "As a newcomer, Your Serenity must find the Untheileneise Court very confusing."

"Yes," Maia said. "It is overwhelming."

Osmin Duchenin trilled with laughter, as if he had said something witty, and launched into a story about someone she knew (Maia did not catch the exact relationship) who had been three and a half hours late to a dinner engagement because he tried to take a shortcut through an unfamiliar part of the palace and became lost. "In the end, he had to be led out by a *boot boy*!" she finished, trilling with laughter again, and mercifully Nurevis was there before Maia had to find a reply—or even worse, a responding anecdote—this time to suggest that perhaps the emperor would like a glass of metheglin and to meet some of Nurevis's friends. Maia caught not one of their names, his memory already water-logged and sinking beneath the weight of the evening's cargo. They were all very much of a type, tall and narrow-faced, eyes pale blue and pale green and pale gray, their features sharp but oddly empty—young men who had never been lonely or afraid or devastated by grief. They ran out the same limp platitudes about Min Vechin's singing that Maia had been listening to all evening, and he responded as best he could.

There was an awkward pause while everyone sought for something to say. One of the young men stepped bravely into the breach and said, "Does Your Serenity hunt? Your late father the emperor was a notable rider."

"How could he, cloth-head?" another young man said amiably, saving Maia from having to grapple with any part of the question, either explicit or implied. "Edonomee is in the western marshes. They hunt grouse out there—or is it goose? Birds, anyway."

"D'you remember," a third young man broke in, "the time Corvis Pashavar flushed that covey of pheasants?"

"He was riding that dish-faced bay mare, wasn't he?" said the first young man. "The one that tried to take a piece out of Solichel at the first meet of the Cairen Hunt three years ago?"

"We had forgotten about that," the third man said, grinning. "Well, Pashavar *warned* him to watch what he was about."

"Even for a mare, that bay of Pashavar's has a filthy temper," said another young man, and within a few minutes, Nurevis's friends had all but forgotten about the emperor, arguing about Corvis Pashavar's bay mare and swapping stories about their own horses and their friends' horses and horses their fathers had told them about. Maia stood and listened, and although he had always disliked metheglin, he drank that entire glass and considered it a very small price to pay.

# 15

## The Problem of Setheris

The morning was bleak; gray clouds heavy with snow loured over the Untheileneise Court. The silence in the emperor's bedroom was as heavy as the clouds outside. The night before, the emperor had returned to the Alcethmeret very late and more than a little drunk. His edocharei, disapproving, did their work in stern silence. Maia, not hungover but with a mood as cold and dull as the sky, stared out the window and tried not to dwell on the memory of Nedaö Vechin's voice.

Matters were no better in the dining room, where he burned his tongue with his first sip of tea. Csevet was as brisk and efficient as ever; today it grated on Maia's nerves, as if there were some veiled reproach or unfavorable judgment behind Csevet's impassive face.

Once the correspondence had been dealt with—and it was much less now that Maia was granting audiences and attending the convenings of the Corazhas—Csevet said with a shade of reluctance, "Serenity, you have promised to speak to Osmer Nelar this morning."

The words were like lead weights. It was an effort not to let his shoulders slump or his chin drop. "We did," he said, and was pleased with how level and uninvolved his voice sounded. "Is that the first item in our docket?"

"Serenity. We thought it best to clear the matter out of the way promptly."

"Thank you," Maia said. "Have you found a position we can grant him?"

"We have done our best, Serenity. As it happens, the Lord Chancellor's office is in rather desperate need of a liaison with the city of Cetho. The previous liaison has just been told he must go south for his health."

Maia thought of the cold gray clouds over the court and shivered in sympathy. "What does this position entail?"

"Paperwork, mostly," Csevet said with a momentary expressive grimace that made Maia smile. "The jurisdictions of court and city are, we have been given to understand, tangled at best, particularly in matters of taxation. The Liaison to the City of Cetho, as the post is styled, er, untangles the tangles."

"We see," Maia said, reflecting that the position sounded well suited to both Setheris's talents and his self-importance. "And you said the position belongs to the Lord Chancellor's office?"

"Serenity. The civil liaison is a position expressly intended to *prevent* these matters taking up the emperor's time. Osmer Nelar would report to the Lord Chancellor." Csevet hesitated, then said, "He would have neither reason nor justification to seek an audience with Your Serenity, and we venture to predict that the Lord Chancellor would be grossly offended were he to try."

And Uleris Chavar, Setheris's old enemy, was just the man to sit on him if necessary. "Thank you, Csevet. It sounds perfect."

"Serenity," Csevet said, bowing.

"When does our cousin await us?"

"Half past nine, Serenity. In the Michen'theileian."

Maia glanced at the clock and was dismayed to discover it was already nearly nine. *Self-indulgent sluggard,* he said bitterly to himself. He looked without pleasure at the array of beautiful dishes Dachensol Ebremis had sent up from the kitchen and poured himself more tea. With Setheris waiting for him, he knew he would taste nothing but ashes, and his stomach was already heavy and cramping without the added insult of food. Even the tea did not offer real solace, but a memory of Setheris sneering at chamomile as fit only for peasants and barbarians.

*It is a good position,* he said to himself, fighting the queasy awareness that Setheris almost certainly wanted more. If he had had visions of featuring prominently in his cousin's new government, Maia hoped that the preceding few days had been enough to dispel them—but he had been an unwilling audience for ten years to Setheris's dreams of glory. Civil liaison would not be what Setheris had in mind.

*He cannot harm thee,* Maia reminded himself. *Thou art emperor. Thou hast guards.* He looked at his nohecharei; they stared back at him solemnly. He drank his tea quickly, lest his hands begin to tremble.

He found himself unwillingly remembering the occasion of his sixteenth birthday, his nominal ascent into adulthood. As with the previous seven birthdays spent at Edonomee, there was no celebration, no gifts, not so much as a grudging "Many happy returns," from Setheris. And, of course, no message from the court. Maia had not expected to be granted his liberty, but it still stung—and led him to the reckless and stupid folly of confronting Setheris.

*I am an adult now,* he had said.

*An if thou art?* Setheris had said, half-drunk and sneering.

*It must change things,* Maia had persisted.

*It changes nothing, boy. Thou art in my guardianship until the emperor says otherwise—not thee and thy vainglorious prating. Thou art the same moon-witted hobgoblin thou wert yesterday, and if thou desirest me to prove it—* He had backhanded Maia across the face, hard enough that Maia fell to one knee, and as he knelt there, tasting blood and the salt of starting tears, he heard Setheris laugh and leave the room.

Setheris was right. Maia's birthday had changed nothing. Setheris was still stronger, angrier, more violent; he still had power that Maia did not, and he was not about to relinquish it. His passion for control could be assuaged only by knowing that Maia feared him, and obeyed him out of that fear. They were not equals, and Setheris did not want them to be.

*Forsooth, we are not equals now,* Maia thought, gulping the last of his tea. *For I am emperor, and he is . . . he is a petitioner to Our Imperial Serenity.*

The idea was so incongruous as to be almost nonsensical. He could feel the bitter lift at the corner of his mouth and consciously smoothed it away as he stood up. Csevet and his nohecharei swept back as gracefully as dancers to follow him out the door.

*I may have power,* he thought, *but in truth I am imprisoned now, laden down with chains that Setheris cannot even imagine. I could dream of escaping Edonomee. There is no escape from the Ethuverazhid Mura, not this side of death.*

And yet no one would believe or understand the nature of his prison, least of all Setheris. *Be grateful thou speakst only in metaphor,* he recommended himself grimly, and put all thoughts of prisons out of his mind.

The Michen'theileian seemed as cold and threatening as the clouds, although he admitted that might be the effect of Setheris standing, waiting, as he always used to when Maia was late for a meal, or a lesson, or in coming when called. He did not actually have his pocket watch open in his hand, but the set of his chin was enough.

"Serenity," he murmured at Maia's approach, and swept a bow. Reflexively, Maia read Setheris's gestures, like a man reading a coded message to which he has memorized the key. Cold anger, nervousness, an underlying smugness of certainty. Despairingly he thought, *I shall never know anyone as well as I know Setheris,* and said in reply, "Cousin."

He let Csevet and his nohecharei take as much time as they liked in settling themselves, although under other circumstances he might have grown impatient with Csevet's arranging and rearranging of his ubiquitous stacks of paper. Setheris stood and smoldered; Maia sat and thought about posture and breathing, about not giving Setheris any kind of leverage.

Only when Csevet signaled himself ready did Maia look directly at Setheris and say, "Cousin, we have considered your desire for a post, and it has come to our attention that the Lord Chancellor's office is in need of a civil liaison to mediate between itself and the City of Cetho. We feel that this post would be well served by a man of your talents, if you are pleased to accept it."

"Liaison," Setheris said thoughtfully. "In the Lord Chancellor's office."

Maia knew that meditative, neutral tone. Setheris used it when someone said something more than usually stupid; it was a chance to retract the stupidity before the consequences erupted in one's face. Maia's hands, in his lap where Setheris could not see them, clasped and clenched so tightly he could feel each individual bone, feel his rings biting into his flesh.

"We had thought, Serenity," Setheris said after a suitable pause, "that we were of more value to you than that."

"It is an excellent and honorable post," Csevet said sharply, "and, we assure you, most valued by both His Serenity and the Lord Chancellor."

He might as well not have spoken for all the attention Setheris paid him. Setheris's eyes were fixed on Maia, unwaveringly.

Like a lump in his throat, Maia could feel the words, *What dost thou want?* His fear of Setheris's temper, the deep-worn rut of doing what Setheris wanted because it was easier and because it did not matter—*thou art emperor,* he said to himself, his hands gripped together now tightly enough to bruise. *Thou art Edrehasivar VII, and it does matter. Give way once to Setheris, and thou shalt bear him on thy back the rest of thy days, and thy people will perforce bear him, too, though they know it not.*

He took a deep breath, almost coughing with the constriction in his throat and chest, and said, "It is the position we offer you. Will you accept it, or decline?" His voice came out thin, and he heard the waver in it. But the words were his words, not the words Setheris wanted him to speak.

The silence in the Michen'theileian held for second after second. Maia could feel the tension in his nohecharei, though surely they knew that Setheris would not attack him. Setheris's self-love was great, but it was not madness. Relegation was far from the worst fate that could meet a man who displeased an emperor.

Maia could not watch Setheris's face, although he knew he should; he stared just past Setheris's shoulder, concentrated on keeping his ears from flattening betrayingly. He turned his fingers so that his nails dug into his palms. The pain counteracted the fear, and he welcomed it.

Then Setheris bowed, a small, stiff gesture barely more

than the bending of his head. "Serenity. We will present ourself to the Lord Chancellor at your demand."

Maia narrowly prevented himself from saying, *Thank you*. Instead, he managed, "You may tell the Lord Chancellor, cousin, that we have every faith in your competence."

"Serenity," Setheris said, unmollified, and bowed himself out.

The door closed behind him, and Csevet said, "Serenity? Are you all right?"

"We are fine, thank you," Maia said, unknotting his hands.

"He should not have spoken to you thus."

"It matters not," Maia said. "Come. We have spent too much time on our cousin already. Tell us what today holds."

"Serenity," Csevet said, fishing obediently through his stacks of paper. But Maia did not miss the sidelong, thoughtful look Csevet gave him and knew the curiosity it betokened.

He said, his voice harsh and brittle with sudden anger, "We do not wish to speak of our cousin again."

"Serenity," his nohecharei said in chorus, and all three men bowed.

*Thou art emperor,* Maia said bitterly to himself. *Behold that thou art obeyed and rejoice.*

The morning passed in a series of small decisions, petty rulings, things that the secretaries of the Witnesses and the Lord Chancellor had to know before the business of governing the empire could proceed. Maia listened and judged as carefully as he could, resolutely asking questions as the need arose, despite the humiliation of revealing his ignorance.

*'Tis better to ask,* he told himself over and over again, gritting his teeth, but all the same he was relieved beyond

his ability to express when Csevet said firmly that the emperor's luncheon awaited and that the secretaries were all dismissed.

But the last of the meek, nervous, indistinguishable chancellery secretaries hadn't even cleared the doorway when Chavar himself swept in, carrying a new set of secretaries in his wake. "Serenity," he said, "we must speak to you at once. About the Archduchess Vedero's marriage."

Csevet began, "His Serenity is—" but Maia held up a hand to stop him. Chavar looked crafty, an expression that Maia instantly distrusted, and he wanted to know *now* what was exercising Chavar, rather than postponing it until it might be worse.

"We understand," said Chavar, "that Your Serenity is not pursuing the late emperor's negotiations with the Tethimada."

Maia's eyebrows shot up despite himself. Someone had been talking, and he was certain it was neither his own household nor Vedero's. "We are undecided," he said, bracing himself to be scolded, but Chavar was already sweeping on.

"We would never have advised the late emperor to make such an alliance, and we are pleased Your Serenity is showing more caution. Especially when, as Your Serenity knows, there is another alliance you are in danger of losing."

Maia, much too bewildered to attempt speech, gestured at him to continue.

"We understand," said Chavar, looking even more crafty under a veneer of patience, "that Your Serenity has received a proposal from the Count Bazhevel."

Much became clear. Prompted by some spark of perversity, Maia said, "You mean his suggestion that we should marry his daughter?"

"What? Preposterous!" Chavar nearly shouted. "You

can no more marry Osmin Bazhevin than you can marry Csoru Zhasanai."

Maia looked at Csevet, who raised his eyebrows in return, his ears tilting satirically. The Lord Chancellor's office could—self-evidently—have done a better job with the Count Bazhevel's letter. But Chavar, inexorable, continued talking. "We were referring to the proposed marriage between the Archduchess Vedero and Osmer Bazhevar."

"The Count Bazhevel did make some such suggestion," Maia said, feeling as wary as a deer who has scented wolves but cannot see them.

"An alliance with the Bazhevada was one of Varenechibel's dearest wishes," Chavar said. He had been advancing steadily into the room as he spoke, using his presence, like the power of his voice, as a weapon. Maia became aware that he himself had just as steadily been backing away. And Chavar had not halted.

*He knows,* Maia thought. *He knows thou fearest conflict and thus he knows he can bully thee—without ever uttering an unkind word.*

Deliberately, he planted his feet. He would give no more ground. "We are considering *both* of the Count Bazhevel's proposals, just as we are considering the claims of the Duke Tethimel. As we were not in our late father's confidence, we can rely only on those of his wishes that were put into writing."

Chavar inflated like a bullfrog, but Maia thought, *He cannot strike thee, and he cannot come to like thee less than he already does. Thou hast nothing to fear from his anger.* He did not entirely believe himself, but he knew he had best pretend he did.

Chavar said, "Do you doubt our word, Serenity?"

It was a dangerous accusation—and a question Maia knew better than to engage with. He said, "We are stating a principle of our government. If Varenechibel the

Fourth did not write his intentions with his own hand, then we must make our judgments without having the benefit of his opinion." He eyed Chavar, who was spluttering but not producing anything coherent, and added, "If you will excuse us, Lord Chancellor, we are late for our luncheon." He sidestepped Chavar, and although he knew he could not sweep grandly as Chavar did, he left the Michen'theileian with all the dignity he could.

Though the Lord Chancellor had caused a delay, luncheon was not unduly rushed. Maia ate sour beet soup, and venison buns with pickled ginger, while Csevet explained the next ordeal in store. Periodically, the emperor had to give audience to individuals of the court who had favors to request, or grievances to impart or other matters they felt must be brought to the emperor's attention directly. There would also be a few commoners, but those (said Csevet) were exceptional cases. As he explained the process by which common petitioners were winnowed, Maia observed, but did not say aloud, that the purpose of the government seemed to be to divide the emperor from his subjects. On a personal level, he was grateful, but his mind was running on principles of government, and he could not help wondering if this was a bad one.

Another of Csevet's lists turned out to be a roster of the afternoon's appointments. "They will be kept strictly to a schedule, Serenity," Csevet assured him, having seen something in his expression or the set of his ears that conveyed his apprehension. Maia nodded and tried to feel comforted, but it was a very long list, full of people he did not know and names he could not place— until Csevet came to a name that Maia knew all too well: "Dach'osmer Eshevis Tethimar has begged permission to present his sister, Dach'osmin Paru Tethimin, to the emperor's notice."

"No one else is presenting their sisters—or their

daughters—to us," Maia said, thinking of Nurevis Chavar's almost offhand introduction of Osmin Duchenin.

"It is a very old-fashioned custom, Serenity," Csevet said. "The Varedeise emperors discouraged it, particularly Your Serenity's grandfather. As you may imagine, it took up much of the time allotted for audiences."

"Yes," Maia said. "Is, therefore, Dach'osmer Tethimar being overly punctilious or deliberately insulting?"

"Or both," Csevet said, then shook his ears out with a jingle of silver rings. "More likely, Serenity, he merely wishes to ensure that Dach'osmin Tethimin is brought to your attention as a potential empress."

"His method is rather clumsy," Maia said, thinking again of Nurevis.

"Dach'osmer Tethimar is not a subtle man," Csevet said. Maia thought he had meant to say it lightly, but it came out flat and dark; there was a pause long enough to be awkward before Csevet looked very deliberately at the clock and said, "We had best go, Serenity. It looks ill for the emperor to arrive late to give an audience."

Every stiff line of Csevet's body was begging Maia to let himself be chivvied on to his next task: to let the question of Eshevis Tethimar go. Maia, despising his own curiosity, said, "Tell us again: who will come first?" And he pretended he did not notice Csevet's almost inaudible sigh of relief.

Audiences had to be held in the great, cold, brooding Untheileian. Maia was oppressed by its empty echoing vastness, and he pitied his petitioners, who had to make the long walk from the doors to the throne under an imperial scrutiny that they could not know was benevolent. Many of them, in fact, seemed to assume it was hostile. There were stammered apologies from the commoners and shows of bravado from the courtiers, and always Maia kept his patience and remembered to smile. In the back of his head, he began composing a prayer of compassion for the living. The requests and questions presented were no difficulty, thanks in large part to Csevet's careful coaching; it was simply a matter of listening through the distractions and defenses to what was actually being asked. Maia was surprised to discover this was something he was good at: he was able, in his turn, to ask the right questions to make the matter clear in both his mind and the petitioner's. Nothing could have been more different from the guilt-ridden bewilderment of attending the meeting of the Corazhas, and although Maia did not exactly relax, he felt a measure of confidence that made it easier to keep his spine straight and his hands still through the long afternoon.

Dach'osmer Tethimar was the last petitioner of the day, whether through some subtle design of Csevet's or mere chance. In either case, the wait had clearly irritated him, for he strode the length of the Untheileian at such a pace that his sister could not keep up.

It was a poor auspice, Maia thought, watching Dach'osmin Tethimin struggle down the hall. She had not the confidence to simply choose her own pace, but keeping abreast of her brother would have required her to trot—possibly, judging by the fierce staccato of Tethimar's shoe heels, to run—which would have been a terrible breach of propriety. And if one left propriety aside, between the tightness of her long sheath skirt and the height of the heels on her shoes, she couldn't have run if her life had depended on it. Maia felt horribly sorry for her, even before she made it close enough that he could see she was shaking with fear.

Paru Tethimin was a pretty girl, though she lacked the strength of feature that made her brother's handsomeness so eye-catching. She had been dressed in the elaborate and sophisticated fashion favored by the widow empress's circle, which did not suit her: she looked like a child caught playing in her mother's wardrobe. Maia tried dutifully to think of her as a possible empress, but aside from her obvious terror, there was nothing to distinguish her from any of the other girls that age whom he had seen at the wake and in the halls of the court.

"Serenity," Tethimar began with a sweeping bow, and then realized his sister was not beside him. For a moment, the expression on his face was more than merely irritated, a there-and-gone look that made Maia's fingers clench on the arms of the throne. Then Tethimar turned and stood watching his sister; Maia was reminded of Setheris and his pocket watch. By the time Dach'osmin Tethimin reached the foot of the dais, she was mortified as well as scared, the perfect elvish whiteness of her skin showing red in unbecoming blotches.

"Serenity," said Tethimar, making his sweeping bow again. At his side, Paru Tethimin made her own bow, quite gracefully—but then, of course, Maia thought with an uncomfortable twinge of cynicism, she would have been well taught. "May we present to you our sister, Paru Tethimin?"

The temptation to crown this disaster by saying no was so severe that Maia was unable to get any other words out. The patchy flush drained away from Dach'osmin Tethimin's cheeks; he saw in her unguardedly horrified stare that by some evil chance of empathy she knew what he was thinking. Even Tethimar was beginning to look concerned by the time Maia finally managed to stammer, "We are most pleased."

He beckoned them closer, even though he felt he was being cruel to make Dach'osmin Tethimin climb the stairs. Now, at least, Tethimar was supporting her with a hand under her elbow, so Maia did not have to worry that she would fall.

At close range, he could see how young she was, and not just chronologically. His nephew Idra was her age, but Idra had been raised at court and formally introduced to its society over a year ago. Maia remembered someone saying Tethimar had "fetched" his sister to court, and he wondered if she had been fetched from somewhere like Edonomee.

Maia knew his duty; he was trying to choose a platitude, such as he had been spouting like a fountain all afternoon, when Tethimar took a step closer and said in a low voice, "We have heard, Serenity, that you favor the Bazhevada over us."

"We do not know how you could have heard such a thing," Maia said, "for it is not true."

"And yet you are considering their suit, when you know—for we distinctly remember telling you—that the late emperor was negotiating with our father. What other reason can there be, Serenity?"

His use of the honorific was like a slap across the face.

Maia's fingers tightened again on the arms of the throne, but he was sick to death of being bullied, and his own voice had an unaccustomed snap when he answered: "Our sister, the Archduchess Vedero, is in deepest mourning for her father and brothers. We will not arrange her marriage until she has had time to grieve, not with you, not with Osmer Bazhevar, not with anyone else. And we do not consider ourself bound by any private agreements our father may have reached. We were not in his confidence and thus cannot rely on anything that has not been put into writing. We regret it extremely if you read into this some judgment upon your person that was not meant."

There was a long, long silence. Tethimar was staring at him, his face blankly unreadable, but Maia could see, just at the downward edge of his vision, Tethimar's hands clenching white-knuckled into fists. Knowing that he was not going to change his answer, and knowing that Tethimar could not actually attack him, Maia waited, and finally, stiffly, Tethimar bowed his head. "Serenity. We are relieved to hear that we are not in disfavor."

"Not at this time," Maia said, and could not help a tiny, malicious flicker of pleasure at the way Tethimar's head jerked back up. "And we are gratified by this evidence that not all of our subjects disdain the old forms of courtesy." He looked very pointedly past Tethimar at Dach'osmin Tethimin, who looked—if possible—even more terrified. "We are delighted to meet you, Dach'osmin Tethimin. Thank you, Dach'osmer Tethimar."

It was a dismissal—he had gotten very good at them very quickly—and Tethimar had no choice but to accept it. Maia was then, blessedly, free to return to the Alcethmeret, where he could replace some of the more uncomfortable layers of his clothing with a heavy fur robe before retiring to the Tortoise Room and Csevet's ever-replenished stack of correspondence.

But there was a matter that had to be addressed first.

"We must speak to you regarding our sister Vedero's suitors," Maia said as he sat down.

"Serenity," Csevet said, bowing his head. "We are at your disposal."

Csevet had a great mass of information about the two proposed candidates for Vedero's hand; he was very careful to distinguish between fact, hearsay, and mere gossip in his telling. Eshevis Tethimar, Varenechibel's choice and persistent thorn in Maia's foot, was the son and heir of one of the most powerful and wealthy landowners in the southeastern quadrant of the empire. Teru Tethimar, the Archprelate, was a cousin in some degree, though not in the current Duke Tethimel's line; Csevet offered to trace the exact genealogy and Maia politely demurred. Eshevis Tethimar was thirty, had distinguished himself in the border wars with the northern barbarians ten years ago, was known as an avid sportsman and something of a political malcontent. "The nobility of the southeast tends that way," Csevet said, and Maia nodded, storing that fact away.

Hearsay and rumor said that Tethimar was an ambitious man, an evil-tempered man, and a man who was carrying a grudge his family had been nursing for generations. "As the then–Duke Tethimel was a great favorite of Edrevechelar the Sixteenth," Csevet said, "so it was inevitably the policy of the first Varenechibel to favor the Tethimada's rivals, the Rohethada and the Ormevada in particular. The Tethimada have never resigned themselves to that loss of power. The current Duke Tethimel and his heir, Dach'osmer Tethimar, have been maneuvering and campaigning for years. The rumors we have heard are that Dach'osmer Tethimar would marry a spavined cart horse if it increased his power at court."

"Why would our father wish a match with him?"

Csevet shrugged uncomfortably. "Serenity. We do not know. But we would guess that it is part of the ongoing difficulties between the Untheileneise Court and the southeastern landowners. There have been petitions and representations in recent years with which Varenechibel was most displeased, and which he was most loath even to consider. Perhaps he hoped that the marriage would placate Dach'osmer Tethimar and his allies, and also that it might give the emperor a way of controlling the Tethimada. When one's wife is an archduchess, one must tread more carefully."

*Yes,* Maia thought, *because that tactic worked so very well for my mother's father.* "What of this other gentleman, the Count Bazhevel's nephew?"

"Dalera Bazhevar, Serenity. Insofar as we have been able to discover, he has nothing to recommend him *beyond* being the Count Bazhevel's nephew. He is a gentleman of good lineage, moderate fortune, and no particular attainments or distinctions."

"Would he make our sister a good husband, do you think?"

"We know nothing to his discredit," Csevet said cautiously.

Maia sighed. "Will you write to both the Duke Tethimel and the Count Bazhevel, please? Tell them that due to the great bereavement suffered by the archduchess and the House Drazhada, we cannot contemplate a marriage alliance between our sister and any house for at least a year."

"Serenity." Csevet stopped, opened his mouth, closed it again, then said, "Are you saying that you are rejecting *both* of them?"

"We reject no one. But we will not negotiate a marriage while the archduchess is in mourning. We are not that heartless. And"—he caught Csevet's gaze—"as we told Dach'osmin Tethimar and Lord Chavar, we do not feel bound by any promises our father may have made or implied. Having never spoken to him, we cannot accept any evidence of his wishes except for what has been written."

Csevet's eyebrows went up in mingled admiration and consternation. "They will be furious, Serenity."

*One of them already is,* Maia thought, remembering that flash of black rage on Dach'osmer Tethimar's face, remembering that long silent stare before he bent his head to the emperor's will. "We will not marry our sister to either a malcontent or a nonentity simply because they do not like our politics or think they can gain advantage over us."

"Yes, Serenity. We will write the letters as you wish."

"We thank you. If you will bring us paper and pen, we will write to our sister ourself."

His letter to Vedero was simple, unadorned with titles or formulas:

*Study the stars.*—M.

# 16

## News from Barizhan

Maia slept well that night, eased by his certainty that he had done the right thing, but in the morning he paid the price: a pile of angry pneumatics from the Count Bazhevel, the Duke Tethimel, Eshevis Tethimar, Dalera Bazhevar, all the Witnesses of the Corazhas, the Lord Chancellor, and a great many other people who Maia thought had no business even knowing the decision he had made, much less giving him their opinion of it. "It is the nature of the Untheileneise Court, Serenity," Csevet said. "Trying to stop the wind from blowing would be no more useless."

There was no message from Vedero; Maia had not expected one, but it still stung a little to have no word of thanks amidst the torrent of rebuke. *Let it go,* he told himself angrily and proceeded to the Michen'theileian, where Chavar appeared to scold him all over again in person.

Maia reiterated everything he had said to Csevet and to Tethimar and to Chavar himself, but he knew full well Chavar wasn't listening, too focused on his own catalog of grievances. Maia would have let him talk himself out, as he had always done with Setheris, but he happened to look at Csevet and he saw by Csevet's deepening frown and the mulish set of his ears that he was about to explode at his former master.

Maia, startled, realized that not only did he have no obligation to let Chavar scold him like this, but he actually had an obligation to stop him, for the sake of Csevet and the other secretaries and every other member of his government who would never dream of berating the emperor in public. *They have the right not to be ruled by a coward,* he thought with a flick of self-contempt, and said sharply, "Lord Chavar, enough!"

Chavar's mouth shut like a portcullis. Maia kept staring at him until he finally bowed his head and muttered, "Our apologies, Serenity."

Csevet was swift to seize the opportunity to move on to other business, but the atmosphere continued strained and thunderous. They maintained a respectable degree of efficiency, though, until they reached the investigations into the wreck of the *Wisdom of Choharo,* which the Lord Chancellor was notably reluctant to discuss. Maia had no difficulty deducing that this meant there had been no immediate and dramatic success, but he persisted in the question—more out of a grim desire not to let Chavar evade him than any wish for the details— and finally Chavar turned and stormed at one of his secretaries for not having brought the correct file, and a page boy was sent running to the Chancellery to retrieve it.

They got through several items of business while he was gone—it was dismally astounding how many townships were in arrears on their taxes—and when the boy returned, panting, with a stack of ledgers and tied quires nearly too high for him to see over, Maia felt it was not unreasonable to say, "We want a *full* report, Lord Chavar, not merely the items you think suitable for our ears."

Chavar began an outraged protest, but Maia cut him

off. "Also, we want a full copy made and delivered to the Alcethmeret."

"Serenity, you need not"

Maia interrupted him again—he was learning that it was easier not to be afraid of the Lord Chancellor if Chavar was never allowed to build up a full oratorical head of steam: *"It is the murder of our father."* And after a long silence, in which Chavar acknowledged defeat by not saying any of the true and ugly things he could have, Maia said quietly, "Please tell us what your Witnesses have found."

They had not found a great deal more than Celehar had, though at much greater length. All the crew members were being investigated, and all the emperor's servants. They had sent Witnesses north to Amalo to talk to the workers who had readied the *Wisdom of Choharo* for what would be her final flight. They had sent a junior Witness to ask the Clocksmiths' Guild how one would go about building a device to explode an airship and who might have the necessary ability. The Clocksmiths had been volubly helpful, but all their information did not, as far as Maia could tell, bring the investigation one step closer to the truth.

It was a long and depressing confession of no progress, and Maia almost wished he had let Chavar weasel out of giving it. But he would give the copy to Celehar. Maybe it would help.

Everyone was glad to leave the Michen'theileian at noon, and Maia said firmly to Csevet as he sat down to lunch, "Talk to us of something else."

Csevet understood and obeyed, and they were deep in a discussion of yet another petition from an exiled enemy of Varenechibel's who hoped Edrehasivar might be more forgiving—they seemed endless, those petitions, like the River of Tears that separated the land of the living from the land of the dead in goblin folklore—when the sound of a considerable commotion in the public space of the Alcethmeret brought both their heads up. Maia nodded to Csevet's inquiring look, and then waited while Csevet went to investigate. It was not an emperor's place to find out anything for himself.

The investigation took longer than Maia expected, and when Csevet returned, he was frowning. "Serenity, it is the ambassador of Barizhan without. He asks an audience with you immediately."

"Immediately?" Maia said, frowning in turn.

"Serenity. He says the matter is of extreme urgency, and for what it is worth, we believe him. He has come himself, and he has *apologized* for not making an appointment through proper channels." And to Maia's raised eyebrows, he added, "Goblins never apologize for anything, especially not in public."

Maia said, "We had best see him. Does it disrupt our schedule entirely?"

"No, Serenity," Csevet said, although he sounded dissatisfied.

"Thank you," Maia said. "We realize it is a shocking nuisance."

"It is our job," Csevet said, bowing, and turned neatly to go escort the ambassador into the imperial presence.

As was appropriate, the ambassador came in alone, but Maia heard the stamp and clank of his soldiers on the landing—and the stamp and clank of Maia's guards in return. His first glance at Ambassador Gormened showed him that Csevet had, if anything, understated the case. Although Gormened's dark skin would show neither blush nor pallor, his eyes were wide and his face was sheened with sweat. He prostrated himself fully, with a mutter in Barizhin out of which Maia understood only the word "respect." *Ordath*. Chenelo had used it in every unanswered letter she had written to her father, and he knew it was part of the proper address to a ruler.

"Please rise, Ambassador," he said, and added, to make a joke of his anxiety, "We trust our grandfather has not decided to declare war."

"Almost, that would be easier," Gormened said, and he did not entirely sound as if he were joking in return. He rose, if not gracefully, then with no evidence of effort. "The Great Avar proposes a state visit."

"He wishes us to travel to Barizhan?"

"No, no," said Gormened, looking even more alarmed at the idea. "He intends to come *here*."

There were several thousand immediate and burning questions. Maia picked one, almost at random. "When?"

"Winternight. He says he wishes to see how it is celebrated in the Ethuveraz."

*Is there any way to stop him?* He did not say it. He did not need to, for he had the answer already in Gormened's distress. He glanced at Csevet, who interpreted his expression correctly and said, "The court can be ready for him, Serenity, although the orders will have to be given very promptly, as there are less than two months remaining before the solstice."

*And my birthday.* He pushed that thought away; he hadn't celebrated his birthday since Chenelo died, and he did not want to celebrate it as befitted an emperor.

"It is the first time the Avar of Avarsin has left Barizhan since the Archipelagar Wars of his youth," said Gormened. "In our memory, he has never gone more than twenty miles from the Corat' Dav Arhos."

Maia began to understand why Gormened was so very rattled. The Great Avar had been an old man already when Chenelo was born; by now he must be over eighty. And it was the ambassador who would be responsible to the avarsin for his well-being.

"Serenity," said Gormened with a new access of determination, "we feel that there must be a wise and careful plan made for the Great Avar's visit, requiring more than the usual—and most commendable—cooperation between your government and our dav." He used a Barizheise word that meant, to Maia's best understanding, something midway between "household" and "office." Goblins did not distinguish between the two. "We would like . . ." He drew himself up a little straighter. "We would like to invite you, your Lord Chancellor, and your Witness for Foreigners to dine with us in three days' time, so that we may all come to a better understanding." Tactfully, he did not specify what was to be better understood, but Maia felt he could make a fairly good guess. He considered the idea with increasing admiration for Gormened, who had come up with an unorthodox but unexceptionable way of asking the emperor to ensure the cooperation of the two men who could most easily make the Great Avar's visit a disaster. Maia's experience of Chavar suggested that nothing, in fact, would be more likely.

"We will be most pleased to attend," he said, and Gormened beamed at him with relief.

Of course, it was not that simple. Schedules had to be juggled; a thousand details of etiquette and security had to be hammered out; Chavar had to be persuaded to agree (Maia carefully did not ask Csevet what that persuasion entailed); and in order that the emperor not be perceived as granting undue favor to Barizhan, Maia had to agree to dine with the Marquess Lanthevel, who presided over the House of Blood in the Parliament. Even worse, the rumor sprang up, faster than seemed possible, that Maia was dining with the goblin ambassador in order to discuss marrying a Barizheise princess. The Alcethmeret was inundated with pneumatic messages, hand-delivered letters, and people seeking personal audiences with the emperor to convince him that he must marry an elvish girl instead. "And there is still the matter, Serenity," Csevet said one morning, and his apologetic tone warned Maia to brace for a new crisis, "of the Count Bazhevel. We are afraid there is no way around it: you must grant him an audience."

"Must we?" Maia said unhappily.

"He feels very ill-used, Serenity. And Osmin Bazhevin is Drazhadeise now, and it is both natural and right that her father should wish to know what will become of her."

"But we do not know what to do with her!" Maia said, and was horrified at himself for sounding so exasperated. It was not Osmin Bazhevin's fault that she was in an ambiguous position, and she and her father both deserved an answer. She had signed the marriage contract with the Archduke Ciris, so she was no longer considered a daughter of the Bazhevada, but the marriage had been neither sworn nor consummated; she had never become Ciris's wife, so she was not now his widow.

It was a tricky and unpleasant question whether she could now marry (*again*, his mind added automatically and he winced), and an even more unpleasant question whether any man would choose to marry her with her ambiguous status. But in the meantime, she was neither a widow, with the right to the income of her husband's properties, nor a daughter of the Bazhevada to be supported by her father's estates, and yet she was also not a *daughter* of the Drazhada.

The easiest solution would be for her to become a votary and join one of the cloisters that dotted the Ethuveraz, principally in the more inaccessible points of topography. Maia knew that many of his imperial ancestors would have made that choice for her whether she felt any calling or not, but he found it too much like relegation, and of all people, Stano Bazhevin had done no wrong.

Maybe, he thought, she would *wish* to enter a cloister.

But he knew it was not something he could—or should—depend upon.

Maia granted an audience to the Count Bazhevel and Osmin Stano Bazhevin on a cold, bleak afternoon when the clouds were nearly the same color as Maia's skin. Because the Count Bazhevel had annoyed him with his scheming, Maia chose to receive them in the Untheileian, even though Osmin Bazhevin's status as the dead archduke's fiancée would have permitted him to use the Michen'theileian or even the receiving room of the Alcethmeret. But he hoped dourly that the frigid expanse of the Untheileian would encourage the Count Bazhevel to be brief.

It was unfortunate that the Count Bazhevel—long-faced and long-nosed—looked so much like a sheep. Maia had heard courtiers drawing the first syllable of *Bazhevel* out into a mocking bleat, and although it was unkind, it was also horribly unforgettable, and even more horribly so when the Count Bazhevel opened his mouth to begin his litany of complaints and produced a high, slightly quavery voice, as sheeplike as his face. Osmin Bazhevin, standing at her father's shoulder, kept her head down and did not meet the emperor's eyes. Maia could see the tension in her shoulders, though, and once her hands started to twist together before she caught herself and brought them to decorous stillness again.

As Csevet had said, the Count Bazhevel felt himself extremely ill-used. Maia chose simply to let him talk himself out rather than either arguing with him or cutting him off, since the essence of his complaint, whether he himself would admit it or not, was that Ciris Drazhar had inconsiderately died before the wedding could take place. Without any imperial response to even the most blatant of his cues, Bazhevel eventually fell silent, although his stance and the set of his ears indicated an obstinate determination to have satisfaction. Maia let the silence stretch long enough that he no longer imagined bleating echoes in the vault of the Untheileian, then said, "Osmin Bazhevin, approach us, please."

Both Bazhevel and his daughter looked alarmed—which heightened the strong resemblance between them, and Maia wondered if the younger courtiers bleated at Osmin Bazhevin now that she was no longer an archduke's fiancée. She climbed the steps of the dais, and Maia said quietly, "We are sorry for your loss."

"Thank you, Serenity," she said, her voice no more than a whisper.

"Osmin Bazhevin," Maia said, "what do *you* want?"

He startled her into a look of honest, almost pained, incredulity, and he winced in agreement. He had put that so badly it was very nearly an insult. "Let us rephrase our question. We understand that you are in a very difficult position and all of your choices are bad. Acknowledging that that is true, what would you choose to do?"

He'd made it worse; she said, still at a whisper, "We would *choose* to have our fiancé alive again."

The next moment, eyes wide and ears flat, she was on her knees apologizing while her father bleated at the foot of the dais.

"Please, Osmin Bazhevin, we do not blame you," Maia said. "Please, stand up." And when she was finally on her feet again, so rattled that he could see her trembling, he said, "You understand that the simplest solution is for you to enter a cloister, but we will not compel you if it is not what you wish."

Her doubtful expression made her look even more like a sheep.

"Truly," Maia said, willing her to believe him.

After what seemed to him a very long silence, she said, "The Princess Sheveän has offered us a place in her household."

"Has she?" Maia said, empty syllables to buy time while his mind raced. He was fairly sure he knew the reason behind Sheveän's offer, and it had nothing to do with charity. Stano would be a meek and obliging companion, exactly to Sheveän's taste. By the same token, Maia wasn't sure it was a good idea for either Sheveän or Stano, but there were limits beyond which he felt he had no right to interfere, even though he knew he was probably the first emperor in generations to make such a distinction. "Is that what you want?"

"Oh yes," said Osmin Bazhevin, stopping herself before she glanced at her father, though her ears twitched uneasily.

"Then we have no objections," Maia said. It was not the truth, but this was, after all, a better solution than the truth could provide and perhaps, he thought—knowing it for callow optimism, but hoping all the same—perhaps having a companion would ease Sheveän's bitterness.

"Thank you, Serenity," Osmin Bazhevin said, curtsying and offering him something that was almost a smile.

Maia nodded his permission for her to leave and raised his voice to say, "Your daughter is provided for, Count Bazhevel. You need trouble yourself no longer." *Nor us,* he thought, but resisted the temptation to say. It was fashionable to be witty at others' expense, but Maia did not need to be told that the emperor could not indulge in fashion, no matter how much Bazhevel irritated him.

He was afraid that Bazhevel would stand his ground, but Osmin Bazhevin did not stop at the foot of the dais; she kept walking, as fast as propriety would allow, toward the distant doors of the hall. Bazhevel hesitated, his gaze flicking from Maia to his daughter and back again. Maia was careful to be looking somewhere else, as if he believed Bazhevel were already gone. A further moment's hesitation, an odd little hopping step of frustration—Bazhevel bowed with a mumbled "Serenity" and hurried after his daughter.

But even with Osmin Bazhevin taken care of, candidates for the honor of becoming Edrehasivar VII's empress were proposed by the battalion; the eldest was forty-two, the youngest barely six months. And Csevet, the evening before Gormened's dinner, insisted that each of them had to be accorded the same serious scrutiny.

"Is this truly necessary?" Maia asked, trying not to sound either sulky or terrified.

Csevet said, "We are afraid it is, Serenity. The great public anxiety about Barizhan means that : . ." He hesitated, twisting the cap of his pen. "Think of it as ritual, perhaps. Or as theater. We must be able to account for every step we take in ways that will seem reasonable and fair."

Maia noticed that "seem," which Csevet might or might not have stressed ever so lightly. And he did understand. He could not say, *We will not marry Osmin Loran Duchenin because she is the niece of our Lord Chancellor, whom we dislike. And because we dislike her as well.* Osmin Duchenin had cornered him— elegantly, unobtrusively—at one of Nurevis's parties, standing just a fraction too close and laughing too much until her laugh started to sound to Maia like the baying of a hunting hound. He had had no idea how to talk to her, beyond even his habitual tongue-tied shyness; there was nothing in her glittering conversation he recognized, nothing he could respond to. And every time he failed, Loran Duchenin just laughed again and pressed closer, fighting grimly on, as if she could make him want her by sheer persistence. Nurevis had not rescued him this time; Maia supposed he had been ordered not to interfere with his cousin's plan of attack. It would be very like Chavar to give such an order, and Maia had learned that while Nurevis might subvert his father's commands in mild and subtle ways, he never disobeyed him directly.

In the end, shamefully, Maia had been rescued by his nohecharei. Telimezh had stepped forward and said, "Serenity, remember that Mer Aisava wishes to speak to you before you retire for the night. And it is growing late." Maia had leaped at the excuse, even if it did make him seem like a child and his nohecharei his nursemaids, and he had been avoiding Osmin Duchenin ever since.

But that was not a *reason*. "Very well," he said. "Then we will tell you plainly that we would choose *not* to marry an infant—and we remember your example of Belmaliven the Fifth, which tells us also that it would be unwise."

"Serenity," murmured Csevet, making a note.

"We suppose," Maia pursued grimly, "that it would equally be folly to choose a woman so near the end of her childbearing years as Osmin Alchenin."

"Yes, Serenity."

"Some of these women must be related to us."

"Most of them, to a greater or lesser degree. The Drazhada have intermarried with most of the noble houses of the Ethuveraz." Csevet coughed uncomfortably, his ears dipping. "We understand that to have been one of the arguments made in favor of Varenechibel's marriage to your mother."

"Ah. Nevertheless, we would prefer not to marry a cousin."

"We will exclude any woman closer than the third degree of kinship," Csevet said, making another note.

"Is there any noble house with which we should *not* ally ourself?" He had not asked the question before, when the matter of choosing an empress had seemed unpleasant but relatively straightforward, but now with this furor over a Barizheise princess who did not exist—he would have to know all the petty, depressing details.

"Serenity." Csevet thought for a moment. "We would suggest—although it is only a suggestion—that further entanglements with the Rohethada and the Imada might be undesirable. Likewise, the Celehada." The families of his half siblings' spouses. And his father's widow. "On the other hand, choosing a wife from the Ceredada might be construed as a graceful and welcome gesture. Your father did not win friends when he put off Arbelan Zhasan."

"We imagine he did not. And do we not remember that there was a Dach'osmin Ceredin among the young women you mentioned to us before?"

"Yes, Serenity. The granddaughter of Arbelan Drazharan's brother. She would be in all ways a fitting match."

"Is she your choice?"

Csevet dropped his pen. The click of the barrel hitting the marble tabletop was perfectly audible. "Serenity, we do not *have* a choice. We would not so presume."

"Chavar would."

"Chavar is your Lord Chancellor, not your secretary." Csevet sounded so prim that Maia realized he was genuinely flustered.

"But we trust neither his judgment nor his loyalties. We trust yours."

Csevet's pale skin flushed rose. "We are honored, Serenity, but we cannot choose your empress."

"Nor can we!" He hadn't meant to shout, and he took no pleasure in the way Csevet and his nohecharei jumped. He lowered his voice again, unclenched cramping fingers. "We cannot . . . We cannot so much as follow the steps of a dance. We cannot possibly choose an empress."

"Serenity?"

"It is a poor metaphor," Maia said, and managed a smile. "It is just as well we never wished to be a poet." He could not sit here any longer, discussing his own marriage as if it were a matter of which stallion should cover a given mare; he knew he would begin shouting again and that was wretched payment for Csevet's service. Maia shoved back from the table and stood. "Surely there is somewhere we are supposed to be this evening."

He saw understanding cross Csevet's face and looked away before it became impatience or pity. "There is one matter, Serenity," Csevet said, "although we have wondered if you were serious about it."

"About what?"

"You asked us to find the lady who was entrusted with your care during the funeral of your mother. We have done so, but we were not sure . . ."

"We were very serious," Maia said. "And we mean the lady no ill. Who is she?"

"Her name is Aro Danivaran. Her husband was Drazhadeise through his mother's line, and your father acknowledged them as cousins. The Danivada are ruinously poor." Csevet paused, glancing at Maia to see if he understood.

Maia understood perfectly. "Like the Nelada," he said.

Csevet winced very slightly. "Yes, Serenity. But Osmer Danivar and his wife were more fortunate—or more politic—than Osmer Nelar. Your father gifted them with a small estate on the birth of their first grandson, some five years ago, and there is hope that the Danivada may be able to right themselves."

"We are pleased at our father's generosity," Maia said, and did not let the words twist into bitterness.

"Osmer Danivar died two years ago. His son runs the

estate, and Osmerrem Danivaran has been maintaining the family presence at court." A note of caution, of regret, had entered Csevet's voice, and Maia was already half expecting it when he said, "Osmerrem Danivaran suffered a brainstorm a few days before your father's death. She is bedridden and not expected to survive to the solstice."

The reminder that other lives had tragedies without reference to his own was both salutary and painful. He said, "We would visit her, if it is allowed."

"Serenity," said Csevet. "Her daughter said she would be both honored and pleased. And that she tends to be most alert in the evenings."

The emperor could not go visiting unannounced, so a page boy was sent at a run to Osmerrem Danivaran's apartments while Maia's edocharei fussed over his clothes and jewels, as what was suitable for an evening spent in the Alcethmeret, where the polite fiction was maintained that the emperor was "at home," was not at all suitable for any endeavor that would take the emperor out into the public halls of the Untheileneise Court. Maia bore it with the best patience he could muster, as his jacket was exchanged for one that had plum and green embroidery on white instead of white embroidery on forest green, and as the achingly heavy amethyst and silver rings were replaced with an equally heavy array in gold set with black opals. Nemer and Avris debated about the amethysts and garnets in his hair but mercifully decided they could stay, merely swapping out the teak and emerald tashin sticks for a pair of gold-chased bone sticks set with pearls. Nemer was deft enough to effect the substitution without disordering a single braid of Maia's hair, and Maia escaped back to the Tortoise Room just as the page boy returned with assurances that the emperor would be both expected and welcome in Osmerrem Danivaran's chambers. Maia collected Dazhis and Telimezh with a glance and set forth.

It was fortunate that he had the page boy, for Osmerrem Danivaran resided in a section of the Untheileneise Court that Maia had not seen before. The courtiers he passed were all middle-aged or older; most of the women curtsied, rather than following the fashion Csoru had set. He reminded himself that it meant nothing, just that they were older and less likely to be swayed by the fads of an empress the same age as their children.

A page boy wearing what had to be the Danivadeise livery was waiting for them; Maia pretended not to notice his heel swing back sharply into the door to alert those inside that the emperor was approaching. Was it a kindness, he wondered suddenly, thus to descend on a household that could not possibly be prepared to receive him? They had not had time, and they did not have the money they doubtless believed to be necessary to fit a room for an emperor. And he could not tell them the truth, that after Isvaroë and Edonomee, it was lavish furnishings that made him uncomfortable, that he still felt like an interloper among the Alcethmeret's splendors.

But it was too late now. The page boy was already throwing open the door, already announcing (in a voice that cracked on the third syllable, and Maia hid a wince of sympathy), "His Imperial Serenity, Edrehasivar the Seventh."

*Learn to think before thou actst, mooncalf,* Maia told himself in a well-practiced imitation of Setheris, but having chosen this action, he was committed to it. He followed Telimezh through the door, Dazhis bringing up the rear.

The receiving room was not nearly as shabby as he had expected; he wondered if he and Csevet had different definitions of "ruinously poor," or if the Danivada chose to bankrupt themselves for brocade wallpaper. The woman standing by the stained glass torchière in the center of the room swept a deep curtsy as Maia entered. When she straightened, he saw that she was middle-aged, plump, with the sort of narrow, pointed face that led to the elvish nobility being satirized as weasels in the comic papers. Although not lavish, her clothes and jewels were tasteful—the lapis lazuli beads in her hair brought some much-needed color to her eyes.

"Osmin Danivin?" Maia said.

She gasped and curtsied again.

"Please. We only wish to assure you that we mean your mother no harm. We will not proceed if you think our visit unwise for her."

"Oh, no," said Osmin Danivin, and then seemed forcibly to pull herself together. "That is to say, Serenity, our mother is very pleased at your visit and most sincerely wishes to see you. She regrets, as do we, that she cannot greet you properly. The brainstorm, you see, it has—"

"Please," Maia said hastily, horrified that she felt she had to apologize for the thing that was killing her mother. "It is no matter. May we go to her?"

"Of course, Serenity," Osmin Danivin said, and led him, nohecharei in tow, down a short hallway to Osmerrem Danivaran's bedroom.

In the dim light, the bed seemed to rise like a lilac and pale blue mountain, all its lace hangings looped back like clouds. Osmerrem Danivaran, propped up on a great bank of pillows, looked infinitely frail, her face as flawlessly white as her hair, the cheerful pinks and yellows of her bed jacket seeming a cruelly chosen irony, although surely nothing could be further from the truth.

She opened her eyes when she heard their approach: pale green and protuberant, they were the only part of her Maia recognized. She croaked a slur of sound that was probably meant to be "Serenity," and Maia said, "Hello, Osmerrem Danivaran. We are pleased to meet you again."

"Pleased," she echoed, more intelligibly, and held out one clawed and trembling hand.

Maia took it, careful of his rings, and obeyed the faint pressure, coming to stand beside the bed. She did not let go. She squinted, as if to focus on his face, and said, "Nice . . . boy."

"She means you were a nice boy, Serenity," Osmin Danivin said. "She told us about you after the funeral, how polite and quiet you were."

"We remembered her," Maia said. He bent his head toward Osmerrem Danivaran and dropped formality; it was ludicrously pointless to play the emperor with a dying woman. He said softly, "I remembered you. But I didn't know your name. I wanted to thank you."

She smiled at him, although the expression was twisted on her ravaged features, and tugged feebly until he let her bring his hand to her face. She pressed her lips against the backs of his fingers, then released him, her eyelids fluttering shut and her body going slack.

"She falls asleep like that," Osmin Danivin said; Maia, who for a dreadful moment had thought that Osmerrem Danivaran had died, saw that her chest was rising and falling. He turned away and allowed Osmin Danivin to lead him back to the receiving room.

He asked her, "Is there anything we can do to make your mother more comfortable? Or to make your task in caring for her easier?"

"Oh! Thank you, Serenity," Osmin Danivin said, more than a little breathlessly. "There is one thing, although we hesitate to mention it."

"Please. Anything. Your mother was kind to us at a

time when we needed that most desperately. We would repay her in any way we can."

He felt more than heard Dazhis's weight shift—an unspoken protest, and he supposed he was being rash. But Osmin Danivin believed him, for she blurted, "Coal!" and then looked dismayed.

"Coal?"

"It's been so cold," she said, half-apologetic and half-despairing. "And the price of coal keeps rising and rising. And Mother is cold all the time, even when the rooms seem comfortable to us. We would take her south, but she cannot travel, and, Serenity, we would not ask it, but we are desperate, and you asked if there was anything, and this truly would make Mother more comfortable"

"We will see to it," Maia said, and Osmin Danivin curtsied so deeply and thanked him so repeatedly that he was grateful to be able to leave.

The first thing he did on returning to the Alcethmeret was to tell Csevet to see that the Danivada's apartments were supplied with coal and not charged, and Csevet said, "Yes, Serenity," and made a note. *Yes,* Maia thought, *we will "see to it" by telling someone else to see to it. Thus do we put ourself out for our benefactors.* But he had no idea how to accomplish the matter himself, and he knew that if he tried, he would succeed only in confusing and frightening a great many people.

On that lowering thought, the Emperor Edrehasivar VII went to bed, where he slept badly.

# 17

## Dinner with the Goblin Ambassador

T**he day of the goblin ambassador's dinner party dawned clear and viciously cold. The frost on the inside of Maia's bedroom windows was too thick to see through, and his edocharei fussed and fretted over whether he would be warm enough or ought they to provide him another layer of silk beneath the wool?

"We beg you not to," Maia said earnestly. He already felt like a Barchakh'kaladim, the Barizheise nesting doll with its series of progressively smaller, fiercer, and more hideous warriors. One more layer could not make him significantly warmer, but it might make it impossible to move.

"If you become chilled, Serenity," Esha said sternly, "you must come back. We will keep the silks by the fire just in case."

"You are very kind," Maia said, and meant it. He had been eight years old the last time anyone had cared whether he was warm enough.

"It is our job, Serenity," Esha said, as Csevet always said, but he thought the three of them were pleased nevertheless.

Breakfast was oatmeal with dried apricots and honey, and the kitchen staff had unearthed a giant, claw-footed, gilt and green enamel samovar that had to be two hundred years old at least. The tea was very strong and very hot, and Maia insisted that Csevet take a cup.

And to Maia's delight, before he was finished eating, and before Csevet was finished explaining the hazards of the upcoming day, his signet was delivered. The messenger was a courier—Dachensol Habrobar was part of the government and thus rated a courier's service, even though the transit was confined to the Untheileneise Court. The courier was goblin-dark and wore scarlet ribbons like defiance in his hair. He was also, unmistakably, a friend of Csevet's; Maia asked him to wait in case there was any problem with the ring, and nodded to Csevet to escort him out of the dining room. He heard one of them laugh as the door closed behind them, and bent his head over the little quilted silk pouch so that neither Beshelar nor Cala could see his face.

The ring was a heavy circle of platinum, unadorned except for the emblem carved into its face with precise and delicate lines. The cat-serpent, with its coiling tail and dramatic whiskers, was perfect, and Maia took an uncomfortable, savage pleasure, as he slid the signet on his right ring finger, in knowing his father had disapproved of the design. The signet was heavy, but no heavier than his other rings (gold today, set with topaz and tiger's-eye), and the weight seemed less cruel, although he knew that was only imagination. But the signet was *his*, and childish fancy or not, it rested more easily on his hand.

Thus fortified, he embarked upon a most wearing morning. Chavar had not had the temerity to refuse Ambassador Gormened's invitation, but Maia almost wished he had. At least everyone would have been spared his unspoken but obvious displeasure, which made itself known in fault-finding and petty obstructionism.

Worse, from Maia's point of view, at midmorning the

Corazhas convened—with the Lord Chancellor in thunderous attendance—for the purpose of selecting the next empress.

The Corazhas were unusually amiable, and he gathered that they approved of his doing something so appropriately emperor-like as taking steps to secure the succession. The Witness for the Judiciate even smiled at him. Once seated, they all looked at Maia expectantly; his mind a horrified blank, he said, "Mer Aisava has done a great deal of the preliminary work in this matter," and turned pointedly to Csevet.

Csevet, as calm, polite, and ferociously organized as ever, responded without either hesitation or discernible chagrin. He bowed slightly to the assembled Witnesses and said, "It is true that we have been assisting the emperor, to the best of our poor ability, to make a wise decision. His Serenity feels that there are three candidates worthy of your consideration: Dach'osmin Paru Tethimin, Dach'osmin Csethiro Ceredin, and Osmin Loran Duchenin."

Maia was more than a little startled to learn that this was his opinion, but he trusted Csevet and held his tongue, and within five minutes, Csevet's strategy was clear. Chavar, inevitably, supported Osmin Duchenin, and ordinarily he would have had the support of Lord Bromar, the Witness for Foreigners, but the Bromadeise estates were in Thu-Athamar, and Bromar—it was plain—knew better than to cross the Tethimada. Maia watched as the Corazhas split into camps. The Witness for the Prelacy supported Chavar, and the Witness for the Universities supported Bromar. Lord Deshehar, the Witness for the Parliament, and Lord Pashavar, the Witness for the Judiciate, found themselves in agreement for the first time that Maia had ever seen, advocating for Dach'osmin Ceredin, and they were joined by the Witness for the Treasury and the Witness for the

Athmaz'are. Maia remembered what Csevet had said about Varenechibel creating ill-feeling when he cast off the Empress Arbelan. Csevet stood and waited, not even smiling, until Chavar and Bromar had argued each other to a standstill, and then said, "We think there can be no objections to Dach'osmin Ceredin."

Lord Pashavar was quick to pick up the cue, and within a very few minutes, the Corazhas had reached consensus in support of Dach'osmin Ceredin; Chavar, glaring more furiously by the second—although now at Csevet—had no choice but to agree.

And then, just like that, it was decided. Edrehasivar VII had chosen his empress. Maia found himself confused and sad and somehow empty-feeling, and he had no appetite for lunch.

Matters did not improve in the afternoon, when Maia gave an audience to the Trade Association of the Western Ethuveraz, which seemed to offend Chavar by its very existence. Maia thought its representatives, including a cousin of the Prince of Thu-Istandaär, seemed very sensible, their goals likely to improve their cities in more ways than just the economic, but Chavar barely let them finish before he was rejecting their ideas, with special scorn being heaped upon their wish for a bridge over the Istandaärtha.

But Maia had listened to their reasons and been impressed, having had no idea that the imperial government charged such exorbitant fees for the use of its airships. "Lord Chavar," he said.

"Serenity?" said Chavar impatiently.

"Whether a bridge over the Istandaärtha is possible or not, these gentlemen should not be censured for desiring one. We see that it would be a great benefit to them."

"We think it *is* possible, Serenity," one of the delegates said eagerly. "We have spoken to—"

"This is not an appropriate matter for you to bring before the emperor!" Chavar sounded sincerely shocked, and glancing at Csevet, Maia saw that he agreed. He himself couldn't understand what was so appalling about it, but he would merely shock Chavar more if he said so. And, the darker thought occurred, it would be one more example of how Edrehasivar was a barbarian, unfit to rule or to go out in polite society. Maia let Chavar and the secretaries resume control of the audience, though he was pleased to note that Chavar did moderate his language. It was the only satisfaction he got that afternoon.

Maia extracted another report on the investigation into the wreck of the *Wisdom of Choharo*. This time, along with all the dead ends (and the pun was so morbidly apt that he had to hide a wince), there was an encouraging sign as well. The Witnesses had determined that the incendiary device must have been brought on board by one of the crew members; thus, they had begun investigating the crew of the *Wisdom of Choharo* with greater rigor, and they had discovered that three crew members had had ties of varying closeness with a dissident group in Cetho. The Witnesses were confident that the answers—and the people responsible for the murder of the emperor—were to be found among the Cetho Workers League.

"That doesn't sound terribly dissident," Maia observed, and got a blistering lecture from Chavar on the danger the league represented, the harm it had done, and the certainty that, given the opportunity, its members would gleefully have conspired to murder the emperor. Maia thought of the mourners in the Ceth'ulimeire and was unconvinced.

When he returned to the Alcethmeret, there was a pneumatic waiting for him, which Csevet took only a glance at before handing over. It was from Lord Berenar, the Witness for the Treasury, a request for a private audience at the emperor's earliest pleasure.

Maia looked helplessly at Csevet. "What can he want with us?"

Csevet said, "Lord Berenar is not a frivolous man, Serenity."

"No," Maia agreed. The Witness for the Treasury did not speak often in the Corazhas, but when he did, he was decisive and to the point. "When can we see him?"

"A formal audience might take several days, but you could speak to him tomorrow morning, if you are willing to meet over breakfast."

"We have no objections," Maia said. The Corazhas politely tolerated his presence during their meetings, but this was the first sign any of them had offered that they were even aware that Maia existed as more than a peculiar decoration in the Verven'theileian. Whatever Berenar wanted, Maia was unwilling to discourage him with delays.

"We will answer his pneumatic," Csevet said. "Your Serenity should dress for dinner."

Between the cold and the occasion, dressing for dinner was something of a carnival. Maia's edocharei had clearly agonized over how he should be dressed, and there were several last-minute flurries of indecisiveness; Avris told him that no emperor had accepted a dinner invitation from a foreign ambassador since the first Varenechibel took the throne.

"Not even when our mother . . ."

"No, Serenity." Maia supposed wearily that he shouldn't be surprised. But even in his grief, Varenechibel should have done better, either entering with good faith into the marriage and the closer relationship with Barizhan it suggested or refusing it altogether—though it was strange to think that if Varenechibel had simply refused that marriage he did not want, he, Maia, would never have existed, and his nephew Idra would now be emperor. A child emperor, controlled by his regents: however inadequate Maia felt himself to be, the long and frequently bloody history of the Ethuveraz suggested he was still better than that alternative.

Nevertheless, he thought it shameful that it had been over 150 years since an emperor had accepted the hospitality of a foreign emissary, so he did not object to the elaborate preparations his edocharei had made. He might wish that less of his clothing were white, but that was a futile wish for an emperor, and he could only hope that the ambassador's kitchens had chosen to prepare something not prone to dripping. At least the velvet brocades were warm. Nemer dressed his hair with frosted glass tashin sticks and strands of pearls, and his rings were white opals set in platinum. Opals in his ears, and he tried not to remember a warm summer morning in Isvaroë and his mother piercing his ears with a needle.

He was pleased to see Beshelar looking as polished as a toy soldier, and even Cala had made an effort, although he must have borrowed the robe from someone else, for while it was a bright, even blue, it was an inch too short in the sleeves. He would have to ask Csevet, he thought, if the emperor's nohecharei didn't get some sort of stipend, or if this was something else Chavar was obstructing. He would not embarrass Cala by asking now.

At precisely seven o'clock, two goblin page boys appeared at the doors of the Alcethmeret, flanked by two enormous warriors, the largest goblins Maia had ever seen, wearing (Csevet told him in a hasty whisper) the full ceremonial regalia of the Hezhethoreise Guard. It seemed Ambassador Gormened was also thinking about those 150 years. The warriors saluted in perfect unison at Maia's approach. He wondered what they thought of all this, in their gleaming spiky armor and elaborately crested helmets, but of course he could not ask. Truly, he thought wryly, curiosity was a useless trait in an emperor.

The page boys he judged to be ten or eleven years old, both of them gray-skinned rather than the true goblin black. One of them, like Maia himself, was slate gray; the other was more the color of winter clouds, but he would never be taken for an elf, not with those vividly orange eyes. The boys were respectful but not at all shy; they talked to him freely on the long trek from the Alcethmeret to the ambassador's dav.

The darker of the two was named Esret; his companion was Teia. They were both from northern Barizhan, where intermarriage between elves and goblins was becoming more and more common. They were the sons of minor avarsin, fostered to the Great Avar's household as a sign of fealty. And, Maia thought, insurance against betrayal. Esret had been at the Untheileneise Court for two years, Teia barely six months. They both preferred it to the Corat' Dav Arhos, the Great Avar's sprawling, half-underground palace, as there was much more to do, and Maia gained a picture of Gormened's efforts to improve his country's standing. Esret knew all about the Lord Chancellor's offices and those of the Witness for Foreigners, while Teia knew all the merchants, both goblin and elvish, who traded between Barizhan and the Ethuveraz and kept an office in Cetho, "and many of them do, Serenity, because it makes it easier to get customs forms approved and visas for travel, and, oh, all sorts of other things that they can only do here." Maia suspected Esret and Teia knew more about trade between Barizhan and the Ethuveraz than he did.

Two more soldiers in the uniform of the Hezhethora were standing at the doors to the ambassador's section of the Untheileneise Court. They saluted and opened the doors, moving in clockwork-perfect unison. Maia was surprised that the ambassador had so many of the Great Avar's warriors, but a whispered confidence from Teia explained it: "Aren't they grand? They came with the courier from Maru'var. Inver and Belu spent all day practicing with the doors and they made Vorzhis send for someone to oil them."

"Vorzhis says he'll be glad when they go back to Barizhan," Esret said, as gleeful as Teia, "but we all know he doesn't mean it. Maybe you could come watch them drill? They're *amazing*."

Maia's gaze crossed that of the soldier holding the left-hand door; he was so astonished when the man winked that he nearly forgot to keep walking. He had known that relations between Barizheise nobles and their dependents were more familial than formal, but it was inexpressibly startling to be included in that. He wondered if it was because of the empress his mother or his kinship to Osmerrem Gormened or if the ambassador had made a particularly astute judgment of his character.

That thought was not a happy one. Maia was frowning as he entered the receiving room, although he had to pull himself together immediately to respond to Osmerrem Gormened's magnificent curtsy, and then the ambassador was there, bowing and smiling and so clearly anxious for Maia to be pleased that he could not hold on to his suspicious detachment. There was a whole host of introductions to be made; Gormened must have prevailed on every Barizheise expatriate in Cetho to attend, and the opportunity to meet the emperor was, of course, a new one for them. Varenechibel would hardly have been welcoming to the goblin community.

They were all shades from goblin-black to elvish-white; some of them had red or orange or gold eyes, others blue or green. Their bone structure varied widely, too, some heavy-boned with the underslung goblin jaw, others with the fine pointed features characteristic of elves. It was the first time in his life Maia had been surrounded by people who were like him instead of only snow-white elves with their pale eyes, and he missed several names in the effort not to faint or hyperventilate or burst into tears. He was steadied by the sight of Chavar's glowering face; it was all too easy to imagine Setheris behind him.

Most of the goblins present were merchants and wealthy. He noticed a distinct divide, though, in that the older goblins seemed to deal primarily in silk, while the younger generation had a diversity of interests: clocks, pens, the machine-woven carpets from Choharo—the goods represented by the Trade Association of the Western Ethuveraz, to put it succinctly. He also noticed that insofar as Chavar could be said to unbend, it was toward the silk merchants. Silk was produced in Thu-Athamar and had been the bedrock of the Ethuverazheise economy for so many centuries that it was practically respectable.

All at once, Maia understood that the conflict over bridging the Istandaärtha was less about either the river or the bridge than it was about trade. The eastern Ethuveraz had always, since Edrevenivar the Conqueror united east and west, been significantly wealthier and more powerful than the western principalities, and their wealth and power were based in large part on the silk trade, which was controlled by a handful of noble families. That had begun to change with the gold rush in Maia's grandfather's day, the founding of Ezho, and was continuing to change as the artisans and merchants of the western cities learned to cooperate among themselves, but the power of the silk monopoly would be dreadfully imperiled, possibly destroyed, by a bridge over the Istandaärtha—a cheap, easy, and safe way, not merely for increasing trade, but also for the peasant families who did all the work of silk production simply to leave. And thus the two sides—quite literally, the east and west banks of the Istandaärtha—one longing ardently for the bridge and the other abhorring even the mention of it. And there stood the emperor in the middle.

It was some time before he was able to find a corner of relative quiet to speak to Gormened. "We must thank you," he said, already embarrassed but determined, "for the nesecho."

"The nesecho?" Gormened's eyes were very sharp, but not unkind. "Did you like it, Serenity?"

"We had to get one of our gardeners to explain it," Maia said, "but we did keep it." He pulled the nesecho, threaded on its golden chain, out of his inner pocket.

Gormened's face lit in an astonished smile. "We are honored, Serenity, and very pleased."

"Thank you," Maia said, tucking the nesecho away again, "but why did you send it to us?" He hoped he sounded like he was asking, *Why are you seeking our imperial favor?* but he was afraid his real question— *Why are you being nice to me?*—was all too apparent.

Certainly, Gormened seemed puzzled, which he would not have been by a purely political question. "Why should we not have?" he said, watching Maia carefully. "Your Serenity was facing—is, indeed, still facing— a formidable task, and we wished to convey"—he shrugged, a wide and comprehensive gesture—"if not our support, precisely, for we are loyal to Maru'var, then our sympathy? Our benevolence? We wished you to know that we were not your enemy. Are not your enemy. For it seemed to us all too probable that you would be in need of that reassurance from at least one quarter."

Involuntarily, Maia's eyes found Chavar, standing like a pillar of thunder among the guests.

"Exactly," said Gormened crisply, and turned to introduce Maia to someone else.

Maia escorted Osmerrem Gormened into dinner; he had so much to think about that he forgot to be anxious and instead asked her a number of questions about what goods were considered luxuries in Barizhan and about trade with other countries across the Chadevan Sea. She was puzzled but cooperative, and ended up enlisting the help of the gentleman on her other side, a silk merchant who had been a sea-trader in his youth—possibly a pirate, if Maia understood the nuances of the conversation correctly—and who knew all about spices and gems and lion-girls and other exotic things that rarely made it as far north as the Ethuveraz. He warmed to his topic as he saw that Maia was truly interested, and he progressed from simple information to wilder and wilder stories. By the time the cucumber salad was cleared and the yam and pork curry served, their entire end of the table was listening unabashedly to Mer Zhidelka. A little later, he was sketching maps on the tablecloth in salt and spilled wine, recounting the adventures of the steamship *Benevolent Lotus* in the Archipelagar Wars, and people farther down the table were craning to listen. Mer Zhidelka's fund of stories seemed inexhaustible, and Maia was both enthralled and grateful.

The curry was removed and replaced with tiny, exquisite lemon sorbets, and Ambassador Gormened rose. "We have an announcement to make," he said, his trained voice cutting easily through Mer Zhidelka's description of the barbaric practices of the Versheleen Islanders, "both delightful and unprecedented. Maru Sevraseched, the Avar of Avarsin, chooses this year to celebrate Winternight at his grandson's court."

Chavar, even though he'd known full well it was

coming, looked as though he'd found pith in his sorbet. The Barizheise guests murmured and exclaimed.

"We are pleased," Gormened continued, "that the emperor and the court have agreed to welcome the Great Avar of Barizhan, and we will be working closely with the Lord Chancellor"—he bowed toward Chavar—"and the Witness for Foreigners"—he bowed toward Lord Bromar—"to ensure that this Winternight is a splendid and fitting celebration of the close ties between our two countries and the beginning of the reign of Edrehasivar the Seventh, may it be long and prosperous!"

Applause, but Gormened and one by one the guests were turning to look at Maia, and he realized they were expecting him to make some sort of speech. His mouth went instantly dry, and his hands were shaking as he pushed back his chair. *Better thee than Chavar,* he told himself; one look at the Lord Chancellor's face was enough to convince him of that.

He stood, gripping the edge of the table so tightly that his rings bit into his fingers, and said, "Thank you, Ambassador Gormened." Horribly, his mind had gone blank except for all the things he *shouldn't* say: *We promise our Lord Chancellor will behave,* for one, *We have always wondered about our grandfather,* for another. Finally, lamely, he said, "We feel this Winternight will be most memorable, and we have utmost faith in you and in Lord Chavar and in Lord Bromar. Thank you." He hoped it was not obvious that he was sitting down to keep his knees from giving out, but even without that humiliation, it had not been much of a speech. He could see from Chavar's expression amidst the polite applause that not only would Varenechibel have done better, but so would Maia's fourteen-year-old nephew Idra. Probably, Idra's little sisters would have done better.

*Setheris punished me for talking too much,* he wanted

to protest, but it would do him no good. He reached for his wine goblet.

Osmerrem Gormened said to Mer Zhidelka, "We fear we have become slightly turned around. Where exactly are the Versheleen Islands?" and Ambassador Gormened signaled to the servitors to bring in the rich, peppery hot chocolate with which goblins finished winter meals. It was a kindness he would not have received from the elvish court. Even if the ambassador and his wife were deliberately seeking his favor, they were doing so with a generosity of spirit for which Maia was deeply grateful.

He looked at Chavar, scowling darkly and ignoring his neighbors, and then looked away quickly and set himself to attend to Mer Zhidelka's stories. He would take goodwill wherever he could find it.

He found himself brooding, though, about goodwill and political alliances and other things, and later, back in the pretend privacy of the Alcethmeret, he asked "What if Dach'osmin Ceredin does not wish to marry us?"

Csevet looked at him as if he'd run mad. "In the first place, Serenity, what likelihood is there of any young woman of birth and breeding *not* wishing to be empress? In the second place, you may be sure the Cere-dada will not let her do anything so foolish as to refuse you."

*In other words*, Maia thought, *her wishes are of no more importance than mine.* "What must we do? Is it all to be handled by secretaries?"

"There will be a formal meeting, Serenity. Other than that, it would be grossly improper for you to have any contact with her before the marriage contract is signed."

"Oh," Maia said, disheartened.

"Although," Csevet said cautiously, "it would not be

improper to include a personal letter with the formal offer of marriage. It is not *always* done, but it is not wrong."

"All right," he said, although the idea was daunting. Then he thought of something even worse. "Is she *here*? At court?"

Csevet's cough might have been a strangled laugh. "She attended your coronation, Serenity." After a moment, he added, his voice carefully noncommittal, "We also understand that she is of the Archduchess Vedero's circle."

"You didn't mention that before," Maia said, and hated how sulky he sounded.

"We have been making inquiries. And—you did not ask."

For all that it was very gently said, it was a rebuke, and one Maia knew he deserved. He felt his face heat and bent his head, biting his tongue against the excuses and complaints that crowded it. Instead, he asked, "Is she an astronomer, too?"

"That, Serenity, we do not know. But the archduchess's circle includes women interested in all branches of learning."

Maia had another question, one that had been bothering him for some time. "The universities are open to women. We know this. Why do these women not—why did our sister not attend?"

There was an unhappy pause before Csevet said, "To do so, Serenity, she would have needed the permission of her father. And a university education is felt to make a woman unfit to be a wife."

"And that was all our father cared for," Maia finished.

"Serenity," said Csevet, not quite openly agreeing.

"We must write to her," Maia said, feeling the truth of it, "but what are we to say?"

"We do not know, Serenity. But you have no other obligations tonight."

Meaning that Csevet thought he should write to Dach'osmin Ceredin now. Maia supposed he was right about that, too.

Although the Untheileneise Court's gaslights meant that the hours of the court were not ruled by the sun, Ambassador Gormened had chosen to follow the older tradition of ending winter meals, if not at sundown, then substantially earlier than most court functions. Maia suspected he had very sensibly found a graceful and plausible pretext to end his party before anything went wrong. Thus, Maia had an unwontedly lengthy stretch of unclaimed time, and he spent it all in laboring over draft after discarded draft of his letter to Dach'osmin Ceredin. When he went to bed—ironically, much later than usual—he was not so much satisfied with the product of his efforts as despairing of any chance that he might do better:

> To Dach'osmin Csethiro Ceredin, greetings:
> We fear this must be strange and awkward for you, as it is for us.
> We are sorry for that. We wish to be a good husband to you. We ask you to be honest with us, to tell us when we offend or wound you, for we will not do so purposely, but only out of ignorance.
> With hopefulness,
> Edrehasivar VII Drazhar

He could not write, *We are not our father,* although his fingers cramped on the pen with the desire to do so.

He sealed his pathetically short missive with his signet, trying to take hope from the clear imprint of the cat-serpent on the wax, and wrote Dach'osmin Ceredin's name on the envelope, then bore it upstairs to his bedroom, for he had realized that he could not let it be sent until he knew for certain that Dach'osmin Ceredin had been informed of the honor which was landing on her shoulders. Nothing could be a worse botch than for his letter to arrive by pneumatic before the courier had even been assigned to bear the formal offer.

He explained the situation to his edocharei, and they gave him a suite of puzzled looks. "Mer Aisava will not be asleep yet, Serenity," said Nemer. "We will fetch him." And he was gone before Maia could tell him not to. He reappeared shortly with Csevet, still fully dressed, and Csevet bowed and took the letter. "It is very well, Serenity. Tomorrow, we will give this to the courier who will carry the formal offer. He will not get things wrong."

Maia knew Csevet would not say so if the man were not fully to be trusted, and tried to put that particular specter of humiliation from his mind. He also tried to apologize. "We did not mean for you to be disturbed so late."

But Csevet, like his edocharei, did not see that there was anything untoward. "Serenity, it is our job, and we are very happy with it."

"But you have no more privacy than we do!" Maia blurted, dismayed, and was even more dismayed when Csevet blushed.

"We assure you, Serenity, we have sufficient privacy for our, ah, needs."

"Oh," Maia said. "That's good. We are glad . . . that is, we are . . . we are going to bed. Good night, Csevet."

"Good night, Serenity," Csevet said, still very pink but smiling. "Sleep well."

Maia got into bed expecting no such thing, but in fact he did sleep well and woke in the morning feeling as if his problems might not be insurmountable after all. He descended to find Lord Berenar waiting for him in the dining room, chatting amiably to Csevet: court gossip that Maia was still too much a newcomer to follow. They both stood and bowed at Maia's entrance; once everyone was seated again, and Maia had a cup of tea warming his hands, he said, "You wished to speak to us privately, Lord Berenar?"

"Yes," Berenar said. He paused then, long enough that Csevet said, "We will await you below, Serenity," and started to get up.

"No, no," Berenar said hastily. "It is not so private a matter as that. Merely . . . Serenity, it seems to us that you need help and no one is providing it."

"What sort of help do you mean?" Maia said, his back stiffening and his ears lowering.

"We mean nothing to your discredit—far from it. Though we do feel the late emperor your father has much to answer for. Serenity, if we are wrong, you need only say so, and we will apologize and trouble you no further, but do you, in truth, understand above half of the proceedings of the Corazhas?"

A scalding blush swept through Maia, leaving cold shame and dizziness in its wake. He heard Csevet say crossly, "Your Lordship's notions of tact leave much to be desired," and he struggled to pull himself together, to keep from betraying himself—but it was already too late for that. Berenar had already seen the truth, seen that he was ignorant and unprepared, unfit to be emperor. Useless, Setheris had called him, and it was true.

"Serenity," Berenar said, sounding anxious, "we did not mean it as an accusation. We wish to offer our help."

"Your . . . help?" Maia echoed from a cotton-dry mouth.

"A lack of knowledge is a remediable problem," Berenar said. "We had assumed that the matter would be seen to—for, certainly, your Lord Chancellor has much experience of the court and familiarity with even its darkest byways—but since it clearly has not, we wish to offer our services."

Maia became aware of the teacup in his hands and drank, giving himself a moment to regroup. It was Csevet who asked, "What do you mean by 'services,' Lord Berenar?"

Berenar flashed a look between Maia and Csevet, as bright and biting as glass in the sun. But he turned courteously to Csevet and said, "Why, education, Mer Aisava, nothing more. We see quite clearly that, through no fault of his own, the emperor lacks the knowledge he needs, and we thought that, having spent much of our life at court, we could supply the deficit."

Maia, well aware that Csevet had been doing his unobtrusive best to teach the emperor the thousands of things he should already have known, looked for signs of offense, but Csevet said, "That is extremely well thought of," and turned, eyebrows raised, to Maia. "Serenity, you do not have to accept if Lord Berenar's offer does not please you."

"No," Maia said. "We mean yes! That is, we are exceedingly grateful to Lord Berenar and will be glad of any information he feels—" He broke off, realizing he was addressing the wrong person.

Berenar seemed unruffled, merely saying, "We are very pleased, Serenity. May we suggest that a regular meeting time will be both more productive and less upsetting to both our schedules?"

"That seems a good notion," Maia said.

Csevet said, "We will arrange it, Serenity. Lord Berenar?" They walked out together, and Maia handed his teacup to Isheian to be refilled.

*There is goodwill to be found,* he thought, as Isheian returned his cup with one of her shy, barely there smiles. *Even in the Untheileneise Court.*

PART THREE

# The Winter Emperor

# 18

## Varenechibel's Legacies

He was called the Winter Emperor, for his reign was brought in with early snow and its first month was characterized by bitter cold; the Istandaärtha froze solid below Ezho for the first time in living memory. It was impossible to keep the Alcethmeret's vast and echoing lower rooms heated, and the public spaces of the court were even worse. Maia was always cold, despite layers of silk and wool and ermine, and he offended Esaran again by asking if the servants were able to stay warm enough. It was Nemer who reassured him: the servants' quarters were built around the kitchens; their rooms were warmer than their emperor's.

It was neither the first nor the last time that Maia wished simply to be a scullery boy.

His days were full of meetings—the Corazhas, the Lord Chancellor and his satellites, representatives of this wealthy family seeking a favor, of that lucrative business seeking a concession. There were formal audiences with each of the ambassadors to the court, Pencharn, Ilinveriär, Estelveriär, Celvaz, and of course Barizhan. The Untheileneise Court itself, like any city, required governance, and he mediated between the courtiers as best he could when he rarely had more than the most academic understanding of the grounds of the quarrel. The courtiers were at least polite about listening to him, though he had no confidence that they heeded him. Matters among the functionaries and servants tended to be far more practical, if no less passionate, but those he only heard about secondhand: Csevet dealt with them lest His Imperial Serenity be "bothered." In the evenings, he dined with the court, as he was expected to do unless he could find some compelling reason to be elsewhere, and then there was dancing or a masque or some other entertainment at which the emperor's presence was understood to be essential. He was late to bed again—and again and again as the days of his reign began to mount—but his eyes were blurry with work, not drink, and the pounding headache came from tension, from the constant, half-crippled feeling of having to make decisions without sufficient information, with an always incomplete understanding of the situations, the motivations, the possible repercussions. Even Berenar's best efforts could not make up the deficit of years in mere weeks.

He tried not to curse his father's memory, but he could not help knowing that it was his father's spite that had crippled him. *Thou wert the fourth son; thy half brothers were healthy, and one had gotten an heir. There was no need for anyone to imagine thou wouldst ever come to the Untheileneise Court, much less rule it.* But he wondered, as petition after petition came before him from those who had been relegated from the court at Varenechibel's command, what his father had intended for him, what his fate would have been if the *Wisdom of Choharo* had not been sabotaged.

The thought was an evil one, but it would not be banished; he wondered morbidly if Varenechibel's tactics had actually brought him peace of mind, or if he had been always aware of those he dismissed from his presence, his first and fourth wives, his son, his cousin, an assortment of other relatives and members of the court who fretted him or angered him or made him uneasy.

It did not help that the letter Maia received from Csethiro Ceredin was brief to the point of brusqueness, written in a cold secretarial hand far more polished than Maia's own. The letter spoke of nothing but duty and loyalty, ignoring entirely Maia's attempts to offer a warmer relationship. Varenechibel had found affection, kindness, even love with Pazhiro Zhasan, but neither the letter nor the prescribed formal meeting held out any hope of the same for Maia.

The Emperor Edrehasivar VII met his future empress for the first time in the Receiving Room of the Alceth-meret. The emperor was immobilized in white brocade and pearls; Dach'osmin Ceredin was austere and im-maculate in pale green watered silk; cloisonné beads, crimson and gold, were wound through her hair and hanging from her ears. The contrast made the vivid blue of her eyes—the same brilliant color as Arbelan Drazharan's—stand out like a shout of defiance in her white, well-bred, characterless face. Maia found it im-possible to meet her gaze steadily.

Dach'osmin Ceredin was accompanied by her father, the Marquess Ceredel. Where she was as unreadable as a porcelain doll, he was visibly nervous, full of bravado one moment and all but cringing the next. The Marquess Ceredel had a guilty conscience, Maia noted; later, he would have to ask Csevet or Berenar why.

This was not a great ceremonial occasion such as the signing of the marriage contract would be, but there was nothing informal about it. Edrehasivar VII announced to the Marquess Ceredel that he had chosen Csethiro Ceredin as his empress; the Marquess Ceredel professed his delight and sense of honor. No mention was made of the property Dach'osmin Ceredin would bring with her to the marriage, nor of the gifts and favors that the emperor would bestow on the Ceredada. Those details were being worked out by secretaries and stewards, and Maia hoped Chavar had as little part in the negotiations as possible. This interlude between the emperor and his father-in-law-to-be was mere theater; Maia wasn't even sure whom it was intended for.

Throughout, Dach'osmin Ceredin stood beside her father, politely impassive, not a flicker on her narrow face or a twitch of her ears to indicate she was even listening. It made Maia both uncomfortable and anxious, and finally, at the point where the audience was meant to conclude, he said, "Dach'osmin Ceredin, are you content with this marriage?"

She raised one eyebrow a fraction in token of her knowledge that his question was useless and even foolish, then dropped a perfect curtsy and said, "We are always content to do our duty, Serenity." Her voice was deep for a woman's, and it carried in the emptiness of the Receiving Room like a tolling bell.

Maia, hot-faced and wretched, could only dismiss them, as Dach'osmin Ceredin had already dismissed him.

His marriage loomed before him like a disaster, but despite his black thoughts, or perhaps even because of them, Maia was pleased to grant an audience to Arbelan Drazharan when she requested one. He received her in the Tortoise Room, and the curtsy she swept him was magnificently formal, fiercely denying her age.

He invited her to sit, taking his own accustomed chair, and said, "What may we do for you, Arbelan Zhasanai?"

She managed to turn a snort into a cough, and said, "You need not give us honors which are not ours, Serenity. We are not zhasanai."

"You were the wife of our father. You were Arbelan Zhasan."

"Thirty years ago. And if you call us zhasanai, you illegitimate yourself. But you know that."

"Yes," Maia agreed. "But we would do you honor, nonetheless."

"Your Serenity is most gracious, and we do appreciate it. But your mother was relegated, too, was she not?" The question was a formality; they both knew the answer.

"Yes."

She folded her hands together and bowed to him across them, an old-fashioned gesture of respect and grief. "Varenechibel was like a killing frost."

They were silent a moment, in token of having survived Varenechibel IV; then Arbelan said, "We wished, Serenity, to discover what your plans are for us."

"We have not made plans on your behalf, nor would presume to. Do you wish to return to Cethoree?"

"No, we thank you," Arbelan said decidedly. "But . . . it is your wish that matters, Serenity, not ours. We are of the House Drazhada." By which she meant not merely that she was Drazhadeise by marriage, but that, like Varenechibel's other wives, both the living and the dead, and like his daughters and his daughter-in-law and granddaughters—like his third son's unfortunate fiancée—she belonged to the Drazhada. She was literally Maia's, to do with as he pleased.

It was no wonder, he thought, that Sheveän hated him, Csoru despised him, Vedero regarded him with distrust and skepticism. No wonder that Csethiro Ceredin would give him nothing of herself but her duty. He was eighteen, ignorant, unsophisticated; he had no right to control their lives—except the right of law. "Arbelan Zhasanai," he said deliberately, "we cannot ask our mother this question, and that saddens us. But it is in her memory that we ask it of you: what do you wish to do?"

She contemplated him, her face unreadable. Then she bowed her head gravely. "If it is not displeasing to Your Serenity, we would wish to stay in the Untheileneise Court. After so long, we have no other home, save Cethoree, where we do not wish to return."

"Then you are welcome here."

"We thank you, Serenity," she said.

"Would you—?" He broke off, feeling his face heat.

"Anything that is within our power, Serenity, you know you have only to command."

"No, it's not like that," he said. "It's nothing . . . it's not a *command*."

Her eyebrows were up. Edrehasivar Half-Tongue Osmin Duchenin had called him when she thought he could not hear; a glance at Telimezh had been enough to tell him it was not the first time. He dug his nails into his palms, forced himself to take a proper breath, said, "We merely wondered if you would consent to dine with us, perhaps once a week?"

She was visibly startled, which in a lady of Arbelan Zhasanai's generation was no small feat. "There is no impropriety," he said hastily. "You are, as you said, Drazhadeise, and widowed and . . ."

"Serenity," she said, and there was something in her voice he did not know how to name, "we would be both pleased and honored."

It was only a small bulwark, but it was a bulwark nonetheless, one evening in seven when he did not have to meet the pale cold faces and glittering eyes of the court. And Arbelan Zhasanai, who owed him her grati- tude, would not bear tales of the emperor's gauche silences, his awkward efforts at conversation. Once she had taken his measure—once, he thought, she had determined that this was not some arcane and hideously subtle trap—she took over the conversation herself, with a power and ease that made him wonder what she had been like when she was Varenechibel's empress, before her body and her husband had betrayed her. Although by tacit agreement they did not speak of Varenechibel himself, she told him stories of her youth, described the court of Varenechibel's father, Vareveséna. And those stories seemed always to lead her to speak of the modern court, of its petty wars and darker treacheries. He understood the worth of what she offered and listened intently, week after week, trying, even in this small way, to make up for the ignorance that was his inheritance.

He had learned the value of gossip from Setheris, from the differences, sometimes small, sometimes vast, between the official communiqués from the court and the letters Setheris received from Hesero. One never relied on gossip, Setheris had said more than once, but it did not do to discount it, either. Therefore, along with his lessons from Arbelan Zhasanai and Lord Berenar, Maia listened to the tidbits his household brought him, his edocharei, his nohecharei, Csevet: each of them heard different stories, different interpretations.

It was Arbelan Zhasanai who told him Sheveän continued to be discontented, Csevet who remarked that several courtiers seemed unnaturally interested in the laws of succession recently. But it was Nemer who, shyly, reluctance and indignation mixed, told him that people were beginning to say Nemolis's son Idra should have taken the throne.

Maia was wearily unsurprised. There was no one in the Untheileneise Court, possibly no one in the whole of the Ethuveraz, who did not know Varenechibel would have preferred to see his grandson succeed him. If Idra had reached his majority before his grandfather's death, he might well have raised his standard against his half uncle—and would almost certainly have defeated him.

But Idra was fourteen; he could not be a player in the machinations of the court, only a pawn. He was also, as things stood, Maia's heir, and thus Maia's instinctive desire to treat Sheveän as his father had treated all who had displeased him—let her see what life was like in Isvaroë or Edonomee or Cethoree—was untenable. He could do it, but either he relegated Sheveän's children with her and did to Idra exactly what Varenechibel had done to Maia himself, or he separated Idra from his mother. And Idra's little sisters—what would one do with them in that case? No, it was not possible. Edrehasivar was not and could not be Varenechibel.

He suffered the miserable certainty that nothing he could say to Sheveän would make the slightest difference. But he remembered that Idra had not seemed to resent him at the coronation, and so he summoned his heir to the garden of the Alcethmeret, where it had become the emperor's custom to walk for half an hour each day, regardless of the weather. Even in the snow, or the miserable frozen rains of winter, he at least walked along the stoa that cradled the garden against the bulk of the palace.

Idra was punctual; if his mother had insisted on coming with him, as Maia had feared she might, the instructions he had left with his household had been effective, and Idra had been divested of her. Idra was perfectly dressed and groomed, his hair in the thick knot that befitted a child, while the amber that glinted warmly among his white braids signalled him to be a child of the ruling house. Like Maia, Idra had the Drazhadeise eyes, gray and pale and clear as water, and he met his emperor's gaze unflinchingly when he straightened from his bow.

It was not a particularly nice day, but the sun shone

fitfully through the clouds, and the wind had less bite than it had had the preceding day. Maia said, "Cousin, will you walk with us?"

"An it please you, cousin," Idra said, meeting Maia on the level of formality he had chosen—"cousin" to acknowledge their kinship, but without oppressive specifics. Maia didn't think he'd be able to force the word "nephew" out of his throat if he tried.

They walked in silence along the first broad curve of the path away from the Alcethmeret, and then Maia, having been able to think of no delicate or tactful way to put it, said simply, bluntly, "You are our heir."

"Yes, cousin," Idra said; Maia saw the wariness in his sideways glance, and hated it. But there was nothing he could do about it. He could not demand that Idra trust him.

"You must know, we imagine, that we are not on the best of terms with your mother."

"Yes, cousin."

"We regret this. Were it in our power, we would make amends."

A silence, thoughtful. Idra said, "We believe you, cousin."

"Do you? Good. Then perhaps you will believe us when we say we wish no enmity with you."

"Yes, cousin."

They were silent for another long sweeping curve of the path. Maia was painfully aware that Idra was only four years his junior—and that Idra was in some ways much older. Not for him the stammering embarrassment of an emperor who had never learned to dance or to choose jewels or to talk politely of nothing over a five-course dinner. He wished that he could unburden himself to Idra, ask his advice. But if they were not enemies, still they were not quite allies, and he could not ask Idra to choose his emperor over his mother.

Well, he *could,* but he did not want to, did not want to make loyalty and love enemies in Idra's heart.

Yet he had to say something, had to reach out to Idra somehow. The Prince of the Untheileneise Court would reach his majority in two years, and unless Maia begot an heir, a thought from which he flinched as a horse shies at a threatening noise, Idra was going to be a fact of his political life until he had no political life left, no life at all. He said abruptly, "Do you grieve for your father, cousin?"

"Yes," Idra said. "We do."

And Maia, who had meant to say something about justice, about sympathy, heard himself say, "We do not grieve for ours."

And Idra said, "Did you ever meet him?"

He had braced for horror or disdain, a remark about goblin savages or an echo of Varenechibel's cruel words about his "unnatural" child. But Idra's voice was simply curious, and when Maia dared glance sidelong at his face, his pale eyes held nothing but a kind of wary sympathy.

"Once," Maia said. "When we were eight. At our mother's funeral. He . . . he did not have much interest in us."

*The damned whelp looks just like his mother.*

"Our father spoke to us once of our grandfather," Idra said, his voice still neutral. "When we were thirteen and expected to take our place in the court."

As Maia should have done five years ago. He nodded to Idra to continue.

"He told us that above all other things, Varenechibel hated to make mistakes, and hated to be seen to have made mistakes. He said that was why Arbelan Drazharan was relegated to Cethoree instead of being allowed simply to return to her kin, and that was why you were . . . we remember how he put it: 'pent at Edonomee.' If our father had lived to succeed our grandfather, he would not have kept you prisoned there."

"We are grateful to know that," Maia said. And he was, although it was as much pain as gratitude that he felt.

"Our grandfather was very kind to us. But we are not so naïve that we did not see he was not thus to all. He did not care for our sisters as he did for us."

"And you found this unworthy in him?"

"They were his grandchildren just as we were. And our father said it was good they were not sons, for too many sons—" He broke off, eyes widening.

"Confuse the succession," Maia finished. "So also we were told."

"By Varenechibel?"

"By our cousin Setheris, who was our guardian."

"He had no right to say such a thing to you," Idra said, with the same indignation with which he had championed his sisters' right to be loved by their grandfather.

"At least Cousin Setheris was honest with us," Maia said, and turned the conversation by asking Idra to tell him what it had been like to grow up at the Untheileneise Court. Idra complied, spoke charmingly and wittily, and Maia listened and smiled and thought, *He would be a better emperor than thee, hobgoblin.*

But at least he stood on good terms with his heir. At least he had that bulwark to shelter behind, as he sheltered behind his dinners with Arbelan Zhasanai. Nurevis proved to be another bulwark, friendly, utterly uninterested in politics, cheerfully ready to explain things that Maia found confusing, forever appearing with invitations to one social event or another. Maia refused more of those than he accepted, but he could not refuse them all. Even if he had wished to, it would be foolish to alienate the only courtier who had offered friendship unencumbered with obligation. And he did not wish to. Nurevis made a particular point of mentioning when Min Vechin would be attending one of his soirées or informal luncheons, and Maia blushed miserably, never having learned how to be teased—but he went. He told himself it was foolish; he told himself it was inexcusable. He knew he was a laughingstock, the hobgoblin emperor, Edrehasivar Half-Tongue, dangling after the opera singer. But Min Vechin smiled at him, and would approach him when invited, and did not seem to mind his failure to make conversation.

He told himself he thought only of companionship and knew he lied.

He did not ask his nohecharei what they thought, and they did not tell him. But he knew Beshelar and Dazhis disapproved, and he thought Telimezh pitied him. *This is what thy life will be, Edrehasivar,* he told himself, and tried not to think about his now-fiancée.

It had taken almost a week for the terms of the marriage contract between Edrehasivar VII Drazhar and Dach'osmin Csethiro Ceredin to be agreed upon. Berenar told Maia that this was uncommonly quick work— "the Marquess Ceredel must fear that you will change your mind."

"Why should we?" Maia said, and then, remembering a forgotten puzzle, "Why is he so afraid of us?"

Berenar snorted. "When the Empress Arbelan was put aside, her brother, the current marquess's father, fell with her. He had traded much too heavily on being the brother of the empress, both financially and politically, and the late emperor your father did not, as it turned out, regard the Marquess Ceredel with any great favor—or, indeed, any favor at all. The Ceredada very nearly went bankrupt, and as the late marquess would never admit to any wrongdoing or flaw in his own person, the current marquess was raised in the belief that the emperor is terrible and capricious and persecutes the hapless House Ceredada. Also, we suspect he may be discomfited by the favor you have shown Arbelan Drazharan."

"But she is his aunt!" Maia protested.

Berenar shook his head. "The Ceredada did not support her."

It took a moment for Maia to assimilate his meaning. "Perhaps the marquess is right to fear us," he said darkly.

"The current marquess, like his late father, is not notable for wisdom," Berenar said dryly, and Maia knew it for a reminder that the emperor, being surrounded by it so much of the time, had to be patient with folly. He would have to hope that Dach'osmin Ceredin took after her mother's line.

Certainly, there seemed to be nothing foolish about her when they met again, this time in the Untheileian to sign the marriage contract with all the court as their witnesses.

The marriage itself would not take place until spring, both for the auspices and because a wedding could not be thrown together at the last minute. Coronations, Csevet said, were much simpler, for there was nothing that had to be *negotiated*, nothing that was not mandated by five thousand years of tradition. Weddings, on the other hand, were nothing *but* negotiations, and—Csevet did not quite say but Maia could tell—on this front the Ceredada were proving difficult to negotiate with.

Signing the contract, with its attendant exchange of oath rings, was a legal ceremony and could be treated purely as business. That was clearly how Dach'osmin Ceredin saw it; she was well, but not lavishly, dressed in pale brown velvet, and her greeting when she came up on the dais was polite and not unamiable, but brisk, like a woman who had a more important appointment to get to.

She signed the contract without histrionics or fuss. In contrast to the perfect, impersonal penmanship of the letter she had sent, her signature was dense and ferociously energetic; he saw that she used the barzhad, the old warrior's alphabet, instead of the secretary's hand favored by the court and thus perforce all of the Ethuveraz who did not have the freedom to be idiosyncratic. His own signature looked like an unformed scrawl next to hers, but he tried to put the comparison from his mind.

The ceremony of the oath rings, like the ceremony of signing, was one that required no spoken words. The iron rings, as plain for an emperor as for a cowherd, were themselves the oath. He was awkward, sliding the ring on Dach'osmin Ceredin's thumb, but she helped, unobtrusively, and at least he did not drop the ring. She was much defter in her turn, and she was not afraid to take an uncompromising grip on his hand.

It was done and she curtsied and then was gone again. They had yet to exchange a total of more than fifty words.

He felt twisted up inside himself, intimidated by his empress, dreading the gossip that would inevitably begin to spread, wound about in self-contempt and the expectation of humiliation. Although he knew he ought to, knew he *needed* to, he could not meditate. Not with two other persons in the room, not with one. He was too self-conscious, too afraid of what would be said. Remembered, too painfully, that his nohecharei were not his friends. He could not bear the thought of their polite incomprehension any better than he could bear the thought of the court's scorn. At night, he lay twisted among the sheets of his great bed and wished for the peace and cool darkness of the vigil-chapel.

And he wished for it more and more as the weeks passed, and to the murmurs that Idra Drazhar had a right to the throne were added new murmurs, rumors, evil things that grew like weeds: the idea that somehow Maia himself had been responsible for the wreck of the *Wisdom of Choharo.*

It was nonsense—but such utter nonsense that it could not even be dealt with. It was not as if the truth of the matter—Maia's confinement at Edonomee, his lack of experience with intrigue and politics, the fact that he had not the slightest idea of how one would go about hiring someone to sabotage an airship—was not well known. It simply did not have enough force against another truth: that Maia, youngest and despised of Varenechibel's children, was now emperor. Even if he could have said, to those who whispered, that he did not wish to be emperor—and he could say no such thing, trapped as he was behind Edrehasivar's mask—he would not have been believed. No one in the Untheileneise Court would ever believe that one could wish *not* to be emperor. It was unthinkable.

The investigation into the Cetho Workers League continued (the Lord Chancellor assured the emperor), but was seemingly no nearer finding the murderer or murderers. Maia called Thara Celehar before him, demanded to know what progress he was making and why it was not more. He frightened Celehar, and was ashamed, later, of having done so, realizing in what a monstrous guise he must have presented himself to make any impression against Mer Celehar's apathy. But for all his browbeating, Celehar could tell him only that he was seeking, questioning the living and, to the best of his ability, the dead. "It is not a matter of machines,

Serenity," he said, white-faced but not apologizing, merely explaining. "It does not happen to schedule."

Csevet gave a small, meaningful cough then, and Maia recollected himself. He said, as gently and as quietly as he could, "Is there anything we can do, Mer Celehar, to help you in your search?"

"We are sorry, Serenity, but there is not. We can only work to the best of our abilities."

"We know. We . . ." Emperors did not apologize, and he remembered Idra saying that the one thing Varenechibel could not forgive was a witness to his mistakes. "We are sorry for implying that you were not so doing."

Celehar's eyes widened, and then he bowed his head, masking his reaction. "Serenity. We shall report to you as soon as we have any information."

"We thank you, Mer Celehar," Maia said, and sank wearily back in his chair as Celehar bowed and left the Michen'theileian. Maia had been emperor, had been Edrehasivar Zhas instead of simply Maia Drazhar, for over a month now. The business of ruling the Ethuveraz had become easier, though no less tedious. He knew the names of most, if not all of his courtiers, was beginning to have a sense of their factions, their allegiances and enmities. Whatever remarks Setheris might be making—and Maia could imagine their tenor only too well—he had not intruded his person on Maia's notice, and for that, Maia was (pathetically, he told himself) grateful. His nohecharei and edocharei did their duties; Csevet organized his emperor as if he had been born to the task. There was discontent, uneasy muttering, but indeed it would have been remarkable if there had not been— and Maia would have had to have the charisma he knew he lacked.

Chavar continued intractable, hostile, but he had not been openly insolent or so egregiously incompetent that Maia was forced to take notice. He still wanted to replace Chavar as Lord Chancellor, but he could not do it until he had a candidate in view, and he had none. Csevet and Chavar's secretaries had worked out an elaborate system to ensure that the emperor and the Lord Chancellor spoke to each other directly as little as possible, and that made it, if not comfortable, then at least bearable for the two of them to work together.

Nurevis Chavar was vastly more obliging than his father. Although his circle of friends barely overlapped with that of Csethiro Ceredin, Nurevis did his best not only to invite Dach'osmin Ceredin to his parties, but also to make the gesture look more neutral by inviting those friends they had in common, as well. Maia was grateful, but he also secretly wished Nurevis wouldn't bother. The Chavadeise public rooms had become a divided camp, with Dach'osmin Ceredin on one side and Osmin Duchenin on the other, and Maia felt miserably sure that he was welcome to neither. Osmin Duchenin made no secret of her anger at being passed over, and Dach'osmin Ceredin was cold and formal and possibly angry as well. When he was not near her, the laughter from her side of the room was uproarious, and he wondered if she, like Osmin Duchenin, was mocking him.

Maia tried to stick to neutral territory: Nurevis, and Nurevis's friends who had not two political thoughts to strike together among the lot of them. They ignored Maia benevolently, and he listened to their incomprehensible conversations about hunting and horses and clothes, and felt at least a little safer. Nurevis talked to him around his duties as host, but Maia was more and more grateful to Min Vechin, who was careful not to be seen to monopolize the emperor but who stopped by him periodically—frequently rescuing him from one or another of the courtiers determined to gain the emperor's favor by sheer force of verbiage—and talked lightly and without expecting more response than yes or no. It was restful and she was beautiful, and he thought she was flirting with him, although he had no idea of how to respond. She made him feel almost normal, almost as if he belonged.

And then one evening, after Min Vechin had drifted gracefully away for the third or fourth time, Dach'osmin Ceredin approached him. She curtsied in a sweep of bronze and red-purple, but she was frowning, and Maia was not entirely surprised that she opened on the attack.

But he *was* surprised when she said bluntly, "Serenity, Min Vechin is using you."

"Of course she is," Maia agreed.

Dach'osmin Ceredin's eyebrows shot upward, and Maia was unable to keep his bitterness pent decently behind his teeth. "How stupid you must believe us to be, to think we are unable to discern that for ourself. We thank you."

She looked as if she'd just been bitten by a cushion. "Serenity, we did not mean—" She stopped herself, and he watched as her colorless skin flushed a hard, painful red. "We beg your pardon. You are correct, and we ought not to have spoken so." He thought she would turn on her heel and flee—it was what he would have done—but she stood her ground, though she bowed her head for some moments. Maia let her be, his own anger having subsided as quickly as it had risen.

When Dach'osmin Ceredin raised her head, there was a light in her vivid eyes that hadn't been there before, and when she spoke, her speech was faster, more clipped, and rich in the animation it had previously lacked: "Since we have disgraced ourself already, we may as well ask: if you know she is using you, Serenity, why do you accept it?" She did not sound judgmental now, merely curious.

But Maia had no answer—at least, none that he could articulate. He said lamely, "She is very beautiful."

"And she has the sense not to frighten you," Dach'osmin Ceredin said, and Maia took a step back, wanting to protest her deduction, but unable to deny its truth.

"We should take lessons from her, we see," Dach'osmin Ceredin said, more than a little sourly, and Maia felt his shoulders hunch, his ears flatten. That tone of voice from Setheris had frequently preceded a blow or a vicious insult. But Dach'osmin Ceredin swept another curtsy—not as graceful as some of the other court ladies, but as precise and sharp as a swordmaster's salute—and said, "Serenity, we do not wish you to be frightened of us." And perhaps to prove the truth of her words, she turned and went back to her friends.

Maia did not stay long after that.

# 19

## Thara Celehar's Grief

The morning began inauspiciously with a letter from Csoru Zhasanai, which was delivered during breakfast.

Csoru, Maia had discovered, throve on the writing of letters, whether because she could take up infinitely more of the emperor's time that way, or for some other reason known only to herself. Maia did not allow himself to sigh; he opened the letter, ran a practiced eye down its contents—then, frowning, read it again more slowly.

"Serenity?" said Csevet, ever sensitive to signs of trouble.

"The widow empress," Maia said, "demands to know by what right we have seconded her kinsman to our service as our chaplain, why we have not, therefore, added him to the rolls of our household, and especially why we did not have the common courtesy—that word underlined heavily and, we suspect, in the widow empress's own hand—to inform her of our intentions." He raised his head, not entirely able to smooth out his frown, although Csevet did not deserve it. "We must speak to Mer Celehar before we reply to the widow empress's letter. Can an audience be fit in today?"

Csevet sorted among his papers. "Yes, Serenity, although it will mean curtailing your luncheon."

"So be it," Maia said, and gave Beshelar and Cala a flat glare, daring them to say anything. They did not, although they both looked as if they wished to.

The afternoon would belong to the Corazhas; Maia spent the morning giving audiences, considering petitions, trying to be the emperor although it still felt like a sham. He was glad to escape the Michen'theileian, although he did not find the Alcethmeret much more comfortable, and it was no refuge, for the emperor's business followed him there, with a page coming into the dining room to announce that Thara Celehar awaited his Serenity's pleasure.

"Pleasure" was so far from being the correct word that Maia was hard-pressed not to laugh in the poor child's earnest and uncomprehending face. "We shall receive him in the Tortoise Room," he said, gratefully abandoning food he had not tasted and had barely touched.

Celehar prostrated himself on the floor of the Tortoise Room when Maia came in.

"Rise, please, Mer Celehar," Maia said, at first astonished, and then remembering with unwelcome distinctness his interview with the Witness for the Dead earlier that week. "We have not brought you here to browbeat you."

"Serenity," Celehar said, getting to his feet, but not lifting his chin to look Maia in the face. And that was not like him.

"We wished to speak to you because we have received a rather peculiar letter from your kinswoman the widow empress—"

"And you wish to know why we lied to her."

Maia felt both Beshelar and Cala become transfixed

with alertness. One did not interrupt an emperor, and especially not in that impatient tone of voice. Maia, though he cared nothing for the interruption, was also watching Celehar closely, warily.

But he did not let that show in his voice when he said, "We have not accused you of lying."

"You should, Serenity. For we did lie to Csoru Zhasanai." Celehar still had not looked up, and his graveled, broken voice was unsteady, his ears flat.

There were many things Maia supposed he might have done or said, but only one that was not cruel. He said, very quietly, "Why?"

"Because we hoped that if we told Csoru Zhasanai that we were your chaplain, it would keep her from revealing to you the truth, which she holds over our head like a poisoned sword."

"Which truth?"

"The truth . . ." His voice cracked rawly. "The truth of why we renounced our prelacy."

Maia considered briefly, said, "Beshelar, will you ask of Mer Aisava, please, how late we may be before the Corazhas will not forgive us?" He met Beshelar's eyes as he said it, saw his meaning received and understood.

"Serenity," Beshelar said, bowed, and departed.

Celehar had the knuckles of one hand pressed hard against his mouth.

Maia said, "We understand that you do not wish to tell this truth to us, but . . ." A deep breath, and a conscious, almost painful shedding of formality: "Wouldst thou tell me?"

The silence held in the Tortoise Room for five thunderous beats of Maia's heart. Celehar's head came up, finally, and he said, "Serenity, we do not deserve the honor you would do us."

"I do not speak of honor," Maia said with something that was almost exasperation. "I speak of compassion.

Thou hast shown great compassion, to both living and dead, and I would show compassion to thee, to the best of my perhaps small ability. If thou wilt tell me, I shall neither tell anyone nor use it against thee."

Celehar looked at Cala, who said, "I, too, shall tell no one. I do swear it."

"The story is not so great as the gift you give me," Celehar said, looking from Cala to Maia. "It is simply told: I convicted the man I loved of the murder of the woman I hated."

Silence again. Maia did not know what to say, and from the look on his face, neither did Cala. But into their silence, Celehar said, "His name was Evru Dalar. The woman was his wife, Oseian Dalaran. She was . . . When I say that I hated her, I do not say it lightly, and I do not say it because I loved Evru. Although watching someone I loved being treated as she treated him—" His voice thickened into nothing. This time Maia did not even search for words, understanding that Celehar needed to speak.

"We were lovers, Evru and I," Celehar said. "The Archprelate has given me forgiveness, and I am still sanctified. But I am not . . . How can I call myself a prelate when I could not help him?"

Cala said, "Ulis is not a—"

"*I know that.*" Celehar stopped himself. "But I could not help him. And the hierophant of the town, knowing that we were lovers and considering it an abomination, would not help him. And so, in fear and hatred and utmost despair, he killed his wife and flung her body in a dry well, hoping it would not be found, and no questions would be asked. But Oseian Dalaran's family was strong in that town, and they did not rest until they had found her, with hunting cats and mongooses following her scent, and then they brought her body to the Ulimeire. To me.

"I was the Witness for the Dead. I could not lie. And the answer was so clear. She had seen her murderer's face, and she had known it well. They asked, and I answered, and Evru was beheaded. He did not even curse me when he died. He had never expected me to value him more than my calling."

Celehar turned away, both hands pressed against his face. He said, muffled, reverting to the formal "you" instead of merely the plural, "You can imagine how filthy the story becomes when it is told by . . ."

*Csoru*, he did not say. "By someone to whom it is nothing but scandal," Cala said gently.

"Yes," Maia said. "We understand why you did not want anyone else to tell us this truth."

A dry, broken chuckle. "Serenity, we did not wish you to be told this truth at all. We *are* marnis. If we had not resigned our prelacy, we doubt we would have been allowed to keep it. The Archprelate is a man of generous mind, but many of the great hierophants feel as our hierophant in Aveio did. We do not blame them."

Maia was not sure how he himself felt about marnei. He had never met one before, knew nothing of them save what Setheris had said, most of it unflattering at the least. He had learned, perforce, the trick of putting something aside to think about later. For now, it would have to be enough that Celehar had done no harm to anyone that Maia knew of, and that he had, however unhappily and at such great cost, held to his duty over his unnatural love. And he was the Witness for the Dead, and as such, the emperor needed him.

"We cannot take you into our household," Maia said. "For it would be said that our favor influenced your findings. But we will speak to Csoru Zhasanai if you wish it."

"Serenity. There is nothing, we fear, that can profitably be said. If you will but assure the widow empress that you command us, and in full knowledge of our unfortunate past, it is more than we have any right to ask from you. We should not have lied."

A painful admission for a man to make, and to a boy fifteen years his junior. Maia said carefully, "Insofar as there was a trespass against us, we forgive it. We leave you to make your own peace with the widow empress."

"Serenity," Celehar said. He prostrated himself again, and as he rose, said, "We are your most grateful and loyal servant."

He left with his head up, and Maia felt obscurely better.

## 20

### The Proposal of the
### Clocksmiths of Zhaö

In truth, Maia was not sorry to be late to the Corazhas. Even with Lord Berenar's help—and Berenar was a better and more patient teacher than Setheris could ever have imagined being—Maia felt as if he were trying to dam the Istandaärtha with a handful of pebbles. He knew *some* of the history of the Ethuveraz, but his knowledge could hardly be called systematic, and it was in no way a sufficient foundation for the fifty years of policy decisions that Berenar was really trying to teach him to follow. Even with the progress he'd made, he still understood half or less of the Corazhas' debates, and asking questions was only getting harder—he felt as if he were accusing Berenar with his ignorance, and his increased consciousness of the interwoven responsibilities of the Witnesses meant that he knew how valuable their time was and how much of it was wasted when he asked for an explanation of something everyone else in the room already understood.

He had stopped asking.

He was ashamed, and angry with himself, but the foreknowledge of another humiliation was like a sword, and he could not force himself to fall on it. He had to trust—he *did* trust—that Csevet would tell him if there was something wrong.

In the middle of an impenetrable debate between the Witness for Foreigners and the Witness for the Parliament about the northern borders, a page brought Maia a note. He recognized Nurevis's paper and signet before he opened it, and was aware of a slight, guilty tingle of pleasure, enhanced by the deliberate withdrawal of his attention from the Corazhas in order to read what Nurevis had written.

It was an invitation to a private dinner with dancing to follow, and Nurevis had added in his own hand:

> *We know Your Serenity does not deign to dance, but we thought perhaps your evening's entertainment would be sufficiently assured by the presence of Min Vechin. She says she is most eager to see you again.*

Blushing, partly with embarrassment and partly with delight, Maia wrote across the bottom, *We will be pleased to attend,* and handed it back to the page to deliver.

After the Corazhas finally closed, the issue between the Witness for Foreigners and the Witness for the Parliament still unresolved, Maia made his way to the Alcethmeret to change from court robes to something suitable for an informal gathering like Nurevis's.

But he was only just past the great grilles of the Alcethmeret when Beshelar lengthened his stride to catch up with him and said, "Serenity, you must tell Osmer Chavar not to send you party invitations when the Corazhas is in session. It reflects not well on you or on him."

"Must we?" Maia stopped, turned to face him. "And

who are you, Lieutenant Beshelar, to tell us how we must behave toward our friends?"

"*Is* Osmer Chavar your friend, Serenity? We ourself would not be quick to say so. And you must understand that favoritism toward the Lord Chancellor's son—"

"Means nothing! Nurevis does not tell us what to do—nor has so much as asked for a favor. We realize, Lieutenant, that we do not measure up to your idea of an emperor, but do us the justice to believe that we are not entirely *stupid*!"

Beshelar actually went back a pace. "Serenity, we did not mean—"

"We know what you meant." And without giving Beshelar another chance to speak, Maia resumed his progress toward his rooms and his waiting edocharei. He did not look to see what Cala thought of his ugly display of temper. *If wilt not be my friend, canst not speak to me of how friends behave.* He was glad—selfishly, vindictively, childishly glad—that the nohecharei's shift changed while Avris and Esha were debating the rival merits of amber and cloisonné beads, and that when he emerged, it was Dazhis and Telimezh waiting for him.

The company in Nurevis's suite was select; Maia had come to be tolerably familiar, if not comfortable, with Nurevis's set, and he was not thrown utterly into confusion by the necessity of making conversation with those next to him at the table. It was still not easy, and he suspected unhappily that his dinner partners found him alternately boring and ridiculous. But he did not disgrace himself. When the floor was cleared for dancing, Min Vechin approached him and, after the initial exchange of courtesies, said, "Serenity, why do you not dance?"

His face heated. "We do not know how."

"No? Truly, your guardian must have been terribly strict."

Maia tried to imagine Setheris teaching him to dance and said, perhaps too quickly, "There was no one with whom we might have danced in any event."

Min Vechin's beautiful eyebrows drew together in a frown. "It sounds to us as if you had no pleasures at all."

He looked down at his hands. Their ugly knuckles were half obscured with rings of silver and amethyst, silver and jet, and under Esha's care, his nails were growing long enough to be worth lacquering; except for the color, they almost didn't look like his hands at all.

"Serenity," said Min Vechin, "we apologize. We did not mean—"

She was within an inch of going down on her knees, and he said quickly, "You did nothing wrong. We were merely . . . discomfited by your acumen." And when, startled, she met his eyes, he managed to give her a smile, although he knew it was crooked. "Osmer Chavar said you wished particularly to speak to us?"

She disclaimed instantly, her hands moving in a graceful, fluttering gesture. "It is of no importance, Serenity."

Ordinarily, he would not have pursued the matter, but he was desperate to sink the topic of the emperor's pathetic childhood. "Please. Is there some service we can do you?"

"It is not for *us*, Serenity," she said, and he felt a pang of disappointment. "But we have a sister, most beloved, who would seek an audience with you. She is an apprentice in the Clocksmiths' Guild of Zhaö. They have presented a proposal for a bridge—"

"Across the Istandaärtha. We remember it."

"The Corazhas will not hear them, but Avro says the design will work and it is very important, and not just for the clocksmiths." She was as animated as he had ever seen her, and he wondered if it was the bridge or the sister that brought forth this passion. "They know they cannot get a formal audience without the approval of the Corazhas, but we thought if you simply came to meet our sister, privately, this evening—"

"Tonight?" Maia said, both startled and more than a little displeased.

"When else may we be sure Your Serenity is free of obligations?" she said unanswerably.

Maia considered, and he tried to consider carefully. Although he did not like the way Min Vechin was trading on his attraction to her, he reminded himself that it was he who had pushed her, and thus he had no one to blame but himself if the favor she wanted was not the favor of his hopeful imaginings. And putting that aspect of the matter aside, he could not help but realize that this was an opportunity for him as much as for Min Vechin's sister. He had wished to know more about the proposed bridge, and he had no one to ask whom he could trust to understand the mechanical aspects any better than he did himself.

"Very well," he said, and pretended he did not feel a rush of warmth when she smiled at him. "Now?"

"If Your Serenity pleases," she said, as if this were all somehow his idea. Maia beckoned to his nohecharei and followed her, first to take leave of Nurevis and then out of the room. Maia was careful not to meet Nurevis's eyes more than briefly, and he tried, though without much success, not to think about the rumors that would have spread throughout the Untheileneise Court by midnight—rumors that would be all the more embarrassing for having not a shred of truth in them.

Graceful and self-assured as a swan, Min Vechin led him to one of the court's many public receiving rooms. Maia had never been in one before—except maybe when his mother died? he couldn't remember clearly enough—and he noticed that while everything was clean and in good repair, the room was austere to the point of hostility, without any decoration save the graceful arch of the windows. It was also extremely chilly.

Min Vechin's sister bolted to her feet as she saw them, and Maia watched her realize that the skinny goblin boy behind her sister had to be the emperor. She bowed—not at all gracefully—and he also saw her kick the ankle of the man seated beside her. His bow was even clumsier, as he was clutching an awkward sheaf of papers to his narrow chest, but Maia did not think he had any intent to offend; he was still blinking dazedly when he straightened, as if he had been lost in thought.

Min Vechin performed introductions. Her sister was Merrem Halezho; the man was Mer Halezh—not her husband, but her husband's elder brother. He was also a member of the Clocksmiths' Guild, of a much higher rank than Merrem Halezho, and although he was reluctant to put himself forward, Maia gathered that the design of the bridge was largely his doing. Certainly, he explained both the scheme for bridging the Istandaärtha and the hydraulic system that would enable river traffic to continue much more clearly and confidently than the Witness for the Parliament had been able to, and he was not stymied by any question Maia put to him. In fact, he seemed delighted; they ended up kneeling on the floor while Mer Halezh drew diagrams of cofferdams and waterwheels on the backs of his plans. Maia glanced over once and saw both Dazhis and Telimezh looking shocked, but neither of them had Beshelar's self-righteous confidence, and they made no verbal protest. Merrem Halezho, kneeling next to her brother-in-law, knew a great deal about traffic on the river, and she explained the system they had already worked out so that barges from Ezho would be able to reach Cairado even in the thick of construction. She was the one who showed him exactly where the clocksmiths proposed building their bridge and explained their reasoning. Maia thought they had chosen well, although he was uneasily aware that he knew rather less about the politics of the situation than Merrem Halezho did.

Min Vechin took no part in the conversation, seeming content to sit on one of the padded benches and observe. Maia feared she must be bored, but he reminded himself that if she was, it was her own doing. And it was not as if this evening would make her *less* likely to want to . . . to do things of which he had only the vaguest understanding. Setheris had told him only as much as was necessary to be sure he fathered no bastards at Edonomee, and there had never been anyone else he could ask.

*Nor is there now,* he thought, flinching away from the thought of having that conversation with Csevet or Cala. Or Beshelar. *Perhaps thou shouldst have told Csevet to find a widow for thee to wed, so that at least* someone *would know what to do on thy wedding night.* That thought was even worse, and Maia shook his head sharply, realizing that his mind had wandered entirely away from the clocksmiths' bridge.

"We beg your pardon," he said to Mer Halezh and Merrem Halezho. "We are very tired, and we need to think on all that you have told us."

"Of course, Serenity," Mer Halezh said. "We are liable to get carried away in our enthusiasm. We did not mean to—"

"We have found it all most interesting," Maia said, interrupting because he did not want Mer Halezh to apologize for having both genius and passion. "But— you understand that we can do nothing ourself? That any decision must be agreed upon by the Corazhas?"

"Oh, yes, Serenity," Merrem Halezho assured him as the three of them stood up again. "We wished only to make our case that the matter *should* be decided by the Corazhas and not merely . . . Nedaö, what is the word?"

"*Veklevezhek*," Min Vechin said. "It is a goblin word, and it means to decide what to do about a prisoner by staking him below the tideline while you argue."

"And *that* is what we wish to avoid," Merrem Halezho said. "We know that the Corazhas frequently practices *veklevezhek*, for if they cannot agree whether to hear a matter—the matter goes unheard."

"Yes, we see," Maia said, thinking of the Witness for the Judiciate shouting down the Witness for the Parliament. "We cannot guarantee anything."

"No," said Mer Halezh, "but you have listened, and we thank you for that." He bowed and Merrem Halezho bowed and Min Vechin rose to sweep a flawless curtsy. She approached him and murmured, "If Your Serenity wishes, we could return to the Alcethmeret with you."

Maia locked up like sabotaged clockwork, as if Min Vechin's words were a handful of sand. He understood exactly what she meant, understood that there had been an implied bargain that he, in his foolish romantic dreaming, would never have thought of pursuing. But Min Vechin was offering.

She was offering, but Maia had no idea how to take. He cringed from the thought of his own awkwardness and knew he would never be able to go through with it—and that would be far more humiliating than simply turning her down now.

The silence had grown long enough to be uncomfortable, but he managed to say, "No, thank you," in a steady, unbothered voice.

Her ears flattened, in surprise and maybe a little offense. "Serenity? You do not wish—?"

"No," Maia said. "Thank you, Min Vechin." He turned away from her with what he hoped was decisiveness rather than petulance. He gave Telimezh the armful of diagrams to carry and returned to the Alcethmeret to sleep alone, except for those who guarded his sleep.

# 21

## *Mer Celehar Goes North*

Maia's dreams were unpleasant, and they lingered about him all morning, although he did his best to attend to the business of the court. Over luncheon, which he pushed around his plate and ate very little of, his dreams like a bad taste in his mouth, he gathered his courage and said, "Csevet, had our father any friends?"

Csevet's teacup clinked against the saucer when he set it down. "Friends, Serenity?"

Maia had nerved himself to ask because Dazhis and Telimezh were still on duty, which they would not be by dinnertime. He could not have raised the subject in front of Cala and Beshelar, who would know so precisely why he was asking. "You must have heard the word before," he said, Setheris to the life. He winced, but Csevet was already answering.

"We beg pardon, Serenity. We were not expecting the question." He cleared his throat. "The Emperor Varenechibel did not generally seek close relationships outside the immediate family circle, so we cannot think of anyone who would fit that description. Perhaps before he came to the throne?" Csevet was frowning, clearly baffled by the question but anxious to help.

"No, we meant when he was emperor. Thank you."

"You are welcome, Serenity," Csevet said, still watching him with some concern, and Maia forced a smile he did not feel.

"We were merely curious. It is no matter."

"The Emperor Varevesena your grandfather had many friends," Csevet offered. "Indeed, he was known for his kindness and generosity to those close to him."

*As opposed to the mass of his subjects,* Maia finished mentally. Setheris had had stories about Varevesena. But he did not want to rebuff Csevet's attempt to help by saying so, which made him perversely grateful that they were interrupted.

The interruption was a page boy in the livery of the Drazhadeise; Maia recognized him: the boy Csoru Zhasanai had sent that first day, the boy Maia had embarrassed. He looked no happier now, and he knelt as if he wished he could simply keep going straight through the floor.

And he was carrying a letter.

Maia did not sigh in exasperation, but said as gently as he could, "You have a letter for us?"

"Yes, Serenity." The boy stood and offered it, carefully not looking any higher than the tabletop. "Csoru Zhasanai dem—that is, she requests the favor of an immediate reply."

Maia appreciated the improvised emendation, although he doubted Csoru would have approved in the slightest. He opened the letter and scanned the contents—and was not feigning bewilderment when he said, "We do not understand. What exactly has occurred in Csoru Zhasanai's household?"

"Serenity." The boy gulped. "Mer Celehar is gone, and the zhasanai says it must be your doing."

"Mer Celehar is *gone*? As in vanished? Does Csoru Zhasanai suspect us of having murdered him?" Maia despaired of himself; what was it about this boy that brought out Setheris in him?

"N-no, Serenity. He had Neraiis, who waits on him, pack a bag, and he said he was going to Thu-Athamar. But he did not seek permission of the zhasanai before he left and . . ."

There, Maia thought uncharitably, was the actual cause of Csoru's distress—not that her kinsman was missing but that he had not asked her permission first. He himself was more interested in another part of the puzzle. "Thu-Athamar? Why would he . . ." But the boy could not possibly know, and Maia was learning that it did not behoove an emperor to ask rhetorical questions. "Csevet, would you check our correspondence, please? It occurs to us that, although he did not inform the zhasanai, Mer Celehar may possibly have sent us a pneumatic."

Csevet murmured, "Serenity," and slipped out of the room, leaving Maia faced with the nervous and unhappy page boy.

*It is no more than thy deserving,* he said to himself mockingly. *Thou wert glad of the interruption.* He considered a moment, but there was really only one thing to do. "What is your name?"

"*My*—I mean—*our* name, Serenity?"

*We know everyone else in the room.* It was exactly what Setheris would have said; Maia could hear the bite in his voice. "Yes, please."

"Oh!" The boy made a visible effort to pull himself together. "Cora, Serenity. Cora Drazhar."

"We are kinsmen, then," Maia said, and Cora flushed an alarming red.

"Only very distantly, Serenity."

"Yes?"

A bare flicker of a glance—pale blue eyes, not the

Drazhadeise gray. "Our great-great-grandfather was the youngest son of Edrevechelar the Sixteenth."

Making them third cousins in the Drazhada—Cora was closer kin to him than Setheris, who was a second cousin but of another house. "Have you served Csoru Zhasanai long?"

Cora's chin came up. "We served the late emperor," he said with unmistakable defiance, as if he thought Maia would have him beheaded for it. "But he was . . . he was displeased with us when he went to Amalo and bid us stay with the empress. We would gladly have died with him."

Here was another who felt more grief for Varenechibel than Maia could imagine. He hesitated, knowing his next question could all too easily be misconstrued, but he had to ask: "Are you happy in the service of Csoru Zhasanai?"

Another pale blue flicker of a glance, but Cora seemed to discern that Maia was not trying to lay claim to his service. "We are well enough, Serenity, though we thank you for asking. It is only until the spring equinox, for we have been accepted as a novice in the Athmaz'are."

"Good," Maia said with quite sincere approval, for if Cora *had* been unhappy, he would have had to do something about it, although he had not the faintest idea what.

Cora actually smiled back, and then Csevet returned, bearing one of the long narrow envelopes used especially for the pneumatic system. "The operators tell us, Serenity, that this came from the widow empress's station just after you left the Alcethmeret this morning."

Maia took the envelope. "We recognize Mer Celehar's handwriting." He broke the seal and extracted the single sheet, reading it far more carefully than he had read Csoru's.

It had clearly been written in haste and some considerable disturbance of spirit:

> *Serenity*—
> *We have been granted a dream of Ulis, which has shown us that which we should already have known: answers are in Amalo, not Cetho. We leave at once, for the airship to Thu-Athamar unmoors in less than an hour.*
> > *Yours obediently,*
> > *Thara Celehar*

"Mer Celehar's notions of obedience are most individual," Maia said wryly.

"Serenity," said Csevet, "we understand that this is most important, and we do not in any way wish to rush you, but—"

The warning note in his voice had made Maia look quite automatically at the clock. "Merciful goddesses, the *time*! Cora, we cannot write the zhasanai now. Will you tell her, please, that . . . oh dear."

His dismay and bafflement were real, but they were also offered to Cora, as much as to Csevet, as both apology and a sign of trust. Cora said, "We could tell her, Serenity, that Mer Celehar wrote to you and said he was very sorry to leave without speaking to Csoru Zhasanai, but he did not wish to wake her. All the zhasanai's household know she never rises before noon unless she must."

"He seems to have been in a terrible hurry," Maia said hopefully.

"Neraiis said so, too."

"And he says he had a dream of Ulis, so really, it *could* not wait."

"No, Serenity," Cora said, sounding shocked.

"You do not mind?"

This time, Cora's smile lit his face. "Serenity, we would not deceive Csoru Zhasanai about anything that would harm her, but this harms no one. And perhaps she will not be so very angry at Mer Celehar when he returns."

"Thank you, Cora," Maia said.

Cora bowed, and finally his movements had the grace that Maia expected from someone raised at court. "We are pleased to serve you, Serenity," he said, and Maia thought maybe he meant it.

# 22

## The Bridge over the Upazhera

Maia had fully intended to bring the matter of the Clocksmiths' bridge up with Csevet, but it was Csevet who spoke first. He approached Maia in the gardens, saying directly, "Serenity, in the Tortoise Room there are papers relating to the bridge proposed by the Clocksmiths' Guild of Zhaö, papers which we do not remember being given to us. Do you know how they came there?"

It was ridiculous to feel like a child detected in wrongdoing; Csevet wasn't going to cane him. Maia straightened his shoulders out of their automatic guilty hunch and said, "They were given us by a Mer Halezh of the guild."

"*When?*" said Csevet, not in anger but in pure astonishment.

*I have done nothing wrong,* Maia said firmly to himself. "The night of Nurevis Chavar's last dancing party. We, ah, have been meaning to speak to you about it."

But Csevet was not to be distracted. "How did a clocksmith gain an invitation to one of Osmer Chavar's parties?"

"He didn't. Min Vechin's sister is his sister-in-law, and a guild apprentice herself."

"And Min Vechin got them into the party?"

"No," Maia said, feeling guiltier and guiltier, although he was still sure he had done nothing wrong. "We went to meet them. In a public receiving room—there was no impropriety."

Csevet probably hadn't even heard that anxious rider. He was staring at Maia in undisguised horror. "You *went* to *meet* them? Have you run *mad*?"

Maia retreated a step, but in the same instant Csevet began apologizing, almost frantically; he prostrated himself on the path before Maia could stop him.

"Please get up," Maia said. "Please. You have done nothing wrong."

Csevet did stand up again, but he was red with mortification. "Your Serenity is very kind, but we should not have raised our voice to you. You would be entirely justified in dismissing us from our post."

"Now it's you who have run mad. We shall do no such thing. And we are sorry to have upset you, but we thought it the right thing to do."

"Serenity . . ." Csevet stopped, took a breath, started again. "Serenity, we do not doubt either your ethics or your concern, but there are *reasons* it is difficult to gain an audience with the emperor. And it does no one any good for you to decide those reasons do not matter."

"We know that," Maia said, but continued obstinately, "The Corazhas refused to hear them, so they could not even petition for a formal audience with us. How else were we to gain the information we needed to decide if the Corazhas was correct?"

Csevet did not bother with arguing for the wisdom and infallibility of the Corazhas. "Serenity, that is what secretaries are *for.*"

"Yes, but we dislike being dependent on another person's judgment of what information we need." He held up a hand to forestall Csevet's protest. "Yes, we know it is necessary lest the government of the Ethuveraz come to a standstill. But this bridge—the idea is so important, so *new*, and withal, so exceedingly contentious, that we would have felt ourself to be most culpably remiss if we had not taken this opportunity."

Csevet, unpersuaded, said, "You must promise us not to do so again."

"We cannot promise that."

"At least—Serenity, *please*—promise you will come to us first. Give us a chance to do our job."

Put like that, Csevet's position was entirely reasonable. "Yes," Maia said. "We promise."

"*Thank you*," said Csevet. "Serenity, you have a dispute to hear in ten minutes." He bowed and went back inside the Alcethmeret, leaving Maia to follow more slowly, trying to gather the armor of Edrehasivar VII about himself again.

The dispute was tedious in the extreme, a matter of rents and water rights and commonholding between the town of Nelozho; the estate of a minor noble house, the Dorashada; and the Prince of Thu-Cethor, the involvement of this last being the reason the emperor had to arbitrate. The representatives for all three sides had detailed maps and histories; while Maia found many instances where two of the three agreed, he found no instances where all three agreed, and when two agreed, it was never the same two from point to point. What was worse was that this ultimately rather petty difference had been festering for so long that it had become a cause for considerable and serious hostility; the Witness for Nelozho Township and the representative of the Dorashada did not make eye contact with each other at all, each speaking past the other as if their enemy were not there, and the representative of Thu-Cethor seemed to feel that the entire issue was an insult to the Cethoreise prince and infuriated everyone—including, after a remarkably short span of time, the emperor—whenever he opened his mouth. By the time each representative had spoken and the history of the judicial proceedings had been summarized, Maia had a splitting headache and wanted nothing more than to tell them all to stop wasting his time, their time, and the time of innumerable secretaries and judges, and settle their damnable petty squabble like adults.

He bit the words back and looked next to the Witnesses *vel ama*, the Witnesses who gave voice to the literally voiceless; there was one for the river and one for the game preserve that had become embroiled in the dispute. Neither Witness spoke at length. They were clearly very junior Witnesses; both of them looked despairing and overwhelmed. If the representatives of town and manor had not been so biased, they could probably have done a better job of Witnessing than these two.

Maia requested a new map, one without lines drawn on it by anyone but the cartographer. The Witness for Nelozho and the representatives of Thu-Cethor and the Dorashada all became very silent and wide-eyed; he couldn't tell if it was trepidation or outrage. The Witnesses *vel ama* began to look a little less squashed. On a clean map, without the dotted lines and shaded areas and bewildering arrows, the situation was much plainer.

"This tributary of the Cethora . . ."

"The Upazhera, Serenity," said its Witness.

Maia nodded. Just as the great rivers of the Ethuveraz—the Cethora, the Evresartha, the Athamara, the Tetara, and the Istandaärtha—were considered in law the property of the emperor, so the waterways in each principate were considered the property of the prince. In this case, that aspect of elvish law contributed to the problem, as the Upazhera ran through part, though not all, of the disputed territory. The solution proposed by the Dorashada was for the emperor to grant the Upazhera to them along with the surrounding land. It was by far the most straightforward of the various schemes put forward, but Maia thought it showed an unbecomingly greedy and encroaching spirit, since if nothing else was clear to him, the fact that a significant portion of the disputed land had originally belonged to Nelozho Township was very clear indeed.

On the other hand, it was also clear that the town had been grazing their sheep on a pasture that belonged to the Dorashada, for which the Dorashada had not been fairly compensated. And both sides had been poaching in the Veremnet Preserve as well as treating the Upazhera as if it were commonheld. The representative of Thu-Cethor had been indignantly eloquent on the subject of waterwheels, and fish farms, and bridges that disappeared whenever the prince's circuit rider came to Nelozho, and the Witness for the Upazhera had nodded dispirited agreement.

And, on yet a third hand which he did not have, he was not pleased with the conduct of the Cethoreise government, either. Someone—what was worse, more than one someone—must have been bribed at some point in the past for the official paperwork to be in the peculiar state it was in, and any number of persons seemed to have been turning a blind eye to the behavior of either Nelozho or the Dorashada as struck their particular fancy.

Maia pinched the bridge of his nose and stared dolefully at the map. The only thing he could be sure of was that any decision he reached would make at least one of the disputants unhappy. As he traced the course of the Upazhera with one finger, that thought abruptly upended itself: *If I must make at least one of them unhappy, and if it cannot be determined that any one disputant deserves to be made unhappy more than the other two, then the only answer is to make* all *of them unhappy.* And if he was not trying to juggle three sets of competing and conflicting demands, the solution was easy.

He straightened his shoulders and said, "We reject all of the claims brought before us."

That won him a chorus of yelps and protests. He waited until they had died away and said, as if they had not happened at all, "The Veremnet and the Upazhera belong to the Prince of Thu-Cethor, as ever they have." The Witnesses *vel ama* bowed gratefully. "On the other hand, there is no evidence that Thu-Cethor has any claim or right beyond that, whereas the claims between the Dorashada and Nelozho Township are so hopelessly entangled that we see no point in considering them further. We are greatly displeased that *anyone* has sought to use this unhappy conflict to enrich their holdings." He glared at all three representatives impartially. "All land in the territory under dispute that is east of the Upazhera we rule belongs to Nelozho Township in common. All land in the territory under dispute that is west of the Upazhera we rule belongs to the Dorashada. We stipulate that Nelozho Township and the Dorashada will work out a fair agreement, acceptable to both sides, for the use of the pasture called the Forty Reach, an agreement that they will present, written, signed, and witnessed, to a representative of the Prince of Thu-Cethor by Winternight. We further stipulate that the Dorashada and Nelozho Township will form a cooperative militia to patrol the Veremnet against the poachers and bandits which apparently haunt it. And finally, we stipulate that the Dorashada and Nelozho Township in cooperation, each bearing an equal share of the cost, will build a bridge over the Upazhera; each will appoint a toll collector, and the toll monies will *not* go to Thu-Cethor, but first to the maintenance of the bridge and second to the relief of the poor of Nelozho. Both these endeavors are to be in place and demonstrated to the prince's circuit rider before midsummer."

He paused, raising his eyebrows at the Witnesses *vel ama*. They, unlike the disputants, had the right to protest his judgment; he was not surprised to find that neither of them was inclined to do so.

"Very well. If any of these stipulations are not met, or if this matter is ever brought to our attention again, all of the disputed territory, including the Veremnet and the Upazhera, will be forfeit to the imperial crown. Have we made ourself clear?"

Representatives, Witnesses, and secretaries alike were suddenly very eager not to meet his eyes. He waited long enough to be sure no one was going to attempt to argue and then, very gratefully, spoke the closing formula: "As we have spoken, so will it be." The emperor's word was law.

He did not bolt out of the Michen'theileian, although he wanted to. He waited while the representatives and Witnesses bowed their way out, followed by their secretaries; waited while his own secretaries—merciful goddesses, there was a *flock* of them, and he didn't know their names—cleared the tables and bowed and departed, except of course for Csevet, who came up on the dais and said, "Serenity, you have"

"No," Maia said. "We have not. We are going back to the Alcethmeret, where we will see no one outside our own household until tomorrow morning, and as few of them as possible. We have a sick headache, and so we bid you tell anyone who may be concerned."

Csevet looked as if he were going to argue, but he must have seen that Maia meant it, for he bowed and said, "Yes, Serenity."

"Thank you," Maia said more fervently than he had wished to.

He maintained a decorous pace through the halls of the Untheileneise Court, though it was fortunate that no one attempted to stop him, for he would not even have slowed. In the Alcethmeret, with the great grilles closed behind him, he felt some portion of his tension recede and was able to speak to his edocharei without snarling as they divested him of his jewels and formal robes, and it was in a less viciously unhappy frame of mind that he descended again to the Tortoise Room and thought suddenly, prompted by nothing, between one step and the next, *If thou canst wrangle townships and petty lords and the representative of the Prince of Thu-Cethor and canst deliver a judgment they do not like—for in sooth it did not kill thee—then thou canst surely deal with the Corazhas.*

He was not stupid and he was not incapable. He remembered the moment when his thoughts had inverted themselves—that shift from not being *able* to please everyone to not *trying*—and the way that change had enabled him to see past the maneuverings and histrionics of the representatives to the deeper structures of the problem; it was the same with the Corazhas. The surface of their words, which intimidated him so much he had all but given up, was not what he needed to see.

*Maybe I* can *do this,* he thought, and he slept better that night than he had expected to.

He began to ask Berenar a different kind of question, began to pay better attention in meetings of the Corazhas to the patterns of the arguments. The Witness for the Judiciate, the oldest of the seven, was contrary and cantankerous; he would disagree reflexively with any proposition put forward by the Witness for the Parliament, but he deeply disliked the Witness for Foreigners, and was liable to become captious when forced into too close an alliance. The Witness for the Prelacy was Chavar's creature, even more than the Witness for Foreigners; Lord Bromar, the Witness for Foreigners, might share Chavar's politics, but Maia came to realize that he shared them out of principle, not out of any thirst for power. The Witness for the Athmaz'are rarely said anything and even more rarely took sides; he often looked as if he were not attending, but none of the traps laid for him by the Witness for the Universities and the Witness for the Prelacy ever succeeded in discomfiting him.

Lord Isthanar, the Witness for the Universities, was friends with the Witness for the Judiciate and could be counted on to follow Lord Pashavar's lead whenever university policy was not sufficient guidance. Of all of them, he was the one who seemed to Maia to be most aptly confined by the official limits of his position, for it was clear he had not had an independent thought in decades, and aside from his status as Corazheise Witness, he was not a powerful man even in the University of Cetho. This put him in sharp distinction to and frequently at jealous odds with Berenar, who was in fact one of the five Lords Treasurer, only one step down from the Lord Chancellor. Berenar, who continued to come regularly to teach the emperor about his empire's political history, had made it clear that there was no sycophancy in what he was doing. He expected no favors in return, and he had not the slightest hesitation in disagreeing with his emperor, either in private or in the Verven'theileian. But he was never offended when Maia's opinion did not march with his own. Of all the Corazhas, Berenar was the one Maia trusted most to be able to see beyond the self-interest and rhetoric that filled the Verven'theileian like fog. And he thought it was not an accident that Lord Berenar so frequently supported Lord Deshehar, the Witness for the Parliament.

Deshehar, who would hold his position only so long as he held his seat in the Parliament, was the outsider among the Corazhas; he was most often the bearer of new ideas and unpopular opinions, and Maia began more and more to dread the day when he decided he had put up with the Corazhas long enough and resigned, for it was hard to imagine any replacement bringing so much enthusiasm to such a thankless role. But Lord Deshehar seemed happy to fight with Lord Pashavar and Lord Bromar, and never seemed in the slightest discouraged by his defeats. Of all of them, he was the one who did not need persuading to listen to the proposal brought by the Clocksmiths' Guild of Zhaö—the only matter that had reached the Corazhas since the beginning of Maia's reign that he felt confident in his own knowledge of—having championed their cause in the first place. Berenar would listen, Maia knew, and he thought the Witness for the Athmaz'are would, as well, although it was always difficult to know Sonevet Athmaza's mind. The Witness for the Prelacy would oppose it because Chavar would oppose it, and Maia could see nothing to be done about that. Lord Bromar would also oppose it, but Maia thought he could be shouted down if a sufficient number of the others were in agreement. It was not, after all, as if he would be agreeing to do anything more than listen, and Maia could point that out as many times as necessary. The Witness for the Universities would follow Lord Pashavar, although he might be baffled at least into silence by evocation of the ideals of education and the pursuit of knowledge. No, the true problem was Lord Pashavar.

Diffidently, he asked Csevet for advice; he could not ask Berenar—that was too uncomfortably close to conspiracy—and he had no one else to ask.

"We will be happy to give you any advice we can," Csevet said at once, and Maia told him the whole, starting with Lord Deshehar and ending with Lord Pashavar. Csevet listened intently, as he always did, and when Maia had finished, he said, "We cannot fault either your observations or your reasoning, Serenity. It is Lord Pashavar you need to sway."

"Have you any suggestions?"

Csevet made a face. "Lord Pashavar is very difficult. Almost, we would suggest waiting for him to die, but that could take years."

Maia was surprised into a snort of laughter. Csevet grinned back momentarily, then said, "Our strategy has heretofore relied on his deep dislike of Lord Chavar, but that will not serve in this instance."

"No, if that were enough, he would already be an eager proponent."

Csevet hesitated.

"What is it?"

"Well, from his point of view, Serenity, he is quite right to dislike the bridge. It will cause a great many changes."

"Yes, but one cannot prevent change simply by wishing it not to happen," Maia said, and did not add, *If one could, our mother would still be alive.* "And if the Istandaärtha *can* be bridged, as Mer Halezh is very sure that it can, we feel that the benefits are considerably greater than the disadvantages."

"Not for the nobility of the eastern principates," Csevet said, not arguing but merely observing.

It took Maia several moments to find the words for what he felt; finally, he said, "Of all our subjects, they are not the ones who need our help."

Csevet's ears dipped and flared with surprise.

"What? Should we not care about our subjects?"

"No, of course—we beg your pardon, Serenity. It is not a sentiment we expected from an emperor."

"We cannot help that," Maia said wearily.

"Serenity, we did not mean—"

"No, but others are bound to make the same observation, and they will say what you do not. They will say it is our mother's Barizheise influence and deplore it. But it does not change that we must do what we think right."

"Edrehasivar the Obstinate, they will call you," Csevet said with something that sounded dangerously close to affection, and promised to think on the matter.

# 23

## The Opposition of the Court

Maia never came nearer to open rebellion than he did over the dinner party hosted by the Presider of Blood, the most powerful member of Parliament. It was not merely that he did not wish to go—for his imperial reign had been one obligation after another that he did not *wish* to fulfill; it was that he was almost ill with fear at the thought of it. It took all of Csevet's considerable powers of persuasion to get him out through the grilles of the Alcethmeret, and if it had not been for his nohecharei, Maia knew that he would have pretended to become lost and accepted every unpleasant consequence thereof, simply in order to escape. But the emperor had no such recourse and was condemned to a punctual appearance at his host's door.

The Marquess Lanthevel, the Presider of the House of Blood, was tall and thin, with graceful, long-fingered hands that Maia could only envy. His eyes were vivid blue, and he dressed to accentuate them: blue brocade jacket and lapis lazuli beads. His bow, when Maia and his nohecharei were ushered into the Lanthevadeise receiving room, was perfect and crisp. "We are pleased at last to meet you, Serenity. You have not the look of your father." Said so blandly that the insult could almost pass unnoticed.

"No," Maia said, "we are generally agreed to favor our mother."

Lanthevel's lips quirked in the slightest of smiles, as if conceding a point to an opponent. "And of course," he continued, with a gesture as softly elegant as an unfurling rose, "Your Serenity knows Lord Pashavar and Captain Orthema, but you must allow us to present our niece, Dach'osmin Iviro Lanthevin; Osmerrem Ailano Pashavaran; and Merrem Reneian Orthemo."

The greetings were all formal and correct, and Maia returned them in kind while trying to keep his glass-edged panic from showing. He had known there would be other guests, but he had not expected Pashavar, who terrified him more than the rest of the Corazhas put together.

Pashavar's wife, a head taller than her husband, had the grim look of a woman determined to do her duty despite her personal feelings. Dach'osmin Lanthevin gave him what might have been a sympathetic quirk of a smile; she was in her forties, a short, brisk, graceful woman who dressed her hair with pale jade combs.

He was disconcerted by Captain Orthema, whom he had never seen before without the sun mask of a knight of Anmura—and had certainly never imagined trying to have a conversation with. The captain's name, Maia knew, was Verer Orthema. He came from far eastern Thu-Tetar, and there was a good deal of goblin in him. His skin was not as dark as Maia's, having only a faint silvery cast, but his hair was black, and his eyes, under heavy brows, were so deep an orange as to be nearly red. He had campaigned several times against the barbarians of the Evressai Steppes before accepting his present position, and bore reminders of warfare on his face: a scar slanting across his forehead and another slashing from one cheekbone to the other across the bridge of his nose.

Although he was almost sixty, his posture was still erect and his stride still vigorous and graceful.

His wife was much younger, only a few years older than Maia himself, and he thought, from the drape of her soft rose dress, that she might be pregnant. She did not look higher than the emperor's collarbones, and he supposed he should take some comfort in the fact that there was someone in the room more terrified than he was.

It was the duty of the unfortunate emperor to begin conversation; although that rule got bent and rather sloppy at some of Nurevis's parties, the cold shine of Lanthevel's vivid blue eyes said there would be no such mercy here. Maia had tried to prepare—as he always tried to prepare—with lists of innocuous but encouraging questions; they all seemed feeble now, like the efforts of a mouse to make conversation with a roomful of hungry cats.

The silence was deepening from awkward to lethal; Maia looked around desperately for something that could at least provide an unexceptionable remark, and saw a wall hanging, not very large and the colors faded with age, but he had taken a step toward it before he knew what he was doing. "We beg your pardon," he said, but could not wrench his gaze away from the delicate embroidered vines and strange wheel-like flowers. "Will you tell us about this wall hanging? Our mother did embroidery like this."

"Did she?" said the Marquess Lanthevel, an odd note in his voice. "That is a wedding stole from Csedo, dated to the reign of Sorchev Zhas." And before Maia had to ask, he added, "Some sixty to a hundred years before Edrevenivar the Conqueror crossed the Istandaärtha."

Maia stepped a little closer. The stole, protected behind a pane of glass, was stained and frayed, and the colors, which must once have been as bright as a celebration, were now almost indistinguishable, red from blue from yellow from green, but his memory supplied a purple cast to the red, a deep golden yellow, a jewel-like blue. Chenelo had used two shades of green, to give the effect of sun and shadow, but it was impossible to tell if the long-ago embroiderer had done the same.

Lanthevel said, "Do you have any pieces of the empress's working?"

"No," Maia said, and forced himself to turn to face his host. "All her personal belongings were burned when she died. We believe it was at our father's command."

"He left you nothing for remembrance?" Pashavar said. He used the ritual word, "ulishenathaän": a token of a dead person.

"No," Maia said. "Possibly he thought we were not old enough to need one."

Pashavar snorted inelegantly, drawing a frown from his wife.

"No one who knew the late emperor your father," she said, "could help but deplore his fourth marriage—not through any fault of the Empress Chenelo's, for indeed we have never heard anything to her discredit, but simply because he should not have made it. The Empress Pazhiro would have been the first to condemn his behavior."

"The third empress was a close friend of our wife's," said Pashavar.

Captain Orthema made a noise that might from another man have been called a sigh. "It is possible to be friends with a man—indeed, to care for him deeply—and yet disapprove of his conduct. We have always felt that the late emperor's treatment of you, Serenity, was foolish, for it created discontent where there was no need to, and we know Lord Pashavar advised him strongly to bring you to the capital."

"When your mother died," said Lord Pashavar, "again when you turned thirteen, and again when you turned sixteen. But he would not listen to us."

"He was always very stubborn," said Lanthevel. "It is a Drazhadeise trait."

*Edrehasivar the Obstinate,* Csevet had said.

"We thought," said Dach'osmin Lanthevin, "although perhaps it is fanciful, that he had come to associate you not with your mother—for indeed, he did not know her—but with the Empress Pazhiro and her stillborn child. That it was not vindictiveness that drove him, but grief."

*The damned whelp looks just like his mother.*

"It is a kind thought," Maia said. "As we were given no chance to know our father, we cannot speak as to its truth."

"A very polite way of saying you disagree," Lanthevel said. "Tact is a fine trait in an emperor. Varenechibel had it not."

"Put tactfully," Pashavar said, and for the rest of the time until dinner was announced, Lanthevel and Pashavar told Maia stories of his father, giving him a glimpse, at least, of the man Idra and Vedero and others who had loved him had known. But Maia kept thinking about the wedding stole, and after the sliced pears in yoghurt were served, he asked Lanthevel, "How did you come by that wedding stole? And—forgive us if this is an impolite question, but why do you hang it in your receiving room?"

"Not impolite at all," Lanthevel said. In fact, he seemed pleased. "Your Serenity knows that we are a scholar of the University of Ashedro?"

"We did not know," Maia said. "We had understood that scholars mostly remain in the universities."

"True," said Lanthevel, "but our elder brother became a votary of Cstheio when he was forty."

"Oh," Maia said.

Lanthevel made a small, ironic nod of acknowledgment. "A scholar may be plucked from his university to sit in the Parliament, but not so a votary. We have found, though, that we are able to continue our studies at least in small ways—and perhaps that makes them more precious to us."

"But what do you *study*, Lanthevel?" Pashavar interrupted. "You'll talk all night and still not have answered the emperor's question."

"Have some more wine, Lord Pashavar," Lanthevel suggested. "Your disposition hasn't mellowed yet."

Pashavar laughed, like a crack of thunder; Maia realized that these two men were genuinely friends, and they were doing him the honor, and the great kindness, of letting him see their friendship.

"As it happens," Lanthevel said, collecting the attention of the table, "we study neither textiles nor the history of Csedo—our studies are in philology—but a close friend left us the stole as an ulishenathaän, and we treasure it."

"Forgive us again," Maia said, dogged because he was trying not to imagine having one of his mother's embroidered pillows to remember her by, "but what is philology?"

The silence was sharp; Lanthevel's raised eyebrows said he suspected Maia of mockery, and Maia said, "We ask in all sincerity. Our education was somewhat erratic."

"Did you not have tutors?" said Pashavar.

"No, only Setheris," Maia said, realizing too late to catch himself the insult in using his cousin's given name unadorned.

Pashavar snorted. "Setheris Nelar must have made the worst teacher the empire has ever seen."

"No, he was a very good teacher, when he could be

bothered." Maia bit his lip, appalled, and only then realized that the warm drifting feeling in his head meant that he was beginning to get drunk. Lanthevel's wine was stronger than he'd thought.

"Yes, but how often *could* he be bothered?" Pashavar said, with a horrible sharp knowingness in his eyes. "We remember Setheris Nelar and the self-importance he wore like a crown."

"We remember," Dach'osmin Lanthevin put in, earning herself a frown from Osmerrem Pashavaran, "his bitter feud with Lord Chavar."

"Osmer Nelar wished to be Lord Chancellor," said Pashavar, "having realized he would never rise as high or as fast as he wished in the Judiciary."

"Arrogance," Lanthevel said.

"Yes," said Pashavar, "but we do not know that he was any *less* qualified than Chavar."

Lanthevel waved this piece of obvious provocation aside. "It is true that Lord Chancellor is in many ways a political post, but it cannot be assumed without *some* knowledge of the workings of the chancellery, and Osmer Nelar had none."

"But the *opportunity* was there," said Pashavar, answering a question Maia was not quite brave enough to ask. "Lord Chancellors do not come and go like dayflowers. If he did not try then, it might easily be forty years before another such opportunity arose. Osmer Nelar was ambitious—and arrogant, as Lanthevel says—and his wife drove him. Or, at least, so Varenechibel always believed. He would not let her accompany her husband to Edonomee because, he said, he did not want them scheming *together*—instead, her energies were consumed in trying to get her husband recalled; and his were spent in . . ." He raised his eyebrows at Maia, but Maia had another question.

"What did he *do*? He would never talk about it, and

no one at Edonomee had the least idea." He'd heard Kevo and Pelchara speculating more than once, but the very wildness of their stories—and the freedom with which they attributed to Setheris the most appalling and extravagant of vices—marked them as make-believe.

"Ah," said Pashavar, and looked at Lanthevel. "You had the story from Chavar, Lanthevel, and he had it direct from Varenechibel."

"Yes," said Lanthevel. "Osmer Nelar made some attempt to persuade Varenechibel against Chavar—which we could have told him was doomed from the outset. But Osmer Nelar said *something* which Varenechibel construed as an attempt to exert undue influence on the emperor."

"Treason," Maia said, his mouth dry from more than just too much wine. Setheris had been exceptionally thorough in teaching Maia about the different kinds of treason—exceptionally thorough and exceptionally vicious.

"Yes," said Pashavar. "And your next question, Serenity, is why Osmer Nelar's head still graces the top of his neck."

"Are you still outraged about that?" Lanthevel said, and Pashavar brought his fist down on the table, rattling the dishes and making Maia and Merrem Orthemo jump.

"The emperor is not above the law," Pashavar said, glaring at Lanthevel with his ears dangerously flattened. "The emperor *is* the law. It sets the vilest kind of precedent for the emperor to ignore due process in that way."

"We do not understand," Maia said as humbly as he could.

"Osmer Nelar was never formally charged with treason—or with anything else," said Captain Orthema.

"He was confined in the Esthoramire at the emperor's command for some three or four months and then relegated to Edonomee, as Your Serenity well knows. It was much the same with Arbelan Zhasan and with the Viscount Ulzhavel and many others."

"My dear Orthema," said Lanthevel, "are you actually offering a *criticism* of the late emperor?"

"No," Orthema said without the slightest hint of offense at the baiting. "Merely stating a fact which Edrehasivar knows to be true."

"Yes," said Maia. "Did the Viscount Ulzhavel die in banishment? For we do not recognize the name."

"He despaired," said Lanthevel, "and killed himself."

"Not the revethvoran?" Maia said, alerted by Lanthevel's phrasing.

"No, for that would have required Varenechibel's command, or at least his permission, and Ulzhavel did not believe he would be granted even that."

"Ulzhavel was unstable," Pashavar said. "He got it from his mother's line. *But.* That does not change the fact that he and many of Varenechibel's other enemies were treated in a way we most heartily condemn."

"And you are confident," said Lanthevel, "that Edrehasivar will not throw *you* in the Esthoramire for criticizing the late emperor his father?"

"Ha!" said Pashavar with such force that Maia was not sure whether it was an exclamation or a laugh. "If Edrehasivar wished to start throwing people in the Esthoramire—or, better yet, the Nevennamire—we are not where he would start." He gave Maia a sidelong look that was angry and mocking, but not entirely unkind. "Are we?"

"No," said Maia, "but we could always change our mind."

There was a moment of arrested silence, and Maia

worried that he had judged Pashavar incorrectly; then Pashavar and Lanthevel burst out laughing, and Pashavar saluted Maia with his glass. "So the kitten has claws, after all."

Maia smiled as best he could, grateful his skin was too dark to show a blush, and Orthema said quietly, "Just because a cat doesn't scratch you doesn't mean he can't—as you well know, Lord Pashavar."

"We are rebuked," said Pashavar, still smiling.

"And there is a question we have not answered," Lanthevel said. "Philology, Serenity, is the study of the origins of words."

"The origins of *words*?" Maia said.

"We study how languages change," said Lanthevel. "Why a word has one form among the silk farmers of the east and another among the herdsmen of the west. Why some words stay in use from generation to generation, while others are discarded. For example, for we see that you are still dubious, the word 'morhath' is the word for 'sky' that was used in the court of Your Serenity's great-great-great-great-great-granduncle, Edrevechelar the Fourteenth. But no one uses it now or even knows its meaning. Our study is to track the course of its disappearance and the emergence of the word that took its place."

"Actually," Orthema said mildly, "that's not quite true. We know the word 'morhath' because we heard it used by the Evressai barbarians."

"You did?" said Lanthevel, all but pouncing on him, and Maia became less worried that this was an elaborate joke to discomfit the emperor. For one thing, he didn't believe Orthema would be party to any such joke; for another, Lanthevel had become so intent on extracting details from Orthema that he seemed almost to have forgotten the emperor's existence. Maia bent his head over his plate and listened as Orthema was slowly encouraged to speak, to describe the people he had spent much of his adult life fighting.

The Evressai Wars had been going on since the reign of Maia's grandfather. The initial cause had been the refusal of the people of the Evressai Steppes to acknowledge Varevesena as their emperor or to pay tithes to the empire. The wars had continued on and off for more than eighty years because the barbarians could not drive the elves out, nor take the Anmur'theileian, the great fortress that had been under siege before it was even built, and the elves could not catch the barbarians.

"You cannot imagine, Serenity, how vast the steppes are. And the Nazhmorhathveras—that is how they name themselves, the People of the Night Sky—the Nazhmorhathveras do not build, nor fortresses nor towns nor even roads. They live in tents and they travel in groups of no more than twenty or thirty. Even if our scouts find a meeting of several houses, they will be scattered and gone before a battalion can reach them. And the Nazhmorhathveras are masters of the art of ambush. It is like trying to hold sand in your fist."

"If the steppes are so vast, why do the Nazhmorhathveras not simply vanish into them?" Maia asked. He feared it was a stupid question, but it was beginning to seem to him that asking stupid questions was what an emperor's job consisted of.

"Brute stubbornness," snapped Pashavar.

"No," said Orthema, "it is not that simple, though we did not understand the truth until we thought to ask a prisoner why the Nazhmorhathveras call the Anmur'theileian 'Memory of Death.' We had thought"—and he used the plural, with a gesture that seemed to encompass generations of knights and foot soldiers fighting and dying far from home—"that they named it that for the uncounted Nazhmorhathvereise dead. But this prisoner . . . do you know anything, Serenity, of the witches of the steppes?"

Maia shook his head; before he remembered that it behooved the emperor—as it behooved everyone (Setheris had said) not raised by goblin mudwalkers—to make a clear spoken response when asked a question, Orthema was speaking again: "The witches are the holy men and women of the Nazhmorhathveras, and they are always albino."

The hiss of indrawn breath was from Dach'osmin Lanthevin; Lord Pashavar's expression merely became more dour, and he muttered, "Barbarians," just softly enough that Maia could not be certain he meant to be heard.

Orthema shrugged a little in acknowledgment—though not, Maia thought, in agreement—and continued: "We captured a witch, by pure stupid luck, nothing more, and for all that he was half-blind, he fought like a nazhcreis, the night-hunting cat of the steppes, which indeed was his usename. Our soldiers were wise enough not to kill him, and certainly his people bargained for his return as they had bargained for nothing and no one else."

Orthema paused for a long swallow of wine. "But bargaining of that sort takes time, and we took over the care of the prisoner to ensure that he was not ill-used, for the common soldiers considered him an abomination and many of our fellow knights expressed the same opinion."

"Which you did not share," Maia said gently.

"Serenity," Orthema said with a much more uncomfortable shrug. "We, too, have been called an abomination." And he made the barest gesture toward his fierce orange-red eyes.

"But that's—" Dach'osmin Lanthevin began, and stopped suddenly.

"Ridiculous?" Pashavar said dryly. "There were many mutters of 'abomination' when Varenechibel's fourth empress bore him a child."

"Please," Maia said before Pashavar could embarrass the table further. "We wish to hear Captain Orthema's story."

"Serenity," Orthema said with a slight inclination of his head; he seemed pleased. "We do not think that Nazhcreis Dein ever entirely trusted us, but he appreciated our care, and one day we asked him why his people called our fortress Memory of Death. For a long time he did not answer, and we thought perhaps he would not—for there were many questions he would not answer—but finally he said, 'Because it is built on our dead.' He gave us an unpleasant smile—we remember it still, for he was sharp-toothed, as all his people are. 'We also call it Carrion-Bones.' And finally, Serenity, we understood that he was speaking *literally*. The Anmur'theileian is built on a great outcropping of rock—they are scattered throughout the eastern steppes, like isolated mountains—and in truth we cannot fault our predecessors who chose to build there, for it offers both vantage and defense, which are otherwise not easily to be found. But what those builders did not know—or did not care, if they did know, and we have our suspicions—was that it was the custom of the Nazhmorhathveras to carry their dead to the top of this rock and leave them there to be stripped by the vultures and the nazhcreian. The rite of adulthood, Nazhcreis Dein told us, was to spend three days and three nights atop the rock with the dead."

"We built our castle on their ulimeire?" Maia said, horrified.

"Essentially, Serenity, yes."

"And is this the *only* rock that will do for their barbarian rites?" Pashavar said.

"That's not the point," Maia said, more sharply than he had ever imagined speaking to Pashavar. "Just because there is a ulimeire in Cetho does not make the tombs in the Untheileneise'meire less sacred."

"Point taken," Pashavar said sourly.

"But if that is true," Maia said, "why have we not returned their ulimeire to them?"

Everyone stared at him in horror. "Serenity," Orthema said finally, clearly struggling for words that would not be insulting or provoking, "it is not that simple."

Pashavar, uninterested in tact, said, "Would you concede defeat in a war which is not of our making and which has claimed the lives of thousands of elvish men?"

"But the war is not of the making of anyone now alive," Maia objected.

"Every effort was made by the late emperor your father to achieve peace," said Lanthevel. "The barbarians—yes, yes, Orthema, the Nazhmorhathveras—refused."

"Yes," Maia said, "and were these efforts through the *current* Witness for Foreigners or the *previous* one?"

There was a short, appalled silence before Orthema rallied. "Serenity, if we simply yield to the Nazhmorhathveras, they will consider the towns of the badlands as no more than prey, as they did before the Anmur'theileian was built, and the people of the badlands are your loyal subjects and deserve protection."

Before Maia could answer, Dach'osmin Lanthevin said, mildly but with a hint of steel all the same, "We feel that this discussion is better suited to the Michen'theileian or the Verven'theileian than to our dining room."

"Of course," Maia said. "We beg your pardon."

There was another uncomfortable silence, in which

Maia was reminded again that emperors did not apologize, and then Merrem Orthemo said bravely, "We are the daughter of the mayor of Vorenzhessar, which lies in the western badlands. We remember our grandmothers' stories about the Evressai raids, and we assure Your Serenity, you have no stauncher subjects than the people of Vorenzhessar and towns like it."

"Thank you, Merrem Orthemo," Maia said. "It is a quandary and we must think on it carefully." But she had also given him an opportunity to shift the conversation with some grace: "Then your town predates Ezho?"

"Oh, yes, Serenity." And when she smiled, he could see that her canine teeth were long and sharp, as Orthema had said of Nazhcreis Dein. "Both our house and the house of our mother's line have lived for centuries in the badlands. There were always people there, even before gold was discovered and the elves came. It is merely that now there are a great many more."

The Ezho gold rush provided innocuous conversation for the rest of the meal; even Osmerrem Pashavaran unbent enough to tell the story of one of her grandmother's brothers, who had gone north looking for gold and had found the mineral springs at Daiano instead— "which made him far more wealthy than a gold strike could ever have done, although even when he was a very old man, he would go out prospecting whenever he had the chance. But he never found gold."

"Our mother went to Daiano for the waters," said Dach'osmin Lanthevin. "They did not keep her alive, but they reduced her pain substantially, and for that we will always be grateful."

Maia wondered if the springs at Daiano could have helped Chenelo, and he lost several turns in the conversation to a wash of futile anger at his father, who would never have granted her permission to try them.

His attention was reclaimed by a question from Lanthevel: "Serenity, do we understand correctly that you have halted negotiations over the Archduchess Vedero's marriage?"

Maia's ears flicked, causing a delicate chime from his silver and jade earrings. "Our sister is in mourning."

"But you have broken off entirely the agreement with the Tethimada, which we have heard was very close to completion."

"Do you trust your sources, Lanthevel?" Pashavar asked, and Lanthevel made an acknowledging gesture.

"But still," he said. "It seems a little rash, Serenity, when you will only have to begin again from the beginning, and very likely from a less advantageous position."

"We see nothing advantageous about our current position. And our sister does not want to be married." He cursed the wine even as he saw everyone at the table become alert.

"For a woman of blood," Osmerrem Pashavaran said harshly, "marriage is not about *wanting*. The archduchess knows that."

"So did our mother," Maia said. "We think it enough to inflict marriage upon our empress."

"You would have done better to choose a daughter of a more traditional house," Osmerrem Pashavaran said. "The Ceredada girls have just as many ridiculous notions as your sister."

"We do not find our sister's notions ridiculous," Maia said. He took a deep breath and tried to let go of the scarlet-eyed rage that had swept over him. Osmerrem Pashavaran didn't look like she minded a bit, but he was scaring Merrem Orthemo. "We do not think marriage is the only thing women are fit for, even if you do."

"It is a vexed question," said Lanthevel. "As is the question of what should become of women who—for whatever reason—cannot find a husband." His gaze crossed his niece's.

Dach'osmin Lanthevin said, "It is hard to find occupation when one has been trained for nothing but child-bearing and then has no children to bear."

"All women have duties," Osmerrem Pashavaran snapped, although the betraying pinkness at the tips of her ears showed that she had not meant to hit a sore spot for the Lanthevada.

"But what do those duties consist of?" Dach'osmin Lanthevin pressed. "Does a woman not have a duty to use her talents, even if they are not talents for the care of children?"

"We had no idea you were so forward-thinking," Osmerrem Pashavaran said, making "forward-thinking" sound like the vilest of insults.

"We have had a certain amount of time to consider the matter," Dach'osmin Lanthevin said. It was clear she was not backing down, and so it was a relief that she chose to turn the conversation to trivial matters while the plates were cleared.

Dessert was a cake made with spices from Anvernel, and from the natural silence of enjoyment, Maia dared finally to approach the subject of the bridge; as he'd expected, Pashavar denounced it instantly, but he had not expected him to describe it as a "cloud-fancy of Varenechibel's. It will come to nothing except the waste of a prodigious amount of money."

"We did not know our father was interested in the building of a bridge."

"Oh yes," said Lanthevel. "He felt that if a way was not found to bring the east and the west together, the Ethuveraz would split apart again. And we think he could not help but see that the Istandaärtha would always be a weakness unless a way could be found to bridge it."

"True enough," said Pashavar, "but not an excuse for encouraging every crazed gear-head he came across."

"We have spoken to the gentleman of the Clock-smiths' Guild," Maia said. "We do not think he is crazed."

"Oh have you now?" said Pashavar, and Maia braced himself. But Pashavar did not seem displeased. "We have thought you were too rule-abiding to be a good ruler—a paradox, you see—but perhaps we were wrong."

"But you're the Witness for the Judiciate!" Maia protested, which made everyone laugh.

"We said *rule*, not *law*," Pashavar said tartly. "There is a difference, Serenity. An emperor who breaks laws is a mad dog and a danger, but an emperor who will never break a rule is nearly as bad, for he will never be able to recognize when a law must be changed."

"We see," Maia said, although he was not entirely sure he did.

"We do not by any means condone it as a *habit*," Lord Pashavar said.

"It would be very disruptive," Maia said with deliberate demureness, and that made them laugh again.

"So," said Pashavar, "you have spoken to the clock-smith. We suppose this means you wish the clocksmith to speak to the Corazhas."

"Yes," Maia said.

"And you would prefer we did not stand in your way."

"Yes, we would."

"Have some brandy, Pashavar," Lanthevel said. "It will make it easier to swallow your objections."

"If your brandy were not so excellent, Lanthevel," Pashavar said, "we would refuse on principle." He said to Maia, "This does not change our opinion."

"Of course it does not."

"And it does not change either our advice or the vote we will cast."

"We would not expect it to. We merely wish the clock-smiths to have a fair hearing."

"Hmmph," Pashavar said, mostly to his brandy snif-ter, but Maia took it as a capitulation, and indeed, at the next meeting of the Corazhas, when he took his courage in both hands and brought the matter of the Clocksmiths' Guild and the bridge forward again, Pashavar did not block him, and the Corazhas agreed that the clocksmiths' ideas should be heard. It was not a unanimous agreement, but Maia had never expected it would be. What mattered was that, without Pasha-var to back him, Bromar could not rally enough sup-port to manage the *veklevezhek* Merrem Halezho had spoken of.

It was an accomplishment on a day that was other-wise full of frustrations. First, Chavar had had to be pinned into confessing that the investigation into the wreck of the *Wisdom of Choharo* was making no head-way. "They just need more time, Serenity," Chavar said, and Maia thought that earnestness sat very badly on him. And then Maia had had an audience with Lord Bromar that went nowhere and achieved nothing ex-cept confirming Maia in his opinion that Bromar was an idiot—and, no doubt, confirming Bromar in his opin-ion that the emperor was a madman. Peace with the Nazhmorhathveras was not even to be considered, and if the Anmur'theileian was built on a barbarian ulimeire, Bromar's blank expression said even before he opened his mouth that he had no idea why Maia considered that either distressing or important. The idea of negotiating with the Nazhmorhathveras didn't even get far enough for the Corazhas to ridicule it.

Maia returned to the Alcethmeret that evening tired and frustrated, but he reminded himself to be pleased that at least he had gotten the clocksmiths their hear-ing. Mer Halezh would be pleased, too, and Merrem

Halezho. He did not know if Min Vechin would be pleased, and he shied away from wondering. Better not to think about her.

Winternight was less than two weeks away; Maia dined privately with Arbelan Zhasanai for the final time until after the last of the guests and dignitaries had left the Untheileneise Court—which would be a week or more after the solstice. "The celebration keeps expanding," he said. "Like the story about the weaver-woman's cat."

"Yarn around every stick of furniture in the house?" Arbelan said, smiling.

"Exactly," Maia said.

"Did your mother tell you that story?"

"Of course," Maia said. "She had a picture book with many wonder-tales in it—destroyed, we suppose, along with her other things when she died. She had brought it from Barizhan."

"You miss her," Arbelan said.

"Of course," Maia said again. "We loved her very much."

Arbelan was silent for a moment, contemplating the wine in her glass. "We miscarried once," she said.

Maia managed not to stare at her, developing a rapt interest in his own glass, and she continued, "It was as close as we ever came to giving Varenechibel a child. He never knew of it."

Maia had to clear his throat. "How far along? . . ."

"Four months, maybe? Only just long enough that we knew for certain it was a miscarriage. Long enough that we had begun to dream—not of Varenechibel's approval, for we had then been married to him ten years and we did know better, but of the child. Of the stories we would tell our child, the songs we would teach him. Or her." She stopped, then said fiercely, "We would have cherished a daughter."

She knew, then, of Varenechibel's disregard for his daughters and granddaughters. "Our mother," Maia said carefully, "told us once, very shortly before she died, that she did not regret her marriage to Varenechibel because it had brought her us. We have never been sure that she should have felt that way, although we know that she told us the truth. She, too, would have cherished a daughter."

"Yes," Arbelan said. She sounded satisfied, as if he had answered a question that had been worrying her, which made him hope that perhaps she would answer a question for him in turn. He said, "Do you know your great-niece Csethiro?"

"The one who is to become your empress?" Arbelan said, her eyebrows raised mockingly. "We do not know her well—we know none of our family very well anymore, for while they were not *forbidden* to visit us at Cethoree . . ."

"Yes," Maia said, remembering what Berenar had told him about Arbelan's brother.

"We know nothing to Csethiro's discredit," Arbelan said, watching him now as if she was not sure what he wanted from her.

"No, we are sure not," Maia said. "We just wondered what sort of a person she is."

"Ah. We are sorry, Edrehasivar. She wrote us a most dutiful letter upon the signing of your marriage contract, and we hope that perhaps we may come to know her better, but we can tell you nothing except she is our brother's grandchild and she is two-and-twenty."

Three years older. It was not so much, really, although it felt like a yawning abysm. And *dutiful*, which he had witnessed for himself.

"Thank you," Maia said, and hoped he did not sound as desolate as he felt. Dach'osmin Ceredin had warned him about Min Vechin, but he wanted a dutiful

companion no more than he wanted a mercenary one.
He wanted a friend, and that, it seemed, was exactly
what he could not have.

He retired to bed early that evening. Nemer and Avris
braided his hair while Esha tidied away the day's jewels and fetched a hot brick for the emperor's bed. Maia
said good night to Dazhis, who guarded the outer chamber this evening, and then good night to Telimezh, who
took his preferred position in the window embrasure
and said softly, "Sleep well, Serenity." Maia then lay and
silently repeated the prayer to Cstheio until he fell asleep.
It was as close to meditation as he could come.

His dreams were chaotic nonsense; he woke suddenly
and was not sure what had woken him. Some noise—a
choked cry? It was pitch black in his bedroom, no hints
of dawn creeping around the curtains. He held his
breath, straining to hear, but there was nothing.

"Telimezh?" he whispered into the darkness, telling
himself that he was a fool, a coward, as bad as a little
boy . . . but Telimezh did not answer.

At that moment, Maia stopped trying to believe nothing was wrong.

"Telimezh?" He sat up, shoved the bedclothes back.
He knew without any need to wonder that if Telimezh
had had to leave the room for any reason, Dazhis
would have taken his place. Therefore, Telimezh was
in the room, but unable to answer him; Maia was
thinking confusedly of the fits suffered by one of the
men who had sometimes helped Haru in the grounds
of Edonomee, and his principal concern, as he groped
for the bedside lamp, was to be sure Telimezh was not
asphyxiating on his own tongue.

But then the door slammed open, and he realized that
he was worried about the wrong thing. The light was
blinding; he got one hand up to shield his eyes, strug-

gled upright, and immediately fell over Telimezh, who was lying on the floor, either insensible or dead.

Hard hands grabbed him, dragging him to his feet, and he had a blurry glimpse of the Drazhadeise crest before a bag dropped over his head. His hands went up to it automatically, but they were caught and pulled back down.

"None of that, Your Grace," said a voice he did not recognize. "We've no orders to hurt you, nor desire neither, but we won't hesitate if you make it necessary. Understand?"

Maia tried to answer and got a choking mouthful of the bag. He nodded, and the voice said, "All right, then—let's go."

He did not know where they took him. There were hallways, and stairs—down which he nearly fell—and a doorway they bent him double to shove him through, and more stairs, narrow and cold, and the scent of stone and water, and then a raised door lintel that he stubbed his toes on and fell, sprawling on cold flagstones. He was lifted to his feet again and the bag was jerked off his head, leaving him blinking at his sister-in-law Shevëan Drazharan, Princess of the Untheileneise Court.

He was not surprised to see her. The Drazhadeise crest had pointed to either Vedero or Shevëan, and aside from the fact that he would not have believed it of Vedero, her household, that of an unmarried woman still under the protection of the head of her house, did not include armsmen. And Vedero had never sought to deny his right to the imperial throne. Shevëan had, and his hope that her muttering and discontent would come to nothing had clearly been ill-founded.

He did not speak, aware that he must be a ludicrous figure in nothing but his nightshirt and with his hair braided down his back, and unwilling to give her further ammunition, either by saying something half-witted or simply by being unable to control his voice. Besides, he was wearily certain he knew what she would say. She stared back at him, her eyes hard, and they might have remained thus for some time, save that a door opened behind her and a man came in.

Uleris Chavar, the Lord Chancellor of the Ethuveraz.

Shevëan's presence had not surprised Maia; Chavar's did. But that was foolish and naïve: Chavar had been opposed to him from the first.

"Your Grace," Chavar said stiffly. "We are sorry for this necessity, but we believe it is what the emperor would want."

He meant Varenechibel.

"You are not fit," Shevëan said furiously. "Consorting with goblins, dishonoring the dead."

"Using your influence to promote the most ludicrous and impossible schemes," Chavar finished. "We cannot let you bring the Ethuveraz into chaos and ruin, as you will most surely do if you are not stopped. We have the papers ready for your signature."

"Papers?"

"For your abdication," Chavar said impatiently.

"You will abdicate in favor of our son," Shevëan said, her voice still tight with the fury she had been nursing for months, "and retire to a monastery in northern Thu-Cethor."

"Dedicated to Cstheio," Chavar said; he seemed reluctant to let Shevëan go uninterrupted for long, whether because she was a woman or for the very good reason that he was afraid of what she might say. "The monks take a vow of silence."

The terrible thing, worse than anything else, was that he was tempted. Silence, austerity, the worship of the Lady of Falling Stars. No responsibility for anyone but himself. What stopped him from capitulating then and there, signing anything they wanted, was not desire for the throne, nor even care for his subjects. It was knowing in the cold marrow of his bones that no matter what Chavar promised—or even believed—Sheveän would have him murdered as soon as she could find someone to do it.

Then other considerations caught up to him: the fact that Idra was a child still; that regencies in the Ethuveraz were a tradition of disasters; that Chavar's policies would lead to the ruin he accused Maia of fostering; that they still did not know who had blown up the *Wisdom of Choharo*; that, truly, the last thing anyone needed was another new emperor before Winternight.

He asked abruptly, "What did you do to our nohecharei?"

"Lieutenant Telimezh is unharmed," Chavar said. "A soporific cantrip, nothing more."

"And Dazhis Athmaza?"

Sheveän laughed, as brittle as new ice. "Who do you think performed the cantrip?"

Maia was swamped with the sick heat of humiliation and betrayal. If even his nohecharei turned against him, maybe Chavar and Sheveän were right. Maybe he merely deluded himself that his rule was preferable to their alternative.

*Pull thyself together.* The voice was sharp, contemptuous—the voice he thought of as Setheris, but Setheris would be exulting in his downfall. Perhaps, he thought in half-hysterical whimsy, it was the Emperor Edrehasivar VII, rebuking Maia Hobgoblin as a steward would a scullery boy.

*Pull thyself together. It is not for thy Lord Chancellor to decide whether thou art emperor or not—and even less for thy sister-in-law.*

He stood straighter, looked Chavar squarely in the face. "We would speak to Idra." Chavar's eyes bulged, and Maia found he was detached enough now to be gratified by it. "If you wish to maintain this charade of abdication, we will speak to our successor. Otherwise, kill us and have done with it."

"Do not speak recklessly, Your Grace," Chavar said.

"We do not, we assure you. Let us speak to Idra or murder us. It is your choice."

Chavar and Shevean retreated into a whispered discussion, quite heated, which resulted in a pair of armsmen being sent to fetch Idra. Maia was relieved by the evidence that Idra had not been involved in his mother's plotting, and found himself thinking again about the nightmarish regencies of previous centuries. It was a rare child emperor who survived to see adulthood; he did not like Idra's chances of joining their number.

It was some ten or fifteen minutes before the Prince of the Untheileneise Court appeared, wrapped in a dressing gown that must have belonged to his father. "Mother, what's toward? Why do—" And then he recognized Maia, and he became very still, his gray eyes going wide.

Maia said, "Greetings, cousin."

"Serenity," Idra said, and managed a passable bow. "Mother, what is the meaning of this?"

She did not answer immediately, and Maia wondered when—and what—she had been planning to tell him. Would she have woken him in the morning with the news that he was emperor? Idra waited, and finally Shevean said, "It is what your grandfather would have wanted. You know he regarded you as his heir as much as your father."

"You are deposing our uncle," Idra said flatly.

"He isn't *fit*," Shevean said. "A half-breed upstart with neither wits nor manners—he is no emperor, Idra!"

"He will ruin the Ethuveraz," Chavar struck in. "He has no notion of business or statecraft."

Idra was frowning. "Surely that is the purpose for which an emperor has advisers."

"You do not understand," Chavar said.

"No one expects you to," Sheveän added. "You are a child still."

"We are only four years younger than our uncle," Idra said. "And if we do not understand, as he does not understand, how is it that we will be a better emperor than he?" Setheris had taught Maia a smattering of rhetoric and logic, enough that he could see Idra had been much more carefully taught.

"You will have regents, Idra," Sheveän said.

Idra's eyes met Maia's. Alarm was visible in his face and ears; and Maia wondered if he, too, had been taught the histories of Beltanthiar V and Edrethelma VIII and all those other wretched boys entombed in the Untheileneise'meire. Idra said, "And what will become of our uncle, Mother? Will you . . . will you have him murdered?"

"Of *course* not," Sheveän said much too warmly.

"He will go to a monastery in northern Thu-Cethor," said Chavar. "The monks will treat him kindly."

Idra was silent for some moments, still frowning. Then he said, "No."

"What?" said Chavar and Sheveän in ragged chorus.

"No," Idra said again. "We will not usurp our uncle's throne."

"Idra!" Sheveän said, but Idra let her get no further.

"We do not think this is what our grandfather would wish."

"Idra, you *know* how he felt about—"

"He was an emperor," Idra said, glaring at his mother. "He would not wish for the laws to be broken in this manner, and merely for personal *preferences*. And our father would be ashamed of you."

It was an oddly childish note against his very adult reasoning, and that made it a particularly vicious blow. It was the first time Maia had seen Sheveän discomfited by anything. She did not answer; Chavar said, "You do not understand the larger reasons"

"You dislike his policies," Idra said. "The entire court knows that, Lord Chavar. But our tutor, Leilis Athmaza, says that that does not mean the policies are bad. And we do not see how you can know that the policies are bad when Edrehasivar has been emperor less than a quarter of a year."

"You know nothing of—"

"Which is why we cannot feel we would be a better emperor than our uncle," Idra said. "We will not do it."

Chavar was beginning to look panicked. "Do you know what you are doing to your mother, boy? Do you know what will happen to her?"

*The same thing that will happen to you,* Maia thought unkindly. But he did not speak. He had to know if Idra could hold to his decision.

Idra said unhappily, "We cannot change what she has done. And surely, Lord Chavar, that is an even worse reason to usurp our uncle than those you have already put forward."

Sheveän said, "Idra, we have come too far to stop now. It is already too late for your qualms."

"Mother," Idra said, and Maia was startled to realize Idra was every bit as furious as Sheveän, "it is useless to say *we* have done anything. *We* knew nothing of this. If we *had* known, *you* would not have 'come too far to stop,' for we would never have agreed to what you have done. We cannot believe you would do this to us."

"To you? Idra, we did this *for* you!"

Idra stepped jerkily back, like a cat discovering it has put its paw in something sticky. "Mother," he said softly, "that is a terrible lie."

Shevëan's face went bone-white, and she snarled, "Enough of this. Talar, take the archduke away."

It was obviously a euphemism, and Maia suspected it was a prearranged one. If she'd had the sense, or ruthlessness, to use it instead of allowing Idra to be brought into the room, it might have worked, but the armsmen had been listening, and they were uncertain now, looking from Shevëan to Idra in obvious expectation of having the order countermanded.

"Talar," Idra said, "we regret to be forced to ask you not to take orders from our mother any longer."

"Idra!" Shevëan looked as much shocked as angry—as if it had never occurred to her that Idra would actively defy her. Idra looked back at her without any outward sign of distress, but Maia could see that he was starting to tremble.

*I never meant to make thee choose,* he thought miserably, and the captain of the armsmen said, "We didn't know, Your Highness."

"We will speak of that later," Idra said. "Serenity, what are your commands?"

At that moment, perhaps anticlimactically and perhaps not, the Untheileneise Guard kicked the door down.

Later, Maia was told the story of how Nemer, struck down by Shevëan's men, had roused himself from the cold marble floor. He had crawled to Telimezh; finding that Telimezh could not be woken, Nemer had managed, despite a severe concussion, to crawl or stagger or fall down three flights of stairs to the pneumatic station, where there was always a girl on duty. The girl had first sent an urgent message to the Untheileneise Guards' pneumatic station, then roused her relief, who woke the

Alcethmeret. Not surprisingly, it had been Csevet who had thought to wonder where Sheveän Drazharan was and what company she was keeping, and from there the rest was inevitable. Maia had only to keep the guardsmen from arresting Idra along with Chavar and Sheveän and Sheveän's armsmen.

It was not yet dawn, although Maia would not have been surprised to find the sun setting. He gave orders for Idra and his sisters to be moved into the Alcethmeret; had guards sent to watch, though not to arrest without good reason, the Chavada and lesser Drazhada who lived in the Untheileneise Court—and what was he supposed to do about Nurevis?; directed a doctor to be fetched to Nemer; and then said defiantly to Csevet, "Everything else can wait another four hours," and went back to his cold, disordered bed.

Where he did not sleep, but lay and made miserable lists of all the things he would have to deal with, starting with the appointment of a new Lord Chancellor and ending with Dazhis.

The thought of Dazhis propelled him out of bed again. Beshelar said, "Serenity?" sounding more than a little startled.

It had barely even registered on him that Beshelar and Cala had been, along with Csevet, the first of his household to reach him in the warren of cellars under the apartments of the Prince of the Untheileneise Court. That was how accustomed to his nohecharei he had become: he didn't even see them. He certainly hadn't seen Dazhis's discontent, and it must have been obvious if Sheveän and Chavar had been able to exploit it.

*Perhaps he merely thought thee unfit to rule*—but he shoved that thought away and demanded of Beshelar, "What will happen to Dazhis?"

Beshelar now looked both startled and unhappy. "Serenity, that is a matter for the Athmaz'are, not—"

Maia stalked across to the bedroom door and flung it open. Cala, alone in the outer room, jerked to his feet. "Serenity, are you—" He had been crying.

"What will happen to Dazhis?"

Cala's color went from bad to worse, but he made no attempt to evade the question. "Serenity, he will commit revethvoran."

Revethvoran. Suicide according to the strict rituals of Ulis. The world wavered distressingly before Maia's eyes, but Cala grabbed his arm and all but forced him to sit. "Put your head down," Cala said, and he did not sound at all like he was talking to an emperor. "Deep breaths. That's it."

"We beg pardon," Maia said, aware of Beshelar looming in the doorway. "We did not mean to."

"Of course not," Cala said, and Maia was weakly grateful for the kindness in his voice. "It was a shock, Serenity. We are to blame."

"No. For we did ask. Is there anything we can do? Can we petition the Adremaza for clemency?"

"Serenity." Cala stopped, and when Maia dared to straighten up, he saw that Cala was struggling for words.

"It was a foolish question," he said, wishing to free Cala from the necessity of answering.

"No, Serenity, not foolish. But . . . Dazhis broke his oath as a nohecharis, and he did so not merely by carelessness, but by choice. He *chose* to betray you, and that is not something—it is not the Adremaza's decision, Serenity, nor is it yours. Nor anyone's. It is the oath itself." He paused, swallowed hard, and added, "If you had died, we"—the plural, and with a flick of a gesture to include Beshelar and the absent Telimezh—"would be committing revethvoran with him."

"It is his deserving," Beshelar growled.

"Oh," Maia said.

Cala said gently, "Dazhis is not the only one who broke an oath last night."

"No," Maia said, but Dazhis was the only one he had liked. *Childish nonsense, this prattle of "liking."* He shook his head. "May we see him? Before—" He had to stop, swallowing hard against the knot in his throat.

"He must come to beg your pardon, Serenity," Cala said, "to make what peace with you he can."

"We hope he will beg Telimezh's pardon as well," Beshelar said.

"Yes," Cala said. "That is another broken oath."

*"Why?"* The question burst out with such force that it left Maia's throat raw. "Why did he do it?"

"Truthfully, Serenity," said Cala, "we cannot imagine. We would—" He stopped quite dead, then lifted his chin and said, *"I* would never do such a thing. I cannot imagine hurting you in that way. Even if it were not a matter of an oath."

"Nor can I," Beshelar said, although he sounded like the words were being dragged from him by main force, and he was quick to change the subject. "Serenity, you need to sleep. We can summon Doctor Ushenar to prescribe a sleeping draft, if you think it would help."

"No," Maia said. "We cannot sleep now. We should not have abandoned our duties as we did."

"Serenity," Cala protested, "you have abandoned nothing."

"And fainting will not accomplish anything," Beshelar said roughly. "We will have Doctor Ushenar sent for."

"No!" Maia said. "We wish no doctor."

"Then at least lie down again," Cala said. "If you wish, you may tell us of the plans you need to make and we will act as your secretary."

It was so obviously a sop to a tantrumy child that Maia flushed and pulled away. "No, we thank you. Summon our edocharei, please."

Avris and Esha were as disapproving as Beshelar and Cala. Maia asked pointedly after Nemer. "He is resting, Serenity," Avris said, and added, every bit as pointedly, "As you should be."

"We are entirely unharmed," Maia said, "and we are not so frail that one night's interrupted sleep will send us into a decline."

"You should look more carefully into your mirror, Serenity," Esha said tartly.

"We do not recall soliciting *anyone's* opinion," Maia said, knowing his anger was disproportionate but unable to banish it. "There is much to be done, and we feel it ill behooves us to coddle ourself."

His edocharei did not attempt to argue further, and Maia descended to the Tortoise Room in a state of cold banked fury he could never remember feeling before in his life. Csevet either observed it or had been warned, for he made no remonstration, but was entirely businesslike. "Serenity, we regret that there is clear evidence Osmin Bazhevin knew of the Princess Shevëan's plot."

"Osmin Bazhevin?" Maia said blankly. "What does . . . oh."

"She confessed as soon as the Untheileneise Guard entered the princess's apartments. She knew the whole, but was too afraid of the princess to speak."

"The woman is an idiot," Maia said before he could stop himself.

Csevet's ears twitched, but he merely said, "Yes, Serenity," and waited.

"Put her in the Esthoramire with Shevëan," Maia said, and closed his teeth sharply on the words that wanted to follow. It was unfair to call Osmin Bazhevin ungrateful when all he had done was allow her to pick the least repellent of the unattractive options before her. But he *had* given her a choice; he *had* permitted her to live with

Sheveän even though he had doubted the wisdom of it. And he was so very tired of betrayal this morning.

Csevet cleared his throat. "Also, Serenity, it has been necessary to detain most of the Lord Chancellor's staff, including your cousin, Osmer Nelar."

"We only wish we were surprised," Maia said. "How much of our government is complicit, do you think?"

"The Witness for the Prelacy," Csevet said promptly. "The monastery seems to have been his idea."

"We must thank him," Maia said bitterly. His discontent had been easier to ignore when he had been unable to imagine an alternative.

"The other Witnesses of the Corazhas are uncompromised, Serenity. They send you messages of support, as do the members of the Parliament—most particularly the Marquess Lanthevel. *Our* staff is pursuing every tendril of this plot." He hesitated, and Maia made a conscious effort to stop scowling.

"What is it, Csevet?"

"We wish only to assure Your Serenity that we have no doubts of the loyalty of your household and secretaries."

"Except for Dazhis."

"Serenity," Csevet agreed unhappily. "And we . . . we would like to assure you, Serenity, of our faithfulness. If you have any doubts, we will resign our post. We would not—"

"Csevet, stop!" Maia stared at him. "Why on earth would you think we doubted you?"

"Not that, Serenity, but we came to you from the Lord Chancellor and we know . . . we know that when you chose us as your secretary, you chose between us and Osmer Nelar. We do not wish you to feel that you are stuck with—"

"We do not," Maia said firmly. "We could not ask for a better secretary, and it has never once occurred to us to doubt your loyalty. Nor do we do so now." He managed a ragged quirk of a smile. "Were you part of Lord Chavar's plot, it would have been much better executed."

He saw the weight fall off Csevet's shoulders, and Csevet's returning smile was better than his own. "Then, Serenity, there is one other personal matter which we think you might deal with this morning."

"Oh?" Maia said.

"The children, Serenity. Prince Idra and his sisters. They have been installed in the Alcethmeret's nursery as you instructed, but the maid assigned to them says they are very fearful and anxious. We think it might help them greatly if you were to speak to them."

"And what are we to say?" Maia asked dismally. "Never speak of your mother the traitor again?"

Csevet said, "They understand what their mother has done, Serenity. Even Ino, the youngest. We think they would be calmer if they knew you did not blame *them.*"

"But of course we do not," Maia said.

"Then that is what you should say."

"But we cannot—Csevet, we know nothing of children!"

"Serenity," Csevet said, "they have no one else."

The truth of it drove Maia to the Alcethmeret's nursery, which was in a side wing off the ground floor with its own set of vast grilles. Empresses, Maia had noticed, might live where they liked in the Untheileneise Court—neither Csoru nor Arbelan had ever lived in the Alcethmeret, nor had Varenechibel's second wife, the Empress Leshan—but an emperor's heirs were a different matter. *Perhaps I should have had Idra here from the start,* he thought, but he knew he could not have done it.

There were a pair of guardsmen at the grilles and another at the door to the nursery sitting room. Maia was relieved to see that no one was taking any chances with the children's safety. One of the guards opened the door and announced, "His Imperial Serenity, Edrehasivar the Seventh."

*Yes, because that will make frightened children feel much safer,* Maia thought—but he could not rebuke the guard merely for doing the correct thing. He entered the nursery, Cala preceding him and Beshelar following, and found Shevëan's children had risen to meet him, each of the girls clutching one of their brother's hands. Idra bowed, and Ino and Mirëan curtsied, all without releasing each other. All three of them were red-eyed and rather blotchy. The Alcethmeret was full of crying people today.

"Please sit down," Maia said, feeling gawky and ill-bred and dark as stormclouds. He sat down himself, in a shabby armchair, and waited until the children were seated again on the sofa. He took a deep breath, grateful that Beshelar had closed the door, and dropped formality. "My name is Maia. I hope that you will feel you can call me by it."

The little girls' eyes widened. Idra bit his lower lip, then said carefully, "Thank you, Maia."

He couldn't reckon how long it had been since anyone had called him by his own name—and there had been only Setheris anyway, since Chenelo's death. The familiar-first felt strange and stiff to his tongue and teeth and lips. "I am very sorry about what has happened."

"It isn't your fault!" Idra flared up, immediately outraged, and Maia had to blink hard to keep his composure.

"Your mother would not agree," he pointed out, "and we—I do not know what she may have said about me."

Idra took his meaning. "She did not speak of you to us," he said—plural, not formal. "We know only that you are our half uncle, the emperor."

Maia forgot himself far enough to make a face. "It

sounds so stuffy," he said apologetically, and was startled and pleased when Ino giggled, though she immediately hid her face against her brother's arm. "And I don't feel I can properly be your uncle; I'm only four years older. Will you call me cousin, instead as you did before?"

"If you wish it," Idra said a little doubtfully.

"I do," Maia said.

"Cousin Maia," said Mireän, "what's going to happen to Mama?"

Maia flinched, then told the truth: "I don't know, Mireän. I do not wish to have her executed, but I do not know if she can be trusted."

"Even if . . ." Idra swallowed hard. "She would have to be imprisoned, wouldn't she?"

"Yes," Maia said. "And she would be forbidden to speak or write to you."

"I am your heir," Idra said somberly.

"Yes."

"What about Ino and me?" Mireän asked. "We aren't your heirs."

Maia met her eyes, although it wasn't easy. "Mer Aisava, our secretary, tells us—I beg your pardon. Mer Aisava tells me that you understand what your mother was trying to do."

"She was trying to make Idra be emperor," Ino said. "But Idra doesn't want to!"

"I know," Maia said.

"And she was going to have you sent away," Mireän said. "Like you're going to do to her."

"Like Papa and Grandpapa got sent away," Ino said, her eyes filling with tears. "So they can't come back."

Maia looked at Idra, who said simply, "It was wrong," before he got out his handkerchief and turned to tend to his younger sister.

"Because *you're* emperor," Mireän said. "We saw you

get crowned and everything. And I still don't understand how Idra could be emperor if you weren't dead."

"I did *tell* thee, Miree," Idra said, perhaps a fraction too quickly. "Mama wished Cousin Maia to abdicate."

"Yes, but I don't—" Mireän began, having her full share of the Drazhadeise stubbornness, then encountered a glare from her brother and subsided.

As he could not honestly reassure Mireän, and yet had no actual proof that Sheveän would have murdered him, Maia thought he would do better to leave that ugly question unanswered. They would have to come to terms with it on their own. He said, "I wished you to know that I do not blame any of you. I know that you must be uncomfortable and unhappy, and I am sorry for that. Idra, is there anything I can do?"

He trusted Idra not to make impossible demands, and Idra, after careful thought, said, "Might we have some of our own household about us? Not the armsmen, we understand that perfectly, but my tutor and the girls' nursery maid?"

"Oh, please, Cousin Maia," Mireän said, "Suler doesn't dislike you or *anything*," as Ino said with perfect conviction, "Suler wouldn't do anything wrong." Maia noticed that the little girls clearly loved their maid in a way they did not love their mother. But of course it was their maid who took care of them; Sheveän was not Chenelo, Barizheise and alone, to tend her children herself.

"I will see what I can do," he said, and got up, uncomfortably aware of the duties that were undoubtedly mounting up on the other side of the nursery grilles.

"Thank you, Cousin Maia," Idra said, with Ino and Mireän a soft chorus behind him. Idra bowed and the girls curtsied, and Maia left them still clinging to each other in the cold and shabby nursery of the Alcethmeret.

# 24

## *The Revethvoran*

Maia's only satisfaction on that long, horrible day was the fact that neither Csevet nor Lieutenant Echana, the officer of the extra cohort of the Untheileneise Guard now assigned to the Alcethmeret, could find any objections to either Leilis Athmaza or Suler Zhavanin. Maia interviewed both the tutor and the nursery maid briefly. Leilis Athmaza was little and bright-eyed and quick-moving; he put Maia in mind of a ferret. He was clearly fond of his pupil, very anxious to know that Idra was all right, and Maia remembered that it had been Leilis Athmaza who had instructed Idra in the difference between a policy that the Lord Chancellor disliked and a policy that was bad. Suler Zhavanin was even easier; she was twenty or so, goblin-dark, scared nearly speechless, but when he told her Mireän and Ino had asked for her, she said at once, "Please, Serenity, let me go to them. Even if only for a few days, until you find someone better."

"We can think of no one better than someone who cares about them and whom they trust. Thank you, Min Zhavanin."

Her smile was as lovely as it was unexpected, and Maia treasured the memory of it against Cala's bloodshot eyes and increasing pallor, as if he were bleeding slowly to death from an invisible wound; against an incoherent letter from Csoru Zhasanai that intemperately mingled self-exculpation with condemnation of Maia's treatment of Shevëan; against a painful interview with Nurevis Chavar, all former friendliness gone; against Telimezh's miserable resolution when he begged an audience late that evening to tell Maia that he was resigning.

"Resigning?" Maia said, his first thought being that he had to have misheard.

"We will leave the court," Telimezh assured him, as if that were a matter of concern. "We do not wish you to be encumbered with us, Serenity."

"Encumbered?" Maia said, as witless as an echo. "Telimezh, please, we do not understand you."

"We failed you, Serenity," Telimezh said with stony unhappiness.

"There was nothing you could have done. We have been told the cantrip was a powerful one."

"We did not see Dazhis Athmaza's treachery. We failed you."

Maia tried exhaustedly to think of a way to handle this new problem. He could see that Telimezh's guilt was all too real; he could even, doubtfully, grant that there might be some justification for it, although still not very much. But . . . "We do not wish you to leave."

"Serenity?" Telimezh seemed astounded.

"You have done nothing to make us doubt you," Maia said. "And . . . we will understand if you no longer wish to be our nohecharis, but we have been most grateful for your service and would wish it to continue."

Telimezh looked as if he'd been hit over the head with a brick. Maia bit the inside of his lower lip to keep from giggling; it was exhaustion and nerves more than humor anyway. "Please," he said, "think on it at least overnight. We would be remiss if we accepted any decision you made today."

It took Telimezh a moment, but he managed to bow and say, "Serenity," and leave the room without walking into the door, although that was at least partly because Beshelar nudged him away from it.

"We don't think he'll resign, Serenity," Cala said after he'd closed the door of the Tortoise Room.

"Not now that he knows you wish him to stay," Beshelar said.

"Oh," Maia said. "Should we not have . . . we did not mean to keep him from resigning if it is truly what he wishes."

"You did not, and it is not," Beshelar said. "Telimezh's heart would always be here."

"Oh," Maia said again, since he was not sure if *good* or *bad* would be a more accurate response.

Csevet, who had politely absented himself during Telimezh's audience, now returned and said, "Serenity, we have bid the guards close the grilles. There is nothing more that can usefully be done today."

"And you think we should go to bed." He was too tired to be angry, all his febrile, furious energy burned away by grief. "We will not argue."

Beshelar and Cala accompanied him silently up the stairs. Maia felt that he should say something to them, but there was nothing in his head but ashes and nails. His edocharei were equally silent, and he found that he missed Nemer, who was much more inclined to chatter and commentary than either of the other two. He was desperately grateful to retreat behind the hangings of his bed, where he could almost pretend he was alone.

He slept poorly and woke to the information that the Adremaza was awaiting his pleasure in the Tortoise Room. Esha was disapproving, but Maia thought that if the Adremaza had come about Dazhis, he'd much rather see him before trying to eat.

The Adremaza was standing by the window in the

Tortoise Room with a young man in a maza's blue robe every bit as shabby as Cala's. *Should I have been suspicious of Dazhis,* Maia thought bleakly, *because his robe was new?*

They bowed. "Serenity," said the Adremaza, "we wish to present Kiru Athmaza, whom we hope you will accept as your new nohecharis."

The young man bowed again, even more deeply, and Maia took stock of him as he straightened. He was quite short and slightly built, with white hair in a long scholar's braid and pale green eyes. His nose tended toward the aquiline, but his chin was softly rounded, and he . . . Maia's gaze skipped down before he could stop it, and then he stared disbelievingly, first at Kiru Athmaza and then at the Adremaza. "Should that not be *nohecharo?*" he asked, and his voice squeaked slightly on the last syllable.

"We told you he would guess," muttered Kiru Athmaza in a voice that was not even close to deep enough to be a man's.

"Serenity—" The Adremaza seemed very nearly flustered. "We assure you, Kiru Athmaza is entirely to be trusted."

"We do not doubt it," Maia said, trying to recover his poise and knowing he was not successful. "But—"

"Serenity," Kiru Athmaza broke in, "we were passed over initially, for the old emperor would never have countenanced such a thing. But we have heard of your kindness to Arbelan Drazharan and to the Archduchess Vedero, and we dared to *hope.*"

"And you?" Maia said to the Adremaza.

The Adremaza *was* flustered; there was a pale pink blush in his cheeks and at the tips of his ears. "Serenity, you must understand that to be nohecharis is no trivial matter. First, one must be dachenmaza, and there are few dachenmazei in the whole of the Athmaz'are, even fewer willing to sacrifice their studies. It has always, *always* been the policy of the Athmaz'are that no one may be forced to take up this burden, and . . ."

He hesitated, and Kiru Athmaza said bluntly, "After losing first the late emperor's nohecharei and now Dazhis—three dachenmazei in as many months—there's no one else left."

"We see," Maia said. He felt rather ill, and was even more glad the Adremaza had not waited for later in the day.

"Serenity?" It was Cala, and of course the Adremaza was right. A new nohecharis had to be found so that Cala and Beshelar could go off duty.

"Yes, Cala?"

"We vouch for Kiru Athmaza," Cala said, though he was even pinker than the Adremaza.

"Thank you," Maia said. He carefully avoided looking at Beshelar and looked instead, searchingly, at Kiru Athmaza.

She returned his gaze steadily; he could see now that she was older than he had thought. She had to be a good ten years older than Cala or Dazhis, if not more. *We were passed over,* she had said, and *we dared to hope.*

"You desire this? Truly?"

"Yes, Serenity. Most truly."

"We must find out if Lieutenant Telimezh objects," Maia said.

"Of course," said the Adremaza.

"Serenity!" Beshelar said explosively. Maia winced, but he noticed Kiru Athmaza did not. "You cannot! What of . . ." For a moment he seemed in danger of strangling. "What of your *bedchamber*? You cannot appear before a woman in only your *nightshirt*!"

"We appeared so before the Princess Sheveän," Maia said, a reminder pointed enough to silence Beshelar.

His objection, though, was not without merit. Maia

looked uneasily at Kiru Athmaza, who was fighting a smile. "We should perhaps mention," she said, "that we are a cleric of Csaivo and have been since before Your Serenity was out of leading strings."

*Make that fifteen years older than Cala*—and clerics of Csaivo practiced strict celibacy; they worked in the great charity hospitals, tending men and women impartially. He wondered, though he knew it immediately for a question that could never be asked, whether it had been her desire, or whether it had been the only way she had to counterbalance the obstacle of her sex. Certainly, she would be far better trained than any court doctor. "And yet you wish to be nohecharis," Maia said. "Why?"

"It is not a matter of one or the other, Serenity. Although we must give up our work at the hospital, there are many here at your court who are in need of our services—even if only in odd hours." Those who could not afford the court doctors, Maia thought; if he had not ordered a doctor to tend to Nemer, Nemer might have had no doctor at all.

Kiru Athmaza was frowning at him. "Do you truly find it so incredible that we should wish to serve you?" She scanned his face, her eyebrows going up. "We see that you do."

"Forgive us," Maia said, breaking eye contact hastily. "We do not mean to doubt either your honesty or your loyalty. If Lieutenant Telimezh does not object to being partnered with you, we will be pleased to accept your service."

Beshelar snorted and muttered something, doubtless uncomplimentary; Maia, summoning up the remains of his dignity, pretended not to hear. Kiru Athmaza's face lit, and she said, "We promise you will not regret your decision, Serenity."

Maia found himself smiling back. "No, we do not think we will."

A clatter on the staircase heralded Telimezh, sufficiently out of breath to make Maia suspect that he, too, had only belatedly remembered that if he did not go on duty, Beshelar could not go off. "Serenity," said Telimezh, bowing, "we hope that you have not changed your mind since yesterday? About continuing to accept our service?" He looked at Maia with mingled anxiety and hope. If Maia found it incredible that anyone should wish so desperately to serve him, Telimezh clearly found it nearly as incredible that Maia should wish for his service.

"Of course we have not changed our mind," he said with as much warmth as he dared show. "But you must tell us if you are willing to be partnered with Kiru Athmaza. The Adremaza assures us she is entirely to be trusted."

Telimezh looked from Kiru Athmaza to the Adremaza to Maia, and Maia sympathized with his bewilderment. He could see that Telimezh wanted to turn and check with Beshelar; although he wouldn't have blamed him, he was glad Telimezh didn't, and not only because Beshelar's scowl would have provided unambiguous guidance.

Finally, Telimezh said, "If you do not object, Serenity, it is not for us to be obstructive. We will be pleased to work with Kiru Athmaza." He turned and bowed to Kiru, and she bowed back.

"Then it is settled!" the Adremaza said, a shade too heartily. "Serenity, we know we are keeping you from your breakfast, but there is one other matter."

"Dazhis," Maia said, his stomach a miserable lead knot. His nohecharei, of one tactful accord, stepped away and began a low-voiced conversation about schedules.

"Yes, Serenity," said the Adremaza. "His revethvoran is tonight, and—we do not know if Cala Athmaza told you—it is customary for the revethvoris to speak to those he has wronged."

"To make peace," Cala said.

"Yes. Properly, Dazhis should come to you, but the, ah, particular circumstances have led Captain Orthema to ask if in this instance Your Serenity might go to the Mazan'theileian instead. There are certain restrictions placed on Dazhis's actions that we cannot assure him will be maintained outside our precincts."

"He cannot believe Dazhis would hurt us."

"Serenity," said the Adremaza, neither agreeing nor disagreeing. "He prefers not to take that chance."

Maia wanted to protest—but he realized before he opened his mouth that he would never have believed Dazhis could conspire to oust him from the throne, either. "When should we come to the Mazan'theileian?"

"Thank you, Serenity," murmured the Adremaza; Maia knew perfectly well that he was being thanked more for not making that futile protest than for his co-operation. "A revethvoran is always performed at moon-set. If you come after you have dined, that will be plenty of time for Dazhis to speak to you and to Lieutenant Telimezh—if you will permit it."

"Of course," Maia said, and wondered how the Adremaza thought he was going to be able to eat after spending the day in miserable anticipation of the night.

By the time his dinner was set before him, however, Maia was ravenously hungry, and for much of the day, he had not thought about Dazhis at all. There were too many other matters demanding his attention. Dates had to be set for the trials of Chavar and Shevëan; Captain Orthema had to be prevented from turning the Un-theileneise Court into a military encampment; the Chavada and the Rohethada had to be heard and reassured that their loyalty was not in doubt. There were astonishing quantities of letters, delivered by pneumatic, by page boy, by courtiers presenting themselves in person at the grilles of the Alcethmeret.

Out of the tremendous stack of letters, Csevet chose one and handed it to Maia. "We thought Your Serenity might wish to respond to this one personally." It was from Dach'osmin Ceredin, who wrote, this time using the barzhad:

To the Emperor Edrehasivar VII Drazhar, greetings & wishes for Your Serenity's continued health & safety & the endurance of your reign. We knew Sheveän was an idiot, but we had no idea she would go so far in her idiocy. We regret extremely that we cannot challenge her to a duel & prove her worthlessness upon her carcase, but we are told that dueling is barbaric & unbefitting a lady & in any event Sheveän would not know how.

Nevertheless, Serenity, if there is any service we can accomplish for you—beyond our loyalty and fidelity, which you have already—you have only to say the word.

And she signed with an elaborate interlocked monogram such as—Maia knew from the blue-backed novels smuggled into Edonomee by the cook and her daughters—the cavaliers of Edrevenivar the Conqueror had used. He did not miss the implication that Dach'osmin Ceredin, unlike the Princess Sheveän, *did* know how to fight a duel. The art of dueling was no longer much practiced among the elves—the Varedeise emperors had disapproved of it wholeheartedly as something fit only for goblins—and it had never been taught to women at all. Maia wondered whom Dach'osmin Ceredin had found to teach her and if her father had the least idea. It occurred to him that there was nothing even remotely dutiful about fighting a duel, and he found himself smiling. He did want to make a personal reply, although he had no hope of matching her tone, and he was in the middle of trying to compose a letter that would be merely stiff rather than embarrassingly awkward when Csevet jerked back from the pile of correspondence as if he'd found it to contain a coiled viper.

"Csevet?" Maia said, more than a little alarmed. There could be no actual snake, but Csevet's ears were flat and his expression too carefully blank. "We beg pardon, Serenity," Csevet said, his voice cool and remote, revealing nothing. But his ears had yet to rise. "We were merely startled."

"Startled?" Maia said with as much polite skepticism as he could muster. "By our correspondence?"

Csevet made a face and conceded, "Perhaps 'repulsed' would be a better word. We are overtired, Serenity. Please disregard our megrims."

For once, Maia ignored Csevet's graceful deflection. "What is it that has repulsed you about our correspondence?"

Csevet hesitated, but he was boxed in and knew it. "It is this letter from Dach'osmer Tethimar, Serenity. We found it . . ."

"Repulsive," Maia finished, when it was clear that Csevet was not going to find an adjective that suited him. Csevet winced.

Maia held out his hand. Csevet said, "Serenity, you need not. It is the job of your secretaries to deal with . . ." He trailed off again, recognizing that Maia was not going to be swayed, and handed over the letter. His reluctance was visible, as if, Maia thought, to Csevet the letter *was* a viper.

Maia scanned it quickly. Like most of Tethimar's other letters, it was verbose and overly intricate, full of hints and insinuations. It also proposed that Maia should allow the House Tethimada to protect him and should retreat to their estate—or fortress, as Dach'osmer Tethimar described it—at Eshoravee until the Untheileneise Court was purged and could again be considered safe. Tethimar also offered to oversee the purging.

It was a remarkable performance, both in its effrontery and in its obvious belief that the emperor lacked enough common sense to open an umbrella against the rain. Maia personally found it more amusing than anything else, but when he looked up, he saw that Csevet's ears were still low, and although he was trying to mask it, the expression in his eyes looked like fear.

"We take it that you would advise us against accepting Dach'osmer Tethimar's kind invitation," Maia said.

He saw the explosion building, but at the last possible second, Csevet realized that he was being baited and said merely, "We would advise against it, yes, Serenity."

"We were not inclined to accept," Maia said as mildly as he could. "We have no reason either to love or to trust Dach'osmer Tethimar."

Csevet assembled his face into something that could almost pass muster as a smile. "Truly, Serenity, we trust your judgment. We are merely overexcitable—it happens when we do not get enough sleep."

Again, Maia disregarded the deflection. "Will you tell us," he said gently, "why you fear Dach'osmer Tethimar?"

Csevet was on the verge of trying to deny the conclusion Maia had drawn, but then his shoulders dropped an almost imperceptible amount. He said, "Serenity, it is not a pleasant story."

"We do not ask for the sake of amusement," Maia said.

"No, Serenity, we know that." Csevet took a deep breath and let it out slowly. "Our memories of Eshoravee are . . . evil. We were sent there, nearly ten years ago now, with a message for the Duke Tethimel. There were ferocious storms and Dach'osmer Tethimar speaks truly when he describes Eshoravee as a fortress. It stands alone on a high hill, and the only road up is narrow and switchbacked and steep. So steep that in some places there are stairs carved out of the rock. Horses cannot climb it. Anyone who wishes to go to Eshoravee goes on foot."

He glanced at Maia, quickly and then away. "We arrived long after nightfall, soaked to the skin and carrying our saddlebags over our shoulder. We had fallen three times on the ascent, and once would have fallen off the road entirely, and doubtless broken our neck, except for the dubious mercy of a thornbush. It is safe to say we hated Eshoravee long before we reached its gates."

"With good reason," Maia murmured, more as encouragement than anything else.

"The Duke Tethimel was drunk but hospitable," Csevet said. "He thanked us for our service and directed the steward to make us comfortable—and then forgot about our existence entirely. The steward despised us—couriers are often accused of promiscuity and wantonness and the worst kind of depravity—but he brought us to the servants' hall and showed us where we could sleep, and then told the scullery boy to show us to the servants' bathhouse.

"The bathhouse—not a separate building, for there are no separate buildings on the height of Eshoravee—was a long cavernous room built along one side of one of Eshoravee's roofed courtyards. The courtyard was serving as a makeshift dog-fighting pit, and as we bathed, we could hear the snarls and howls of the dogs and the snarls and howls of the men.

"The scullery boy, overworked and sullen, had not thought to tell us how to get back to the servants' hall, and although our sense of direction is normally quite acute, it is perhaps not surprising that we became lost. No matter which way we turned, we could not seem to get away from that courtyard and the stench of blood and smoke, and finally we went out to see if someone could spare their attention from the dog fights long enough to give us directions.

"Eshoravee has long been the favorite manor of the Dukes Tethimel, despite the fact that it is both inaccessible and primitive. It is staffed almost entirely by locals, and they do not fear outsiders so much as they despise them. The first man we approached shrugged us away; the second man cursed us. We were trying to choose a third man who might be less hostile when Dach'osmer Tethimar found us.

"We were fifteen, Serenity, and it was not the first time we had been propositioned—as we said, couriers are known to be . . ." He hesitated, searching for a word. "Amenable. But Dach'osmer Tethimar did not so much proposition as *grab*. We did not know who he was, and we disengaged ourself with more force and less tact than we would have if we had known. In point of fact, for he was very determined and, of course, very skilled in unarmed combat, we bit him."

"You *bit* Dach'osmer Tethimar."

"It is very likely that he still has the scar," Csevet said. "It made him angry, Serenity. He cursed us and slammed us against the wall of the courtyard and pinned us there, and we saw murder in his face.

"He backhanded us, knocking us to the ground, and by then there was a clear space, and all attention was on us. 'What do you say, boys?' cried Dach'osmer Tethimar. 'Fox and hounds?' There was a roar of approval, for this was something better than a dog fight, and Dach'osmer Tethimar said to us, 'We will give you five minutes' head start.' He pulled out his pocket watch—and that was when we realized who he was, for he dressed no differently than any of his men—and said, 'Starting . . . *now*.'

"Serenity, we bolted. We did not know Eshoravee, which we knew was what Dach'osmer Tethimar was counting on, but every minute we could buy ourself would be one more minute that he had not caught us. And Osreian or Salezheio or *someone* offered us a blessing that evening, for we found a staircase before the 'hounds' found us. We heard them laughing and shouting, and it did sound like the baying of hounds. We do not think Dach'osmer Tethimar made them wait the full five minutes, either.

"The stair we found was a servants' stair, for it was narrow and steep pitched and we climbed it in the dark, using our hands as much as our feet, but it twisted all the way up to the attics, and there we found a ladder, which led us to a trapdoor, which led us to the roofs. And there we spent the night, curled against a chimney for warmth. In the morning, we descended as soon as there was enough light to see, hiding from every noise of footsteps or voices. We made it out of Eshoravee without meeting anyone save the guard at the gate, and he did not recognize us as the 'fox'—or had not been part of the hunt at all. We abandoned our saddlebags and everything in them, and made our way down the switchbacked road, skidding and half-crawling and praying that no one had sent a message to the ostlers to hold us for Dach'osmer Tethimar's pleasure. No one had, and we were away from Eshoravee before the sun had fully cleared the hills. Before it set that evening— before we reached Puzhvarno—we were feverish with a charcarsa that nearly killed us. And that, Serenity, is why we fear Dach'osmer Tethimar."

The pause was uncomfortable—Csevet was clearly longing to be anywhere else—but there was one more question Maia had to ask. "What do you think they would have done to you if they had caught you?"

"We imagine," Csevet said, dry and bitter, "that being beaten to death is the best we could have hoped for. And, Serenity, we must tell you that no one would have cared. The Duke Tethimel received his message, and that, after all, is what matters."

"According to *whom*?"

Csevet's ears dipped and he sounded taken aback when he said, "Serenity, it was many years ago. And we survived."

"Yes. We are sorry. We are . . ."

"Shaken and fatigued," Kiru struck in, and Maia smiled at her gratefully.

"We will not accept the Tethimada's hospitality," he said to Csevet. "You need have no fear on that account."

"Just so, Serenity," Csevet said, and gracefully changed the subject to Maia's next responsibility. There were people who had to be reassured in person, including the mayor of Cetho and the preceptors of the Vigilant Chapters of both northern and southern Thu-Cethor. The preceptors glared and stalked around each other like rival tomcats, and Maia made a mental note that perhaps an inquiry into the conduct of the Vigilant Brotherhood would not be amiss. He was not at all sure whose authority they came under: the Archprelate or Captain Orthema? He would have to ask Csevet—merciful goddesses, how often in a day did he think that? He remembered Csevet's anxiety the day before and realized that, from a certain angle, it was not as unfounded as it had seemed to him. *Thou must become less dependent,* he told himself as Isheian cleared the plates from a dinner he had barely noticed eating, and wondered how he thought he was going to manage it.

And then he looked at the clock and realized it was time to go.

He set out for the Mazan'theileian accompanied only by Telimezh and Kiru, saying rather tartly to Lieutenant Echana that if armed soldiers were going to overrun the Untheileneise Court, they would already have done so, and his nohecharei could defend him for anything less. "It is, after all, their purpose," he said, and Echana unhappily gave way.

The Mazan'theileian was not part of the Untheileneise Court proper, but had been connected to it by a covered bridge during the reign of Edretanthiar III, in the delicate lacelike stonework typical of that era. The bridge was called Usharsu's Ladder, for the Adremaza who had commissioned it, and aspirants to the Athmaz'are spoke of "climbing the Ladder" or "falling off the Ladder" in describing their progress.

Kiru told Maia all this, not as one attempting to make conversation—which Maia would almost certainly have rejected—but simply as if she wished to share the information with him and Telimezh and the stones of the bridge. And Maia listened with a desperation he prayed did not show, trying not to think about what awaited him.

They were met at the end of the bridge by a boy of sixteen or so with a bad complexion and hair too fine to stay neatly in a braid. Unprepossessing, but his bow was graceful and his voice, when he spoke, the antithesis of his appearance: deep and warm and astonishingly well controlled for a boy so young. "Serenity," he said, "the Adremaza bade us welcome you and escort you to the Visitors' Room. We are Ozhis, a novice of the Athmaz'are."

"Thank you," Maia said, and could only be grateful his voice didn't crack.

The Visitors' Room was small and rather bare, but shining with cleanliness. There was only one chair, which both Ozhis and Kiru indicated strongly Maia was to sit in. He sat, composed himself, and waited. It was no more than five minutes before Dazhis was brought in. His hair had been cropped, and he wore, rather than the maza's blue robe to which he was no longer entitled, a black and shapeless garment that would be his shroud. He was flanked by two grim-faced mazei who bore the black stripe on their robes betokening them canons of Ulis. Dazhis went down on his knees almost before he cleared the doorway. He was weeping, in horrible racking sobs.

Maia had not the least idea what to do.

There was no comfort he could offer—Dazhis had committed a dreadful crime, and Maia could not help him escape the consequences. Nor could he say that he forgave him, for the truth was that he was not sure he did. Nor could he say he understood. But to stay silent was agonizing.

He had almost made up his mind to say something, though he did not know what, when one of the canons said, "Revethvoris, you must speak." His tone was not cruel, but it was perfectly inflexible, and Dazhis responded to it, gulping against his sobs and finally achieving a state in which he could force his voice out.

"Serenity, I am to beg your pardon." No formal-first, and Maia understood that even as he instinctively recoiled from the nakedness of it.

"Yes?" he said; Setheris, with a lawyer's eye for logic-chopping, had made very sure that Maia understood the difference between an apology and a statement about an apology, and in this instance, he found he could not settle for the lesser.

"I . . . I am sorry for what I did."

It wouldn't have been enough for Setheris, who would have made him spell out what he had done, but Maia did not have that kind of viciousness in him. And there was something he needed very badly to know: "Why? Why did you do it?"

Dazhis began sobbing again; Maia had the unwelcome suspicion that this was more an effort to evade the question than any sign of true grief.

"Revethvoris," said that same canon.

"*You* know," Dazhis cried, turning to him. "Why can't *you* tell him?"

"Because it was thy choice," the canon said flatly. "Not ours."

"Thou must answer," said the other canon.

Dazhis got himself under control again and said, "They promised me, the Princess Shevëan and Lord Chavar, that if I helped them, I should become Adremaza when Sehalis Adremaza dies."

*And possibly,* Maia thought, *the Adremaza's death would be sooner rather than later. As my own would have been.*

"And?" said one of the canons.

"And they promised I should be Prince Idra's First Nohecharis," Dazhis said in a whisper. "And they would not . . . his government would not . . ."

"We understand," Maia said, and flinched at the coldness of his own voice. Dazhis had lacked the courage to rebuke him to his face, but Maia had been a fool to think that meant his disapproval could be discounted.

*No,* said that astringent inner voice that was not Setheris. *Thou art emperor. It is no place of thy nohecharei to approve or disapprove of thee, and it is certainly no place of thine to court their approval. It is Dazhis who is in the wrong here. Not thee. Do thou remember that, Edrehasivar.*

He would try, but it was hard not to feel that he had done something wrong, something that had led to this.

"Have you anything else to ask the revethvoris, Serenity?" said one of the canons.

"No," Maia said. He had other questions, but none that he could bear to ask.

"Revethvoris?" prompted the other canon.

And Dazhis looked up at him for the first time and said, "Serenity, will you stay?"

"Stay?" Maia said. "You wish us to witness your revethvoran?"

Dazhis nodded. "I know it is an . . . an imposition and I should not ask it. And I will not fault you, Serenity, I promise, if you will not. But . . . Please, Serenity."

"But why would you wish . . . ?" He couldn't even find a way to finish the question.

One of the canons said, "Serenity, you are under no obligation to the revethvoris," but under that he heard Dazhis's reply: "I have no one else."

Maia was ashamed, suddenly and bitterly, that he did not know enough about Dazhis to know whether he meant that he was an orphan, that his family lived far away, that he was alienated from them already, or simply that they would not come. Chenelo would have known; Chenelo would have expected *him* to know. He said, "We will stay."

"Thank you," Dazhis said.

The canons looked at him dubiously, but seemed to decide they did not have the authority to argue with the emperor. "The revethvoris must also speak to Lieutenant Telimezh," one said.

"Yes," Maia said. "We will step outside with Kiru Athmaza, for what is between them is no business of ours." Also, he had to escape from this tiny, imprisoning room, from Dazhis's misery and his own inability to respond.

Kiru followed him and stood beside him in the great

vaulted hall of the Mazan'theileian, saying nothing. The hall was almost empty, and there was a hushed tension in the atmosphere that Maia hoped was not usual. The one or two mazei who passed them were almost scurrying, heads down—although perhaps that was his fault for being here?

He turned to ask Kiru, but at that moment the door to the Visitors' Room opened and Telimezh came out with one of the canons. Telimezh's face was bone-white and grim, and he did not meet Maia's eyes. The canon bowed and said, "Serenity, the revethvoran will take place at moonset, two hours from now, in the Lesser Courtyard, which Kiru Athmaza can show you. You may return to the Alcethmeret to wait if you wish, or if you prefer . . ."

It was the first sign of hesitation Maia had seen in either canon. "Yes?" he said.

"It is customary, Serenity, though by no means required, for the witnesses to a revethvoran to spend some time in prayer beforehand. We would be honored to open the Ulimeire of the Mazan'theileian to you and to Lieutenant Telimezh."

Maia did not need the twitch of Kiru's ears to tell him he was being accorded a signal honor, nor did he need any further explanation of the canon's hesitancy in broaching the subject. Piety was not fashionable at court, was in fact regarded with a certain amount of suspicion: another reason Chenelo had been so bitterly unhappy. The canon must have expected to be turned down—and possibly with a stinging rebuke.

Even if Maia had shared the court's opinion, he didn't think he could have rejected the offer—not knowing how rare it was for an outsider to be invited into any of the mazei's precincts, much less a holy place. He could not think why they would make him such an offer—emperors had been denied before, and at least one of them had had an army at his back—but he said, "We, too, would be honored. Telimezh?"

"Y-yes, Serenity." Telimezh was still badly rattled, but he bowed and said, "Our thanks, maza."

The Ulimeire of the Mazan'theileian was much larger than the Ulimeire of Cetho, but very nearly as shabby. The walls were undressed stone, and all the furniture was worn and much mended, sometimes by skillful hands and sometimes not. There was a cluster of mazei, all blue robed, with their heads bent in prayer; a little distant from them, the Adremaza knelt, alone, but he looked up as Maia entered and then got to his feet.

He was haggard and unkempt, as though he'd been digging his fingers into his hair, but he bowed and said, "Serenity, you are welcome here," with gentle tranquillity.

"Thank you," Maia said. "We would not intrude, but—"

"Dazhis asked you. It is a great kindness in you to agree."

It was guilt, not kindness, but there was no need to distress the Adremaza by saying so. "Where may we sit and not be in the way?" Maia asked instead, and the Adremaza showed him, with Telimezh and Kiru following, to a prayer bench along the west wall. Maia settled himself gratefully; for the next two hours he would not have to speak to anyone or guard his expression or behave like an emperor.

He knew only a few of the Barizheise prayers to Ulis, for his mother—perhaps superstitiously—had given him minimal instruction in Ulis's worship. One of the prayers he knew was inappropriate, being intended for a sickbed; of the others, he chose the one of which he was most sure. It took him some time to settle, but he remembered that it was always so after a break in custom, and he persevered without worrying, repeating the prayer carefully and mindfully, trying as best he could to mean it. Even if he could not truly forgive Dazhis, he did not wish either his death or what came after to be . . .

*Any worse than thine own would have been, Edre-hasivar?*

Maia shuddered away from that thought; he had been trying for two days now not to imagine how he would have died—if Sheveän would have instructed her men to make it look natural, or like an accident, or if she would have disdained subterfuge, safe in the knowledge that no one would dare protest. He was quite sure she would not have cared whether his death was painful or peaceful, fast or slow. There would have been no chance for him to make amends with those he had wronged.

*Dazhis had no thought of murdering me,* he rebuked himself, but the rejoinder came instantly: *Would he have said a word to prevent it?*

He forced his attention back to the words of the prayer. It didn't matter what Dazhis would or wouldn't have done in a situation that had not come to pass. *No, what he* did *do is quite bad enough.*

Maia winced as if those unforgiving words had been spoken aloud. *I cannot afford this anger. The Emperor of the Ethuveraz cannot become vengeful, for once begun, there will never be an end of it.*

*Ulis,* he prayed, abandoning the set words, *let my anger die with him. Let both of us be freed from the burden of his actions. Even if I cannot forgive him, help me not to hate him.*

Ulis was a cold god, a god of night and shadows and dust. His love was found in emptiness, his kindness in silence. And that was what Maia needed. Silence, coldness, kindness. He focused his thoughts carefully on the familiar iconography, the image of Ulis's open hands; the god of letting go was surely the god who would listen to an unwilling emperor. *Help me not to feel hatred,* he prayed, and after a while it became easier to ask that Dazhis find peace, that Maia's anger not be added to the weight against his soul.

When the canon rang the great deep-voiced revetha-hal, the death bell, Maia felt as close to serene as he thought could ever be possible under the circumstances, and he followed Kiru to the Lesser Courtyard with nothing in his heart beyond that prayer for peace.

The Lesser Courtyard looked like an accident of architecture; it was a narrow quadrangle between the main building of the Mazan'theileian and an obvious and much later addition—made even narrower in perception by the height of the walls on every side. Its primary purpose was clearly as a water collector, as the gutters, the pitch of the flagstones, and the grated drain in the center showed, but that made it ideally suited for a revethvoran, as well. It would be easy to wash away the blood.

It was bitterly cold; Maia pulled his hands back into the shelter of his quilted oversleeves and wished the imperial regalia ran more to woolly hats than diamond chokers. He shifted a little to whisper to Kiru, "You do not have to stay out here, Kiru Athmaza. We do not wish you to freeze."

"Thank you, Serenity," she murmured back, "but we are fine." There was nothing else she could say, and he knew it, but at least he had tried.

They did not have long to wait. First the Adremaza appeared on the opposite side of the courtyard, and then Dazhis came out, flanked by the canons. He was shuddering violently; Maia couldn't tell if it was from fear or cold. But he saw Maia and managed something that was almost a smile.

There was no spoken ritual: the canons escorted Dazhis to the center of the courtyard, where first one and then the other bowed to him and retreated to stand beside the Adremaza. Then the Adremaza stepped forward. He said something to Dazhis that Maia couldn't hear, then handed him the revethvoreis'atha and stepped back.

The revethvoreis'atha glinted in the lantern light. Its blade was long and narrow, its haft unadorned. Dazhis stared at it for a long moment; then he lifted his head, searching out Maia again. Maia still could not imagine how his presence could mean anything but more guilt to Dazhis, but he could not deny that somehow it must, for Dazhis's mouth firmed with what looked like genuine resolution, and he bared his right arm to make the first cut.

The revethvoreis'atha slid through his flesh like water. In theory, a revethvoris or revethvoro was to make five cuts: across each wrist, along each forearm, and the fifth cut across the throat. Few, however, were strong enough for the fifth cut, and it was not considered profanation of the ritual if they did not make it. Dazhis didn't. The revethvoreis'atha fell from his hand halfway through the fourth cut and was lost immediately in the spreading, glinting blackness of his blood. He kept his feet barely any longer, falling in an awkward sideways sprawl which had little dignity but did keep his face clear. His breath was coming in whimpers, but they did not form words. Maia forced himself to watch, forced himself to see that his anger was unnecessary. Presently, Dazhis fell silent; some time after that, the canons came forward again, kneeling without compunction or repugnance in Dazhis's blood to confer over him. One of them touched his face, then his throat; the other lifted his right wrist, apparently inspecting the cuts. They nodded to each other, then rose and returned to the Adremaza. A brief colloquy, and the Adremaza said in a carrying voice, "The revethvoran is completed."

Maia became aware that he was shivering and that Telimezh was saying, "Come inside, Serenity," in an anxious voice. It was hard to obey; he felt as if he'd frozen solid to the ground. But he forced himself to move, to return to the shocking warmth of the Mazan'theileian, where the Adremaza appeared out of nowhere to ask, "Are you all right, Serenity?"

*Was* he all right? Maia had his doubts. "We are fine, thank you,"

The Adremaza didn't look convinced; he said, "We must thank you again for witnessing, Serenity. We were afraid Dazhis would not . . ."

Maia didn't want to make him finish that sentence, so although he'd sworn not to, he asked, "He said he didn't have anyone else. Was he an orphan?"

"No," the Adremaza said with a tired sigh. "He was exaggerating."

"Oh."

"We are unfair. We beg your pardon. Dazhis was the third of eight children of a schoolmaster in eastern Thu-Athamar. We believe he was not happy as a child. He did not visit his parents after he was accepted as a novice to the Athmaz'are, and so far as we know, he did not correspond with them. He did not write to them today, although he was encouraged to."

"And no friends?" He knew *nothing* of Dazhis, nothing save his betrayal and his death.

"None who would witness a revethvoran," the Adremaza said, almost brusquely.

"No, of course not. Forgive us—it was a foolish question. Good night, Adremaza."

"Good night, Serenity," the Adremaza answered, bowing, and Maia walked back to the Alcethmeret in cold silence.

He did not sleep that night—could not, and could not bear to try. There would be no wake for Dazhis, and this was not one either. This was pent-up rage and grief and fear that had no outlet. He could not stay cold, much as he longed to, and he paced from room to room of the Alcethmeret, up and down its echoing staircase, only barely choking back the urge to scream at his no-hecharei, merely for doing their jobs. He was sure they were grateful when morning came and they could escape.

Beshelar was as picture-perfect as ever; Cala was pale and tired-looking, but no longer seemed distraught. They did not attempt to speak to him, but somehow he found himself herded into the dining room, where the samovar was singing its odd little song and Isheian was waiting to pour him a cup of tea.

There was no point, he thought wearily, in refusing comfort. He sat down, accepted the teacup, and tried to find some of the cold and quiet peace he had achieved in the Ulimeire. He did not think he was notably successful, but when he had drunk his tea, he went up to his rooms and let his edocharei bathe and dress him, and when he descended again for the day officially to begin, he no longer wanted to scream at anyone, so perhaps that was progress.

But then, as Csevet was edifying Maia's breakfast with an account of all the things that had to be accomplished, starting with a meeting of the Corazhas and ending with increasing the emperor's household budget to account for Idra and his sisters, a page boy brought a message from Hesero Nelaran, imploring him to grant her an audience, and Maia realized there was one consequence of that unsuccessful coup with which he had simply and utterly failed to come to grips.

His cousin, Setheris Nelar.

# 25

## *Matters of the Aftermath*

Maia received Hesero Nelaran in the Tortoise Room. It had been, he thought, a month and a half since he had first been introduced to her, and he was almost, oddly, sad to find that she no longer overwhelmed him as she had his first day in the Untheileneise Court. She was still a beautiful, sophisticated woman, but he had been surrounded by women like her for weeks, and she no longer stood out for him except by virtue—if "virtue" was what one ought to call it—of being Setheris's wife.

"Serenity," she murmured with a low and exquisitely graceful curtsy. "We thank you for granting this audience, which we know we should not have presumed to ask for."

"Osmerrem Nelaran, we don't—"

"Please," she said, and she smiled a brave, fake smile at him. "Did we not agree we were cousins?"

"Cousin Hesero," he amended. "What is it you wish?"

"Serenity, please, we ask that you grant an audience to our husband, your cousin."

"Why should we?"

"He is your cousin," she said, frowning.

"And the princess is our sister-in-law."

"He raised you!" she protested. "Serenity, we know

you do not favor him, though we do not understand why, but can you not see past whatever grudge it is you hold against him? Is it just of you to—"

"*Grudge?*" He could hear that his voice had risen, but he could not find the wherewithal to care. "Osmerrem Nelaran—Cousin Hesero—we hold no *grudge*. We have tried our most desperate best not to act from spite or malice. We did not send him back to Edonomee, although we could have. We offered him a position that was honorable and useful. What more could we do?"

"Serenity—"

"No." He realized distantly that he was trembling. "We could not. *I* could not. He bullied me. He reviled me. He beat me—not for discipline, but for his own anger and helplessness." He fumbled with his left cuff, shoved the sleeve up to show the scars, thick silver lines on slate-gray skin. "This is his handiwork, Cousin Hesero. And while I . . . I understand, truly, and I forgive him as best I may, I will not show him favor. Nor do I think it *just* that he demands it of me." He choked the words off, ashamed that he had said that much, and bent his head to fasten his cuff again. But his fingers were too unsteady for the tiny pearl buttons, and he was about to forsake it when a voice said softly, "Serenity, will you permit me?"

It was Cala. Maia could not meet his eyes, but he extended his wrist. Cala's long white fingers were quick and deft; he had fastened the last button before Maia registered his use of the first-familiar. He looked up, and where he had feared to find pity or contempt, Cala said, "I could not be as forgiving," and bowed deeply before returning to his place beside Beshelar.

*Later*, Maia told himself. *Think about it later*. He had the threads of another conversation to pick up; Hesero had backed away and was staring, stricken. Maia had wondered if Setheris had ever raised his hand against his wife, and now he supposed he had his answer in her horror-filled eyes and ashen face.

"Sit down, Cousin Hesero," he said.

She sat, the first graceless motion he had seen from her. "He was cruel to you?" she said in a bare, breathless whisper.

"Yes," Maia said. There was no point now in trying to soften the truth. He sat down himself, suddenly uncertain whether his legs would hold him if he remained standing. "I am sorry. I should not have—"

She shook her head dazedly. "No, it isn't—that isn't . . . I cannot—Serenity, I do not understand how we can be speaking of the same person."

"I am sorry," Maia said again, helplessly. "I don't understand either. But . . . he was very unhappy. We both were. And we were very isolated."

Although she was trying to meet his eyes, her gaze kept going back to his left forearm. "It was a firescreen," he said. "He . . . he didn't mean to."

She nodded and then by force of will dragged her gaze back to his face. "Will you see him?"

Maia resumed the armor of formality. "We suppose we must."

"He is innocent of treason," she said, her voice barely a whisper. "He does not deserve . . ." She stopped, and he could see her composure was as fragile as a soap bubble. "Whatever he may have done, he is our husband. Please, we beg you, if you will condemn him, at least do it yourself."

He did not understand her, but then, he could not imagine loving Setheris that much. He supposed many things would be different if he could. "We will grant him an audience," he said. "Now." His glance at Csevet was not a question, and Csevet's drawn-down mouth and dipped ears acknowledged it.

After considerable and careful thought, Maia had

Setheris brought to the Tortoise Room. It did not provide him the shield of impersonal public grandeur that the Untheileian or even the Michen'theileian would have, but he decided it was worth sacrificing that shield for a greater feeling of comfort and security and therefore confidence.

Setheris, when he arrived, escorted by a pair of guardsmen, looked tired and shabby and . . . it took Maia several seconds to identify what he was seeing in Setheris's posture and the carriage of his ears, and several more to believe it: Setheris Nelar was afraid.

It wasn't that Setheris *shouldn't* be afraid, Maia thought; it was that Maia had never seen Setheris afraid, never *imagined* Setheris afraid, and now that it was in front of him, he did not know what to do.

Setheris knelt and stayed there. For once, Maia felt no qualms about leaving a petitioner on his knees.

"We have spoken to thy wife," Maia said.

Setheris flinched as if he'd been burned, and Maia realized that that must have been the one thing he had most wanted to prevent. Maia wondered if he should feel somehow victorious; he didn't.

"She tells us," he pursued grimly, "that thou art loyal to us."

"I am, Serenity," Setheris said, his voice as flat as his ears, as if he did not expect to be believed. "I swear it."

"Why?"

Maia's guards and nohecharei stared at him like stunned carp. Setheris did not—Setheris did not even look up. He knew why Maia was asking.

Maia waited; he had never seen Setheris at a loss for words before. Finally, Setheris said, something between a plea and a snarl, "Because Uleris Chavar is an idiot. And I believe in the law. I believe that *you* believe in the law." Which was a shocking admission from Setheris, as close to a compliment as Maia had ever had from him. Setheris looked up then, and his eyes were wild. "I am many things, Serenity, but I am not a traitor."

And Maia understood: Setheris had been here before, accused of treason, on his knees before the emperor. But that confrontation had gone very differently. Maia asked, for the question burned him like a live coal, "Why wert thou relegated to Edonomee?"

Setheris's laugh was as bitter as Maia remembered it. "I told the late emperor your father that if he believed I had committed treason, he should put me on trial, not lock me up in the Esthoramire like a misbehaving dog. I thought he was going to kill me. For I had *not* committed treason, and he knew it. But I had tried to manipulate him, and he could not forsake his anger. Could *never* forsake his anger. And thus I was sent to Edonomee. With you."

The history between them made the air thick. Slowly, thoughtfully, Maia said, "We could send thee back there."

"Serenity, I have done nothing wrong!" The protest was anguished, clearly ripped from him despite his own better judgment.

"I know that," Maia said. "But I hate thee, as thou well knowest, and if thou art at court, I will always have to wonder what thou art saying, and to whom."

Setheris's face was bloodless to the lips. He said, his voice dropping to a whisper, "I swear I will say nothing—I *have* said nothing, even to my wife. It is the past and it will stay there. I am loyal, Serenity, and I understand the danger of words—as *thou* knowest."

Maia thought of all the things Setheris had called him, from "moon-witted hobgoblin" to "misbegotten blot," and had to admire his cousin's courage—if not outright insanity—in invoking those memories. "I will not send thee to Edonomee, but I cannot have thee here." He held Setheris's gaze steadily, for the first time in his life not flinching away from his cousin's cold eyes. And it was Setheris who looked down. Who muttered grudgingly, unhappily, "I suppose I have earned this from you."

Maia said, "We suppose so also." He saw Cala's wince out of the corner of his eye.

"Just—Serenity, please. We are—I am loyal and competent. Give me a job, a responsibility, *something*. Do not leave me to rot as Varenechibel did."

"We cannot punish thee for *not* conspiring against us," Maia said, and watched some of the fear bleed out of Setheris's body. He deliberately looked away from Setheris to find Csevet, noticing distantly how difficult it was to do so. Csevet was blank-faced, but his ears were ever-so-slightly flattened with disapproval. Maia glared at him, and Csevet, coming back to himself with a jump, bowed his head in acquiescence and slipped silently out of the room.

"Something will be found for you," Maia said to Setheris, "and we do not think you need stay in the Esthoramire any longer."

Setheris's head had jerked up when Maia granted him the second-person formal, and by the end of the sentence, his eyes were shining in a way that Maia found disconcerting and embarrassing. It was no part of their relationship for Setheris to be grateful to him—he did not, he realized, even *want* Setheris's gratitude.

He looked at Hesero Nelaran, standing against the wall, her arms crossed tightly across her chest. "You have your husband back, Cousin Hesero."

She said, "We thank you, Serenity," and Maia thought she meant it. Or, at least, she was trying to. Her curtsy was still exquisite, and she left, beside her husband, with her head up, as if she bore no burdens on her shoulders at all.

In the silence, Maia gripped his courage together as best he could and turned to face his nohecharei. Beshelar was scarlet in the face. Maia looked hastily past him at Cala, who said, "How old were you when—?" and he nodded toward Maia's arm.

"This? Oh, fourteen or so." He added, still not sure in his own mind if it made things better or worse, "He was drunk."

Beshelar said, grinding the words viciously between his teeth, "He should be flogged through the streets. He should be flogged to the river and thrown in." He fixed Maia with a furious glare and demanded, "Did the emperor know?"

"We have no idea," Maia said blankly; this was not the reaction he had expected from Beshelar. "If he was told, he did not care."

"Monstrous!" Beshelar shouted, very nearly at the top of his lungs. Csevet, coming into the room, startled back and almost dropped the sheaf of papers he was carrying. There was a moment of supreme awkwardness, and then Maia was simply unable to keep from laughing. He sat down, still laughing, and waved Csevet into the other chair. Csevet sat, looking bewildered and a little alarmed. Beshelar said, very stiffly, "Serenity, we will await you on the landing," and stalked out.

Csevet looked from Beshelar's retreating form to Cala to Maia, who had managed to calm himself. "Serenity, should we—?"

"No, it's fine," Maia said. "Beshelar was talking about something else. And you have a matter to lay before us?"

"Serenity," Csevet said, agreeing and accepting. "This first order of business before the Corazhas must be the selection of a new Lord Chancellor, and we thought—unless you have a candidate of your own to put forward?"

"We would choose you in a heartbeat," Maia said, "except that we would be lost without you."

Csevet blushed a delicate, pleased pink and said, "We are far too young, Serenity."

*As am I,* Maia thought, but he bit the words back as unprofitable. Instead, he thought carefully about the men he had encountered in the government of the Ethuveraz, those who supported Chavar's policies (and who now might be backtracking in haste), those who did not, those who balanced carefully and noncommittally between, and he thought that, out of all of them, only one had both seen that the emperor was out of his depth and had chosen to do something about it. And had continued to offer help without asking anything in return. And that man, he thought, was the man he wanted in charge of his government. "Our choice would be Lord Berenar," he said.

"Serenity," Csevet said, making a note. "Do you wish to announce it to the Corazhas? You are unlikely to meet with opposition, and it would certainly expedite matters."

"Will we seem to be biased if we do? It is not always clear to us."

"No, Serenity. You have every right to propose a candidate to the Corazhas, just as you have the power to refuse any candidate *they* propose. Lord Berenar is universally respected, and indeed we think him an excellent choice. They *may* refuse him, as is *their* right, but they, too, are anxious to see this matter dealt with, and we do not think they will be, ah, fractious."

"Thank you. Then, yes, we will recommend Lord Berenar to the Corazhas."

And an hour later, he got up and did so, feeling awkward and inarticulate and much too young, particularly as the Archprelate had taken the place of the Witness for the Prelacy until such time as the Prelates' Council should be able to meet to choose a new one, and the Archprelate made Maia unsettled—not guilty, exactly, but too aware of his failure to meditate, to worship as his mother had taught him. But the Witnesses heard him respectfully, and when he had sat down again, Lord Berenar murmured, "Thank you, Serenity," before rising to announce that he was willing, if the Corazhas agreed.

The Corazhas *did* agree. Maia was amazed at the lack of squabbling. The concerns raised were legitimate and dealt with responsibly, and in only slightly more than an hour the Ethuveraz had a new Lord Chancellor. The formal investiture would have to be scheduled and suffered through, but Lord Berenar knelt and swore a personal oath then and there in the Verven'theileian, and said he did not wish to wait as things were already in a terrible snarl and only getting worse with delay.

"Proceed with our blessing," Maia said, and now the Corazhas was down two members, a state of affairs that, however inconvenient and deplorable, provided an unexceptionable reason for ending this meeting. Maia did so thankfully and turned toward Csevet to be told the next item in his never-ending agenda, only to discover Csevet had been buttonholed by Lord Berenar's personal secretary.

Maia knew perfectly well that he could interrupt, but if he didn't, he might have as much as five minutes of peace before Csevet extricated himself. He leaned back a little in his chair, refraining with difficulty from a sigh—and realized that Archprelate Tethimar was watching him closely.

Maia straightened again, feeling guilty even though he knew it was ridiculous. "Did you wish to speak to us, Archprelate?"

The Archprelate considered him, head cocked a little to one side, like a bird. "Are you well, Serenity?"

Bewildered, Maia said, "Why would we not be?"

"Forgive us," the Archprelate said. "We do not wish

to pry. But we know that the strain you are under must be considerable."

Maia supposed that it was, but there was nothing to be done about it. "We thank you for your concern."

The Archprelate smiled at him, as sudden and dazzling as sun on snow. "A gracefully noncommittal answer, Serenity. You have learned quickly the arts of being politic."

Maia saw Lord Berenar's secretary bow to Csevet and hurry out of the room. "Forgive us," he said, hoping his relief did not show. "We fear we may already be late for our next obligation."

"Of course, Serenity," the Archprelate said—although Maia had the feeling that those bright eyes saw right through his feeble excuse—and he, too, bowed and left.

Maia turned to Csevet and said, "What now?"

"Luncheon," Csevet said firmly. "And this afternoon must be given to the Witness for the Emperor, who is preparing for the trial of Lord Chavar and the Princess Sheveän."

"Of course," Maia said, and tried not to feel the great hollow coldness opening inside him. But he had no appetite for luncheon.

Again, Maia chose the Tortoise Room for this audience that he expected to be uncomfortable. Csevet had assured him it was his choice, and although he feared he was betraying weakness by not choosing the Michen'theileian, the Tortoise Room was the only place in all of the Untheileneise Court that felt in the least homelike to him.

The Witness for the Emperor was a small, neat man, very precise in all his movements. His name was Tanet Csovar. In face and voice he was entirely unremarkable; his clothes were sober and unostentatious, and his hair was obviously a wig, for although it was dressed very plainly, with only a single pair of tashin sticks, it was sleek and lustrous, unlike his sparse eyebrows. He was a judicial Witness of more than twenty years' experience, and there could be no doubt he knew his job very well. He asked his questions respectfully, but remorselessly, and if the answer he got was not adequate, he asked another question. He showed neither impatience nor disappointment; it was simply that he could not be deterred. The most disconcerting thing, though, was that he did not take notes. He simply *listened,* his cold eyes watching Maia's face intently, and his questions quickly revealed that he forgot nothing of what he heard.

He first had Maia tell him the events of the attempted coup, asking him to be as accurate as he could, particularly in recounting what each person had said. That was not so bad, but then the Witness began to ask about previous encounters with Lord Chavar, with the Princess Shevëan, about what Maia thought their reasons might be; then, even worse, he asked about how Maia had felt.

"We do not see that our emotions have any relevance," Maia said, trying to sound annoyed rather than trapped.

"We cannot witness if we do not know the truth," said Csovar, "and emotions are part of the truth of any person."

"But surely it isn't necessary."

"Serenity, we will not think less of you for your feelings, if that is what troubles you."

"No, we are sure you will not." Defeat. It was not Mer Csovar's bad opinion he dreaded, but he wasn't supposed to care for his nohecharei's opinions, either. "We were afraid," he said finally, determined to get the words out and be done with them, "for we know enough history to predict the fate of an emperor once dethroned."

Mer Csovar frowned. "We understood from what you told us that there was no intent to harm you."

"Not then, no. But our person, if alive, would always

be inconvenient and potentially dangerous, would it not? And we could see that the Princess Shevëan would not hesitate. Would perhaps even be pleased. She seems to hate us very much."

He was grateful that Mer Csovar did not attempt to convince him he was mistaken, merely nodding and saying, "You feared, very naturally, for your life."

"Yes. We feared also for our nephew Idra and for the Ethuveraz. It is not a secret, now, that we and Lord Chavar disagree most fundamentally about the needs of our empire, and it did not seem to us that the Princess Shevëan was interested in the needs of the *empire* at all."

"Do you feel she cared only for her son? Or only for her own access to power?"

It was a good question—a better question than most of the fruitless ones Maia had been asking himself. He stopped and thought, and Mer Csovar made no attempt to hurry him. At length, he said, "We do not know. We do not know what plans she and Lord Chavar had made about governance. We believe that she was acting in what she saw as her son's best interests—and to honor her husband's memory, for we have always felt that it is that for which she most hates us, that we are alive when her husband is not. We do not think her motives were . . . were *political*."

"It is a subtle distinction, Serenity," Mer Csovar said.

"We know. We do not understand the Princess Shevëan, so truly, it is only a guess. But," he said slowly, as it became clear to him, "either she was acting out of a desire for power which left no room to consider the welfare of her son—or her daughters—or she was acting out of a blind self-righteousness which would make her easily manipulated—or indeed disposed of—by those who called themselves her allies. We did not see any chance of a beneficial outcome."

"And so you demanded to see Prince Idra. Did you expect him to support you?"

Maia stared at Mer Csovar. "The question did not occur to us. We could not . . ."

"There is no hurry, Serenity," Mer Csovar murmured.

Maia pressed his hands together before his chest, palm to palm and fingertip to fingertip. It was a Barizheise meditation technique, and if any of them cared, he was betraying all sorts of things, but it steadied him enough that he could say, "We thought only that if we were not fit to be emperor, it was not for our Lord Chancellor to decide, nor for our sister-in-law. It was Idra who would live—or die—with the consequences, and we felt we had to speak to him. We expected . . ." What had he expected? He wasn't even sure now, that cold cellar seeming as far away and improbable as something dreamed. He let his hands fall, and his shoulders sagged with them. "We expected to die."

He thought there was a noise behind him, but did not turn to look. "We wished to ensure, whatever happened, that Idra *knew*. We did not expect him to defy his mother."

"Would you have signed the abdication papers?"

"Yes," Maia said bleakly. "If it had come to that, we would have. We could not subject our people to a civil war, not when we are unsure—" He stopped himself, but it was already too late.

"Unsure, Serenity?"

"We believe that our rule is better for the Ethuveraz than a regency government led by Lord Chavar, but what if we are wrong? What if we *are* leading our people into chaos and disaster? What right have we to impose our rule on those who do not wish it?"

"You are the only surviving son of Varenechibel the Fourth," said Csovar. "If nothing else, Serenity, it is the law."

"We did not think we could be sure of anyone's support," Maia said. That was definitely a noise, Beshelar biting back an intemperate comment, no doubt. Maia kept his attention on Csovar. "The coup was led by the most important official of our government and a member of our family, and they were assisted by one of our nohecharei."

"Yes. We understand." Csovar considered him for an uncomfortable moment. "Serenity, were you angry?"

"We were furious," Maia said, and was ashamed at how quickly the words came to his tongue. "And sick with betrayal, although perhaps that was foolish of us."

Csovar's eyebrows went up. "If Lord Chavar did not wish to serve you, the appropriate thing to do was resign." He coughed, looking a little embarrassed. "Many members of your government also feel betrayed, Serenity."

"Do they? Thank you." He was weak and foolish, but it *did* help to know that. "We were—we *are*—very angry. We are trying to forgive, but we find it very difficult."

"What would you wish to be done with those who have wronged you in this matter?"

"We know not," Maia said wearily. "It will be our decision in the end, regardless."

"Yes, Serenity, but we did not ask what you *will* do with them."

"You ask dangerous questions, Mer Csovar."

"Serenity," Csovar said with a briskness that was as near to impatience as he seemed likely ever to come, "it is our task to witness for you precisely *because* there are things that you, as the Emperor Edrehasivar the Seventh, cannot say. It is the calling of Witnesses, to speak for those who cannot speak for themselves."

"You are a Witness *vel ama,*" Maia said. The idea was bitterly amusing.

"Yes, Serenity."

"And if we say we want them dead? As slowly and painfully as possible?"

Csovar did not look away. "Is it the truth?"

"No," Maia said. *Weak. Foolish.* He folded his hands in his lap against the urge to rub his eyes. "We did not even wish Dazhis Athmaza dead, and it was he who betrayed us most . . . most nearly."

"Would you spare them all punishment?"

"No," Maia said, and struggled with it. Csovar waited. "In our inmost and secret heart, which you ask us to bare to you, we wish to banish them as we were banished, to a cold and lonely house, in the charge of a man who hated us. And we wish them trapped there as we were trapped."

"You consider that unjust, Serenity?"

"We consider it cruel," Maia said. "And we do not think that cruelty is ever just. Are we finished, Mer Csovar?"

Csovar gave him a long, dry, thoughtful look. "Unless there is something Your Serenity wishes to add?"

"No, we thank you," Maia said, and Csovar bowed and unhurriedly made his way out, neat and precise and impartial, witnessing Maia's weakness without judging it, carrying that burden of darkness beneath his shining wig without being weighed down by it. Maia only wished he could do the same.

# 26

## The Clocksmiths and the Corazhas

The one thing that Maia had been determined to achieve before the celebration of Winternight began was the presentation of the Clocksmiths' Guild of Zhaö before the Corazhas. Most of the things hanging over his head were things he could not control (and there had been no word from Thara Celehar since his precipitous departure for the north), but this thing at least could happen, and the Corazhas could have two weeks or more to think about it before there would be time for a discussion and a vote. His control was mostly an illusion, especially as he did nothing himself but merely told Csevet what he wished done, but it was better than throwing temper tantrums or going into a decline or any of the other more ostentatious responses to being emperor that occurred to him.

In fact, the Corazhas did not grant an audience to the Clocksmiths' Guild until the day before the Avar of Barizhan's scheduled arrival, and even that, Maia was given to understand, was the result of a vast quantity of pushing and prodding. The Prelates' Council still had not chosen a new Witness for the Prelacy. The new Witness for the Treasury was a very young man, by Corazheise standards, and it looked as if it might be three or four years before he found the confidence to open his mouth. Maia almost regretted Lord Berenar, who had yet to emerge from his first plunge into the depths of the Lord Chancellor's office, but he reminded himself of just how much more he wanted Berenar *there* than *here* and did not repine.

The Clocksmiths' Guild was represented again by Mer Halezh and Merrem Halezho, this time supported by (or supporting—Maia couldn't quite tell from their demeanor) another man, older than Mer Halezh and showing a clocksmith's crouch: even when he straightened from his bow to the emperor, his shoulders stayed hunched. He was introduced as Dachensol Evet Polchina; Maia did not know what precisely that title betokened in the guild, but several of the Corazhas were looking impressed, as if Dachensol Polchina's presence reassured them that they were not wasting time on a mere cloud-fancy of the emperor's, as Lord Pashavar had so eloquently put it.

And when the emperor formally invited the Clocksmiths of Zhaö to speak to the Corazhas, it was Dachensol Polchina who stepped forward. He made a deep formal bow to Maia and then bowed, less deeply, to each of the Corazhas in turn. Then he beckoned, and Mer Halezh and Merrem Halezho carried forward a massive draped shape and set it on the table in front of Maia's chair.

"What is this?" Csevet said, with a cold glance at one of the junior secretaries, who apparently should have known better than to allow any such object in the room without Csevet's approval. Telimezh moved forward as if he were preparing to fling himself on it.

Dachensol Polchina's face creased into a beatific smile. "That is the bridge." Another gesture, and Mer Halezh and Merrem Halezho carefully lifted the linen drape.

Maia's breath caught.

Beneath the drape was a model of a section of a

river—of the Istandaärtha. There were tiny houses on one side and pasture on the other, with little black-and-white dairy cows grazing on green velvet. The road on each side was paved with tiny quartz pebbles, smooth and gleaming like cobbles after rain. The river banks were rocky, with twisted verashme trees showing defiant golden-red blossoms. The river itself was brown and roiling, rendered, he thought, with silk and clusters of fish scales. At one point, a tree trunk surged angrily out of the water; he was amazed at the impression of movement and ferocity, at how deftly the model-maker had conveyed the power of the Istandaärtha.

And in the center of this marvel, the focus and anchor, was the bridge. To Maia's eye, instantly adapted to the delicacy of the world the model showed, it was a massive thing, a brass and iron monster, four great square towers, two on each bank, throwing out arm after arm toward each other until they met and clasped claws in the middle. He saw, with a jolt that was not surprise, that the spars of the bridge had been engraved to suggest the claws he had fancied. He leaned closer and saw the ugly, benevolent faces of four tangrishi at the top of each tower.

"What better protectors for a steam-powered bridge?" Dachensol Polchina murmured, only loud enough for Maia to hear—although that was partly because the Corazhas' muttering was growing louder, from the initial gasps of astonishment and admiration on one side and angry disbelief on the other.

"The thing's ridiculous," snapped Lord Pashavar.

"It will break under its own weight," Lord Deshehar protested.

"No boat could possibly get past this monstrosity," said Lord Isthanar, the Witness for the Universities, and that was apparently the opening Dachensol Polchina wanted.

"Aha!" he said, and nodded to Merrem Halezho. She touched something beneath the model cow pasture, and she must have had a touch of the maza's gift, for there was a spark and the smell of burning.

"It will take a few minutes to generate enough steam," Dachensol Polchina said, "though for the real bridge, there would of course be employment for stokers to be sure the river traffic doesn't have to wait. In the meantime, we will be happy to answer your questions."

Maia barely heard the ensuing discussion, vehement though it was. He was too entranced by the model. As he looked closer, he could see that there were tiny people among the houses: a woman hanging laundry, a man weeding his vegetable garden, two children playing hider and seeker. There was even a tiny tabby cat sunning itself in a window. On the road toward the bridge, a wagon pulled by two dappled horses had stopped while the driver rummaged for something beneath his seat. Looking to the other side of the river, Maia suddenly spotted the cowherd among the cows, and he barely restrained a crow of delight. The cowherd, goblin-dark, was sitting cross-legged beneath the only tree in the pasture and playing a flute so carefully rendered that each fingerhole was distinctly visible.

Maia straightened up and said decisively, cutting through the increasingly acrimonious discussion between Corazhas and clocksmiths, "We wish to see the bridge work."

Lord Pashavar glared at him. "Your Serenity is determined to go ahead with this foolishness?"

"We do not find it foolish," Maia said, and was surprised at the calmness of his own voice, "and we do not believe that Dachensol Polchina finds it foolish, either."

"It is not foolish," Dachensol Polchina agreed. "It is new, which is not the same thing."

"It is hardly a clock," said Isthanar, sneering. "Are you quite sure you understand what you are doing?"

"If you find our understanding flawed, you are welcome to explain it to us," Dachensol Polchina said mildly, with a gesture toward the model.

Isthanar's stricken silence was covered by the Archprelate saying, "How can you possibly know that when you come to build the real thing, it will support its own weight?"

"It's not as heavy as it looks," Mer Halezh said. "You'll see in a minute."

At first, Maia could not identify the noise coming from beneath the model, for it had no place in the Verven'theileian, no place in the life of an emperor. It was the whistle of a teakettle coming to the boil.

Merrem Halezho said, triumph snaking out around the corners of her mouth, "We are ready, Serenity."

"Then, please," Maia said, and hoped he did not sound as pompous as he felt he must, "show us your bridge."

Merrem Halezho did something beneath the model, and the whistling stopped. They waited—and even Pashavar seemed to be holding his breath—and then with a slow, jerky movement, two of the bridge's claws released their grasp and folded back. The rest followed, pair by pair, and then the spars of the bridge lifted like wings and pulled back, one pair at a time, starting in the middle. Maia's chest felt full of amazement, like a great glowing ball he could barely breathe around.

"The process can be halted at any point," Dachensol Polchina said, as if he did not know that emperor, Corazhas, secretaries, and all were struck dumb with wonder. "But in case of storms or floods, the bridge can be pulled back onto the banks, as you see. And thus any amount of river traffic can be accommodated."

It did not happen swiftly or quietly, but as Dachensol Polchina had said, the bridge pulled back almost entirely into its towers.

"It *is* a tangrisha," Maia said, and then blushed painfully.

"The tangrisha was one of our inspirations," Mer Halezh said kindly, "though we also watched a great many spiders."

"But if it is light enough to do that," said Lord Deshehar, "how much weight of traffic can it bear?"

The question was like a pebble starting a rockslide. Questions poured forth from the Corazhas, a tumult that enveloped Dachensol Polchina and Mer Halezh, though both of them maintained their composure and their courtesy, which was more than Maia thought he could have done himself.

He leaned closer to Merrem Halezho and said, "Can you make it extend again?"

"Of course, Serenity," she said, and adjusted something beneath the pasture. Maia watched as the two ends of the bridge reached slowly and yearningly for each other, knowing he was as wide-eyed and entranced as a child listening to a wonder-tale and in that moment not caring. The bridge was more marvelous than any amount of imperial dignity was worth. He watched especially closely as the claws clasped again, seeing the jointed spurs curl around each other into an unbreakable hold. The dappled horses could draw the wagon safely across this bridge; the cowherd and his flute could drive the black-and-white cows back to the barn that waited beyond the houses.

He looked up finally. The Corazhas still surrounded Dachensol Polchina and Mer Halezh, but Lord Pashavar had withdrawn—no more than a few steps, but distinctly putting himself outside the melee.

Maia circled the table to approach him. "You still disapprove, Lord Pashavar?"

"It is a toy," Pashavar said, angry and contemptuous and perhaps, behind that, a little afraid. "It will waste money and time and no doubt lives—have you considered that, Serenity? The men who will die building this cloud-castle of yours? And in the end, the Istandaärtha will remain unbridged, because it is unbridgeable, and it is naught but a wonder-tale to imagine otherwise."

Maia flinched a little, both at the twisted echo of his own thoughts and at what amounted to an accusation of murder, but he said steadily, "Our grandfathers must once have said the same thing about airships. But they are now commonplace, and neither our government nor our economy could function without them."

"A poor choice of analogy, *Edrehasivar*," Pashavar said with a sparking glance.

But Maia was ready for that gambit. "No," he said, "for the wreck that caused our father's death was not an accident. The blame does not lie with the *Wisdom of Choharo*, but with the person who made her explode." Seeing Pashavar was about to argue, he added, "That person could just as easily have sabotaged the axle of a traveling coach. Or the girth of a saddle."

"None of this means this foolish bridge can possibly be built," Pashavar said, his ears flicking almost petulantly.

"We trust the judgment of the Clocksmiths' Guild. In the end, that is the question on which any decision must be based, for we do not have the knowledge to judge the design ourself—and neither do you." He resisted the urge to use the informal *thou*, even though he wanted to signal how exasperated he was with Pashavar's obstinacy. No amount of obstinacy made Pashavar deserving of the insult.

"But *should* we trust the Clocksmiths' judgment?" Pashavar said, using the plural "we" and gesturing widely. "If the advances necessary to make this bridge more than a cunning toy have truly happened, should the universities not be the ones making the demonstration?"

Maia looked across the room at Lord Isthanar, who had also withdrawn from the excited—and more than slightly tempestuous—discussion around the clocksmiths. He had a dour expression on his face, as closed as a miser's strongbox.

"We think that is an excellent question, Lord Pashavar," Maia said, "but we would not ask it of the *clocksmiths.*"

Pashavar caught his meaning, and from the scowl on his face, it did not please him. Perhaps it would divide the force of his resistance. At least, however, Lord Isthanar was about to have some very pointed questions to answer, as Pashavar offered a hint of a bow and strode across to his colleague.

Maia returned to the model and asked Merrem Halezho to make the bridge work one more time.

# PART FOUR

~∞∞∞~

# Winternight

## 27

## The Great Avar Arrives

The Great Avar of Barizhan arrived at the Untheileneise Court at noon of a brutally cold day that was as bright as it was brief. Forewarned by a courier from Uvesho, where the Avar and his train had spent the night, the emperor was waiting at the great formal entrance to the palace, which he had never seen before. As each leaf of the doors took four men to swing open, it was not much used.

The Avar of Avarsin did not travel by airship; he did not, Ambassador Gormened explained, feel it consonant with the dignity of a great ruler to go bobbing about in the air like a child's balloon. He was making the journey—the first time he had left his own dominions in fifty years or more—by coach.

The first outriders reached the Square of the Empress Parmeno nearly an hour and a half in advance of the Avar. Although they could not be formally welcomed or admitted to the palace before their ruler, Maia had servants take hot tea to them, and then to each successive wave as it arrived. Servants, baggage, a full sixteen-man eshpekh of the Hezhethoreise Guard, and then finally, a single man on a horse, who rode directly to the sentries before the doors of the Untheileneise Court and announced the arrival of the Great Avar.

By this time, a significant crowd of citizens had gathered despite the cold, and they cheered as the great doors were swung open. They cheered again when Maia came out. He was startled and for a moment alarmed, but Kiru said, just loudly enough for him to hear her, "They would be pleased if you acknowledged them," and he realized that, of course, many of them were probably out here freezing for the chance to see their emperor in person. He raised one hand in an awkward wave, and the cheering, unbelievably, redoubled. Maia froze—and was saved by a tremendous, thunderous clatter of hooves and the arrival of the Great Avar's traveling coach. It was a ponderous monstrosity, painted red and gilded like a samovar, with tremendous staring eyes carved beneath the coachman's seat, and a mouth like a bullfrog's cunningly made between them. More carving along the sides indicated elbows and haunches, and there was a spiked crest along the top and down the oddly curved back. The coach was drawn by ten black horses with red and gold enameled harness, perfectly matching the coachman and footmen, pure-blooded goblins in red and gold livery.

The footmen leaped down almost before the coach had stopped moving. They swept a bow to Maia and his entourage and then became very busy setting blocks before the coach wheels and unfolding the steps built into the belly of the coach beneath the door. The Hezhethora advanced to create an aisle, eight men on each side, and their captain mounted halfway up the palace steps and removed his fabulous snarling-faced helmet, tucking it beneath his arm like an extra head. The footmen glanced to see that he was in place, glanced at each other, and one opened the door of the coach while the other stood ready to assist the Avar. All without a syllable being spoken.

One of the ten black horses stamped a foot.

Maru Sevraseched, the Avar of Avarsin of Barizhan, emerged from the coach.

It took all Maia's willpower not to let his jaw sag perceptibly. The Great Avar was aptly styled; Maia's first thought was amazement that that vast coach had been big enough to hold him. He was six and a half feet tall, if not more, and mountainously fat. His skin was jet black, his protuberant eyes lurid orange. His hair, white-streaked with age but very thick, was caught in a soldier's topknot, with braids, brightly ribboned, accenting rather than containing the hip-length mass. His mustache was equally luxuriant, hanging in thick braids well below his jaw. In contrast to his beautifully liveried servants and soldiers, he was dressed very simply in a vast blue robe, and although he wore fire opals in his ears, he had no other jewelry.

Maia watched in mingled awe and dismay as the Avar came down the steps, realizing that if he should lose his balance, there was no way the footman, less than half his master's size, would be able to save him. But, although the Avar went slowly, he was perfectly steady. Once on the ground, he seemed to become impossibly larger, for he towered over even the soldiers of the Hezhethoreise Guard.

The crowd had gone completely silent, as if the Avar were a man-eating ogre like those said to live in the mountains above Ezho. But after one comprehensive look around the square, he waved amiably and set off at a rolling, ground-eating stride along the aisle made by his soldiers. Behind him, the coach began disgorging more liveried servants—his edocharei and secretaries and whatever else the Great Avar felt necessary to his comfort while traveling.

Maia was cravenly grateful that it was Gormened's job to step forward and receive the double handclap on the shoulders that was the affectionate greeting between goblin men. There was a quick, low-voiced exchange in Barizhin, and then Gormened stepped back and said loudly in Ethuverazhin, "The Great Avar of Barizhan greets the Emperor of the Ethuveraz and thanks him for his hospitality this Winternight."

The crowd recognized their cue and cheered enthusiastically; the Great Avar heaved his bulk up the last of the steps, and Maia, tilting his head back, was face-to-face with his grandfather. Properly, Maia knew, he ought to give some sort of speech, but looking into his grandfather's round orange eyes, he could not believe the Avar would be impressed if he tried—or even if he succeeded. Therefore, he said only, "We welcome you. Please, come inside where it is warmer."

The Avar stared at him a moment longer, unblinking and unreadable, and then his laughter boomed across Parmeno Square. "Perhaps you are more a goblin than you look!" He clouted Maia hard, though not actually painfully, on both shoulders, and gestured to his soldiers and servants without bothering to turn around. "We agree—let's go in!"

Csevet had very carefully shielded Maia from the discussions, decisions, and feuds over where and in what style to house the Avar; Maia had caught unconnected, ragged fragments of debate here and there—enough to know that there was a vast and bitter war that he was not being allowed to see. All His Serenity had been informed of was the outcome: the Avar had been granted the rooms known as the Archduke Ermezhis's Suite. The suite was in a currently unfashionable quarter of the palace, and thus unoccupied; moreover, due to the circumstance that the Archduke Ermezhis had contracted a wasting fever in early childhood and had been an invalid all the rest of his life, it was one of the few suites in the Untheileneise Court which could be evenly and adequately heated for an elderly goblin. The Great Avar declared himself satisfied after a cursory glance around, but his edocharei immediately began a silent and thorough investigation. Maia knew it was Csevet who would hear their opinion; he could only hope it would be favorable.

The next item on the agenda was a reception luncheon in the Ambassador's dav, with all the most respectable goblins in Cetho and all the elvish courtiers who were willing to attend. That night, there would be a reception ball in the Untheileian, to which the entire court would come whether they approved of the Avar's visit or not. After that, the days were arranged in an endless rotation of receptions, performances, galas, and celebrations until the Avar departed again. If Maia wished to say anything private to his grandfather—insofar as the word had any meaning at all in his life—it would have to be now.

He had thought, imagining this meeting, that he would have too many questions to be able to choose, but he found that there was only one: "Why did you not answer her letters?"

All of the Barizheisei within earshot froze for a moment; the Avar, who was inspecting the view from the sitting room windows, stiffened perceptibly, but when he turned around, his face was sad. "It seemed better. She was not ours. We could not help her. What else was there to say?"

Goblin and elvish law were the same on this point: a woman belonged to her husband's family. Interference from her own kin was, at best, a matter for the farcical novels of Budarezh and Omdar—a light in which no man with any pride wished to be seen. And if that was all the Avar had had to offer his daughter, then he was right. There was nothing to say.

"The ambassador is waiting for us," Maia said. "We had best go."

# 28

## *A Letter from Mer Celehar*

Apparently, when left to their own devices, goblins liked to have meals that lasted for half a day, one course of tiny, beautiful foods after another. They also disdained the business of seating all the guests around a table and making them stay there, preferring to set the courses out on small tables where one could sit if one chose, but one could also simply wander the room. It unnerved Maia, because he couldn't tell how to be polite.

He observed that the elvish courtiers in attendance were all from lesser families, and almost all from the western principalities, the exception being a lord of the Zherinada from the southern borders of Thu-Tetar. All of them seemed to speak fluent Barizhin, as well, and Maia sat and thought about all the things he was missing due to the protocols and safeguards that kept the emperor separated from all but the very highest tier of his subjects. They were not comfortable thoughts.

Ambassador Gormened approached, dropped to one knee.

"Please," Maia said, and only barely stopped himself from saying *don't*. "Please rise, Ambassador."

"Thank you, Serenity." The ambassador looked worried. "Are you well? May we fetch you anything?"

"No, we thank you. We are well." And of course he was worried: the emperor sitting in a corner like this. Maia screwed up his courage and asked, "Will you introduce us to someone?"

"Of course, Serenity. To whom?"

"Anyone," Maia said helplessly.

"Any . . . oh." The ambassador's expression was briefly distant; then he said, "Perhaps Your Serenity would be pleased to join our wife? She is speaking to the wife of the Hezhethoreise captain."

"We would be very pleased," Maia said. He was grateful not to be dropped into any of the heavily political and financial conversations being pursued in various parts of the room, even if he suspected Gormened's motive was to spare the lords and merchants the emperor's presence, and he gladly followed the ambassador to the widely bowed window recess, where Osmerrem Gormened sat with a young goblin woman. Maia wondered if he ought to inflict himself on them, but both women rose and curtsied with perfect composure, and Merrem Vizhenka smiled and said in excellent, if heavily accented, Ethuverazhin, "We are most pleased and honored to meet you, Serenity." Her skin was charcoal gray, darker than Maia's though not quite the perfect goblin-black, and her eyes were pale yellow. She was much taller than Osmerrem Gormened—an inch taller than Maia himself—and her figure was opulent, even in a heavy winter court dress.

"Thank you," Maia said. "We are glad to be able to welcome the Avar and his people."

It was a trite sentiment, and awkwardly phrased, but Merrem Vizhenka did not seem to notice. She said, "Is he what you expected, your grandfather?"

It was not a question Maia had been prepared for *anyone* to ask, and that must have shown on his face, for she said, "We should inform you, we suppose, that we are your aunt."

"Aunt?" Maia croaked.

"We are the Avar's youngest daughter." She cleared her throat. "He was not married to our mother."

"Then you aren't the mad one?" Maia said and was immediately mortified, but Merrem Vizhenka threw her head back and laughed; her laugh was very like the Avar's.

"No, our sister Thever does not travel," she said. "And we would not call her *mad*, though much given to nervous fancies."

"Have we other aunts?" He did not need to ask about uncles; even an illegitimate son of the Great Avar of Barizhan would have been brought to the emperor's attention.

"Three others," Merrem Vizhenka said. "We doubt your mother knew of them, any more than she knew of us. It is only since her death that the Avar has chosen to acknowledge us. Your aunt Ursu is a sea captain's wife; your aunt Holitho is in the Convent of the Lighthouse Keepers in Urvekh'; and your aunt Shaleän, the oldest of the Avar's daughters, ran away in her youth, disguised herself as a boy, and became a sailor. She is now a sea *captain*, and in truth no one in Barizhan quite knows what to do with her. The Avar acknowledges her, but he does not *discuss* her."

"What is the name of her ship?" Maia asked, and learned the difference between Merrem Vizhenka's polite smile and her real smile.

"Her ship is the *Glorious Dragon*, and her home port is not in Barizhan at all. Shaleän has a wife in Solunee-over-the-Water."

Osmerrem Gormened said mildly, "Nadeian, perhaps

you should not explode all your boilers at once? He is your nephew, not your enemy."

"But we wish him to *know*," Merrem Vizhenka said passionately. "And how will he know if we do not tell him? For we know full well the Avar's ministers have decided it is better that we his daughters not be spoken of, even if we are acknowledged. Besides, why else would Vorzhis introduce him to us and then *leave*?"

Maia was also wondering that, and had come up with no more plausible answer. Osmerrem Gormened sighed. "Our husband is ever serpentine. But, Nadeian, we do not wish you to get in trouble."

"She will not," Maia said. "We are grateful—thank you, Merrem Vizhenka. We loved our mother very much, and we are *glad* to know of her sisters." He managed to smile at her. "We are glad that you told us."

"Then we care not for the ministers," said Merrem Vizhenka. "There was not time between the Avar's decision and our departure for messages to reach either Holitho or Shaleän, but Ursu and her children send warm regards and their hopes that perhaps someday they may meet you."

"It is very kind of them," Maia managed, feeling a rush of prickling tears, which he blinked back. "Will you tell us of the Convent of the Lighthouse Keepers? For we have not heard of it before, and are curious."

Merrem Vizhenka agreed willingly, and she was still explaining the treacherous rocks and currents of Urvekh', and the three lighthouses maintained by the votaries of Ashevezhkho, the Barizheise goddess of the sea, when Csevet apologetically approached. "Serenity, ladies." He knelt. "Serenity, we regret the intrusion, but there is a matter which we think you will wish to attend to."

And if Csevet thought so, he was most probably correct. "Excuse us, please," Maia said to Osmerrem

Gormened and Merrem Vizhenka. They rose with him and curtsied, and he followed Csevet out of the ambassador's dav. The Hezhethorei on guard saluted magnificently.

Csevet led him to a small withdrawing room, hung with badly faded pink silk wallpaper. It had clearly not been used in a very long time, and Maia supposed that was as good a promise of privacy as could be had without making the long journey back to the Alcethmeret—and an absence that prolonged would lead to inquiries, from the ambassador if from no one else.

"Serenity," Csevet said, "a letter has arrived from Mer Celehar." He held it out—a thick sheaf of brownish paper—and Maia exercised all his good breeding and did not snatch it out of Csevet's hand. The seal was broken, and he raised his eyebrows at Csevet.

"No, Serenity. It was broken when it reached our hands. We have set an undersecretary to make inquiries, but it is not likely anything will come of it. Someone was probably well paid to learn its contents, and also well paid to hold his, or her, tongue. The, er, clumsiness of the method also suggests that this is someone who has not made a habit of reading other persons' mail clandestinely, so there is little hope of finding out on the basis of other crimes."

"Could you have done it more neatly?"

"Yes, Serenity," Csevet said, sounding almost offended. "We do not wish to alarm you, but it is common practice among many of the great houses to 'buy' couriers, and pneumatic operators, and many other such persons. We guard the probity of your household as best we can, but it would be naïve to think your mail was not routinely being read."

"We thank you," Maia said, a little dismally, and opened Celehar's letter:

*To the Emperor Edrehasivar VII, greetings and loyal good wishes.*

We realize, Serenity, that you may be vexed with us for our hasty departure from the Untheileneise Court. We ask your forgiveness, but we could do nothing else when granted a message so unmistakable. We do not and cannot consider ourself worthy of Ulis, but it is clear that He finds us, if nothing else, a suitable tool.

We write to you, Serenity, as we would once have written to our superior, so that you may understand how we came to the conclusions that we did and so that, if something should happen to us before we are able to speak with you again, you will nevertheless have a record of our findings.

We came to Amalo because our dream showed us that we were making a fundamental error in pursuing our inquiries among the families of the crew of the <u>Wisdom of Choharo,</u> for her home port was Cetho, and her destruction did not find her in Cetho— she did not reach Cetho on her last flight. It found her in Amalo.

We knew also that we would have to proceed carefully. While the families in Cetho were very willing to speak to a Witness for the Dead, almost desperate to help us in any way they could, people in Amalo would have no such willingness, and the person we sought might even be driven to flight. Therefore, we took a cheap room in the Airmen's Quarter and began looking for work.

We had not realized, Serenity, that Amalo was so deeply involved in the manufacturing of airships, but it is apparently the chief source of the principality's revenue, and nearly a third of the city's citizens are involved in one way or another. We had no difficulty *in finding employment in one of the hangars where the ships come to be tested when they are new, and where they come to be repaired, and to be refitted after they have been in service five years. We were able to learn very quickly that the Wisdom of Choharo had in fact undergone such a refit barely a week before she was destroyed—in preparation, of course, for serving the emperor.*

*We followed this trail further and discovered that the airship which bore His Serenity to Amalo, the Strength of Rosiro, had not been refitted, or repaired, in the months before her service as an imperial vessel, as she had been refitted entirely only last winter. While inconclusive in itself, this was nevertheless useful information, for it suggested that the device had been planted on the Wisdom of Choharo during her refitting. We had already determined that the device must have had a clock of some kind attached to it to ensure that it would not explode until the emperor was on board, for the idea that one of the crew members had chosen to commit suicide in order to murder the emperor, an idea which we know the Lord Chancellor's investigation has been pursuing strenuously, was an idea for which we could find no support either from the dead or in our conversations with the families. Regardless of when the device was put on the ship, it would have to have been so carefully hidden that the Emperor's nohecharei would not find it. Therefore, if it was governed by a clock, we could see no reason that the clock could not have run for a week, or even two. We decided we would have to learn more about the workers who refitted airships, and particularly those who had refitted the Wisdom of Choharo.*

*It was not difficult to gain a position on a refitting*

crew, nor was it difficult to encourage our coworkers to talk. In truth, they needed little encouragement at all, merely the occasional question to turn their talk in the direction we wished. We have learned much more about airships than we ever thought to know, and we have also learned a great deal about the men and women who work on them. Most of it was irrelevant to our purpose, but we learned that among the airship workers of Amalo, there is a devoted following of the philosopher Curnar. We had not previously known much of Curnar, and we find we do not care for his teachings. He argues that the gods are made by men rather than the other way around and—that being so—there is no reason why men cannot make themselves gods as well. He says that rank and wealth and power are the ways in which men aspire to godhood, and that the power that one man accumulates can be taken by another man. And that it should be, if the first man is not striving to advance, for men cannot ascend to godhood if power is allowed to stagnate—in, for example, the elvish devotion to our houses. Old men should not be allowed to rule young men simply because they fathered them, or their younger brothers fathered them. Power is not inherent, says Curnar, and all men may become gods. This is the doctrine of Universal Ascendance, and it is no wonder that Curnar was executed in the reign of Your Serenity's grandfather. We find his writings full of deliberate mysticization and empty rhetoric, but the workers we have talked to seem to believe his teachings very fervently. Most of them do not follow Curnar to the logical conclusion, that they should take power from their supervisors or the owners of the airship company or the Prince of Thu-Athamar, but they like to feel that they would be justified in *doing so. And—as we are sure Your Serenity has already observed—it makes a very convenient belief for a man who sets out to murder an emperor.*

*We were easily able to find the most fervent Curneisei, and we cultivated them cautiously. They are angry men, Serenity, and in truth our caution was but little needed, for their anger makes them blind and easy to deceive, and it makes them very eager to talk, first about their grievances—and although it is no business of ours, Serenity, we do think that some investigation should be made of the Amal-Athamareise Airship Company, for some of their grievances desperately need to be addressed—and then about their plans for glory and vengeance and godhood. Most of these plans are mere cloud-fancies, and all involved are well aware of and content with that state of affairs. Most of the workers we talked to were shocked and grieved at the death of Varenechibel IV, and although they did not seem to know that it had been deliberate, they were as passionate in defense of their airships as they were in defense of their Curneise ideals.*

*We might still be there, Serenity, in an airmen's bar called the Cloud Horses, watching men drink cheap metheglin and listening to bad philosophy—and of all the ways we have envisaged spending the rest of our life, it is not the worst—were it not for the chance that put us one day on the same workcrew as Evrenis Bralchenar.*

*Bralchenar talked to us freely, almost unstoppably; the other workers were no longer willing to listen to him. He is an ardent Curneisis, and we noticed very quickly that he did not regard Universal Ascendance as something hypothetical or something that would doubtless take place, but in the far distant future. For Bralchenar, it was going to happen <u>soon</u>. We asked* *him why he thought Universal Ascendance was, as he put it "within the grasp of all men now alive," and he looked mysterious and said he knew men in power, great men, who were already taking action. It was not what we had expected him to say, and we were puzzled; what "great men," by his or any other standard, could Bralchenar know? Rushing ruins the bread. We asked no more questions of him that day.*

*We did not work with Bralchenar the next day, but we asked the men we did work with about "great men" visiting the hangars and found out two things. First, that tours of the hangars were to be expected when the Prince of Thu-Athamar had guests. Second, that in the protracted negotiations leading up to the prince's recent marriage—attendance at which was, of course, the reason the emperor was on board the* Wisdom of Choharo—*everyone had become quite accustomed to seeing men of the bride's family "hanging around." We did not ask for many details, but we believe the prince's interest in the Amal-Athamareise Airship Company may have been part of the settlement negotiations. In any event, Tethi-madeise men were inspecting everything and asking questions of everyone, and we received hints, although no one said so outright, that they had been very free with their money as well. Someone said sourly that Bralchenar had been trying to get himself adopted, and that, we thought, completed the circle. We were still puzzled, Serenity, for by no means did Bral-chenar have either the knowledge or the ability to make a device such as the one which destroyed the* Wisdom of Choharo. *We decided to continue to encourage him to talk to us when we worked with him again, for we felt sure that he was involved, and we felt sure that he would not be able to resist indefinitely the lure of a sympathetic listener. In this we* were correct, for on only the third time that we worked together, Bralchenar told us that he could see we were a true ascender (as the Curneisei style themselves) and invited us to come with him that evening to a teahouse called the Stone Tree, where he promised to introduce us to men we would appreciate. His efforts to make us feel that we were one of a select group were very clumsy, but we began to understand the appeal of Curneise philosophy to men like him. For if all men are your brothers in the struggle for godhood, it doesn't matter so much if you are unskilled at making friends, just as it does not matter if you are a younger son, or the son of a younger son—or if your house has no inheritance at all.

We accompanied him that evening to the Stone Tree, which is a teahouse in the Athamareise style: a warren of small, inconvenient, interconnected rooms, each the particular territory of one group or another. Many of the rooms seemed to be occupied by Curneisei; Bralchenar was hailed as "kinsman" on all sides—"zhornu," the north-country word for cousin. The Curneisei all call each other that, to signify their rejection of bloodties in favor of the brotherhood of struggle. It makes them sound very warm toward each other—even affectionate—which we think may be another reason young men like Bralchenar are drawn to them. There were women in some of the Curneise rooms, and they called each other "zhornu" with the rest. In fact, the group Bralchenar eventually sat down with had two women along with four or five men. Bralchenar introduced us proudly as "our new zhornu," and none of the others seemed at all inclined to question either him or us.

We listened without speaking much that first night and for several nights thereafter, and we learned that the motivating force behind Bralchenar's cadre of Curneisei was an intense young man, part goblin, who had come to Amalo from Zhaö; he had, in fact, been apprenticed to the Clocksmiths' Guild and been thrown out as a troublemaker. His name is Aina Shulivar, and we saw very quickly that here was one who would have no difficulty in either imagining or constructing a device such as the one which destroyed the <u>Wisdom of Choharo</u> and all aboard her. Shulivar and one of the women, Atho Narchanezhen, are the two most intelligent of the Curneisei we met, and we noticed in listening to them that, although they use the <u>words</u> Universal Ascendance, what they mean by them has nothing to do with godhood and everything to do with power here among the living. In other words, they choose to read Curnar metaphorically, and imagine Universal Ascendance as a world in which no man holds power over any other. Or, for Narchanezhen, over any woman (and we heard many long arguments between her and Shulivar about whether man's power over woman is natural—and therefore unchangeable—or not). And they believe this world is achievable.

Personally, Serenity, we think this as much a cloud-fancy as the more typical Curneise dream of becoming gods, for it requires men not to desire power, and that, we think, is impossible—we notice that as much as the Curneisei speak of taking power away from the powerful, they speak just as much of holding power themselves. But that is not truly the point; the point is what people like Shulivar and Bralchenar and Narchanezhen, holding this belief, are prepared to do in its service.

They took silence for assent, as the zealous often do, and the longer we sat among them and said nothing, the more loquacious and fervent they became, the more inclined to hint at great deeds already accomplished as well as great deeds still to be done. We sat and we listened and we thought of the dead— not merely of the emperor and his sons, but of all those who died stathan, who died terribly, in agony and fear, merely because someone wanted Varenechibel out of the way. We can understand and even sympathize with the Curneisei's desire to improve their lives, their desire to change the world, but we cannot abide the deaths they caused uncaringly, the grief and fear and desperation they left among the living in their wake—the people whom they condemned to the sort of struggle and hopelessness that they avow themselves to be eradicating. The widows we talked to in Cetho all said the same thing, even when their words varied. They did not know how they and their children would survive. And they may *not* survive, Serenity, the smaller children killed by diseases they could survive if they were properly fed, the older children killed in the factories. Before we were sent to Aveio, we served as a curate in the Ulimeire of Sevezho, where the factories run from dawn to dusk in summer, and in winter the workers rise in darkness and return home in darkness and never see the sun at all. We know how many children die in those factories because they aren't strong enough or fast enough or tall enough for the jobs they have been hired—at cruelly low wages—to do.

But we have wandered from our point. Again, we must ask your pardon, Serenity. We have heard enough from the Curneisei, and from the workers at the Amal-Athamareise Airship Company, to be confident that Aina Shulivar made the device which destroyed the Wisdom of Choharo and Evrenis Bralchenar concealed it in the airship's armature where it would not be detected. We believe that they were inspired to this task, as well as paid to complete it, by a man or men

*of the House Tethimada, but of that we cannot find*
*proof without questioning them officially. We do not*
*know what part Atho Narchanezhen played in the*
*plot, although we are sure she knew of it. We believe,*
*however, that all the other Curneisei of Amalo are in-*
*nocent. Tomorrow, Serenity, we will speak to the*
*Amalo Chapter of the Vigilant Brotherhood. We have*
*the priest of the Amalo Ulimeire to vouch for us—he is*
*an old colleague and we think perhaps a friend. We*
*hope most fervently that in less than a week we will*
*be able to return to the Untheileneise Court with all*
*the answers you asked us to find.*

> *In loyalty and gratitude,*
> *Thara Celehar*

Maia folded the pages carefully and returned them to
Csevet. "And again where there is trouble, we find the
House Tethimada. What can you tell us of the Prince
of Thu-Athamar's wedding?"

"Ah," Csevet said. "We know nothing to the detri-
ment of the young lady, and it was certainly a very favorable match. There was speculation that your father's
attendance at the wedding of the Prince of Thu-Athamar
to a daughter of the Tethimada was a harbinger of peace
between them."

"If Mer Celehar is right, that irony must have amused
someone very much," Maia said. As succinctly as he
could, he put Csevet in possession of Mer Celehar's
facts.

Csevet's eyes widened as he listened. "We believe the
Tethimadeise wealth to have been a strong motivation
in Prince Orchenis's marriage."

"Indeed," Maia said grimly.

Csevet eyed him uneasily. "We must hope Mer Celehar will be able to move as swiftly as he predicts. At
the moment, Serenity, we have no proof of anything."

"We know," Maia said. Csevet did not sigh with relief, but it was clearly only willpower that stopped him; Maia remembered Lord Pashavar's comment about mad dogs and knew what Csevet had feared. "Will you, please, put Mer Celehar's letter somewhere that is both safe and unlikely?"

Csevet's eyebrows went up, but after a moment, he said, "Yes. We understand, Serenity, and we will do so." A momentary gleeful grin made him look no older than Idra. "We have already thought of several promising options."

"We thank you. We must return to the reception, as we are certain we have already been missed."

Csevet walked with him back to the ambassador's dav, as if he would otherwise be leaving his emperor alone if he did not. Maia's nohecharei padded invisibly behind them, and Maia thought unhappily that he understood why Cala had said they could not be friends.

Gormened was there as soon as Maia had cleared the door and the saluting guards. "Serenity, the Avar requests a moment of your time."

That was almost certainly not how the matter had originally been phrased; Maia followed Gormened to one of the small tables, this one offering puff pastries filled with pate of duck and sour cherries. The Avar, expansive and possibly slightly drunk (Maia had confined himself to tea after one experimental sip of sorcho, the hot rice wine the goblins preferred), was telling a mixed audience of goblin merchants and elvish courtiers about the visit of the self-styled king of the Chadevaneise pirates to the Corat' Dav Arhos. "*Eight* lion-girls he brought with him," the Avar was saying as Maia approached. "Poor things, they were freezing, and even King Khel-Avezher didn't have the heart to make them—" He broke off when he saw Maia. "Grandson! We are told you have been introduced to our daughter Nadeian."

Inwardly, Maia quailed; he had promised Merrem Vizhenka that she would not get in trouble. "Yes," he said. "We were most pleased to meet her."

"Excellent," said the Avar with such a twinklingly malicious look that Maia could not help smiling back. Apparently the Avar was as fretted by his ministers and their strictures as Maia was by the Corazhas and its squabbles. "Our daughter Thever sends you many good wishes, and we believe there is a gift. Selthevis! Where is our daughter Thever's gift to the emperor?"

Selthevis emerged from the crowd as if conjured. He was middle-aged, soberly dressed, unremarkable except for the dark, almost purplish red of his eyes, which was emphasized by the rubies braided in his hair and hanging from his ears. "We have it, Maru'var," he said and, bowing low to Maia, presented an ornately lacquered box.

For a moment, Maia quite literally could not think what to do. The last time he had had a present of any sort had been his eighth birthday, when his mother had given him the only set of her earrings that were at all suitable for a boy. Setheris, he remembered, had nearly fainted when he realized the delicate rings in Maia's ears were genuine Ilinverieise work and the jewels were not glass and fish-scales, but real pearls.

He took the box and fumbled awkwardly until he found the catch. Inside, each in its own blue silk hollow, was a complete set of ivory combs, tashin sticks, and two strands of amber and rubies. The combs were carved in a pattern of scales, and the tashin sticks each ended in a dragon's head with brilliant, faceted ruby eyes. He closed the box and saw what he had not managed to assimilate at first: it was emblazoned with a magnificent carved and lacquered dragon.

"A glorious dragon," Maia murmured, feeling his face move in a smile as if it belonged to someone else.

"Exactly so," said the Avar.

Perhaps he had learned something from Chenelo's death. Maia wondered, but he knew there was no way to ask. He could only bow to his grandfather over the box—for it might be a gift from his mother's sister, but he would never have received it if his grandfather had not approved—and say, "Thank you."

From the Avar's return nod, Maia thought he understood.

# 29

## A Ball and a Deathbed

Maia didn't know whose job it was to decorate the Untheileian, but they had done a splendid job, with crimson and gold and blue banners which artfully suggested the colors of both Barizhan and the Ethuveraz. Maia's uncomfortable throne had been outfitted with gold-embroidered blue cushions, and he silently blessed whichever servant had had the wits to think of that. He sat and watched the dancing and told himself this was practice for the Winternight Ball when the dancing would start at sunset and go on—with pauses for the banquet and for the midnight celebration in the Untheileneise'meire—until dawn. "Like a wake," he had said, and Csevet had smiled and said, "Yes, Serenity. It is called dancing the old year down, and it is the one night of the year when servants may join their masters in the dance."

It was also Maia's birthday, and although he had tried to explain that he did not want any particular festivity, Csevet had stared at him in horror and said, "You are the *emperor*. Your birthday will be—and should be—celebrated in every corner of the Elflands. You *cannot* ask people not to celebrate, Serenity."

"No," Maia had said, defeated. "We suppose we cannot," But he was oppressed by the thought, appalled at the idea that children would be forced to celebrate his birthday as he had been forced to celebrate his father's.

*'Tis not the same thing,* he pointed out to himself, striving to be reasonable. *What reason has any child to resent thee as thou didst resent thy father?*

*Idra,* a darker voice responded promptly. *Ino. Mireän.*

*I will tell them they need not.* And then he realized his own absurdity and had to stifle a laugh.

"Serenity?" Cala said. "Are you well?"

"Yes, we thank you. Merely ridiculous."

"Serenity?" Beshelar, instantly disapproving.

"It is nothing," Maia said. "Is not the dancing beautiful?"

"It will be better on Winternight," said Beshelar, who passed judgment the same way he breathed.

Cala must have caught some echo of that thought on Maia's face for he said quickly, "We see that the Avar enjoys dancing."

"Yes," Maia said. His grandfather had been escorting one elvish lady after another onto the floor; he dwarfed them to the point that he should have looked ridiculous, but he moved with such unerring accuracy and grace that he was somehow beautiful instead—although Maia was not about to tell him that.

He realized that the lady currently partnered with the Avar was Arbelan Zhasanai; his eye tracked back along their path—people cleared well out of the Avar's way as he moved—and he saw that the woman sitting beside Arbelan's vacated seat was Csethiro Ceredin.

She met his gaze and raised her eyebrows in a clear question. Maia nodded, and she stood and made her way to the dais. Her hair shone beneath the candles of the Untheileian's myriad chandeliers, and she had eschewed the obvious lapis lazuli, dressing it instead with black lacquer combs and strands of emeralds to pick up the subtle green embroidery on her gray gown. She curtsied when she reached the top of the steps and said in a voice designed to carry no farther than Maia's ears, "You need not speak to us if you do not wish to."

"You are our future empress," Maia said. "Even if it is only duty, we would rather that duty were a pleasant one."

He did not mean to sound bitter, but Dach'osmin Ceredin said, "Oh *damn*," in an unexpectedly heart-felt tone. "We must apologize to you, Edrehasivar. We were angry with our father—and our stepmother—but we should not have taken it out on you."

"You thought we were too stupid to matter," Maia said, realizing.

"We were grossly misled by—by gossip from a source we will not trust again," Dach'osmin Ceredin said stiffly. "But it seemed as if duty was all there was, and we prefer to be allowed to *choose* our duties."

"We feared as much," Maia said, "but there seemed to be nothing we could do."

She waved it off. "We wrote to Great-Aunt Arbelan in that same spirit—to spite our father. We have already begged her pardon, and now we beg yours."

She curtsied deeply, bowing her head, and Maia said, "Forgiven. Please."

She rose and smiled at him for the first time. "Really, you should make us grovel more than *that*. But we thank you."

"We will make you answer a question, then," Maia said, feeling very daring. "You said you wrote to your great-aunt to spite your father. How . . ."

"Well, more to *embarrass* him than spite him," Dach'osmin Ceredin said; she seemed not at all both-ered by the question. "Our father, you see, did not . . . ah, well, it is not that he did not *recognize* her, for of course he *did*, but he did not *dwell* on the relationship. He did not visit her or write to her, and our sisters and ourself knew that we had a Great-Aunt Arbelan only because our grandfather would talk of her sometimes. Father gambled that she would not return to favor—or court—in her lifetime."

"It must have seemed a very safe gamble," Maia ventured.

"Yes, though rather cold-blooded—and not, we think, likely to increase his standing with the late emperor regardless." She grinned suddenly, an urchin's expression. "He certainly did not expect you to be *kind* to her."

"We like Arbelan Zhasanai," Maia said, a little stiffly, unsure whether she was mocking him or her father.

Her eyebrows shot up. "You recognize her as your father's widow?"

"Yes," Maia said, even more stiffly.

"Csoru must *hate* you," she said, and when Maia stared at her in bewilderment, she laughed outright. "We beg your pardon, Serenity—as it seems we will be making a habit of doing. Our father, you see, was fostered in the household of Csoru's grandfather and became inextricably close friends with her father. 'Heart-brother,' they call each other, which we find rather sentimental, but no mind. It was their great wish to see an alliance between their houses, but they were cursed by a plague of daughters. Our father has five daughters, although there are hopes, we are told, that our stepmother will be delivered of a son when she is brought to bed in the spring. And Csoru is her father's only child, for he would not marry again upon her mother's death, despite the strongest representations of his father, our father, his mother, his wife's father and mother . . . So." She quirked an eyebrow at him. "Still listening?"

"Yes," he said.

"You are patience itself. But thus it happened that the Count Celehel and the Marquess Ceredel—our second sister wrote a *very* rude rhyme based on the similarity in family names, which we will not embarrass you by repeating—could not achieve a marriage, and so they became determined that their daughters should be closest friends—heart-sisters." Her smile was sharp. "On our first introduction—for as we are the same age as Csoru, all but a handful of months, and named after her dead mother, so it was considered our fate to be her beloved friend—we lasted slightly less than ten minutes before we hit her. Now, of course, that we are an adult, we can hold out for nearly an hour." He couldn't quite tell if she was joking. "When she was betrothed to the late emperor, our father all but forced us to 'reconcile' with her—which Csoru accepted in exactly the same spirit in which we offered it—and he has been imploring us ever since to be friendlier to her, when he does not command it outright."

"No wonder you wished to spite him," Maia said, and made her laugh again.

"We will find it much more pleasant to be amiable to Arbelan Zhasanai than to Csoru Zhasanai." Her brows drew together in a slight frown. "And you, Serenity? How do you find the drunken hornet's nest that is the Untheileneise Court?"

"Bewildering," Maia said before he managed to censor himself. It was the way she asked—as if she actually desired to hear his answer.

"It would be," she said thoughtfully. "We must beg your pardon that we know very little of you. As you might imagine from his attitude toward his aunt, our father has ever behaved as if relegation were contagious. We know that you are the child of Chenelo Zhasan, and that you were relegated at the time of her death to somewhere in Thu-Evresar."

"Edonomee," Maia said. "In the western marshes."

"That must be a bleak landscape."

"Yes," he said.

"And you lived there until your father's death?"

"Yes."

"How many people made the household of Edonomee?"

"Ourself and our guardian. Two menservants, one for the inside work and one for the outside. A cook and two maids, although they all slept out."

"And you saw the occasional courier, we would imagine."

"Very occasional," he agreed.

"*Very* bleak," she said.

He did not know how he would have answered her, for it was at that moment that Csevet approached, bowed, and was on the dais before Maia had even registered his appearance. "Serenity." He bowed again. "Dach'osmin Ceredin."

"What is it, Csevet?"

Maia couldn't entirely keep annoyance out of his voice, and Csevet spread his hands apologetically as he answered, "It is Osmerrem Danivaran, Serenity. Osmin Danivin says she is dying, and did you wish to come?"

There was a horrible, jolting moment when first he couldn't remember who Osmerrem Danivaran was or why he cared about her death and then *did* remember and was hit with grief like a stone to his chest. "Yes," he said. "Yes, we wish to come. Dach'osmin Ceredin, please forgive us. We must—"

"But where are you going?" she said. "Who is Osmerrem Danivaran?"

"She was very kind to us at our mother's funeral. The only person who was. She had a brainstorm, and has been . . . it is not unexpected, but . . ."

"Then you must go," Dach'osmin Ceredin said. "Do not give us a second thought, Serenity. You need have no doubt you will see us again." And with an odd quirked smile that made her face seem properly lived in for the first time, she curtsied and descended from the dais.

Maia barely saw her go. "Do we need to say anything?" he said with a desperate, wide gesture at the Untheileian. "Will they—?"

"Do not concern yourself, Serenity. We have spoken to Lord Berenar and to the Great Avar's steward and certain other people. Nothing will be disordered by your absence."

"*Thank you,*" Maia said, and with his nohecharei, followed Csevet out of the Untheileian. He was not surprised to find that Csevet knew the way to the Danivadeise apartments, although he supposed he should have been. But Csevet knew everything, and Maia was profoundly grateful for it.

Osmin Danivin met them at the door. She had been weeping, but had achieved both poise and dignity in her grief. "Serenity, we thank you for coming," she said, sweeping a curtsy. "We will not ask you to stay for long, but Mother is lucid now, and we know that . . ." She bit her lip and fought herself back under control. "We know that she was so very pleased by your visit, and we thought—"

"Osmin Danivin," he said, realizing that interrupting her was the only way out of an increasingly painful sentence. "A visit costs us nothing, and if we can repay kindness for kindness, we are pleased to do so."

"Thank you, Serenity," she said, and led him into her mother's bedroom.

It was unchanged since his previous visit—except possibly warmer, and if that was so, he was gratified by it—and the woman on the bed was only more frail, more swallowed by her clothes. Her eyes were open, and as he approached the bed, he could see that she saw him.

"Serrrrrr," she croaked. *Serenity.*

"Hello, Osmerrem Danivaran," he said, and he smiled at her.

"Come to . . ." She heaved a deep and obviously difficult breath. "Good-bye?"

"Yes," he said. As Osmin Danivin had said, she was lucid. She knew that she was dying. "I wanted to."

That made her smile, the same twisted smile as before. "Nissss." *Nice boy,* she'd said last time.

He took her hand carefully. There was nothing, he thought, that needed to be said, and he remembered from his own mother's death that she had not wanted to speak very much in the last two or three days that she was cognizant. She had wanted to look at him, to hold his hand. To know that he was there. And he thought there was a light of relief in Osmerrem Danivaran's eyes when she realized he wasn't going to make her struggle either to speak or to listen. He held her hand and thought about how kind she had been to him when he was eight, and thought about Thara Celehar saying the prayer of compassion for the dead with the same attention the last time as the first. And when he could see that she was beginning to fade away from this moment of clarity, he stooped and kissed her forehead.

Her hand clutched his more tightly for a moment. "Good," she said. "Good emprrrrr."

And whether she meant, *be a good emperor* or *you are a good emperor,* there was only one answer, "Thank you, Osmerrem Danivaran," Maia said. "Thank you for everything."

She smiled again and released his hand. He stepped back, letting her daughter resume her place at the bedside. "Thank you," Osmin Danivin whispered in passing.

He inclined his head to her, then turned and left before he became too blinded with tears to move.

"Will you return to the Untheileian, Serenity?" Beshelar asked when they were out in the hall.

"Must we?" Maia asked wearily, swiping an impatient and futile hand across his face.

"Later," Csevet said firmly. "The dancing will go on for hours yet. Come back to the Alcethmeret, Serenity, and compose yourself. There is no hurry."

When Maia woke the next morning, he could not remember how he had gotten from the Tortoise Room, where he had agreed to sit quietly for half an hour, to his bedroom, and could not imagine how Csevet had persuaded him to go. But he was grateful.

Waiting for him on the breakfast table was a black-bordered note from Osmin Danivin: her mother had died the previous night, less than an hour after his visit.

And no one would understand, Maia thought, if the emperor wore mourning for her.

# 30

## The Nineteenth Birthday of Edrehasivar VII
## and the Winternight Ball

On Maia's nineteenth birthday, he was woken before dawn by the wind howling around the spires of the Alcethmeret. The noise was mournful and furious at the same time, and he realized after only a few minutes that he had no hope of going back to sleep. He sat up and lit the candle beside his bed, and Telimezh said, "Serenity?" from his post by the window.

"The wind," Maia said apologetically.

"It is terrible, isn't it?" Telimezh said, and then looked taken aback at his own daring.

"And lying here listening to it only makes it worse. There was a ballad one of the maids at Edonomee used to sing, about a woman who let her lover murder her husband and then went mad and murdered him—"

"And after the townspeople put her to death, her ghost walked the streets screaming first for one man, then the other," Telimezh finished. "Our sisters sang it together with a descant that sounded just like this wind."

"Are you from Thu-Evresar?"

"Yes, Serenity. We were born in Calestho."

Twenty miles from Edonomee. "We did not hear it in your voice," Maia said, half question, half apology. The accent of western Thu-Evresar was distinctive.

"No, Serenity," Telimezh said, apologetic in turn. "We were schooled most carefully when we were accepted into the Untheileneise Guard."

"Of course," Maia said, feeling foolish. He slid out of bed; the coldness of the floor struck instantly through his socks, making him wince. "What's the clock?"

"Half past five, Serenity. Shall we summon your edocharei?"

"Yes, please." Not so much as a dressing gown was ever left out where an unattended emperor could find it; although it fretted Maia to be waited on in this way, as if he were as helpless as a toddling child, he knew what would be said if he expressed the desire to dress himself. And he knew how hurt his edocharei would be.

An hour and a half later, he descended to the dining room to find the table invisible beneath towering, tottering piles of packages and envelopes. There were more piles on the floor. Around the table, Csevet, Esaran, Isheian, and two other servants whose names he couldn't think of looked up with unmistakable guilt written across their faces.

"What on earth—?"

Csevet shot to his feet. "We hoped to . . . that is, we weren't expecting . . ."

"But what is it?" Maia said, beginning to be alarmed. He had never seen Csevet this flustered.

There was an ominously long silence before Isheian said, her voice barely more than a whisper, "Your birthday gifts, Serenity."

"Birthday gifts?" He stared at the piles heaping the room. "*Our* birthday . . . gifts?"

"Yes, Serenity," Csevet said, pulling himself together. "We—with Merrem Esaran's gracious help—have been keeping a tally so that letters of thanks can be written.

We did not intend you to be bothered with all of these, but the task needs to be completed and we were not expecting you to come down so early."

Maia barely noticed the note of reproach. "But who—who are they all *from*?"

*Thy grammar is atrocious,* said that dry, rebarbative voice that was no longer Setheris.

"From everyone, Serenity," said Isheian.

"We expected the messages from the princes, the Corazhas, Lord Berenar, and the members of Parliament," said Csevet. "The Marquess Lanthevel has sent you a scholarly book about embroidery. We even expected the emperor-clock from the Clocksmiths' Guild of Zhaö." He paused, then corrected himself primly: "We should say, we were not surprised they sent a gift. The clock itself is . . ."

"Surprising," Esaran said, and Maia was startled to realize that she and Csevet were friends.

"Yes," Csevet agreed. "But, Serenity, you have also gifts from a number of Barizheisei merchants in Cetho, and from the Trade Association of the Western Ethuveraz. There are messages from mayors and hierophants in every principality. The people of Nelozho have sent you a letter with nearly five hundred signatures, which must be the entire population. The crew of the *Radiance of Cairado* have sent you a model airship. The families of the crew of the *Wisdom of Choharo* have sent you message after message. And that doesn't even begin to account for—Serenity?"

"We don't understand," Maia said helplessly, sinking into a chair. "What do they want?"

Csevet frowned. "They want you to have a happy birthday." Csevet looked at him, still frowning, a moment longer, then turned and began issuing brisk orders. Within minutes, the room was clear, and Isheian was presenting Maia with a cup of tea. "Dachensol Ebremis says you may have breakfast whenever you please, Serenity, but as it's still so early, he wasn't sure . . ."

"Just tea is lovely," Maia said. He took a sip and realized that Csevet was hovering. "What is't?"

"We thought, Serenity," Csevet said promptly, "that perhaps you would like to have breakfast with your nieces and nephew this morning."

By which he meant, of course, that he thought Maia *should*. "Do you think they would like that?" Maia said doubtfully.

"We hear from Leilis Athmaza that they talk about you frequently and that they call you Cousin Maia as you asked them to."

"All right," Maia said, accepting defeat. "But let them come here." He shrugged at Csevet's inquiring eyebrow, and said, a touch guiltily, "They will find it more exciting." *And I will not invade their family space.* He doubted the nursery was "home" to them, or that it ever would be.

The emperor sat and drank tea and pretended to be unaware of the various commotions in his household. Csevet appeared occasionally to offer his emperor such updates as he felt suitable and to provide reading material: the birthday felicitations from the five princes, the Corazhas, and Lord Berenar. Maia would have preferred the messages from the families of the *Wisdom of Choharo*'s crew, but that request could be made later.

Dach'osmin Ceredin had sent a sword, a long, thin, shining blade that made Telimezh's eyes go wide. Maia, who could see that the sword was very old and beautifully made but nothing more, raised his eyebrows invitingly. Telimezh said, "It is a sunblade, Serenity, the weapon of the ancient princes, before Edrevenivar the Conqueror united the Ethuveraz. We did not know the Ceredada still had one."

"It is a gift of great honor," Kiru added softly.

"Although a trifle opaque as to meaning," Csevet said with a frown.

"We trust Dach'osmin Ceredin to mean us nothing but good," Maia said.

"It signifies loyalty," Telimezh said almost impatiently. "If the Ceredada have kept this sunblade all these centuries, then to offer it to the emperor *now*—" He broke off and regrouped. "Serenity, she is giving you a gift that Arbelan Zhasan did not give the late emperor your father."

"No," Maia said thoughtfully. "She did not."

The messages from the princes were, he supposed, exactly what they should be from vassals who had met their emperor exactly once: excruciatingly correct and devoid of either warmth or individuality. The messages from the Corazhas were more varied; though most were perfectly formal, Lord Pashavar's was unapologetically laden with advice and Lord Deshehar's included a number of quick, clever caricatures, obviously drawn during Corazhas sessions: Lord Pashavar looking superbly waspish; Lord Bromar holding forth; Lord Isthanar obviously on the verge of falling asleep; Maia himself, pinching the bridge of his nose in exasperated dismay. He might have been offended or embarrassed or even alarmed, had there not been such obvious fondness in all the sketches. And he understood the gift Lord Deshehar was giving him with his trust.

Lord Berenar's letter, although he remembered to include the appropriate birthday wishes, was actually the shameless exploitation of a chance to tell the emperor about what he had discovered in the Lord Chancellor's office. To Maia's great relief, Lord Berenar and his staff had proved that Chavar was honest—

*although the same cannot be said, Serenity, of all those who were subject to his oversight. Some of the dis-*

crepancies we have found go back a decade or more. We fear that Lord Chavar cared a good deal more for the _political_ aspects of his position than the _administrative_. And while we do not deny the importance of the Lord Chancellor's advice to the emperor, we do not understand how he can have presumed to give that advice without the knowledge which he clearly did not bother to gather. Too much of the necessary work of his office had become the burden of his secretaries, and Lord Chavar was not the man to inspire personal loyalty in his underlings: we have not found any secretary of his who has been with him for more than three years. We had some inkling of the state of affairs, of course, as the Chancellery and the Treasury must work very closely together, but we had not known how deeply—and how widely—the rot went. The same can be said of the Courier General's office, only to an even greater extent, as Osmer Orimar seems to have been actively deceiving Lord Chavar, as well as being shiftless, stupid, and undisciplined. One need look no further than the state of his personal office to understand why he chose to back Chavar—anything to ensure he was left alone to continue his venal and incompetent reign. Mercifully, the couriers themselves seem to be honest and loyal, unaware of the disgraceful behavior of those above them, and we feel that the situation is, with some work, salvageable.

Berenar also reported on the investigation into the wreck of the _Wisdom of Choharo_:

The Witnesses are both honest and loyal, Serenity, but we feel there are too many of them—and too few who have ever had to do this kind of work. They could follow a simple logical trail, but when that trail turned

*out to be false—for we must tell you, Serenity, that
the Cetho Workers League is entirely innocent, and
their innocence has been clear for several weeks—they
were paralyzed by indecision and (we regret to say)
petty squabbling. Lord Chavar seems to have exac-
erbated the problem by refusing to believe the Cetho
Workers League was innocent. We understand that he
continued to assure you of their guilt long after their
innocence was fully attested. Thus, the investigation
has stagnated and must now be pushed into motion
again. We have no doubt that this can be done, but it
seems that today, when we should be offering you
gifts, we must ask a gift of you instead: your patience.*

Csevet came back in, and Maia interrupted whatever
he had been going to say. "Osmer Orimar?"

Csevet winced. "A puppet for Lord Chavar."

"Lord Berenar says Osmer Orimar was concealing
dishonesty of some considerable scope from Chavar."

"Gracious," said Csevet. "We would not have thought
he had the intelligence."

"It does not seem to have been very difficult."

"Ah," said Csevet.

"Lord Berenar says he believes the couriers to be
honest and loyal. Would you agree?"

"Serenity, we do not—"

"Would you?"

"Yes, Serenity." Csevet gave him an odd look—
assessing, Maia realized, when Csevet continued, "Couriers, Serenity, are not like clerks and secretaries. For one
thing, a courier does not have to be able to read."

Maia bit back every one of the questions that sprang
to mind, and Csevet gave him an approving nod. "Those
who can't are taught by their fellows, as with any other
piece of education they might need. But, for all of us,
the courier system gave us a chance, sometimes our *only*

chance, at an honest job. And one where we did not have to work on our knees. Or our backs."

Another infinity of questions not to be asked.

Csevet said, "While couriers are as prone to petty dishonesty as any other group of people, none would think of theft or blackmail or anything he understood as treason. And all couriers have the insatiable and impertinent curiosity of ferrets."

"That night at Edonomee, had you read Chavar's letter?"

Csevet hesitated, then said staunchly, "Yes, Serenity."

Maia nodded. "Thank you. And we do not blame you for it."

"Thank you, Serenity." Csevet started to speak again, but Maia stopped him with an upraised hand.

"If not Osmer Orimar, then who is it who commands the couriers? Someone must."

"Yes, Serenity. He is called Captain Volsharezh, although we know not whether he earned any captaincy in truth. He has been doing Osmer Orimar's work for years. It is he who keeps the courier system honest."

"Will you supply Lord Berenar with his name, please? We do not wish the good to be cleared away with the bad. And we suspect that Lord Berenar's position will be easier if he knows there is someone on whom he can rely."

"Serenity." Csevet bowed. This time Maia let him continue with his original purpose: "We must ask what you want done with the gift from the Tethimada."

"What *is* the gift from the Tethimada?"

"A full set of summer hangings. In white sharadansho silk."

Someone muttered a curse. Sharadansho silk—so called, with a pun on snow-blindness, because the laborers who made it went blind over its intricacies—was the most diaphanous of the silk weights, taken and worked into a kind of half embroidered, half lace state. It looked like snowflakes, and white was the worst of the colors, said to destroy sight at twice the rate of indigo.

"A full set," Maia said.

"Bed hangings, canopy, curtains . . . We brought," Csevet said, beckoning to a page boy waiting outside the door, "the parasol."

The boy brought it in and gave it to Csevet, who proffered it with straight-faced formality to Maia.

Maia accepted it reluctantly. The haft was rosewood, the metalwork delicately engraved like tree branches with glass flowers hanging from the end of each spar. The sharadansho was leaf-patterned, and there were tiny mirrors attached in a scrupulously random pattern, so that the parasol's user would sparkle in the sun.

It was a beautiful object, and by itself it would have been an ostentatious gift. "A full set," Maia said again.

"We fear the meaning is not at all opaque," Csevet said.

"No," Maia agreed, putting the parasol down and resisting the urge to wipe his hands on his trousers. "A little ambiguity from the Tethimada would almost be welcome. We understand that we cannot reject this gift, but must we *use* it?"

"Serenity, the emperor could not use all the gifts he is given even if there were five of him," Csevet said. "If you approved of this gift, it would be suitable for you to respond with some especial mark of your favor to the Tethimada, but as you do not, you may leave the matter in our hands."

"The workmanship is beautiful," Maia said reluctantly. "We would gladly show favor to the craftspersons—and to those who no doubt went blind in the making of the Tethimada's gift."

"Serenity?" Csevet said uncertainly.

Maia realized he was on the brink of setting his secretary an impossible task. "Never mind. Please, present us with the next item on the agenda."

"Serenity," Csevet said, the dip and flick of his ears showing that he had decided he should let the matter go. He picked up the parasol and handed it to the page, who bowed to Maia and departed. Maia wondered what happened to all the gifts the emperor could not use. He had to shake himself free from visions of storerooms like an ogre's cavern in a wonder-tale to attend to what Csevet was saying: a listing of the gifts and messages from the other great houses, none of which was as ostentatious or inappropriate as that of the Tethimada.

Idra and his sisters arrived only a few minutes later, all three looking immaculate and very alert. Idra bowed, and Ino and Mireän curtsied, and there was a soft and ragged chorus of, "Happy birthday, Cousin Maia."

"Thank you," Maia said, and bade them be seated—then had to ask Isheian to fetch a cushion so that Ino could reach the tabletop. There was no moment of awkward silence, for Mireän said as soon as she was settled, "Cousin Maia, have you seen your *clock*?"

"Clock?" said Maia.

"The emperor-clock from the Clocksmiths' Guild, Serenity," said Csevet.

"It's . . . *magnificent*," Mireän said.

"I haven't seen it yet," Maia said. "Tell me about it?"

Mireän began describing the wonders of the clock, but it wasn't long before Ino interrupted her, and by the time breakfast was served, Idra had entered the discussion, too, and there was no need for Maia to worry about keeping the conversation going, for the three children did that effortlessly. Idra tried once to initiate a more adult conversation, asking Maia how the Great Avar's visit was faring, but Mireän intervened immediately.

"He's the biggest goblin I've ever seen! Cousin Maia, are you going to be that big?"

"No," Maia said. "I shall probably grow no taller than I am now."

"He's your grandpapa," Ino said. "Does that mean your mama was a goblin?"

"Yes," Maia said.

"Dinan says goblins are going to invade and eat us. Is that why your grandpapa's here?"

"Ino!" Idra said. "Cousin Maia, I beg your pardon."

"No, it seems like a very reasonable question," Maia said. "Who is Dinan?"

Idra looked at Mireän, who said, "Dinan Cambeshin, Idra."

"Oh," said Idra. "The daughter of one of Mama's bosom bows. She's Ino's age, and I guess they play together?"

"I don't like Dinan," Ino said. "She's mean. But Mama says we have to be friends."

Maia was reminded of Csethiro Ceredin being forced into "friendship" with Csoru, and he was glad that Idra said firmly, "Thou'rt not obliged to be friends with anyone thou likest not, Ino. But why did she say that about goblins? It's not true."

"Isn't it? But Mama said the goblins were going to take over now that Cousin Maia was on the throne, so I thought Dinan was right."

Idra looked so horrified that Maia was hard-pressed not to laugh. He took a sip of tea and said, "No, the goblins aren't going to take over. They're certainly not going to eat anyone. And my grandfather is just here to celebrate Winternight."

"Oh!" Mireän said. "Like when we went to stay with our *other* grandpapa *last* Winternight. Remember, Ino? Grandmama Zharo gave us oranges?"

"Yes," Ino said, a little doubtfully.

"Oh, thou *must* remember," Idra said. "Grandpapa Idra showed us his dogs—one of them had a litter of puppies."

"I remember the puppies!" Ino said. "And the mama dog licked my fingers. Grandpapa said she liked me."

"That's right," Idra said. "And Grandmama Zharo took us to see the puppet theater."

"What is a puppet theater?" Maia asked, and the rest of breakfast was occupied with explanations, Idra as bright-eyed and breathless as his sisters, all adulthood forgotten. Maia was sorry when Csevet appeared to enforce the emperor's unforgiving schedule—but at least in leaving the Alcethmeret, he had to pass the emperor-clock, and even Csevet did not chide him for pausing. Mireän and Esaran were both right, Maia decided: it was magnificent *and* surprising.

The short hours of daylight passed quickly; Maia's schedule was crammed with dedications and performances—one by Min Vechin that was so damnably beautiful that he forgot to feel resentful and embarrassed at the sight of her—and then the Great Avar insisted on visiting the Horsemarket of Cetho, regardless alike of the weather and of the disruptions it caused. Maia had never been to a horse market before, much less *the* Horsemarket, and he trailed, fascinated, in his grandfather's wake until the Avar turned from inspecting a horse and boomed a question at him.

It made no sense, and Maia apologetically said so. "We know nothing of horses."

"Nothing?" The Great Avar choked and spluttered and then erupted, demanding to know how any grandson of his could stand there and say he knew nothing of horses.

"We were never taught to ride," Maia said, doing his best not to flinch. "Our mother was much too ill, and there were no saddle horses at Edonomee. Even an there were, our guardian would never have permitted us to learn."

The Avar looked very grim. "And your father permitted this?"

"Our father did not—" *Care.* He caught himself just in time, remembering that they were in a very public place. "Our father did not concern himself with our education," he said, and met the Avar's eyes steadily, lowering his voice: "Nor did you."

The Avar looked even grimmer. "It is surely neither the first nor the last time that we have been a fool," he said. "Come. Let us buy you a horse."

And that, despite Maia's protests, was exactly what he proceeded to do, giving Maia a rapidly comprehensive lesson in horses and horsemanship along the way. The part Maia liked best was being taught how to make friends with the horses the Avar considered: how to hold his hand, how to offer bits of apple. He loved their soft noses and clever lips and the whuffle of their breath as they investigated.

The Avar was splendid in his refusal to be rushed; Maia watched and took mental notes. Finally, as the lamps of the Horsemarket were being lit against the drawing down of the day, he chose a white horse—which he immediately taught Maia to call a gray—a ten-year-old gelding replete with mysterious but apparently important traits. His name was Velvet, and Maia was bemused and bewildered at the thought of owning a horse.

There was no time for more; even the Avar could not hold out any longer against the combined efforts of secretaries, nohecharei, and Hezhethoreisei. They were returned to the Untheileneise Court at a speed Maia thought was not permitted on the streets of Cetho—and thought certainly should *not* have been permitted with the snow and the wind—and Maia spent a frantic hour being stripped and bathed and perfumed and dressed in white robes stiff with lace and silver embroidery. Instead of combs and tashin sticks, his hair was caught in an elaborate silver webbing with tiny diamonds at every node, and a veil over it so fine it almost wasn't there. Diamonds on his fingers, in his ears, around his neck, and he understood when he caught a glimpse of himself in the mirror: he was white and cold and sparkling, like a snowfield under moonlight. The only flaw in the resemblance was his skin, and even that might be but cloud shadows over the moon.

His nohecharei—Cala and Beshelar, and he couldn't remember when their shift had changed—whisked him away to the Untheileian and deposited the emperor on his throne just as the musicians began to tune their instruments. Beshelar was muttering darkly about haste and disrespect to the gods, but Cala said, "If that's the worst the gods have to contend with tonight, we may all count ourselves holy men," and Beshelar fell silent.

The musicians signaled their readiness with a brief flourish of a tune called "The Snow Queen," and Maia rose. He had been taught the ritual words and he spoke them carefully, words that were both invitation and request that the old year should be seen out with dancing and music, that no one should lack a partner, that anyone who wished to dance should be welcomed. He sat again, exerting himself to be sure it was controlled and graceful and not the emperor collapsing like a suit of armor knocked off its stand. But he was grateful to be able to sit and watch, rather than having to participate.

He saw immediately that what Csevet had said was true; the glittering courtiers were being joined by people in plainer clothes, people who wore no jewels, whose hair was dressed only with pins. The dark faces did not belong only to the Great Avar and his retinue. He saw the blue robes of the mazei at several points around the room, and young men in couriers' leathers, and he recognized at least one of the girls from the Alcethmeret's pneumatic station. She was dancing with Lord Pashavar, and Maia was delighted.

After three hours, the dancing was interrupted for a fireworks display and a banquet, both equally magnificent, in the Emperor's honor. Maia sat with Ambassador Gormened on one side and Osmerrem Berenaran on the other. He had been unfairly surprised to discover that Lord Berenar was married; he was even more surprised by the lady, who was stout and rather plain and made no effort to conceal either. She did not demand conversation from him, but provided a brightly funny monologue about moving the Berenadeise household from the apartments they had occupied for thirty years to the apartments which came with the Lord Chancellor's office. Chavar had never used them. "Our husband says that's part of the problem," Osmerrem Berenaran said, "but we do not pretend to understand his reasoning."

"It must be very uncomfortable," Maia said, "moving after so many years."

She snorted, an unladylike but unmistakably good-humored sound. "'Uncomfortable' is one word. 'Welcome' is another. We have no love for the Berenadeise apartments, and we have not seen Eiru so happy in his work since our children were small."

"Happy? From what we understand, we have landed Lord Berenar in a bramble bush—if no worse than that."

"He thrives on brambles. The thornier a problem is, the happier he seems to be in the solving of it." Her smile made her lovely. "Our thanks is worth little, to be sure, but nevertheless, we thank you, Serenity. For landing him in the brambles."

Maia smiled back. "We believe your thanks to be

worth a great deal, Osmerrem Berenaran. And we are glad of them."

They smiled at each other a moment longer; then Gormened attracted Maia's attention to ask about the Great Avar's trip to the Horsemarket. Maia wished for Lady Berenaran's ability to make a funny story out of trifles, but he could at least assure Gormened that the Avar had neither taken nor caused offense.

Gormened let out a gusty sigh of relief, and Maia said, "Surely we are not your only source of information."

"No, Serenity, but we can trust you to tell us the truth, for you need fear neither our anger nor the Avar's."

"Would he be angry?"

Gormened made an expressive face. "He did not gain his power—nor hold it for so many years—by being amiable and obliging." He visibly shook off the mood. "But a horse! This is splendid, Serenity. Tell us about him."

Maia was not able to comply as fully as he knew he ought to, but Gormened nobly took the burden on his own shoulders and filled the rest of the time before the procession from the banqueting hall to the Untheileneise'meire in telling Maia stories of his childhood pony, to which Maia listened raptly.

The ceremony bidding farewell to the old year and welcoming the new was simple, and Archprelate Tethimar kept it short, knowing that his congregation was eager to return to the Untheileian and dance till dawn. Maia felt as if he was spending the night being herded from one uncomfortable vantage to another, but at least in the Untheileian he could sit down. And the dancing was very beautiful to watch. He saw the Great Avar dancing with Nadeian Vizhenka; Csevet dancing with Arbelan; the Marquess Lanthevel dancing with Csoru—and he was surprised at how attractive Csoru looked when she forgot herself.

Csethiro Ceredin came out of the dance to join him on the dais for a time, and he misused his nohecharei to the extent of sending Beshelar to fetch the nearest chair. Dach'osmin Ceredin was pleased and told him stories of the Winternight celebrations of her childhood, giving such a vivid picture of her affectionate relationship with her sisters that he found himself envious.

She broke off in the middle of telling him about her eldest sister's first grown-up Winternight Ball and what the younger sisters had done to, as she said, "even the score," and he saw that his half sister Vedero was standing patiently at the foot of the dais. Dach'osmin Ceredin stood up, smoothing her skirts with an expert flick of her wrists, and said, "You must learn to take care, Serenity, lest we wear your ears out with our endless talking." She departed with an elegant curtsy; he noticed that she and Vedero pressed hands as she passed, as friends did, and the archduchess climbed the stairs. Vedero's curtsy was deeper than it had to be, and she took the chair beside the throne without hesitation when Maia offered it.

She said, "We need to thank you, Serenity, and we do not know how."

"You needn't—"

"Yes, we do. For all that you should not have done it, we are grateful. Especially as we know we gave you no reason to be kind to us."

Deeply uncomfortable, Maia said, "We would not wish *anyone* to be as ill-treated and unhappy as our mother was."

"We know," said Vedero, "and that is why we must thank you."

He looked at her so blankly that her mouth twitched into a smile. "You did not do it for us, and you would have done the same for Sheveän, would you not?"

"Yes," Maia said, "we suppose we would have."

"And so we thank you," Vedero said briskly, as if everything should now make sense. She rose again. "There will be an eclipse of the moon in a fortnight's time, Serenity. If you would care to come watch with us, we would be very pleased."

"Yes," Maia said, startled and delighted. "We would like that very much."

Vedero's smile looked stiff and unpracticed, but he thought that she meant it. She curtsied and descended from the dais, where her hand was promptly claimed by a young man in courier's leathers. Maia sat and watched and tried to keep from smiling foolishly.

It was much later, and he had had conversations with a number of other people, when Eshevis Tethimar went down on one knee at the foot of the dais.

Maia thought, *I am too tired for this,* and knew it was true. But he had no choice. "You may approach, Dach'osmer Tethimar," he said, retreating into careful formality.

Dach'osmer Tethimar came up the stairs and knelt again, to Maia's irritation. "What is your concern, Dach'osmer Tethimar?" Csevet had taken him very stringently to task only a week ago for saying *What may we do for you?* with its implications that the emperor was at the command of the suppliant, and Maia was working diligently to find more acceptable alternatives.

"Our concern?" Dach'osmer Tethimar raised his head. Whereas everyone else Maia had spoken with had been flushed with dancing, Dach'osmer Tethimar was white as snow. "Our concern does not interest you, *Serenity.*" He spat the honorific as if it were a curse. "But this will." And he leaped forward like a hunting beast, a thin dagger glinting in his hand.

Maia had nowhere he could dodge to, trapped as he was in the uncomfortable grandeur of the throne, but even as he was pressing futilely against the back of the chair, his thoughts a jumble of prayer and disbelief, something came between him and Tethimar and there was a crack like lightning, and the sharp reek of ozone. Maia could not see what happened then, a moment of violent confusion, and then he found he was pinned against the throne by the weight of Deret Beshelar, who was lying, bleeding, in his lap. Tethimar was a huddle of velvet and silk at Maia's feet, and Cala was shaking his hands out as if they hurt.

Belatedly, Csoru Zhasanai screamed.

Maia swallowed down the desire to do the same and said to Beshelar, "Is it very bad?"

Beshelar twitched. "Oh, gods, sorry. Sorry." He jerked himself to his feet. "We beg pardon, Serenity."

"For saving our life? Beshelar, you most incomparable idiot—" His voice cracked and he didn't even care. "Are you all right?"

"I . . ." Beshelar stared down at Tethimar, who was not moving.

"Let me look," Cala said firmly, and Beshelar extended his bleeding arm as obediently as a child.

"Serenity!" Csevet scrambled up on the dais, and Maia lost track of Beshelar and Cala in the whirling chaos that ensued, as several women had hysterics; a number of valuable dignitaries were hustled away by their personal guards; the Hezhethora formed a bristling square around the Great Avar; and the Untheileneise Guard had hysterics of its own, as it tried to simultaneously guard the emperor and scour the court for further threats.

What Maia remembered most clearly, later, was his grandfather's voice raised above the tumult, apostrophizing his soldiers as a bunch of moon-witted ninnies.

It took some time for Csevet and Lord Berenar—each working, as it were, from opposite ends of the problem—to meet in the middle and restore order. Maia was of no use to them and was ashamed of it, but the thing came crashing down on him in stages—first that Dach'osmer Tethimar had actually tried to kill him; then that Dach'osmer Tethimar was dead ("Oh yes," he heard Cala's voice in answer to someone's question, "very dead."); then that Dach'osmer Tethimar had been killed by *Cala* and that the smell of ozone had come from a death-spell ("revethmaz" was the word, and it jangled unstoppably in his head); and then finally that Dach'osmer Tethimar had to be the person who had been behind his father's death—and he could do nothing but sit and shake and once make a desperately hasty trip to the nearest lavatory, where he remained afterwards in a huddle, unwilling to trust either his knees or his guts, until someone got alarmed enough to fetch Csevet and Csevet had the sense to send someone else to fetch Kiru, who came and said impatiently, "It's a perfectly understandable reaction to being very nearly assassinated. We would suggest letting His Serenity go to bed, but if you feel you cannot, then fetch some strong, sweet tea and someone to take charge of this nonsensical jewelry." She came into the lavatory, and he found he was grateful that she had been a cleric of Csaivo when he was still in leading strings, for she helped him put himself back together without scolding and without making things worse by being shocked or sympathetic. He could tell that she was not as calm as she was trying to seem, but that just made it more like a conspiracy between them, and he appreciated it.

The tea arrived with his edocharei, who were *very* shocked and *very* sympathetic, but he could bear up under it by then and was glad for their deft and much practiced help in shedding the jewels and the ornate and uncomfortable jacket (which was now stained with Beshelar's blood). Avris had brought the fur-lined robe that Maia was normally not allowed to wear beyond the grilles of the Alcethmeret, and he wrapped himself in that while Nemer repinned his hair, and when he emerged again (*like a butterfly from a most unusual chrysalis*, he thought, and had to turn a choke of laughter into a cough), he was able to say, "Let us remove to the Verven'theileian, where we will not all *echo* at each other," and be obeyed.

The chairs in the Verven'theileian were comfortable, and none of them was a throne. Maia sat and cradled his teacup in both hands and watched Csevet and Lord Berenar use the choke point of the door as a way to reduce the number of persons involved. There was a great deal of arguing, which Maia decided he did not need to listen to, until his attention was caught by a woman's voice, deep and clear and carrying.

"Let her in," he said to Csevet.

"Serenity," Csevet began, turning to face him, and his body no longer blocked Maia's view of Dach'osmin Ceredin. They stared at each other; then she dropped a curtsy and said, "No, we need not encumber you. We wished merely to see for ourself that you are unharmed. Good night, Serenity." She took two strides, then turned back to say, sharp and sudden, a sword sliding out of a scabbard, "We would have *gutted* him, if he were not already dead."

She was absolutely true to her word. She did not linger, and the silence she left behind her lasted only a moment, only long enough for Maia to recognize a feeling almost like warmth at her concern. And then the arguing started again. In the end, it was the three of them—Maia, Csevet, and Berenar—plus all four of Maia's nohecharei, Captain Orthema, and Captain Vizhenka of the Hezhethora—the Great Avar had allowed himself to be persuaded to bed only on the understanding that he should have a representative in the Verven'theileian, and Maia, seeing both that his obstrep-

erousness came from genuine fury and concern and that
arguing with him was doing nothing but taking up time
and energy, had agreed. "Would you rather have Gormened?" he had muttered to Lord Berenar, and Berenar had reluctantly agreed. Better a soldier than a
courtier in this council.

Captain Vizhenka, who pacified Captain Orthema by
saying outright that he was here at the Avar's request,
not in any official capacity as a representative of the
Hezhethora or of Barizhan, swiftly proved invaluable.
He had been watching the dancers rather than partici-
pating, and he had observed Eshevis Tethimar's progress through the Untheileian. "He attracted the eye," the
captain said, "because he did not dance and because
when he stopped to speak to someone, it was always a
man. We could tell that his business was very important, but we did not realize it was deadly. We are sorry,
Serenity."

"We didn't realize either," Beshelar said gruffly. His
arm had been bandaged and he was reluctantly drink-
ing a cup of Kiru's strong sweet tea; he was glowering
at everyone.

"Did you recognize any of the men Dach'osmer Tethimar spoke to?" said Lord Berenar. "At the least, we
should ask them what he said."

Vizhenka said, "We have been at some pains to learn
your court, for Maru'var desired it of us. He says that
he is old and his memory is failing, but the truth is that
he has never had a good memory for names. We saw
Dach'osmer Tethimar speak first to the Count Solichel,
then to the Count Nethenel and Mer Reshema, and finally to Dach'osmer Ubezhar."

Everyone looked increasingly dismal as Vizhenka's list
grew. All of them were lords of Thu-Tetar and Thu-
Athamar. "All," said Csevet, "are related, on the mother's side or through marriage, to the Tethimada. And we

know Dach'osmer Ubezhar went to Amalo to assist in the negotiations surrounding his kinswoman's marriage."

Berenar, Orthema, and Vizhenka looked bewildered. "Serenity?" asked Berenar.

"Csevet, will you fetch the letter, please?" Maia said, and while Csevet was gone, he told the others of Mer Celehar's investigations.

"Why did you not tell us?" Lord Berenar demanded when he had finished; from his fulminating expression, Captain Orthema was wondering the same thing.

"Because we had—and have—no proof. Mer Celehar's suspicions, although we believe them to be correct, are nothing more than that. Even now, we do not have *proof* that Dach'osmer Tethimar was involved in the murder of our father."

"But—!" said Telimezh, and subsided. Maia thought Kiru had kicked his ankle.

"We think, however," Lord Berenar was beginning briskly, when Csevet returned, slightly out of breath and frowning.

"Serenity," he said, "we have the letter. But we also have an urgent request—if you feel that you can, perhaps while these gentlemen are reading Mer Celehar's words, your presence is greatly desired in the nursery."

"The children!" Maia realized he had jolted to his feet. "Are they—"

"They are unharmed," Csevet said quickly. "No attempt had been made against them. But they have heard of the, ah, disturbance in the Untheileian and they are . . ." He bit his lip and finally offered, "distraught."

"Oh." He could imagine it, losing father, grandfather, uncles, then their mother, and now not knowing what had happened to the person who had taken on the mantle of their protector. "We will come at once," he said. "Gentlemen, you must excuse us. Please, read Mer Celehar's letter. We believe Mer Aisava knows as much about this matter as we do. He will stay and answer your questions. If you can come up with a way to proceed from here, we shall be very pleased to hear about it upon our return."

He started for the door, and all four of his nohecharei sprang up.

Maia stopped, baffled. "We do not need all four of you."

Beshelar and Kiru both began to speak and subsided, glaring at each other.

Maia picked Kiru as the more likely to be both reasonable and concise and said to her, "Well?"

"Lieutenant Beshelar is injured," Kiru said. "He should not be on duty. We have already told him he should be in bed."

"We are perfectly well," Beshelar said.

"You're the color of old cheese," Cala said, quite audibly. "But *we* are perfectly well, Serenity, and there is no need for Kiru Athmaza to lose any more sleep."

Cala was not "perfectly well"; Maia could see the tremor in his hands, and the way in which it periodically racked his whole body with a shudder. *He killed a man tonight,* Maia thought, and felt oddly as if his heart were breaking.

"There's no need for Telimezh to lose sleep, either," Beshelar was saying fiercely. "The second nohecharei must come on duty this evening whether we go to bed now or not, and it seems ill-advised to us for them to go needlessly without rest."

"As ill-advised as guarding the emperor with a great bloody rent in your arm?" Cala said, and his voice was too sharp, not like him.

"It is not—"

"Stop!" They turned and looked at him, wide-eyed, and he realized he had come very close to yelling.

"Cala, Beshelar, go to bed," he said firmly. "Kiru and Telimezh may guard us until this evening, when you may pick up the next shift. Unless there is something sacred about the First Nohecharei guarding us on even-numbered midnights?"

All four nohecharei went shades of red; Cala recovered first. "No; Serenity. Come on, Beshelar. You know you'll feel better for some sleep." And for all Beshelar's bravado, he seemed relieved to be able to stop arguing. Maia jerked his head at Kiru and Telimezh and at last made it out of the Verven'theileian.

When he reached the Alcethmeret, he found Leilis Athmaza fidgeting anxiously in the hall outside the nursery grilles. "Serenity. We are . . . we are very pleased to see that you are unharmed."

"Thank you. Mer Aisava said the children were distressed?"

"Yes, Serenity. It was impossible to be unaware of the commotion, you see, and Prince Idra desired us to find out what was going on. Unfortunately, we could get no clear answers, but we all knew you had not returned to the Alcethmeret, and . . ."

"We understand," Maia said and added, to the guilt in Leilis Athmaza's face, "We do not see that you are to blame. It is not your fault that you could not find anyone to give you answers. Now where are the children?"

"This way, Serenity," Leilis Athmaza said, bowing. He opened the grilles to the nursery, closing them carefully behind them and tucking the key on its long black ribbon back into his robes. He took Maia past the sitting room to a door that stood open, light pooling warmly on the floor.

It was Ino and Mireän's bedroom, judging by the two small beds, but all three children were there, Idra sitting on one bed holding Ino on his lap with Mireän pressed tightly against his side. They were in their night clothes, hair braided down their backs. Both little girls were crying, and Idra looked blotchy and red-eyed himself. They all looked up as Maia came in, and before he had a chance to say anything, Mireän leaped off the bed and rushed to him, flinging her arms around his waist. Ino pulled free of Idra; Maia, realizing that she was about to join her sister, knelt on the floor so that they would not knock him over.

"Mireän, Ino," Idra said, trying to be reproving, but his voice wobbled.

"It's all right," Maia said. "I'm sorry. I should have thought to have someone tell you—"

"You had more important things to think about," Idra said, and looked away.

Ino's hot, damp face was pressed against his neck and Mireän was sobbing exhaustedly somewhere around his armpit. "I'm not sure I did," Maia said. "But I *am* all right. Truly."

"What happened?" Idra said.

Maia swallowed hard. It was not getting easier to think about. "Eshevis Tethimar tried to kill me."

Idra frowned. "The man Aunt Vedero is supposed to marry?"

"Not anymore," Maia said grimly. "Did you know him?"

"He made a point of being nice to me," Idra said with an uncomfortable shrug. "But Mama . . ."

"It's all right," Maia said; Setheris had forbidden him to speak of Chenelo, and he understood Idra's hesitation. "I don't expect you to pretend she does not exist."

That got a bare flicker of a smile. "Mama said Dach'osmer Tethimar wasn't someone I should wish to be friends with, and indeed I did not like him, even when he was nice."

"No," Maia said. "I did not like him, either."

"But he tried to *kill* you?"

"Yes."

"Did he want to be emperor?" Mireän asked, lifting her head and relaxing her grip, for which Maia was thankful as it had been getting difficult to breathe.

"I don't know," Maia said.

"Is he going to kill Idra?" Ino said.

"No. He's dead." He thought how horrible it was to be offering that as reassurance, and then thought that it seemed a suitable epitaph for Eshevis Tethimar.

Idra said, "There must be a great deal to—I mean, you must be busy."

"Somewhat," Maia admitted. "I should not stay."

"Thank you for coming," Idra said. "We were . . . concerned."

"I don't wonder at it," Maia said gently; he met Idra's eyes over Ino's head and let Idra see that he knew "concerned" was a euphemism. "I was concerned, too."

That got a guilty crack of laughter out of Idra, and he got off the bed to come kneel by Maia. "Ino, Cousin Maia has to go."

Ino clung tighter for a moment, then let go. She looked up at Maia, swollen eyed and sniffling. "Wilt come back?"

"Yes, I will, I promise thee," Maia said. "Although it may not be soon."

"May we come visit thee again?" Mireän asked, and added with hasty conscientiousness, "Sometime. Not while thou'rt busy."

"I would like that," Maia said. He got up, and Idra rose with him, looking at him as anxiously as Ino.

"I'm all right," Maia said to Idra. "Thou needst not fear for me. I am well guarded."

"Of course," Idra said, and did not add, *So was my grandfather.*

"It is different when one knows to be careful," Maia

said, mindful of the little girls now clinging to Idra's hands.

Idra's eyes lightened a little. "I suppose it is. Thank you."

Maia touched his shoulder gently, recognizing it as he did so for a strange muted echo of the Barizheise gesture he'd gotten used to seeing in the past few days, and said, "Try to get some sleep. *Somebody* ought to."

And Idra actually smiled and said, "I'll try."

# 31

## A Conspiracy Unearthed

In the Verven'theileian, Maia found Lord Berenar and Captain Orthema engaged in a heated debate, while Captain Vizhenka watched resignedly. Csevet was consulting with a pair of secretaries whom Maia recognized but could not put names to. Everyone stopped and bowed as Maia came in, and he thought he had better make use of the interruption before Berenar and Orthema started in again.

"Captain Orthema," he said, "we remember that the Untheileneise Guard has been stationed to prevent anyone leaving the court."

"Yes, Serenity."

"Would you go and find out whether your men have actually had to stop anyone? We feel that that information might be very interesting."

Orthema hesitated only fractionally before saying, "Yes, Serenity," which, given the glare he directed at Berenar, was much to his credit. He bowed and departed, and Maia asked Berenar, "What were you and Orthema arguing about?"

Berenar sighed ruefully. "He wished to have all of the Tethimada currently in the Untheileneise Court arrested, along with the men Captain Vizhenka observed talking to Dach'osmer Tethimar. And while we do indeed see and sympathize with his point of view, we could not countenance it without Your Serenity's direct order." He gave Maia a cautious look, as if worried now that Maia would support Orthema.

"No," Maia said. "We do not think we have reason yet to arrest anyone—although we would very much like to speak to the men to whom Dach'osmer Tethimar spoke."

"Serenity," Csevet said, interrupting politely. "The Count Nethenel and Mer Reshema have expressed their desire to cooperate and are waiting in the public meeting room across the hall. The Count Solichel's manservant informs our page boy that he is ill and cannot speak to anyone."

"A very sudden illness," Lord Berenar said.

"Indeed," said Maia. "And Dach'osmer Ubezhar?"

"Cannot be found, Serenity. Although perhaps Captain Orthema will have news of him when he returns."

"Perhaps. Very well. Let us speak to the Count Nethenel." Maia sat in his accustomed seat at the Verven'theileian's long table, and Csevet slipped out, returning almost immediately with Pazhis Nethenel, the Count Nethenel, who was nearly gray with strain but otherwise composed.

The House Nethenada, Maia remembered from Berenar's lessons, was a minor house of western Thu-Tetar, noted principally for their centuries-long stewardship of the Nethen Ford, where by a combination of causeways, dredging, and some fortuitously placed islands, they maintained the only reliable crossing of the Tetara for well over fifty miles. The current Count Nethenel was some six years older than Maia and had been named for the Empress Pazhiro, although if this had been an effort to curry favor with Varenechibel, it could not have been said to have succeeded. The Nethenada were one of the poorest noble families of Thu-Tetar, for of course the Tetara belonged to the crown, and the Nethenada could not charge tolls without permission which had never yet been granted. Maia, examining the ferret-faced lord in front of him, thought that perhaps a little more consideration was due the Nethenada than they had received.

"Count Nethenel," he said, "thank you for agreeing to speak to us."

"Serenity," said the Count Nethenel with a jerky bow.

"We do not suspect you of anything," Maia said as gently as he could. "We merely wish to know what Dach'osmer Tethimar said when he spoke to you this evening."

Nethenel swallowed hard. "It was . . . it was in the nature of a threat, Serenity."

"A threat?" said Lord Berenar.

"We . . ." Nethenel coughed and began again. "The House Nethenada and the House Tethimada have been in disagreement for some time about . . . well, about Dach'osmer Tethimar's political ideas. We had only this summer again refused him our support in a complaint he was bringing to the emperor. This evening, he said that we would soon be sorry for our loyalties."

He coughed again, and Maia said, "Some water for the Count Nethenel, please."

Csevet poured a glass from the carafe sitting beside the samovar and brought it over. Nethenel's hand was shaking when he took it, and he sipped it carefully. "Thank you, Serenity. We regret that we are . . . we are a little overcome still."

"We do not blame you," Maia said, and as it had with Idra, the wry understatement worked with Nethenel, for he managed to meet Maia's eyes and even to offer a shaky smile.

"We would speak to Mer Reshema, please," Maia said to Csevet.

"Serenity, he knows nothing of this!" Nethenel said in sudden desperation. "Please. He didn't even know who Eshevis was."

"We have no suspicions of him, either," Maia said, puzzled. "But he is also a witness."

The Count Nethenel looked as if he wished to protest further, but Csevet had already left the room.

Mer Reshema turned out to be barely older than Maia. He was, in fact, the young man in courier's leathers whom Maia had seen dancing with Vedero. He was part goblin; although his skin was somewhat paler than Maia's, his hair was black and his eyes were fiery orange. He had a better command of himself than the Count Nethenel, and Maia wondered, looking from him to Csevet, if couriers were chosen for their unflappable calm or if it was part of the education Csevet had spoken of. Mer Reshema confirmed Nethenel's account: "He was gloating, Serenity. We thought—the Count Nethenel and ourself—that he must have gained some important concession from you, although we could not imagine what."

"We did not expect," Nethenel put in anxiously, "that he would—that he meant to—"

"How could you have?" Maia said. "We admit, it does not improve our picture of Dach'osmer Tethimar that he would stop on his way to murder us to indulge in petty gloating, but certainly you could not be expected to discern that he would go from petty gloating to murder." He looked at Lord Berenar. "Have you any other questions for these gentlemen?"

"No, we do not think so. It is Dach'osmer Tethimar's friends from whom we must seek further answers, not his enemies. Thank you, gentlemen."

"Yes," said Maia. "Thank you. We appreciate your help."

"We only wish we could be of *more* help, Serenity,"

said Mer Reshema, and the Count Nethenel murmured agreement. They bowed and departed.

"The Count Nethenel was very nervous," Maia remarked.

"He should be," Lord Berenar said. "The Winternight Ball is one thing, but bringing your baseborn lover to it is quite another."

"What?" Maia said.

"Did you not know, Serenity? It seemed to us even the sparrows were gossiping about it. The Count Nethenel has been making an unseemly spectacle of himself since the spring equinox."

"We found nothing distasteful in Mer Reshema."

"And we know nothing to the young man's discredit," Berenar agreed. "It is Nethenel who is teasing the quicksand. And truly, that is neither here nor there, for imprudence is a far cry from treason, and the Nethenada have always been stupidly loyal."

"We *beg* your pardon," Maia said in mock outrage and was pleased when Berenar laughed.

"We did not mean in respect to yourself, Serenity. But previous emperors have . . . well, Varevesena for one gave them no reason to love him. But no matter. The question is what to do about Solichel and Ubezhar—once Ubezhar is found, of course."

"We believe," said Csevet, tilting his head, "that that may even now be happening."

Maia heard it, too, a commotion in the corridor commingled of the chink and scrape of armor and a voice yelling indistinguishable words. Csevet opened the door just as the tumult reached the Verven'theileian; two soldiers entered, half-dragging a third man between them—not out of any desire to be brutal, but because he was struggling against them. By his clothing he was a courtier, and Maia guessed from his clear unwillingness to be brought before the emperor that he was the elusive

Dach'osmer Ubezhar. Captain Orthema brought up the rear.

"Serenity." The soldiers saluted—a little awkwardly because of their need to keep a grip on their prisoner. Captain Orthema stepped fastidiously around them, and Csevet closed the door and then stood with his back to it. Dach'osmer Ubezhar became abruptly silent—and intensely focused on the task of straightening his clothes.

"Serenity," said Captain Orthema, "Dach'osmer Ubezhar was discovered in the south stables, attempting to bribe a groom to open the gate. We commend Khever, the groom, to your attention, for he refused most vehemently, and our corporal says that he threatened to punch Dach'osmer Ubezhar in the nose."

"We have nothing to say," Dach'osmer Ubezhar announced—which was interesting, Maia thought, as no one had yet asked him to say anything at all. He was not a prepossessing man, with none of Eshevis Tethimar's power, and his attempt at hauteur fared badly, although it would have been hard for any man to carry it off with his hair coming down.

"I think," said Captain Orthema, and no one in the room was foolish enough to think his use of the familiar-first was in any way friendly, "that you will find that you do."

"Captain," Maia said—not quite a rebuke, but definitely a warning. Orthema gave him a grudging nod and came around the table to stand by Berenar's chair. But neither he nor Maia ordered the soldiers to step back.

Dach'osmer Ubezhar said, "Are you a boggart to frighten children, Captain? We are not a child." His sneer was too clearly a copy of Tethimar's, and Maia thought that under the bluster he was badly scared.

"Dach'osmer Ubezhar," Maia said, and waited until Ubezhar was at least looking in his direction—although not coming even close to meeting his eyes. "We regret if we are the first to inform you, but Dach'osmer Tethimar is dead."

Dach'osmer Ubezhar said nothing, although Maia could see it was an effort. He did not seem at all surprised.

Maia said, "He spoke to you this evening."

If Ubezhar had had the wit or the nerve to stay silent, Maia was uncomfortably aware he would have been at a stand, with Orthema's solution all too tempting. But Ubezhar said, instantly defensive, "Doubtless he spoke to many persons."

"Including us," Maia agreed, and was unworthily pleased at Ubezhar's wince. "We have spoken already to some of the others and will speak to the rest, but that is no concern of yours. What did he say to you?"

"Surely that is a private matter between us and our dead friend."

"Not when your dead friend went from your side to an assassination attempt," Lord Berenar said.

Ubezhar winced again, although Maia, watching him closely, thought it was more for Berenar's lack of tact than for the idea that his friend had intended to murder the emperor.

"If he spoke to you of unrelated matters, we will—"

"He did!" Ubezhar said, much too eagerly. "Nothing to do with . . . that is, we had no idea that . . ."

"Because," Orthema said silkily, "if you *had* known, you would—of course—have stopped him."

"Of course," Ubezhar said, but he was not a good liar.

"Dach'osmer Ubezhar," Berenar said, "do you know the penalty for treason?"

"Treason?" Ubezhar said, his voice squeaking.

"That is generally what the murder of an emperor is called."

Ubezhar went white and blurted, "I had nothing to do with it! It was all Eshevis's idea!"

Berenar raised his eyebrows. "The murder of Edre-hasivar the Seventh? Or the murder of Varenechibel the Fourth?"

Ubezhar stared at Berenar in mingled fury and panic, and then wrenched free of the soldiers and lunged for the door. And Csevet, making good on the groom's threat, punched him in the nose.

Once Ubezhar cracked, he cracked completely and the details came pouring out around the bloodstained hand-kerchief pressed to his face: Tethimar's dissatisfaction, shared as it was by many nobles of Thu-Athamar and Thu-Tetar; their increasing impatience with Varenechi-bel's refusal to heed them. "It was never like this under Varevesena," Ubezhar said indignantly, although he was not old enough to remember for himself. Tethimar had had little difficulty in gathering a number of like-minded men about him, little difficulty in convincing them they were ill-used. And from there, it required unfortunately little imagination to follow the path they had taken to murder and treason. Sick at heart, Maia said to Bere-nar, "Is our presence needed?"

Berenar looked startled, then something illuminated his face that Maia shied away from understanding. "No, Serenity. Not at all. Please, go and sleep."

And Maia had no strength left to resist kindness. It took all his attention to get back to the Alcethmeret without falling over his own feet, and there he found himself an obedient puppet as his edocharei undressed him, bathed him, offered him food which he could not face, and put him to bed. He lay and stared at the wres-tling cats and was so exhausted that the room seemed to be spinning very slowly around him, and he could not sleep.

After what felt like a very long time, a voice said softly, "Serenity?"

Kiru. He had never figured out how his nohecharei

decided which of them stayed in his bedroom and which did not, and it seemed somehow rude to ask. "Yes, Kiru Athmaza?" He was careful not to look at her.

"You are not sleeping," she said, a gently voiced statement of fact.

"We cannot," he said bleakly. "It is all . . . If we close our eyes, we see him again."

"Tethimar."

"Yes. The look on his face—" He shivered and then found he was unable to stop.

"Serenity?" Kiru's voice was closer.

"No!" he gasped. *We cannot be your friend.* "We are all right. Just . . . just cold."

He could tell by the quality of her silence that she did not believe him, but if there was an advantage to being emperor, it was that she could not call him a liar to his face. He rolled onto his side, facing away from her, and curled himself into the tightest ball he could manage. *Just cold,* he told himself. *Just very cold.*

Quietly, Kiru began to sing. Maia didn't know the song—something about dead women luring faithless lovers to drown in the Tetara—but it didn't matter. Kiru's voice was soft and rather rough, but she held strongly to the melody, and the kindness of it made his throat hurt in a way that Min Vechin's beautiful voice never would. If he made any betraying noises, Kiru gave no sign of hearing, and when he finally fell asleep in the gray stormy daylight that crept around the curtains, she was still singing.

He slept heavily for four hours and woke feeling better than he thought he had any right to. Over a late luncheon, Csevet told him of the progress being made against Tethimar's conspiracy. Two of the men Ubezhar had named had killed themselves before they could be arrested, but the other four were in custody, and only one, Dach'osmer Veschar, was attempting to claim innocence. Moreover, Mer Celehar had arrived on the noon airship from Amalo and wished to see Maia as soon as possible.

"Did he *say* that?" Maia said before he could stop himself, it being quite contrary to his experience of Thara Celehar.

Csevet cleared his throat. "He is very distressed, Serenity, that he was not fast enough to prevent Dach'osmer Tethimar's attempt to murder you. We believe that he does, indeed, wish to see you so that he may beg your pardon. Also," and Csevet was now very carefully not looking at Maia, "we have heard that Csoru Zhasanai has thrown him out."

"Oh dear," Maia said. "For it *is* our fault."

"Serenity," Csevet said, not quite agreeing. "We do not, however, believe that Mer Celehar will mention that fact if you do not force him to."

"Thank you," Maia said. "When will we have time to see him?"

"Um," said Csevet, consulting part of his inevitable sheaf of papers. "If you will grant him an audience now, Serenity—we have told everyone else that you will not be available until your nohecharei have changed shifts again." He gave an odd, one-shouldered shrug. "Unlike an hour designated on the clock, it does not allow of arguing that five minutes earlier cannot hurt."

"Do you suffer a great deal from such arguments?"

"It is our job, Serenity," Csevet said, and smiled at him. "Will you see Mer Celehar now?"

"Yes," Maia said.

He took a fresh cup of tea to the Tortoise Room and sat as close to the fireplace as he could; as if to make his half lie to Kiru a truth in earnest, he was bitterly cold and could not seem to get warm. Celehar must have been waiting for the summons, for he was almost immediately there, prostrating himself on the floor.

*Merciful goddesses, not again.* "Get up," Maia said. "Please. We do not wish for—"

"We failed you, Serenity," Celehar said, unmoving.

"You failed . . . *what*?" Maia pinched the bridge of his nose. "Mer Celehar, making all allowances for the upsetting nature of what happened last night, we *cannot* understand why you would say such a thing."

Celehar looked up. "But—"

"*No.*" He had to stop, as surprised as anyone else by the brusque power of his voice. He tried again: "You are not responsible for Dach'osmer Tethimar's self-love, nor for his remarkably poor judgment. You did what we asked you to do, and you did it very well. Nothing else is within your responsibility, and we ask you, most sincerely, not to pick up further burdens."

Celehar finally got up; he looked simply bewildered. "But if we had not . . . it was clearly our investigations which caused Dach'osmer Tethimar to . . ."

"If it hadn't been you, it would have been something else," Maia said. "He was . . ." But he didn't have a way to put into words the thing he had seen in Tethimar, the cruel fury, the self-love so deep that it could not abide to be crossed even in the smallest matter. "He would never—that is, he had come much too far to accept anything less than complete compliance with his wishes, and he would never have achieved it. In fact, we are grateful to you, for if your investigations had not threatened him, he might have taken the time to come up with a better plan. As he did in murdering our father."

"Serenity," Celehar said, appalled.

Maia looked at him. His color was bad and his eyes bloodshot. "Mer Celehar, when did you last sleep?"

"Um." Celehar rubbed his face. "We do not . . . what is today?"

"We believe it is still the twenty-second," Maia said.

"Ah." Celehar frowned. "We must have slept on the

twentieth. Yes, for we remember the Vigilant Brother-hood offered us the use of a cell."

"Then you need to sleep," Maia said. "We feel sure that none of this will seem so much like your fault when you awake."

The hesitation before Celehar said, "Yes, Serenity," was perfectly palpable, and Maia wondered how much of Celehar's willingness to accept blame for things which were not his fault was due to Csoru Zhasanai and what must have been, at best, a very unpleasant scene.

"We will take you into our household," he said, "for as Csoru Zhasanai is our kinswoman, so must you be our kinsman, and you have done us, moreover, a great service. Csevet, will you ask Merrem Esaran, please, to grant Mer Celehar a room?"

"Of course, Serenity," Csevet said. "This way, Mer Celehar."

Celehar stood frozen for a moment, then he said, his broken voice barely more than a whisper, "Thank you, Serenity," and let Csevet herd him out of the room.

Maia sighed with relief and turned his attention to the documents Csevet had brought him, a neat summa-tion from Lord Berenar of the progress of the investi-gation. Csevet had told him most of it already, but he read carefully anyway, and was glad to see that Bere-nar had already begun to establish innocence as well as guilt; although Eshevis Tethimar's father was as guilty as his son, the rest of the Tethimada seemed to be guilty of nothing more than trusting the head of their house to be honorable, and Dach'osmerrem Ubezharan was distraught with horror at her husband's scheming. Bere-nar added that he had advised her to petition for a divorce—scandalous advice from a Lord Chancellor, but Maia agreed; if she was not part of Ubezhar and Tethi-mar's plot, she did not deserve to be left holding the bur-den of their shame.

And he was deeply, dizzyingly relieved that the Archprelate was not implicated. It was more than bad enough that his reign had begun with two attempted coups, one led by his Lord Chancellor, without having the Archprelate of Cetho involved as well.

When Berenar was admitted—hard on the heels of Cala and Beshelar, and Maia remembered what Csevet had said about "five minutes earlier"—he told Maia the rest of what Ubezhar had said: "The wreck of the *Wisdom of Choharo* was not, as it turns out, Tethimar's plan."

"It wasn't?"

"Do not mistake us, Serenity. Tethimar intended the emperor and his sons to die. But not *then*. He intended them to die after his own wedding."

"We beg your pardon?"

"Tethimar's plan," said Berenar, "was that the emperor's airship would be destroyed as it returned to Cetho from Puzhvarno, the city nearest to the Tethimada's manor of Eshoravee."

"We know of it," Maia said with a glance at Csevet, who gave him a grave nod in return. "Do you mean, then, that he had indeed been promised our sister Vedero in marriage?"

"It seems so, Serenity. Certainly he and his allies thought he had been. They intended the *Wisdom of Choharo* as . . . as practice."

"*Practice?*"

"Ubezhar said that Tethimar wished to be certain that the device could indeed be hidden successfully. The plan was that an object of the same size and shape should be placed on the *Wisdom of Choharo,* and if it reached Cetho undetected, they would know that the actual device would be secure. But there was some miscommunication."

"So he *intended,*" Maia said slowly, "that he should

marry our sister, and then our father and brothers should be killed."

"Putting Eshevis Tethimar in an ideal position to assume the regency for Prince Idra," Berenar agreed.

"But then what did he intend to do with us? For he cannot have imagined that we should be allowed to attend his wedding?"

Berenar coughed, his ears dipping. "We believe, Serenity, although Ubezhar did not exactly say so, that Tethimar had all but forgotten about you. You were not regarded as a threat."

"A lunatic inbred cretin," Maia said sourly, and Berenar's ears dipped even farther before he recovered himself.

"But the device wrecked the *Wisdom of Choharo,* and Tethimar was not only not married to the archduchess, he didn't even have a signed marriage contract. You were coronated more quickly than anyone expected. And Tethimar's attempts to regroup were blocked."

"Repeatedly," Csevet said with audible satisfaction.

"You would not agree to his marriage to the archduchess. The Lord Chancellor made his own attempt to seize power. The investigator you sent to Amalo discovered the man who made the device. Tethimar spent the past several days, according to Ubezhar, in seeking some way out of the snare he had laid for himself. And when he could not find one . . . well, Ubezhar did not want to say, but, Serenity, we believe that Tethimar had come to think that you were the author of all his problems. The last thing he said to Ubezhar was that he was content to die if it meant that you would die with him."

"It did seem that he hated us," Maia said, and was embarrassed by the thinness of his own voice.

"Well, no matter," Berenar said briskly, changing the subject. "He is dead, and we believe his conspiracy will die with him." He explained, lucidly and completely, the plans he and Orthema had made to be sure that the conspiracy was not merely uncovered, but entirely uprooted. "We advise, Serenity, that the next head of each implicated house be required to come and swear his loyalty to you personally. And we advise most strongly that the House Tethimada be extirpated. Let its holdings be divided among Eshevis Tethimar's unmarried sisters, so that each may have a generous dowry, and let it be heard of no more."

"How many sisters had he?" Maia said.

"Four. But the eldest, of course, is married to Prince Orchenis."

"Yes," Maia said uneasily. "Berenar, have you . . . that is, we do not believe that the prince is in any way . . . we do not wish to . . ." He subsided, unable to make himself ask, *Are you satisfied that the Prince of Thu-Athamar was not conspiring against us?*

Berenar waited politely until it was clear Maia was not going to find a way to end his sentence, then said, "We do not feel that there is any reason to doubt Orchenis's loyalty. We would recommend that you summon him and his wife here, as it is rather too important a matter to be left in any way doubtful—in fact, from our knowledge of Orchenis, we feel that he will wish to tell you, personally and unequivocally, that he is loyal—but . . . well, Serenity, if Orchenis had been part of the plot, we would have expected him to raise his banner upon your father's death."

"Ah," Maia said. "Yes. We see what you mean." He shook his head to clear it and said, "How old are Dach'osmer Tethimar's unmarried sisters?"

"Serenity." Berenar cleared his throat. "Fifteen, twelve, and seven."

"And he had no brothers?"

"There was a younger brother, Serenity, but he died

some years ago. A hunting accident, we believe, although we do not remember the details."

"It matters not. Who becomes the girls' guardian, then?"

"Serenity?"

"Their brother is dead; their father soon will be. Is their mother—?"

"Dead, Serenity. In childbirth of the youngest daughter."

"And if they are to carry the wealth of the Tethimada to other houses, one does not wish to put them in the care of a Tethimadeise cousin," Maia said. "Their mother's house?"

Berenar looked pained. "Ubezhada, Serenity."

"Ah. No." He had a vision of the nursery of the Alcethmeret filled with the children of his enemies, and then the solution came to him: "Prince Orchenis."

"Serenity?"

"He is their brother-in-law. And if, as you say and we also believe, he is loyal, there can be no more suitable person."

Berenar was silent, as if contemplating the idea from several sides, and then he nodded. "Yes. We concur. It will do very well."

"Are there other matters?" Maia asked.

"We have spoken with Mer Celehar," Berenar said, "and with the officers of the Vigilant Brotherhood who accompanied him and the prisoners."

"The prisoners?" Maia said sharply.

Berenar consulted his notes. "Shulivar, Bralchenar, and Narchanezhen. The persons responsible for the device which destroyed the *Wisdom of Choharo*. They have been remanded to the Judiciate, but we wondered if . . . Serenity, it would be entirely legal to forgo trial and execute them tomorrow. The officers tell us that they do not deny what they have done, and offer no defense."

"No," Maia said instinctively and so harshly that he said immediately, "We beg your pardon. But no. We will not stoop to vengeance. But—"

"Serenity?"

He heard his own words and only barely believed them: "We wish to speak to them."

# 32

## Shulivar, Bralchenar, and Narchanezhen

Berenar, Csevet, Beshelar, Cala, Lieutenant Echana, and indeed every other member of Maia's household had done their best to dissuade him. And he had no rational arguments to put against them, merely a feeling so strong that he could not disregard it. These were the people most directly responsible for making him emperor; he needed to see them, as if their reality might prove his own.

Between his staff's reluctance and his obligations—another banquet for the Avar, this one followed by a performance of the Municipal Choir of Cetho, and a seemingly endless procession of people who had to be reassured that he was all right—it was past midnight by the time he could descend to the ancient prison of the Untheileneise Court, the Nevennamire. It was older, in fact, than the court that Edrethelema III had designed, and Maia found its narrow halls and strange rounded rooms a disconcerting suggestion of what the palace had once looked like.

The Nevennamire was the place where a great many different jurisdictions converged: the Untheileneise Guard, the Vigilant Brotherhood of Cetho, and of Thu-Cethor, and then the Judiciate Guard, a small but honorable body that guarded its autonomy as ferociously as its prisoners. The guardroom was rather crowded, since the officers from Amalo had also to be accommodated, and all of them leaped to their feet in consternation when Beshelar said loudly, "His Imperial Serenity, Edrehasivar the Seventh."

Maia had refused to have the prisoners brought to the Alcethmeret, or even to the Michen'theileian. Here he received unexpected support from Lieutenant Echana, who said that it would be far easier to contain the prisoners in the Nevennamire than in the wide halls of the court.

"If His Serenity would be sensible," Beshelar said, "there would be no need to contain them."

Echana had smiled suddenly. "Yes, but it is clear that we cannot have that, so let us work with what we do have." And so the emperor came to the Nevennamire, which Cala said he was fairly sure hadn't happened since the Empress Valestho had been wrongly imprisoned by the brother of the Emperor Belthelema IX, and the emperor himself came to unlock her chains.

"We will set another precedent," Maia said grimly. "It may go in the history books next to our two attempted coups in less than a month."

"Serenity—"

"Never mind. We apologize."

"Don't," Cala said unhappily.

Maia shrugged, just as unhappily—*we cannot be your friend*—and kept walking.

And now, in the Nevennamire, the guards seemed very nearly panicked by his presence, which did not make him feel better. Fortunately, the duty officer, one Corporal Ishilar, managed to keep his head, and even if he did not understand why the emperor was here or what he hoped to accomplish, he was willing to cooperate. He refused to allow Maia past the guardroom into the prison itself, but he had no hesitation in rearranging the guardroom into an impromptu audience chamber—which, while not exactly what Maia wanted, he recognized as the best he was likely to get. He sat in the chair Corporal Ishilar had placed for him, with Cala on his right and Beshelar on his left, and the eight guards like pilasters along the walls, and waited while Ishilar fetched the prisoners.

Ishilar had also flatly refused to bring more than one at a time—and had been vehemently supported by Beshelar—so Maia had asked to see Min Narchanezhen first, then Mer Bralchenar, and finally Mer Shulivar. He felt that he would need practice before he could speak to the person who had actually constructed the device, who must, better than anyone else, have known what it would do.

Min Narchanezhen had the full-blood elf's ferret face and wore her white hair in a worker's crop. He could tell that she was determined not to be impressed by him; he didn't care. She had been the courier between Ubezhar and Shulivar—the two men had apparently agreed on their plan of destruction and murder without ever meeting face-to-face. He looked at her for a long time, while she found it progressively harder to meet his eyes; finally he asked, "Did you know what it would do?" It was the only question that seemed to matter.

"Yes, and I would do it again," she spat at him. "It is the only way to force you vile parasites to relinquish your power."

Corporal Ishilar cuffed her. "You speak to your emperor, Narchanezhen."

"*My* emperor?" She laughed, and it was a horrible noise, jagged as the scars on Maia's arm. "This is no emperor of mine. What cares he for me—or I for him? He would never know my name if it were not for the glorious strike we made against the stagnant power he represents."

"Is that what you think it?" Maia said. "Glorious?"

"Glorious," she said with defiant emphasis.

He thought of the congregation of the Ulimeire of Cetho and felt sick. "Then there is nothing further to be said."

She shouted at him as Ishilar and one of the officers from Amalo dragged her out, her voice rising and rising until it was a shriek as terrible as the wind.

"Serenity," Cala said, "you do not have to do this. No one requires it of you."

"I do," Maia said tiredly, and Cala retreated again.

Bralchenar was almost worse than Narchanezhen; groveling and terrified, he was all too clearly prepared to say anything that might save his life. There was no point in questioning him, for he would say only what he thought Maia wanted to hear. Maia listened for a few minutes, feeling that he owed it, if not to Bralchenar, then to all the people Bralchenar had killed. Finally, he said, "Your choices were your own, Mer Bralchenar," and nodded to Ishilar.

Mer Shulivar was not what Maia had been expecting—although, in truth, he couldn't have said what that would have been. Shulivar was tall, a little gawky, with short-cropped black hair and vividly blue eyes; his skin was the same slate gray color as Maia's. They looked at each other; Shulivar was neither frightened nor hostile, and Maia found it strangely easy to say, "Why did you do it?"

"Because it had to be done," Shulivar said. Maia saw that he was absolutely certain, that his calm came not merely from courage, but from conviction.

"*Had* to?"

"It is the nature of all persons to hold on to power when they have it," Shulivar said. "Thus it stagnates and becomes clouded, poisonous. Radical action is necessary to free it. And if you look, you will see that it is already working. If I had not done what I did, a half-goblin such as yourself would never have gained the throne of the Ethuveraz."

Maia opened his mouth, then closed it again. On that point, Shulivar was right.

"I can already see the changes," Shulivar said. "You do not hold on to power as your father and grandfather did. You are not afraid to let it go. And you have new ideas, ideas that no emperor before you has ever had."

"No," Maia protested.

"Yes," Shulivar said. "No other emperor would ever have attended the funeral of his father's servants. No other emperor would have accepted a woman as his nohecharis. You bring change, Edrehasivar, and you bring it because I opened the way for you."

"No. It is not worth the price."

"Twenty-three lives," Shulivar said. "Do you know how many people the factories of Choharo and Rosiro and Sevezho kill in a year? In a month?"

"But I haven't"

"You will," said Shulivar, and his eyes were blue, serene, and utterly mad. And yet, dear blessed goddesses, he was right. Maia knew he *would*.

"Our father was working to improve conditions in the west," he said.

"Against the stiff opposition of the east," said Shulivar, "which he would always have had to compromise with. And yet, that opposition is *already* dismantled by your rule."

"That's not—" Maia almost bit his tongue. "It wasn't a miscommunication, was it? You betrayed Tethimar on purpose."

"Does it matter?" said Shulivar. "I regret all the deaths,

but I repeat. It had to be done." He bowed his head, the first gesture toward conventional etiquette which he had made. "There is nothing more to say, Serenity. Truly."

It was a dismissal, and Maia was too horrified to argue with it. He nodded to Ishilar, and Shulivar was taken away.

"*Now* will you leave?" Beshelar muttered.

Maia stood up, and he did not miss the expressions of relief on the faces of all the guards. When Corporal Ishilar returned, Maia said, "Thank you for your help. And your patience."

Ishilar went pink. "It is our honor to serve you, Serenity," he said, and all the guards saluted. Maia went back to the Alcethmeret and tried not to think about Shulivar. Tried not to think about Shulivar's terrible philosophy and his father's lace-veiled corpse. For the first time, he understood why Setheris had spent so much time drunk. If it would stop the clamor in his head, it would be worth it.

But not worth having to ask Isheian or Nemer or someone to bring him a decanter of metheglin. Not worth the way Beshelar would look at him. Instead, he let his edocharei prepare him for bed, although he was almost certain he would be unable to sleep.

He lay on the bed and closed his eyes so he wouldn't look at Beshelar, and the next thing he knew was Avris saying, "Serenity, it is a beautiful morning and the Great Avar has sent you three messages already about meeting him in the east stables."

*That's right,* Maia thought, *I have a horse now.*

He sat up. "Do we have time?"

"Yes, Serenity," Avris said. "The Great Avar has made that very plain."

"Avris?"

Avris said, "The Great Avar, Serenity, has spoken very firmly on the subject to Lord Berenar and Mer Aisava and we know not whom else. He says that you must be allowed time to do things that are for yourself or you will go mad."

"Oh." Maia felt his face heating.

"So you have the entire morning, Serenity," Avris said encouragingly. "And the Great Avar is waiting."

Maia was aware of the irony, but he was too grateful for his grandfather's interference to resent it.

And he pushed the memory of Shulivar's blue eyes, of his father's ragged face beneath the funeral veil, as far from himself as he could.

# 33

## The Great Avar Departs

The Great Avar did not himself ride, being, as he said, far too fat and far too old, but he seemed happy to spend mornings in the east stables while Maia was taught the rudiments of staying on a horse. Maia heard snatches of his conversation with Dachensol Rosharis, the head groom of the Untheileneise Court; as best he could tell, both men were enjoying themselves, although he understood no more than one word in five. Certainly, the Great Avar seemed very smug on the last day of his stay when he and Dachensol Rosharis presented the elaborate plan of buying and selling and borrowing and gifting between the stables of the Untheileneise Court and the stables of the Corat' Dav Arhos that they had worked out. If Rosharis hadn't seemed equally smug, Maia would have been worried.

The Great Avar chose to leave after luncheon; he could make Uvezho easily, he said, and he had approved greatly of the hotel there. The luncheon was, predictably, magnificent; once again in Gormened's dav and surrounded by Barizheise cuisine, Maia found himself bewildered by the options offered and had to stick to the mushroom and venison pie, which was the first thing Gormened mentioned that he felt relatively confident about. And he did *not* accept a cup of sorcho.

Luncheon was perhaps two-thirds over (as Maia judged—he still had no idea how the goblins reckoned the length of a meal) when the Great Avar settled himself in the chair next to Maia's.

Maia became instantly tense.

"We shan't eat you, boy," the Great Avar said, but his expression was forbidding. Maia said nothing, waiting, and the Great Avar finally sighed and said, "We have no sons."

"Yes," Maia said cautiously.

"When we die, the avarsin will have to fight among themselves to choose the next Great Avar, for such is the custom when the Great Avar has no son and sometimes even when he has."

"Yes," Maia said even more cautiously.

The Great Avar gave him a hard look. "We would be more pleased an we could name you our heir."

"*Me?*" His voice was shrill and almost soundless with the shock.

"Half-elvish though thou art," the Great Avar agreed, seeming to take Maia's inadvertent use of the first-familiar as a cue to change his own level of formality. "Thou wouldst be a sword plunged into the anthill of the avarsin, truly, and I should take the thought most happily to my grave. But it cannot be done without destroying Barizhan, and that I do not want."

"No," Maia agreed—perhaps too hastily, for it made the Avar smirk.

"However, I am not pleased at leaving thee here among these elves. We have always thought them a cold people, but I tell you, any goblin would be ashamed to behave as hotly to his avar as they have behaved to thee. Attempts to usurp thee! Attempts to murder thee! Among the avarsin, it is at least an honest fight."

"It is not typical," Maia offered.

The Avar snorted. "That is what they say, but I must

tell you I am not so sure." His fierce orange eyes pinned Maia. "I wish you to know that, if you need it, Gormened will give you sanctuary. And I am leaving a half eshpekh stationed here, with Vizhenka as their captain."

"Vizhenka?" Maia said.

"If I have trusted him with myself, and with my daughter, I think I can trust him with my grandson."

"But—"

"And I think Nadeian will be happier out of the Corat' Dav Arhos."

That stopped Maia's next protest. The Great Avar was glowering at him, as if daring him to draw any conclusion at all, but Maia remembered Nadeian's passionate disregard for political decisions, and thought he understood.

The Great Avar nodded sharply. "If thou needst them, know that they are here," he said, and hauled himself to his feet again. "Gormened! You promised us khevaral!"

Maia was rather abstracted for several minutes; when he pulled his attention back to his surroundings, he found Captain Vizhenka standing in front of him, looking as uncertain as it was possible for a man of his physique and temperament to look.

"Captain?"

"Serenity." Vizhenka saluted. "We know that you cannot be happy about having a foreign army posted in your court."

"It is a very small army," Maia said.

Vizhenka ignored that. "We wished to assure you that we have no orders except to safeguard your person—and this dav—in the event of there being," he coughed politely, "any excitement."

"We thank you, Captain," Maia said, understanding that Vizhenka was pushing very near the edge of his maneuvering room as a Hezhethoreise captain to make that assurance. "We understand that our grandfather is concerned for our safety. We think it unnecessary, yet we admit we are . . ." He stopped, for he could not find the word he wanted, and finally settled, lamely, on "grateful."

"Serenity." Vizhenka saluted again. "It will be an honor to serve you in the event that it should become necessary."

And Maia had the odd feeling that he meant it, that somehow Vizhenka approved of him.

*Grateful,* he thought. It was not the right word, but it would have to do. He said, "We hope that we may be allowed to invite you and Merrem Vizhenka to an occasional, er, family gathering? Would that be inappropriate?"

"Not at all, Serenity," Vizhenka said. "We will be very pleased—and we know that we may safely say the same for Merrem Vizhenka."

"Good," Maia said.

And then Vizhenka was called away, and Maia was approached by one of the Barizheise merchants who lived in Cetho, who wished to know if it was true that the emperor was planning to bridge the Istandaärtha.

"The idea has been presented to the Corazhas," Maia said and, barely half a minute later, found himself surrounded by goblin merchants, eagerly telling him what a boon and a blessing such a bridge would be, and he could not free himself until the tumult of the Avar's departure.

They progressed once again to Parmeno Square, where the Avar's traveling coach waited. The Avar exchanged salutes with Vizhenka, kissed his daughter's hands, and thumped Maia on the shoulders hard enough to stagger him. Then he heaved himself into his coach;

the coachman touched his cockaded hat in the direction of the emperor and cried, "Hai!" to the ten black horses.

In the center of his own private thunderstorm, the Great Avar departed.

# 34

## Building Bridges

The first two months of the new year were consumed in the trials of the Princess Shevëan, Lord Chavar, the Duke Tethimel, Dach'osmer Ubezhar, Mer Shulivar, Mer Bralchenar, Min Narchanezhen, and a dizzying host of other persons associated with one or the other of the attempts to remove Edrehasivar VII from the throne. Maia was unable to decide if it was a relief or a further burden that no one could be charged in both attempts. Shevëan and Chavar had apparently been entirely unaware of Tethimar's machinations and vice versa. What *was* a relief was the fact that the specter of Eshevis Tethimar made it acceptable, and even reasonable, for the emperor to show clemency to Shevëan and Chavar. They had, after all, sincerely believed that what they did was for the good of the Ethuveraz and faithful to the wishes of Varenechibel IV. The Tethimadeise Conspiracy, as it came quickly to be called, had had no interest in the good of the empire, and its members had seen the emperor merely as an inconvenience to be removed from their path.

The executions were public and horrible and gave Maia nightmares.

He had refused flatly to command Eshevis Tethimar's sisters to attend, as some members of his government seemed to think he should. The girls were guilty of nothing except their birth, and he could think of no surer way to teach them that their brother and father had been correct in their resentment. It had given him a private, defiant sense of satisfaction to give the girls into Prince Orchenis's keeping before the Tethimadeise trial was even completed and see them off to Amalo on the *Loyalty of Lohaiso*—a name so appropriate as to be painful, for Orchenis's loyalty proved to be as solid as the mountains that were his home. He began his audience with the emperor by offering revethvoran, and Maia had seen in his grim face, heard in his flat voice, that he would do it if ordered and think it no more than he deserved.

But Orchenis had known nothing of the Tethimada's schemes—from what he said, Maia gathered that in fact the conspirators had been very careful to keep even discussions of their discontent away from him. And his wife, pretty and colorless and obviously, shyly, worshipful of her husband: whether she would have sympathized with her brother and father's aims was immaterial, for she was never told of them.

With the Tethimadeise girls taken care of, Maia had to decide what was to be done with the members of the first conspiracy. Chavar was comparatively easy; the Chavada had a country estate in the corner of Thu-Athamar between the Tetara and the Tetareise border, and the Viscount Chavel had accepted the responsibility for the terms of his brother's confinement there.

Maia had done everything he could to prevent the Chavada being dragged down with the Lord Chancellor; he believed without reservation that Chavar, a widower and not close to either his son or his brother, had taken none of his family into his confidence. Certainly, the Viscount Chavel, when he appeared before the emperor some three days after the failed coup and offered

revethvoran—which was more than Chavar had bothered to do—had had no idea. And if Nurevis had known,
there would have been no need for the dramatic assault
on the Alcethmeret; Maia could simply have been waylaid in the Chavadeise apartments.

But even so, there were penalties Maia could not
gainsay. Chavar's extensive properties were forfeit, and
without them, the Chavada returned to the ranks of
the shabby patch-pocket nobility with the Nelada and
the Danivada and all the rest of them. And Nurevis
didn't even have that. He was not his uncle's heir.

Dissuaded from revethvoran, the Viscount Chavel had
offered to stay at court, so that the emperor might keep
an eye on him and be sure he was not plotting treason.
The idea clearly revolted him. Maia had declined that
offer as well, and the Viscount Chavel had gratefully begun the long and ugly process of putting the Chavadeise
court apartments into mothballs. Most of the furnishings were going straight to an auction house in Cetho,
where Maia hoped, perhaps a little viciously, that they
would be bought by the goblin merchants Chavar so
despised.

The work was not finished by Winternight, and Maia
did not blame Chavel for the panic-stricken declarations
of innocence he sent by hourly pneumatic until he got an
answer with the emperor's own signet. Nor did he blame
Chavel for wanting to avoid a second audience; the first
had been nerve-racking enough on both sides. But it
seemed like cruelty to send Nurevis, of all people, to inform the emperor that the Chavada were finally leaving
the Untheileneise Court.

Perhaps it *was* cruelty. The Viscount Chavel was honest and loyal, but that was no guarantee he was not like
his brother in other ways.

Nurevis was haggard, his ears low, and he was dressed
in clothes nearly as shabby as those in which Maia had

first come to court. His own wardrobe would also have gone to the auction house; Maia remembered Setheris, in their first weeks at Edonomee, poring gloomily over the invoices from the sale of his clothing.

Nurevis recited the formulas of leave-taking quickly, stiltedly, and then fell silent. For the first time in Maia's acquaintance with him, he seemed awkward, his poise gone along with his father's power.

Out of his own grief and regret, Maia blurted, "We are sorry." He knew it was the wrong thing to say before the words were entirely out of his mouth. It sounded as if he were apologizing to Nurevis, and even a backwards goblin emperor knew that the emperor did not apologize for someone else's attempted treason.

Nurevis's ears flattened even further and he said, "Serenity, you should not be."

"But we are," Maia said with mulish truthfulness and added, "We did like you."

Nurevis gaped, thrown into a momentary resemblance to his father by the shock. Finally, he said slowly, "You are the only person still willing to admit to having been our friend. Thank you, Serenity."

"They are frightened," Maia said, thinking of the bright, laughing crowds in the Chavada's salon, the young men who spoke of nothing but hunting.

"So are we," said Nurevis, his voice no more than a whisper.

Any comfort Maia offered would be false, and therefore unkind. Maia did the only thing he could. He dismissed Nurevis, who bowed his head and left, shoulders slumped and ears down, looking more like a beaten dog than a courtier, and Maia hated Chavar for it. Hated him and was glad he was going to a poverty-stricken country estate where he would be the Chavada's problem.

But Shevëan was the problem of the House Drazhada,

both to house and to guard. With Csevet's help, Maia made a list of all the Drazhadeise estates and considered each one in turn. He rejected Isvaroë and Edonomee out of hand, and decided that Cethoree was too close to the capital, and to the principal estate of the Rohethada. Varenechibel, he thought dourly, had been lucky that Arbelan was loyal.

The Drazhada had estates scattered throughout the Ethuveraz; Maia could send Shevëan almost anywhere he wanted to. In the end, he chose the manor of Bakhoree in northern Thu-Cethor—not for spite, although Bakhoree was very close to the monastery where Chavar and Shevëan had planned to send him, but because it was a long way from the nearest town, and the estate was almost entirely self-sufficient. Any strangers, as Maia knew from Edonomee, would be noticed, and Shevëan would be able neither to escape nor to send clandestine messages. She would undoubtably consider it primitive and uncomfortable, but Maia could not find it in himself to care.

He cared more about how her children would take the news. He brought a map to the nursery of the Alcethmeret and showed Idra exactly where Bakhoree was. "She will be well treated," he said awkwardly. "The people of the manor are accustomed to relegated nobles—there was a series of them there during my father's reign—and she will have Osmin Bazhevin for company."

"Osmin Bazhevin did not take part in the conspiracy," Idra said.

"She did nothing to stop it, either," Maia said. "Your mother bullied her into silence and she let herself be bullied."

"As it has ever been with our mother's companions," Idra said wearily. "Our father asked her once if she wouldn't prefer an actual sheep, for at least she would get the benefit of the wool. Mother was not amused."

"I am sorry I never got the chance to know your father," Maia said cautiously.

Idra smiled at him. "I am, too. Although it is a little strange to say, I think you would have liked each other."

"Of *course* Papa would have liked Cousin Maia," Mireän said indignantly. "Show me where Mama's going to live, Cousin Maia?"

He pointed out Bakhoree again. Mireän touched her finger to the delicately drawn keep and sounded out the syllables written beneath it. "It's in the mountains," she said. "Are there ogres?"

"None at Bakhoree," Maia said promptly.

"Good," Mireän said.

"But what if they come out of the mountains?" Ino said. Ino, Maia had learned, was a worrier. "Will they eat Mama?"

"No," Maia said. "Bakhoree is an old house, like a tiny castle. And your mother will have soldiers to protect her."

Idra gave Maia a sardonic look, but was far too kind a brother to say anything. And Ino was comforted.

Maia was glad that none of them asked to be allowed to say good-bye to their mother, for if they'd asked, he thought he would have had to agree, and he did not trust Sheveän not to attempt to capitalize on the pathos of being separated from her children. He himself did get up at dawn to see her off at the court's mooring mast, mostly so that he would be certain, beyond any shadow of tortured midnight imaginings, that she was gone. Sheveän was unimpressed by the emperor's condescension; she barely bent her knees at all when she curtsied, and her gaze was fixed on something beyond him. Stano Bazhevin could not meet his eyes at all. He felt sorry for her, but that was nothing compared to the great wash of relief he felt when the *Honor of Csedo* cast off and carried Shevëan away from the Untheileneise Court.

He tried not to let his relief show that evening, when he told Idra privately that his mother had left the court, but Idra said, "Thou must be glad."

There was no accusation in his tone, but Maia knew it was a test, even if not one Idra had planned. He said, "Not *glad*. I would have been *glad* if she would have accepted me, even if she never liked me. But, yes, I am relieved. I was afraid she would do . . ." He trailed off and shrugged; he already knew his imagination wasn't as good as Shevëan's. "Something."

"My father—" Idra's voice cracked, but he continued doggedly: "My father said once that Mother should have been a soldier. She was very offended, but my father said that she would have been a general by the time she was forty, and that pleased her. It is true. She is very fierce."

"Yes," Maia said, having been on the other end of that ferocity.

"And she . . ." He stared at his hands as if they displeased him, then looked up and met Maia's eyes. "I want better for my sisters. Mother would not be . . ."

There was no good word, and Maia knew it. "What she is," he offered.

"Yes, thank you. She would not be what she is if she had ever had something given her that was a burden equal to her strength. One hears people say it all the time—'she should have been a son to her father'—but it is *true*. If she had been a son, she would have had a duty that went beyond children. And that duty is not congenial to everyone."

Maia tried to protest, but Idra shook his head. "I saw the look on thy face when thou realized my sisters love their nurse more than their mother."

Apologetically, Maia said, "I loved my mother very much."

"I try to have compassion for mine," Idra said wryly.

"Then thou dost not . . . I wondered if it was my fault, that she hated me so much."

"No," Idra said at once and with some vehemence. "She would have hated anyone who came between her and what she saw as her right."

"To be empress?"

"No. That's why Csoru hates thee." Idra grimaced. "I'm sorry. That was an awful thing to say."

"But it's true," Maia said. "I knew that the first time I met her."

"Mother didn't care about that—although I don't say she wouldn't have *liked* being the Empress Sheveän. But no. She believed her right was to be the *mother* of the emperor."

"Then she was championing thee after all. I had thought—"

"No," Idra said again. "Or, well, in a way. But it wasn't about *me*." He hesitated. "I have never said this to anyone, not even my father, although it was he who helped me to understand that Mother's ferocity—like a beast, yes? not a choice, but something she cannot take off, as a beast cannot take off its fur—that that was not something I had done, or that Mireän and Ino had done, and that it was not something we could undo. But he loved her, and I did not want to upset him."

"Of course not," Maia said.

Idra gave him a grateful smile. "But maybe thou canst tell me if I am wrong—it seems to me that Mother does not care very much about people as people. She never saw you as a *person*, just as something wrong. And when I say she wanted to be the mother of the emperor, I don't mean that she wanted *me* to be emperor. She wanted *her son* to be emperor. And she has always gotten very angry at people who won't play the roles she puts them in. I think that's why she always wants people like Osmin Bazhevin around her."

"And it was not my place to be emperor."

"Yes. And thou didst not abdicate. I remembered, later, that's what she'd said when she realized thou wert the only one left. That thou shouldst abdicate. And I think that's really what she thought."

"And so she was angry at me because I didn't." It made sense, and in a peculiar way, it made him feel better. It meant there really was nothing he could have done.

"Yes. And because thou didst things that Varenechibel would not have done." Idra added hastily, "I do not mean it as a criticism!" and Maia realized that he had winced, remembering Shulivar.

"No, I know. I'm sorry." He hesitated, then offered a partial truth: "I find being compared to him . . . oppressive."

Shyly, Idra offered a truth in return, "I hope thou wilt have a son quickly. For I do not want to be emperor."

"I understand," Maia said. They smiled at each other, bound together in that moment by the responsibility that neither of them wanted and that one of them still might escape.

Maia thought about that, and he thought about Vedero, who had kept her promise to let him watch the eclipse with her. She kept her telescope on the roof of her apartments, reached through a trap and by means of a ladder that was nothing more than iron rungs bolted to the wall. He was glad she was wearing trousers, although she had apologized for them, glad also that she had warned him, through his edocharei, not only to dress warmly, but to bring two pairs of gloves. The thick fur-lined mittens, while deeply appreciated on the roof, would have been worse than useless on the ladder, but the rungs were deathly cold even through the leather of his thinner pair of gloves.

He was pleased and impressed by Vedero's arrangements on her flat bit of roof. She used the adjacent chimney both for warmth and as a windbreak, and she had a squat brazier in the shape of a toad to mark the opposite corner of her observatory. Between the two and the roof railings, there was enough room for four people, but only if they stayed very close together. Maia was glad it was Beshelar and Cala tonight, both because Cala was genuinely interested and because if he was going to be huddling into someone's body heat, he'd rather it was one of those two.

The eclipse was beautiful and fascinating; all four of them ended up taking turns with Vedero's telescope—a remarkable thing engraved like a unicorn's horn. Maia commented on it, and she said, "It is a gift from our friend, Dach'osmin Tativin. She made the horn for her automaton, but found the telescoping was prone to retracting or extending itself at just the wrong moment."

"An automaton? Of a unicorn?"

"Yes. Steam-powered—by a pipe from her furnace at the moment, for while she can get it to raise and lower its head, she has not yet figured out how to make it walk, so it does not matter that it is tethered to her study wall. She uses it as a coatrack—as she is very short, it is convenient for her to have a coatrack that will duck its head."

"Truly?" Maia said, afraid that it was merely an elaborate joke.

"Yes," said Vedero. "She will come to the court in the summer, when it is too hot for her experiments, and you may meet her. If you are not careful, she will show you all her drawings."

"We should like that," Maia said; Vedero looked at him sharply, but in the minimal light thrown by the brazier and by one dark lantern, mostly shuttered, he could not read her face.

He got her to talk more, in bits and pieces, about her friends and the work they were doing. One of her friends was translating the Barizheise poet Amu Carcethlened, who had written fabulous adventure tales about the voyages of the steamship *Lion of Orpezhkhahar*. Another friend was writing a treatise on the principles of inheritance as observed from her family's millennium-worth of horsebreeding records. Another had started an unofficial school for girls with mazeise talents. There were others and others, and at some point Vedero said, "Of course, when we say 'friend,' we do not necessarily mean that we like the person particularly. We mean that she shares with us the belief that women can and should do the same intellectual work as men." Her shoulders were stiffly defensive, and Maia wondered what she expected him to say.

Except that he knew. She expected condemnation, or to be told that it was all very well for a hobby, but the only work women were fitted for was the bearing of children. He said, gently, "We would be honored to meet your friends—both those you like and those you don't."

She swung around so forcefully to stare at him that she nearly knocked Cala into the railings. "You are serious," she said, not quite a question, but not quite a statement either.

"We were not considered worth educating, either," Maia said.

She bowed her head and said, "We take your point, Serenity."

It was not friendship he found with Idra and Vedero—either in the usual sense or in her particular sense—but it was something that was *like* friendship, kinship in a metaphorical rather than a literal fashion, something that was maybe as close as an emperor could get.

He found the beginnings of something similar with Dach'osmin Ceredin. She came up onto the dais in the Michen'theileian during the first ball held after Winternight, as everyone was dancing very cautiously and alertly, and said, "Serenity, why do you not dance?"

"We do not know how," Maia said, and did his best to sound indifferent.

She considered him; none of the pity that Min Vechin had shown was visible on her face, only a kind of disinterested curiosity. "We could teach you, if you wanted."

"Teach . . . us?"

She snorted. "We learned when we were five years old. We assure you, Serenity, it is not that difficult."

"Thank you," he said. "If it would not be a great bother to you—"

She shrugged impatiently. "What else is there to do in the winter?"

So another piece of time was carved out of the emperor's schedule, like the three mornings a week he now spent learning equitation on Velvet's patient back, and Csethiro Ceredin taught him to dance. She was a better teacher than he had expected, patient and funny and very clever about finding ways to explain things he did not understand. And gradually he learned not to trip over his own feet, gradually learned not to flinch every time their hands met. "By our wedding," she said, "we will not be afraid to dance with you in public, Edrehasivar."

"Please," Maia said. He was standing close to her, one hand on her waist, the other holding one of her hands. Her other hand was on his shoulder, and he was as aware of it as of a burning coal. "My name is Maia."

She was very still for a moment; then she looked up at him. She was not at all pretty, her nose too long and her chin too weak, but her eyes were sharp and full of light, and even of kindness. "And mine is Csethiro. It is probably good for a husband and wife to be on familiar terms with each other." And then, with a pause he would have thought was mocking except that he was close enough to hear her nervous inhalation, "Thinkst thou?"

"Yes," he said, and daringly turned her in the move she had just been teaching him. "I do think so."

And she laughed with delight and said, "Not bad. Now let's try the whole thing again, and this time remember that thy spine is not an iron rod."

"Yes, Csethiro," he said, and they grinned at each other all the way back to the top of the dance.

It was because of that new warmth between himself and his future empress that when he was petitioned for an audience by Min Nedaö Vechin, he did not refuse. He did not even tell Csevet to schedule her among his public audiences; instead, he received her in the Alcethmeret—although not in the Tortoise Room.

She was as beautiful as she had been the first time he saw her, although not quite so simply dressed; she had found patronage at court, then, aside from her maneuverings with him. He found that he was not resentful; he had learned too much about the way the court worked.

She approached, curtsied exquisitely, and said without further preamble—or, indeed, waiting for permission to speak—"Serenity, we have come to apologize."

He looked at her more closely, seeing past the armor of her clothes, the armor of her beauty. She was nervous, her color too high, her teeth catching at her lip: nervous and determined, and he realized with a sudden odd sense of kinship that she had blurted the words out—*rushed the fence* in the hunting cant he was learning to decipher—because she was afraid that if she didn't, she wouldn't manage to say them at all.

Forgiveness was on the tip of his tongue, but Csevet

had finally taught him not to say anything in an audience without thinking it through, and by the time he was certain that, yes, he did forgive her, he had become curious. "What have you done that warrants an apology?" Because he knew why he thought she should apologize, but he had no idea if it looked the same way to her, if she was even talking about the same thing.

"Serenity." She folded down onto her knees. "We knew that you were prepared to enter into a . . ." She hesitated, ears flicking, and said carefully, "a *closer relationship* with us, and we used that against you."

"It was very much to our advantage," he said, "for we did in truth need to speak to the Clocksmiths' Guild."

"No," said Min Vechin, "that is not what we mean. It is not about the outcome, although we understand that the outcome is indeed felicitous. It is about what we *did*." She looked up. "We should have asked you properly. Honorably."

"You didn't do anything dishonorable," Maia protested.

"Only because you did not let us," she said. "And so we must thank you, as well as apologize to you."

Her words hung awkwardly, and then Maia felt his eyebrows shoot up. "You hadn't . . . that is, we beg your pardon. Of course you had not."

"Not all opera singers are—" Her voice cracked and she pressed the tips of her lacquered fingernails against her mouth.

Maia had a moment's inadvertent imagination of what the scene would have looked like if he had said yes: two embarrassed virgins trying to pretend they knew what they were doing. And he still didn't know what he was supposed to do about his nohecharei in that situation. "We were angry," he admitted. "But we are not any longer."

"We did not *think*," said Min Vechin vehemently. "We

wanted to help and we saw that we could, and we did not remember that you are a person, not just the emperor."

"You were helping your sister," Maia said, trying to be reassuring, but she shook her head.

"Mer Halezh," she said, and the expression in her eyes said everything else.

"Oh," said Maia. He remembered wondering if she were bored, during that long, slightly feverish conversation about the bridge over the Istandaärtha; now he knew she had not been.

"We have apologized to him, also. He has forgiven us." Maia heard the wonderment in her voice, although whether it was over the forgiveness or Mer Halezh he could not tell and had—he reminded himself—no right to ask. "And we are returning to Zhaö to begin rehearsals for *The Tiger's Bride,* but we had to apologize first. Because it was a rotten thing to do."

The phrase was clearly one from her childhood; her accent deepened even as her voice lifted, and when she realized what she'd said, she blushed as deep a red as any rose.

"Min Vechin," Maia said, and smiled at her. "We forgive you."

She smiled back, and he knew that when she left for Zhaö, it would mean he had a friend there.

Idra, Csethiro, Nedaö, Vedero: instead of bulwarks, he began to feel that he had alliances, that his life—for perhaps the first time since his mother died—was not merely a matter of surviving from one hostile encounter to the next. It was strange to him, and he did not entirely trust it, so that when Thara Celehar asked for an audience, Maia granted it expecting the worst, even though he did not know exactly what the worst might be.

He was not reassured when Celehar appeared in the

company of the Archprelate. The Council of Prelates had still not succeeded in choosing a replacement for the Witness for the Prelacy, and Maia was becoming more and more uneasy with the thoughtful way the Archprelate watched him in sessions of the Corazhas, especially as he could think of no reason for it.

"Serenity," Celehar said, "we have come to ask a favor of you."

"If it is within our power, we will grant it," Maia said. Csevet, in his usual position in the corner, grimaced, but Maia had spoken no more than the truth. He owed Celehar any favor the man desired.

"We . . ." Celehar coughed, as if trying to clear his throat, although it had no effect on his graveled voice. "We deeply appreciate Your Serenity's kindness in taking us into your household, and we do not in any way wish you to think that we are discontent or unhappy or . . . or anything of the sort."

"We have no proper position for you," Maia said.

"That is . . ." Celehar trailed off, seeming simply unable to find the words he wanted. He looked imploringly at the Archprelate, who nodded at him and stepped forward.

"That is why Thara asked us to come with him."

"Oh?" said Maia, noting the use of Celehar's given name, although he was not sure what it signaled.

"It is difficult for any man to articulate the nature of his calling," said the Archprelate. "Thara wished us to help him explain to you that although he would be very proud to be your chaplain, it is not a role he can fulfill."

"We never thought he should," Maia said, more than a little appalled. "We did not intend any such implication in our action—we wished merely to ensure that he was not left homeless by Csoru Zhasanai's anger."

Celehar bowed profoundly. "And we thank you for

that, Serenity. But if we are not to be your chaplain—which, as the Archprelate says, we cannot feel ourself suited to be—then there *is* nothing for us to do in your household. There was nothing for us to do in Csoru Zhasanai's household either, and it was not until we went to Amalo that we realized how much that fretted us."

"Then you must have a suggestion," Maia said, looking from Celehar to the Archprelate.

"Thara wishes to resume his priesthood," said the Archprelate.

"Then he should," Maia said immediately. "We do not know if we have an ulimeire in our benefices—but surely we must. Csevet?"

"Serenity," Csevet said in acknowledgment. "We will inquire."

"No!" Celehar said hastily and then flushed beet-red.

"No?" Maia said.

"That is not the favor we wished to ask," Celehar said, mostly to the floor. "We would not trespass so on Your Serenity's generosity. We wished merely to be released from your household so that we might return to the prelacy for assignment. We do not deserve a benefice."

"That is a matter of opinion, Mer Celehar," Maia said, and was surprised and pleased when the Archprelate smiled at him.

"In truth . . ."

"Go on, Thara," the Archprelate said.

"In truth, Serenity, although we appreciate . . . although we cannot ever repay your generosity, a benefice is not what we want."

"All right," Maia said. "We admit, we are very ignorant as to the options before you. What is your wish?"

"We wish to be a Witness *vel ama*," said Celehar. "They are often clerics of Ulis."

"It is a little unusual for someone to come to the position from the other side," said the Archprelate, "but in point of fact, the prelacy has a considerable need for such Witnesses."

"We thought all priests of Ulis were Witnesses for the Dead."

"They can be called upon to do so," the Archprelate said, "but it is not part of their routine duties, and many of them—to be frank, Serenity—do not have any particular aptitude for it. It has always been *possible* for a priest who knows himself to be unequal to the task to ask the prelacy to send a Witness, but it means a delay, and sometimes it means a delay of months, if the prelacy does not have anyone who can be spared. If Thara returned to us *as* a Witness, we would be able to do several things which seem to us desirable. For one, we would be able to *encourage* priests to ask a Witness to be sent. For another, we would be able to encourage young priests to enter this path. There are always some whose devotion to Ulis is sincere and intensely strong, but who—just as their brothers have no gift for speaking to the dead— have no gift for speaking to the living. And the more of these dedicated Witnesses we have, the less either we or the judiciate has to rely on the unpredictable abilities of local priests."

"We understand," Maia said. "It seems to us a very worthy task. If that is truly all you desire of us, Mer Celehar, we will grant it gladly, but please know that we would grant you a much greater favor with equal happiness."

Celehar actually smiled. "Thank you, Serenity, but this is our desiring. Nothing more."

There was a light in his eyes that Maia had never seen there before, and it was clear he meant what he said.

"Then whatever obligation you may feel you have to

us, we release you from it," Maia said. "And we wish you well."

Celehar bowed again and said, "You may call on us, Serenity, if ever you need us. And although we hope you will never need our particular skills, we also hope that if you need our friendship, you will not hesitate."

"Thank you," Maia said. "We are . . . we will remember."

Celehar then left, but the Archprelate remained. Maia looked at him uneasily. "Archprelate?"

"Serenity. In considering Thara's situation, it occurred to us that, even though he is quite right in thinking himself unsuited for a chaplaincy, that does not mean that you do not, perhaps, need one."

"A chaplain? Ought we to—"

"We are not reproaching you," the Archprelate said. "It is not a requirement. Your late father chose to do without, and we assure you, our loyalty was in no way diminished. But you are not your father."

"No," Maia said, "we are not."

"And we know that Chenelo Zhasan was a woman of deep spirituality," the Archprelate said.

"How do you know that?"

"We were at the Untheileneise Court when she was," said the Archprelate. "We were a canon of the Untheileneise'meire—it is a customary step for those destined for the higher offices of the prelacy—and we saw her there often. We spoke to her once."

"You did?" Maia said, and hoped his eagerness did not show.

"She asked if she was intruding, or making our job more difficult. We told her that the Untheileneise'meire was *supposed* to be a place of prayer, even if the emperors of the Ethuveraz have tended to treat it only as a tomb, and she thanked us, then asked if there was somewhere she might light candles. She explained a little of the place candle-lighting holds in Barizheise ritual, and it was clear that it was very important to her. We found a place where she could do so without the candle wax attracting attention, and—"

"Where?" Maia said, and if he'd wanted to appear disinterested, he had just failed utterly. "Will you show us?"

"Of course, Serenity," the Archprelate said, more than a little startled but not displeased, and they went in a small procession to the Untheileneise'meire, Maia, the Archprelate, Beshelar, and Cala. On the way, the Archprelate said, with some hesitation, "We are grateful, Serenity, that you did not consider us a collaborator with our cousin Eshevis."

"We were sure you were not," Maia said.

"Many emperors would not have bothered with a distinction."

"Including our grandfather, yes. We hope that, in this instance, our father would have approved of our decisions."

The Archprelate gave him a thoughtful, sidelong look, but said only, "In any event, thank you, Serenity. Your trust means much to us, and for greater reasons than the preservation of our own skin."

"We are pleased," Maia said awkwardly. "That is, thank you?"

The Archprelate gave him a smile that absolved him from having to try again, and moved ahead to open the doors of the Untheileneise'meire.

The two canons there looked very alarmed at being descended upon by both their Archprelate and their emperor, but bowed gratefully and obediently when the Archprelate waved them away. He led Maia around the outer ring of tombs to one of the chapels—and Maia realized for the first time that there were six chapels, rather than five. "This is the Chapel of All Gods," said the Archprelate. "The Mich'othasmeire. It is not much used, since even celebrations for a single god tend to be too large for the chapels, and people who come to pray privately wish most often to pray to Osreian or Cstheio. Once, when we first came to the Untheileneise Court, we remember a divine of Akhalarna appeared—a very old woman with the ritual scars. She was making a pilgrimage from her home to Valno, where Akhalarna fell to earth, and she stopped to make an offering here. But other than that . . ." He shrugged. "Chenelo Zhasan was very anxious not to disturb anyone, and we assured her she would not. We did not observe her after that, but when she was sent to Isvaroë, we came to clean the chapel. She had put candles in all the windows, and we imagine the effect must have been very beautiful."

"Thank you," Maia said, looking around. Like the Untheileneise'meire, the chapel was circular; it was devoid of ornament save the gold mosaic triskelion in the center of the floor. The windows were tall and narrow and spaced evenly about its circumference. It would not have been very like the shrine Chenelo had assembled at Isvaroë—but then, that had not been very like the goblin churches with which she had grown up. And the Archprelate was right; this small, peaceful space would have been beautiful by candlelight. "May we—?" He stopped, for the question was ridiculous. He was the emperor; technically, this chapel, like every other inch of the Untheileneise Court, was his property.

"You would be welcome," the Archprelate said gently. "And that is related to what we wanted to say to you."

"Yes?" Maia said.

"Just as it is not a crime to do without a chaplain, Serenity, it is no crime to wish to have one. Few emperors are publicly observant—a habit which dates back to the suppression of the cult of Chevarimai—but few of them are as sternly separate from the church as your late father. And we guess that you must have been raised in the Barizheise tradition?"

"Until we were eight," Maia said, wishing there were somewhere to hide.

"Then you are accustomed to meditation more than ritual," the archprelate said thoughtfully. "May we consider the matter and present you with an option of chaplains? We have several young priests who have been trained in Barizheise practice—it has become popular in Thu-Tetar and Thu-Istandaär—and in fact we would like to encourage the Barizheise habit of contemplation in both our clergy and our congregations."

"And the emperor makes a fine example," Maia said, only slightly sourly.

"It is the truth, Serenity," the Archprelate said, unfazed.

"Very well," Maia said. "For we cannot deny that you are correct, and meditation would be a solace to us." He hoped that was put mildly enough. "As would a teacher—for we know only what our mother taught us before her death."

"Of course, Serenity. We will think on it."

"Thank you, Archprelate," said Maia, and they parted.

On the return trip to the Alcethmeret, Cala caught up to him and said, "Serenity, we did not know you meditated."

"We have not," said Maia. "Not since coming to the court."

"But why not?"

"The emperor," Maia said dryly, "is never alone."

"Oh." Cala nearly stumbled, and he was silent for several moments before he said, "Did you think we would mock you?"

"No," Maia said. "For surely any nohecharis who mocked the emperor would be dismissed forthwith. But we feared . . . we feared you would think less of us."

Cala said, "No," as if the idea horrified him, and over him, Beshelar said, "We would not, Serenity."

"Thank you," Maia said. Two steps later, he realized that neither of them had said, *It is not the nohecharei's place to disapprove of the emperor,* and that came together suddenly with his thoughts about alliances and relationships that were like friendship, and he turned suddenly and fiercely on both of them and said, "The Adremaza was *wrong.*"

"Serenity?" Beshelar said, even as Cala, alarmed, went back a pace.

"When he said you could not be our friend. For if he meant by that that we could not be fond of you, or you could not be fond of us, then he simply lied. It is nonsensical. It denies the truth, which is that we—" He broke off, dropped formality as deliberately as smashing a plate. "I am fond of both of you. If I were not, how could I possibly bear to spend *half my life* in your company? And surely the same must be true in reverse. At least, I hope it must."

Cala and Beshelar were both going red, but they mumbled something that sounded like agreement.

Almost breathless with his own ferocity, Maia said, "It is true that we cannot be *friends* in the commonly understood sense, but I have never in all my life had such a friend, and I do not think I ever will. I am the emperor. I *can't.* But that doesn't mean I can't have friends at all, just that they can't be that *sort* of friend. I believe that the Adremaza meant his advice for the best, but he was cruelly wrong. I do not ask, or expect, you to be friends with me as you are friends with other mazei, or other soldiers in the Untheileneise Guard. But it . . . it's *silly* to deny that we hold each other in affection." He stopped, swallowed hard. "If, of course, you do."

"Of course we do," Beshelar said, using the plural rather than the formal.

"For my part," Cala said, "I have never been able to stop thinking of you as—you are right, not as a friend, exactly, but . . . I would die for you, Serenity, and not only because I swore an oath."

"As would I," said Beshelar.

Maia blinked hard and said, "Then we will be a different sort of friends."

Cala's smile was beautiful, and although Beshelar didn't smile, he saluted with élan.

"All right," said Maia, smiling back. "Then let us return to the Alcethmeret before Csevet sends to find if we have been lost."

He entered the Alcethmeret, and for the first time it felt like coming home.

# 35

## The Bridge over the Istandaärtha

The Corazhas met to decide on the question of the bridge over the Istandaärtha on the first day of the spring rains. The sound of rain was everywhere, and in the Verven'theileian, someone had flung all the curtains back. The view was ugly with mud and the great louring clouds, but hopeful.

At long last, there was a new Witness for the Prelacy, a dry, decisive young man who—unlike the Witness for the Treasury, who was still meek as a mouse—showed no signs of being overawed. He assured Maia before the session proper began that he had studied the matter carefully and would not cast his vote out of ignorance or laziness. Maia was inclined to approve of him.

The Corazhas had been grimly businesslike throughout the trials, and Maia was not surprised when the debate over the bridge became very vocal. Lord Pashavar still opposed it, partly on the grounds that it could not be done, and partly on the grounds that even if it could, it shouldn't. He was supported by the Witness for Foreigners and the Witness for the Universities, opposed loudly by the Witness for the Parliament and quietly by the Witness for the Athmaz'are. The Witness for the Prelacy proved his quality by flinging himself into the argument, and although at first he seemed inclined to support the anti-bridge side, the answers to some of his questions caused him to change his mind. The Witness for the Treasury sat and watched and said nothing.

When at last it came to a vote, the split was perfectly predictable: three yeses and three noes, right down the middle, and the Witness for the Treasury, looking terrified, said, "We abstain."

"You can't *abstain*," Lord Pashavar said in outrage.

"Yes, he can," said Lord Deshehar. "Although we admit we would prefer he did not."

"We cannot decide," the Witness for the Treasury said. "We are sorry, but it is the truth."

"May we suggest that indecisiveness is hardly a desirable trait in a member of the Corazhas?" Lord Pashavar said.

"We will give our resignation if His Serenity asks it," the Witness for the Treasury said, looking at Maia.

"You are very decisive in your indecision," Maia said, which surprised several members of the Corazhas into laughing. "We do not ask your resignation. But, if you find that the responsibilities of the Corazhas are more than you can bear, we will certainly permit you to step down."

The Witness bowed his head. "Thank you, Serenity. We are . . . We did not expect to find it so overwhelming, and we would ask for more time to consider."

"Of course."

"But even so," he added, with a hint of steel in his voice, "on the question of the bridge, we cannot vote. We abstain."

"Well," said Lord Pashavar, sour as vinegar, "then it is up to you, Serenity, to break the tie."

"You cannot keep change from happening, Lord Pashavar," Maia said sympathetically, and Lord Pashavar flapped a hand at him to get on with things.

"We vote in favor of the bridge," Maia said, as surely everyone in the room had known he would.

"Thank you, Serenity," Lord Deshehar said. "And may we propose that it be named the Varenechibel Bridge, in memory of your late father."

*No,* Maia thought. And then, quite suddenly, he knew what would be right. "It is an excellent thought," he said, "but we would prefer that it be called the Wisdom Bridge, in memory of all those who died. And in hope."

And all the members of the Corazhas, even Lord Pashavar, bowed their heads in agreement.

The session ended shortly thereafter; Maia sat and waited for Csevet as the room emptied. When it was only the two of them, and Telimezh and Kiru behind Maia's chair, Csevet said, "Between this and Nelozho, they will start calling you Edrehasivar the Bridge-Builder."

Maia thought about it. "We suppose you are right." He thought about it some more, thought about alliances, about Idra and Csethiro and Gormened, about Lord Pashavar and Captain Orthema, about Vedero and Mer Celehar and Arbelan. About Cala and Beshelar, Kiru and Telimezh. About Csevet himself. He regretted the bridges he had not built, Setheris and Sheveän and Chavar, and the bridges he had never had a chance to build—his brother Nemolis, for one. And he knew that if the rest of his life was spent in building bridges, it would be no bad thing.

"We would like that," he said finally. "We would like that very much."

EXTRACTS FROM

# A HANDBOOK FOR
# TRAVELERS IN THE ELFLANDS

(published by the Press of the Crooked Stair for the
Royal Merchants Guild of Pencharn)

## PRONUNCIATION

There are no silent letters in Ethuverazhin. Two vowels
written together signify length, unless the second vowel
carries an umlaut, as in the name of the great central
river, Istandaärtha, in which case, they are to be pronounced separately. *Ai* is the vowel of "line"; *ei* is the
vowel of "lane"; *ee,* which occurs rarely and is largely
archaic, is the vowel of "lean."

Ethuverazhin has a number of aspirated consonants.
*Ch* is pronounced as in "churn"; *kh,* a consonant common only in Ethuverazhin and its sister tongue, Barizhin,
is pronounced rather like a cough in the back of the
throat. The traveler is not advised to attempt it until
great familiarity and comfort with the language have
been achieved. *Th* is pronounced as in "theater." *Sh* is
pronounced as in "show." *Zh,* like *kh,* is rarely heard
outside the Ethuveraz and the goblin lands; it is pronounced more or less as a slurred *j.*

The consonant *c* is always hard (the elves along the
border with Barizhan have even started to borrow the
*k* of goblin orthography), and the consonant pair *cs*
should be pronounced, as best as possible, as a hard *c*

and *s* elided together. Apostrophes indicate only a dropped syllable and should not be marked in any way in speech. In other respects, the traveler will find the orthography of the Ethuveraz perfectly straightforward.

## NAMES

*Personal names* are marked by gender. Male names end in -*a*, -*is*, and -*et*, as in the popular wonder-tale about the brothers Vana, Vanis, and Vanet, in which Vanet, the youngest and weakest, is the only one who can lift the sword Cartheio from the ogre's anvil. Female names end in -*o* and -*an*. The ending -*u* appears in names of both genders.

*Family names* are of paramount importance to the people of the Elflands. The traveler should remember that each family name is a root to which suffixes are added to mark gender and marital status. Men use the suffix -*ar*, married women use -*aran*, and unmarried women use -*in*. The suffix -*ada* signifies "many," and is used to denote the family—or "house" as the elves call it—as a collective body. Among the common people of the south, along the border with the goblin lands, the suffixes -*a*, -*o*, -*eth* are still to be found, and the herders of the western plains inflect their names with -*ezh*, -*ezho*, -*ezhen*.

*Place names* also carry markers. Note that cities and rivers are both named for their tutelary spirits, and thus cities are always female and rivers always male. The traveler is *strongly* advised to ignore the rude rhymes about the river Istandaärtha and the city of Cairado that may be heard among the more vulgar parts of the populace. The suffix -*ee* denotes a dwelling, while the suffix -*an* denotes a gathering place. *Theileian,* the word for "hall," carries a specifically governmental or juridical connotation. The *Untheileian,* the emperor's hall, bears an archaic prefix, the exact meaning of which has been lost. Philologists are divided between those who believe it derives from the word for "wisdom" and those who believe it derives from the word for "center."

## FORMS OF ADDRESS

The elves are an ancient and punctilious people. Travelers are advised always to err on the side of politeness. Never address an elf with the informal second, "thou" or "thee," even such humble folk as chamber maids and waiters. Excessive formality will be forgiven from a foreigner; rudeness will not.

Elvish titles are likewise complicated and likely to trip up the unwary traveler. Children under thirteen should all be addressed as *michen,* "little." Although the age of legal adulthood in the Ethuveraz is sixteen, children of thirteen are frequently expected to begin to take their place in the adult world, and thus should be addressed as adults.

Men are *mer,* married women are *merrem,* single women are *min.* (The traveler may look for the iron oath ring on the woman's right hand.) Even the merest pocket baron, however, must be addressed as *osmer,* his wife as *osmerrem,* his daughter as *osmin.* Those of more exalted rank—and rest assured, traveler, you will not encounter them unawares—have the prefix *dach'* (shortened from *dachen,* "greater") added in front of the prefix *os* (which means "honorable"), making their forms of address *dach'osmer, dach'osmerrem, dach'osmin.* The emperor is addressed always and only as "Serenity."

The artisans' guilds of the Elflands have their own

hierarchy and titles, with which the traveler need not be concerned. Persons of the artisan class may always be correctly addressed as *mer, merrem,* and *min.*

## THE EMPERORS

The Elflands have been ruled by the family Drazh for more than two thousand years, although it must be confessed that the continuity of this dynasty is in some ways a politic fiction due to strategic adoptions by the emperors of their chosen heirs. The emperors assume a cognomen upon ascending the throne; these are invariably archaic and cumbersome names that the traveler will not hear otherwise used, and they are further marked by the imperial prefix. Before the unification of the eastern and western Elflands by Edrevenivar, commonly called the Conquerer, the imperial prefix was always Bel-. Since Edrevenivar, although no emperor has taken his cognomen, the imperial prefix has been Edre- in his honor. Most recently, Varenechibel I chose to adopt the prefix Vare-, which the common people consider an insult to his ancestors and thus a harbinger of ill luck.

*A Listing of Persons, Places, Things, and Gods*

**Aäno:** maid at Edonomee; daughter of Kevo
**Adremaza:** the master of the Athmaz'are
**Aisava, Csevet:** a courier; later Edrehasivar VII's secretary
**Aizheveth:** Witness for the *Wisdom of Choharo*; scholar of the second rank
**Akhalarna:** a god
**Alcethmeret:** the emperor's residence within the Untheileneise Court
**Alchenada:** a noble house
**Alchenin, Doru:** a noblewoman
**Amalo:** a city in Thu-Athamar
**Anmura:** god of the sun and god of war
**Anmur'theileian:** a fortress built by the elves in the Evressai Steppes; called Memory of Death and Carrion-Bones by the Nazhmorhathveras
**Anvernel:** a country across the Chadevan Sea
**Ashedro:** a city in Thu-Athamar; seat of a university
**Ashevezhko:** the Barizheise goddess of the sea
**Athmaz'are:** the institution of the mazei of the Ethuveraz
**Athamara:** a river of the Ethuveraz; meets the Istandaärtha at Cairado
**Atterezh, Clemis:** the emperor's Master of Wardrobe
**Aveio:** a town in Thu-Evresar
**Avris:** one of the emperor's edocharei

**Bakhoree:** a manor belonging to the Drazhada in Thu-Cethor

**Barizhan:** the Ethuveraz's southern neighbor; the land of goblins

**Barizhin:** the language of Barizhan

**Bazhevada:** a noble house

**Bazhevar, Dalera:** nephew of the Count Bazhevel

**Bazhevel:** a count of Thu-Tetar

**Bazhevin, Stano:** fiancée of Ciris Drazhar; daughter of the Count Bazhevel

**Belmaliven IV (dec.):** Belmaliven Zhas, the 123rd Emperor of the Elflands; brother of Belmaliven V; father of Belvesena XI and Belmaliven VI

**Belmaliven V (dec.):** Belmaliven Zhas, the 124th Emperor of the Elflands; brother of Belmaliven IV

**Belmaliven VI (dec.):** Belmaliven Zhas, the 126th Emperor of the Elflands; son of Belmaliven IV; brother of Belvesena XI

**Beltanthiar III (dec.):** Beltanthiar Zhas, the 113th Emperor of the Elflands; defended by Hanevis Athmaza from Orava the Usurper

**Beltanthiar V (dec.):** Beltanthiar Zhas, the 121st Emperor of the Elflands; a child emperor who did not live to see adulthood

**Belthelema IX (dec.):** Belthelema Zhas, the 88th Emperor of the Elflands; husband of Valestho Drazharan

**Belu:** a soldier of the Hezhethora

**Belvesena XI (dec.):** Belvesena Zhas, the 125th Emperor of the Elflands; son of Belmaliven IV; brother of Belmaliven VI

**Berenada:** a noble house

**Berenar, Eiru:** the Witness for the Treasury; later Lord Chancellor; husband of Anzhevo Berenaran

**Berenaran, Anzhevo:** wife of Eiru Berenar

*Benevolent Lotus:* a Barizheise steamship

**Chavel:** a viscount of Thu-Athamar; brother of Uleris Chavar

**Chevarimai:** a god whose cult was suppressed

**Choharo:** a city in Thu-Istandaär

**Cloud Horses, the:** a bar in Amalo

**Clunethada:** the principal house of Thu-Athamar

**Clunethar, Orchenis:** Prince of Thu-Athamar; husband of Uleviän Clunetharan

**Clunetharan, Ebreneän (dec.):** sister of Varenechibel IV

**Clunetharan, Uleviän:** daughter of the Duke Tethimel; wife of Orchenis Clunethar, Prince of Thu-Athamar

**Convent of the Lighthouse-Keepers:** a convent for votaries of Ashevezhkho in Urvekh'

**Corat' Arhos:** Cruelty of Water; the sea serpent

**Corat' Dav Arhos:** the palace of the Great Avar of Barizhan

**Corazhas:** advisers to the emperor; the Corazhas is composed of seven Witnesses: the Witness for the Judiciate, the Witness for the Prelacy, the Witness for the Universities, the Witness for the Treasury, the Witness for the Athmaz'are, the Witness for Foreigners, and the Witness for the Parliament

**Csaivo:** goddess of rivers, water, birth, and healing

**Csedo:** a town in Thu-Istandaär

**Csovar, Tanet:** the Witness for the Emperor

**Cstheio Caireizhasan:** goddess of the stars, of wisdom, and of magic

**Curnar, Olvaris (dec.):** a philosopher; executed in the reign of Varevesena

**Dachen Mura:** the Greater Jewels of the emperor

**Daiano:** a town in Thu-Cethor, north of Ezho; noted for its mineral springs

**Dalar, Evru (dec.):** husband of Oseian Dalaran; lover of Thara Celehar

**Dalaran, Oseian (dec.):** wife of Evru Dalar

**Danivada:** a noble house

**Danivaran, Aro:** a noblewoman

**Danivin, Thiriän:** Aro Danivaran's daughter

**Dazhis Athmaza:** Second Nohecharis to Edrehasivar VII

**Deshehar:** the Witness for the Parliament

**Dorashada:** a noble house of Thu-Cethor

**Drazhada:** the ruling house of the Ethuveraz

**Drazhar, Cora:** page boy in Csoru Drazharan's household; Maia Drazhar's third cousin

**Drazhar, Ciris (dec.):** second son of Varenechibel IV and Pazhiro Drazharan (third son of the emperor); fiancé of Stano Bazhevin; killed in the crash of the *Wisdom of Choharo*

**Drazhar, Ermezhis (dec.):** an archduke of the Drazhada; an invalid

**Drazhar, Idra:** Prince of the Untheileneise Court; son of Nemolis Drazhar and Sheveän Drazharan; brother of Ino Drazhin and Mireän Drazhin

**Drazhar, Maia:** only child of Chenelo Drazharan and Varenechibel IV (fourth son of the emperor); relegated by his father first to Isvaroë (with Chenelo Drazharan) and then to Edonomee (with Setheris Nelar); see also Edrehasivar VII

**Drazhar, Nazhira (dec.):** elder son of Varenechibel IV and Pazhiro Drazharan (second son of the emperor); killed in the crash of the *Wisdom of Choharo*

**Drazhar, Nemera (dec.):** see Varenechibel IV

**Drazhar, Nemolis (dec.):** Prince of the Untheileneise Court; son of Varenechibel IV and Leshan Drazharan; husband of Sheveän Drazharan; father of Idra Drazhar, Mireän Drazhar, Ino Drazhar; killed in the crash of the *Wisdom of Choharo*

**Drazharan, Arbelan:** first wife of Varenechibel IV; put aside for barrenness and relegated to Cethoree

**Drazharan, Chenelo** (dec.): second legitimate daughter of Maru Sevraseched, the Great Avar of Barizhan; fourth wife of Varenechibel IV; mother of Maia Drazhar; relegated to Isvaroë by Varenechibel IV, where she died

**Drazharan, Corivero** (dec.): an empress; an opera, *The Dream of the Empress Corivero,* was written about her

**Drazharan, Csoru:** fifth wife of Varenechibel IV; kinswoman to Thara Celehar

**Drazharan, Leshan** (dec.): second wife of Varenechibel IV; mother of Nemolis Drazhar and Nemriän Imaran

**Drazharan, Parmeno** (dec.): an empress

**Drazharan, Pazhiro** (dec.): third wife of Varenechibel IV; mother of Nazhira Drazhar, Ciris Drazhar, and Vedero Drazhin; died in childbirth

**Drazharan, Valestho:** the empress of Belthelema IX

**Drazharan, Sheveän:** Princess of the Untheileneise Court; wife of Nemolis Drazhar; mother of Idra Drazhar, Mireän Drazhin, and Ino Drazhin

**Drazhin, Ino:** younger daughter of Nemolis Drazhar and Sheveän Drazharan; sister of Idra Drazhar and Mireän Drazhin

**Drazhin, Mireän:** elder daughter of Nemolis Drazhar and Sheveän Drazharan; sister of Idra Drazhar and Ino Drazhin

**Drazhin, Vedero:** daughter of Varenechibel IV and Pazhiro Drazharan

**Duchenada:** a noble house

**Duchenel:** a count of Thu-Cethor

**Duchenin, Loran:** second daughter of the Count Duchenel; niece of Uleris Chavar

**Ebremis:** master chef of the Alcethmeret

**Echana:** a lieutenant of the Untheileneise Guard

**Edonara:** the marshes of western Thu-Evresar

**Edonomee:** a manor belonging to the Drazhada;
 Maia Drazhar and Setheris Nelar were relegated
 here by Varenechibel IV

**Edrehasivar VI (dec.):** Edrehasivar Zhas, the 182nd
 Emperor of the Elflands

**Edrehasivar VII:** Edrehasivar Zhas, the 209th
 Emperor of the Elflands; see also Maia Drazhar

**Edretanthiar III (dec.):** Edretanthiar Zhas, the
 172nd Emperor of the Elflands

**Edrethelema III (dec.):** Edrethelema Zhas, the 185th
 Emperor of the Elflands; the architect of the current
 Untheileneise Court

**Edrethelema IV (dec.):** Edrethelema Zhas, the 186th
 Emperor of the Elflands; son of Edrethelema III;
 builder of the Untheileneise Court

**Edrethelema V (dec.):** Edrethelema Zhas, the 187th
 Emperor of the Elflands; son of Edrethelema IV;
 builder of the Untheileneise Court; had Lisethu
 Pevennin put to death

**Edrethelema VI (dec.):** Edrethelema Zhas, the 188th
 Emperor of the Elflands; son of Edrethelema V;
 builder of the Untheileneise Court

**Edrethelema VIII (dec.):** Edrethelema Zhas, the
 192nd Emperor of the Elflands; a child emperor
 who did not live to see adulthood

**Edrevechelar XIV (dec.):** Edrevechelar Zhas, the
 201st Emperor of the Elflands; great-great-great-
 great-great-granduncle of Maia Drazhar

**Edrevechelar XVI (dec.):** Edrevechelar Zhas, the
 203rd Emperor of the Elflands; father of
 Varenechibel I

**Edrevenivar (dec.):** Edrevenivar Zhas, the 157th
 Emperor of the Elflands; known as Edrevenivar the
 Conqueror; united the eastern and western
 Ethuveraz

**Erimada:** a noble house

**Esaran, Echelo:** steward of the Alcethmeret

**Esha:** one of the emperor's edocharei

**Eshoravee:** a manor belonging to the Tethimada

**Esret:** a Barizheise page boy in the service of Vorzhis Gormened

**Estelveriär:** a country bordering the Ethuveraz

**Esthoramire:** the prison of the Untheileneise Court

**Ethuveraz:** the Elflands

**Ethuverazhid Mura:** the crown of the Elflands

**Ethuverazhid Zhas:** the Emperor of the Elflands

**Ethuverazhin:** the language of the Elflands

**Evresartha:** a river of the Ethuveraz; meets the Istandaärtha at Ezho

**Evressai Steppes:** home of the Nazhmorhathveras

**Ezho:** a city in Thu-Cethor; founded in the gold rush of Varenechibel III's reign

*Glorious Dragon:* the ship of Shaleän Sevraseched

**Gormened, Nadaro:** wife of Vorzhis Gormened; cousin of Chenelo Drazharan

**Gormened, Vorzhis:** Barizheise ambassador to the Untheileneise Court; husband of Nadaro Gormened

**Habrobar:** a maker of signets

**Halezh:** a master of the Clocksmiths' Guild

**Halezho, Avro:** a member of the Clocksmiths' Guild; sister of Nedaö Vechin

**Hanevis Athmaza (dec.):** nohecharis of Beltanthiar III

**Haru:** servant at Edonomee

**Hezhethora:** the traditional guards of the Great Avar of Barizhan

*Honor of Csedo:* an airship

**Ilinveriär:** a country bordering the Ethuveraz

**Imada:** a noble house

**Imaran, Nemriän:** daughter of Varenechibel IV and Leshan Drazharan; wife of the Marquess Imel

**Imel:** a marquess of Thu-Athamar; husband of Nemriän Imaran

**Inver:** a soldier of the Hezhethora

**Isheian:** servant in the Alcethmeret

**Ishilar:** a corporal of the Untheileneise Guard

**Istandaärtha:** the principal river of the Ethuveraz

**Isthanada:** a minor house

**Isthanar:** the Witness for the Universities

**Isvaroë:** a manor belonging to the Drazhada; Chenelo Drazharan and Maia Drazhar were relegated here by Varenechibel IV

**Kevo:** cook at Edonomee; mother of Aäno

**Khel-Avezher:** self-styled king of the Chadevan pirates

**Khever:** a groom in the Untheileneise Court

**Kiru Athmaza:** Second Nohecharis of Edrehasivar VII; a cleric of Csaivo

**Lanthevada:** a noble house

**Lanthevel:** a marquess of Thu-Athamar; Presider of the House of Blood

**Lanthevin, Iviro:** niece of the Marquess Lanthevel

**Leilis Athmaza:** tutor of Idra Drazhar

**Lohaiso:** a city of Thu-Evresar

*Loyalty of Lohaiso:* an airship

**Mazan'theileian:** the hall of the Athmaz'are in the Untheileneise Court

**Michen Mura:** the Lesser Jewels of the emperor

**Michen'theileian:** the emperor's audience hall

**Mich'othasmeire:** the Chapel of All Gods in the Untheileneise'meire

**Narchanezhen, Atho:** an airship worker; a follower of Curnar

**Nazhmorhathveras:** the People of the Night Sky, the inhabitants of the Evressai Steppes; at war with the Ethuveraz

**Pashavaran, Ailano:** wife of Lord Pashavar

**Pashavel:** a duke of Thu-Cethor

**Pelar:** Witness for the *Wisdom of Choharo;* scholar of the second rank

**Pelchara:** servant at Edonomee

**Perenched, Ursu:** natural daughter of Maru Sevraseched; a sea captain's wife

**Pevennada:** an extinct noble house

**Pevennin, Lisethu (dec.):** a lady of the last house to lead a rebellion against the Drazhada

**Polchina, Evet:** a master of the Clocksmiths' Guild

**Pencharn:** a country bordering the Ethuveraz

**Puzhvarno:** a city in Thu-Athamar, near Eshoravee

*Radiance of Cairado:* an airship

**Reshema:** a courier

**Rohethada:** a noble house

**Rohethar, Idra:** father of Sheveän Drazharan

**Rohetharan, Zharo:** mother of Sheveän Drazharan

**Rosharis:** the head groom of the Untheileneise Court

**Salezheio:** goddess of wind, winter, couriers, and storytellers

**Sehalis Athmaza:** Adremaza of the Athmaz'are

**Selthevis:** the secretary of Maru Sevraseched

**Sevesar:** Witness for the *Wisdom of Choharo;* scholar of the second rank

**Sevezho:** a town in Thu-Istandaär

**Sevraseched, Holitho:** a natural daughter of Maru Sevraseched; a votary in Urvekh'

**Sevraseched, Maru:** the Great Avar of Barizhan; father of Shaleän Sevraseched, Thever Sevraseched, Ursu Perenched, Holitho Sevraseched, Chenelo Drazharan, and Nadeian Vizhenka

**Sevraseched, Shaleän:** a natural daughter of Maru Sevraseched; a sea captain; her ship is the *Glorious Dragon* and her home port Solunee-over-the-Water, where she has a wife

**Sevraseched, Thever:** elder legitimate daughter of Maru Sevraseched

**Shulihada:** a noble house

**Shulivar, Aina:** an airship worker; a follower of Curnar

**Solichel:** a count of Thu-Tetar

**Solunee-over-the-Water:** a port across the Chadevan Sea

**Sonevet Athmaza:** the Witness for the Athmaz'are

**Sorchev Zhas (dec.):** a ruler of Csedo before the unification of the Ethuveraz

**Stone Tree, the:** a teahouse in Amalo

*Strength of Rosiro:* an airship

**Talar:** a Drazhadeise armsman

**Tativada:** a noble house

**Tativin, Aizheän:** a friend of Vedero Drazhin

**Teia:** a Barizheise page boy in the service of Vorzhis Gormened

**Telimezh:** Second Nohecharis to Edrehasivar VII

**Tetara:** a river of the Ethuveraz; meets the Istandaärtha near the border with Barizhan

**Tethimada:** a ducal house of Thu-Athamar

**Tethimar, Eshevis:** son of the Duke Tethimel

**Tethimar, Teru:** the Archprelate of Cetho

**Tethimel:** a duke of Thu-Athamar; one of the wealthiest landowners of the Ethuveraz

**Tethimin, Paru:** daughter of the Duke Tethimel

**Thorchelezhen:** a junior canon of the Untheileneise'meire

**Thu-Athamar:** a principality of the Ethuveraz

**Thu-Cethor:** a principality of the Ethuveraz

**Thu-Evresar:** a principality of the Ethuveraz

**Thu-Istandaär:** a principality of the Ethuveraz

**Thu-Tetar:** a principality of the Ethuveraz

**Ubezhada:** a noble house

Ubezhar, Odris: a friend of Eshevis Tethimar

Ubezharan, Medo: wife of Odris Ubezhar

Ulis: the god of death and the moon

Ulzhavada: a noble house

Ulzhavel (dec.): a viscount of Thu-Cethor; committed suicide after being banished by Varenechibel IV

Untheileian: the hall of the Ethuverazhid Zhas, the emperor; the center of the Untheileneise Court

Untheileneise Court: the palace of the Emperors of the Ethuveraz; also houses the Judiciate, the Parliament, the Corazhas, the Mazan'theileian of the Athmaz'are, and the Archprelacy of Cetho

Untheileneise Guard: the guards of the Untheileneise Court; mostly, but not entirely, ceremonial

Untheileneise'meire: the othasmeire of the Untheileneise Court

Upazhera: a tributary of the Cethora

Urvekh': a town in Barizhan, on the coast

Usharsu Athmaza (dec.): Adremaza of the Athmaz'are in the reign of Edretanthiar III

Ushenar: a doctor in the Untheileneise Court

Uvezho: a town in Thu-Cethor

Valno: a town in Thu-Evresar; where Akhalarana fell to earth

Varenechibel I (dec.): Varenechibel Zhas, the 204th Emperor of the Elflands; son of Edrevechelar XVI

Varenechibel II (dec.): Varenechibel Zhas, the 205th Emperor of the Elflands; son of Varenechibel I

Varenechibel III (dec.): Varenechibel Zhas, the 206th Emperor of the Elflands; son of Varenechibel II

Varenechibel IV (dec.): Varenechibel Zhas, the 208th Emperor of the Elflands; son of Varevesena; husband, in sequence, of Arbelan Drazharan, Leshan Drazharan, Pazhiro Drazharan, Chenelo Drazharan, Csoru Drazharan; father of Nemolis